Great Irish Stories of the Supernatural

Great Irish Stories of the Supernatural

Edited by Peter Haining

BARNES
&NOBLE
BOOKS
NEW YORK

CONTENTS

INTRODUCTION

According to a recent estimation, the Irish Folklore Commission has in its archives well in excess of two million pages of stories taken verbatim from native story-tellers. Yet so rich is the oral tradition in Ireland that one collector, Sean O'Sullivan, maintains that in a single rural parish, Carna in West Galway, there still remain more unrecorded folk-tales than in the whole of continental Europe.

Some readers may regard such claims with scepticism, or even dismiss them as typical examples of the 'tall story' for which the Irish are famous, but there is no doubt that the folk material from Celtic Ireland is far more abundant than that from any other part of the British Isles—or indeed from almost anywhere else. Of these stories, a very substantial number consists of hero tales glorying in Ireland's great heritage; but equally impressive is the quantity whose theme is the twilight world and the figures that dwell on the borders of consciousness and reality: the ghosts and banshees, the fairies and leprechauns, the devils and revenants.

Since Ireland was young, the story-tellers—the *seanchaí* —have sat around the hearths enthralling their audiences, young and old, with tales of the wild, grotesque and fantastic beings prowling just outside the door. Sometimes, they said, the unknown was closer still than that—in the very room where they were sitting. And then the listeners would huddle closer as the shadows lengthened—for the fear of what cannot be seen or touched or smelt but which all the senses insist is there is a universal fear.

7

From this ancient tradition have evolved the stories collected in this book. They have been developed from folklore; shaped by the narrative powers of Irish writers; and built into a library of stories that are the envy of the world. For the Irish are pre-eminent not only in the art of the short story: since the middle of the eighteenth century they have shown themselves second to none in creating tales of the supernatural. Some famous names have been involved in this immensely fruitful period—a number of them wholly associated with the genre, others better known for their more general literary works but nonetheless skilled at writing tales of mystery inspired by folk-memory. For although these stories are labelled fiction, every one is rooted in the Irish supernatural tradition.

The stories have been grouped by subject and, in the main, in chronological order of composition, to show how successive generations of authors have differed in their approach to a particular supernatural figure, though never lost belief in it. Among the writers are some important pioneers who went out into the countryside to collect at first hand the raw material for their work: Thomas Crofton Croker, Patrick Kennedy, William Carleton, Gerald Griffin and Douglas Hyde. There are others whose books have had a profound influence on modern supernatural fiction: Joseph Sheridan Le Fanu, creator of the modern ghost story; Charlotte Riddell, writer of that key collection, *Weird Stories*; and Bram Stoker, author of the most famous of all vampire novels, *Dracula*. In their wake follows an impressive company whose work has dictated the development of the modern Irish short story—George Moore, Daniel Corkery, Liam O'Flaherty, Sean O'Faolain, Frank O'Connor, Elizabeth Bowen, Benedict Kiely, William Trevor and Mary Lavin. Lastly come a few, perhaps surprising, inclusions, such as W. B. Yeats, James Joyce, J. M. Synge and Michael MacLiammoir.

A great friend of mine, the American fantasy writer Ray Bradbury, once remarked to me that the Irish constantly take the rest of the world unawares. Ray himself first went to Ireland in 1956, to write the script for John Huston's film of *Moby Dick*, and thereafter found himself bewitched by the magic of the country and its people.

'There are times when I wish the Irish would no longer surprise us,' he wrote to me after one visit. 'They are much too clever, move too quickly on their feet, vanish here to reappear there, and they write so damn well that suicide seems most appealing.'

Having spent the last few months reading through the massive corpus of Irish supernatural fiction, I know exactly how Ray feels. The stories here may not include everyone's choice, but you can be sure that they will surprise and delight you—and may even send a chill or two up your spine.

Welcome, then, to the unique world of the Irish supernatural. As James Joyce wrote in *A Portrait of the Artist as a Young Man*, 'This race and this country and this life produced me—I shall express myself as I am.'

Peter Haining
May 1992

1
GHOSTS

There is probably no supernatural figure more widely recorded in the folklore of Ireland than the ghost, known as the *Thevshi* or *Tash*. Irish ghosts appear in a variety of forms including human, animal, and even disembodied bits of the human anatomy such as legs and hands! Many are said to be the spirits of people who have been killed or met violent deaths, and of all the specific types the banshee, or *Bean Si*, a wailing female figure who heralds death, is the best known.

In the mid-nineteenth century Irish ghosts became the inspiration for a series of short tales which proved to be the forerunners of the modern ghost story as we know it today. These were the work of Joseph Sheridan Le Fanu (1814–1873), the Dublin-born great-grand-nephew of the playwright Richard Brinsley Sheridan, and they have led to Le Fanu being hailed by Everett F. Bleiler, in his definitive *Guide to Supernatural Fiction*, as 'the foremost writer of supernatural fiction in English literature'. According to James F. Kilroy, in *The Irish Short Story: A Critical History*, these stories 'anticipate not only the formal purity of the modern short story, but also, in their exploration of psychological reality, many of the concerns of twentieth-century fiction.'

What Le Fanu did was transform the old-fashioned Gothic novels—which were invariably set in haunted castles peopled by double-dyed villains and helpless heroines—into tales of psychological horror set in everyday situations. In so doing he earned for himself the accolade of the 'British Poe', but paid for his obsession by becoming an eccentric recluse (although the sudden death of his beloved wife was probably a contributing factor) and taking to his bed where he wrote much of his later fiction. Eventually he met his death by a heart attack, and was found lying in this same bed with every sign on his agonised features that his last moments had been nightmarish. This, however, was only after he had worked for some years as editor of the *Dublin University Magazine* which became a repository for the new style of ghost story, including a substantial number of his own.

Several of the most influential of Le Fanu's stories are set in the Dublin suburb of Chapelizod, once the headquarters of the Royal Irish Artillery—among them the tale of 'The Spectre Lovers'. First published in the *Dublin University Magazine* in 1851, it describes how the hapless Peter Brien finds himself beset by some strange and ominous military ghosts. Le Fanu's inventive combination of past and present make the story an ideal one with which to start this collection.

One Irish writer who was deeply influenced by Le Fanu was Patrick Kennedy (1801–1873), the author of a story with the intriguing title 'The Ghosts and the Game of Football'. The son of a peasant farmer from County Wexford, Kennedy had become fascinated while still a youngster with the folk tales of his neighbourhood. Thanks to an education paid for by a local landowning family, he was able to secure a job as a teacher in Dublin, which provided him with the means to start writing down these tales and contributing them to local magazines. One of the first editors to encourage his undoubted gifts was Le Fanu, and when in 1866 Kennedy published a selection of these stories in book form, under the title *Legendary Fictions of the Irish Celts*, he dedicated the work to his editor, 'in consideration of your being a truly good man, and in gratitude for your kind encouragement of my own literary attempts—without that encouragement I should probably never have had an opportunity of penning a dedication to any one.'

It seems appropriate that Kennedy's story of some racketing ghosts who persecute a young man should follow that of his mentor, and it deserves reprinting in its own right, for it is a tale unique in both supernatural and soccer literature!

The Irish banshee is also unique to Ireland, although it can pursue members of old Irish families far beyond the confines of the country—as Charlotte Riddell (1832–1906) describes in her remarkable story 'Hertford O'Donnell's Warning'. This ghost, emitting its unearthly wail, only appears immediately prior to a death, and it may materialise either as a beautiful young maiden in trailing garments or as an old hag clothed in winding sheets. Some accounts say it has red eyes from constant weeping. The banshee has apparently been seen by Irish families as far away from their native soil as Europe, America and even Australia.

'Hertford O'Donnell's Warning', written in 1874, has been described as the finest tale on this theme, justifying Bleiler's praise of Mrs Riddell as 'with the exception of J. S. Le Fanu, the foremost British High Victorian author of supernatural fiction'. Born Charlotte Elizabeth Cowan into a wealthy Carrickfergus family, she was thrown into a life of poverty when her father was bankrupted, and was only able to restore her own fortunes by turning to writing. Her style, characterisation and psychological insight soon made her a popular magazine contributor, and when a collection of her best supernatural tales was published in 1882 as *Weird Stories*, the book was hailed as a 'landmark volume'. She also received considerable acclaim for a series of realistic novels about business and financial life, which earned her the soubriquet, 'novelist of the city'. 'Hertford O'Donnell's Warning' was written while she was living in an old haunted mill-house on the River Thames, and she later used the place as the setting for one of her most popular novels, *The Haunted River* (1877).

Elizabeth Bowen (1899–1973) left her native County Cork for England in 1906, when a psychological illness struck down her father and shortly afterwards her mother died of cancer. In London she managed to recover from these traumas (although occasionally drawing on them for her fiction) and there established her enduring fame as a writer with *The House in Paris* (1935), *The Death of the Heart* (1938) and *The Heat of the Day* (1949). She also became fascinated by the supernatural and produced a number of stories which were later published in collections—*Encounters* (1923), *The Cat Jumps* (1934) and *The Demon Lover* (1945). The title story of the last volume, about a woman's fickleness generating its own terror, has since become one of the most anthologised horror stories of this century. Elizabeth Bowen often returned to stay in her ancestral home in Ireland, a magnificent 800-acre estate called Bowen's Court, and it was during one visit that she conceived 'Hand In Glove', a compelling story of supernatural revenge in which she makes full use of her intimate knowledge of the privileged classes from which she had sprung.

Echoes from the past are also to be found in the last story, 'The End of the Record'. The author, Sean O'Faolain (1900–   ), is generally listed with Liam O'Flaherty and Frank O'Connor as one of the three masters of the modern Irish short story, the writers who have set the standards for artistic achievement in the genre. O'Faolain, who was born John Whelan and changed his name to its Irish equivalent at the age of 18, was the son of a Dublin policeman. He served on the Republican side in the Irish Civil War before graduating through University College, Cork, and going on to do an MA at Harvard. He taught in America and England before becoming a full-time writer and, for some time, editor of the Dublin literary magazine, *The Bell*.

O'Faolain's tales are often held up as examples of the short story writer's exacting craft at its very best, and 'The End of the Record', with its authentic flavour of the traditional tale well told, also demonstrates the author's fascination with his nation's folk history. The story is certainly one of the most haunting in this collection; the final lines—like the theme itself—echo long in the mind.

THE SPECTRE LOVERS

Joseph Sheridan Le Fanu

There lived some fifteen years since in a small and ruinous house, little better than a hovel, an old woman who was reported to have considerably exceeded her eightieth year, and who rejoiced in the name of Alice, or popularly, Ally Moran. Her society was not much courted, for she was neither rich, nor, as the reader may suppose, beautiful. In addition to a lean cur and a cat she had one human companion, her grandson, Peter Brien, whom, with laudable goodnature, she had supported from the period of his orphanage down to that of my story, which finds him in his twentieth year. Peter was a goodnatured slob of a fellow, much more addicted to wrestling, dancing, and love-making, than to hard work, and fonder of whiskey punch than good advice. His grandmother had a high opinion of his accomplishments, which indeed was but natural, and also of his genius, for Peter had of late years begun to apply his mind to politics; and as it was plain that he had a mortal hatred of honest labour, his grandmother predicted, like a true fortune-teller, that he was born to marry an heiress, and Peter himself (who had no mind to forego his freedom even on such terms) that he was destined to find a pot of gold. Upon one point both agreed, that being unfitted by the peculiar bias of his genius for work, he was to acquire the immense fortune to which his merits entitled him by means of a pure run of good luck. This solution of Peter's future had the double effect of reconciling both himself and his grandmother to his idle courses, and also of maintaining that

18

even flow of hilarious spirits which made him everywhere welcome, and which was in truth the natural result of his consciousness of approaching affluence.

It happened one night that Peter had enjoyed himself to a very late hour with two or three choice spirits near Palmerstown. They had talked politics and love, sung songs, and told stories, and, above all, had swallowed, in the chastened disguise of punch, at least a pint of good whiskey, every man.

It was considerably past one o'clock when Peter bid his companions goodbye, with a sigh and a hiccough, and lighting his pipe set forth on his solitary homeward way.

The bridge of Chapelizod was pretty nearly the midway point of his night march, and from one cause or another his progress was rather slow, and it was past two o'clock by the time he found himself leaning over its old battlements, and looking up the river, over whose winding current and wooded banks the soft moonlight was falling.

The cold breeze that blew lightly down the stream was grateful to him. It cooled his throbbing head, and he drank it in at his hot lips. The scene, too, had, without his being well sensible of it, a secret fascination. The village was sunk in the profoundest slumber, not a mortal stirring, not a sound afloat, a soft haze covered it all, and the fairy moonlight hovered over the entire landscape.

In a state between rumination and rapture, Peter continued to lean over the battlements of the old bridge, and as he did so he saw, or fancied he saw, emerging one after another along the river bank in the little gardens and enclosures in the rear of the street of Chapelizod, the queerest little white-washed huts and cabins he had ever seen there before. They had not been there that evening when he passed the bridge on the way to his merry tryst. But the most remarkable thing about it was the odd way in which these quaint little cabins showed themselves. First he saw one or two of them just with the corner of his eye, and when he looked full at them, strange to say, they faded away and disappeared. Then another and another came in view, but all in the same coy way, just appearing and gone again before he could well fix his gaze upon them; in a little while, however, they began to bear a fuller gaze, and he found, as it seemed to himself, that he was able by an effort of attention to fix the vision for a longer and a longer time, and when they waxed faint and nearly vanished, he had the power of recalling them into light and substance, until at last their vacillating indistinctness became less and less, and they assumed a permanent place in the moonlit landscape.

'Be the hokey,' said Peter, lost in amazement, and dropping his pipe into the river unconsciously, 'them is the quarist bits iv mud cabins I ever seen, growing up like musharoons in the dew of an evening, and poppin' up here and down again there, and up again in another place, like so many white rabbits in a warren; and there they stand at last as firm and fast as if they were there from the Deluge; bedad it's enough to make a man a'most believe in the fairies.'

This latter was a large concession from Peter, who was a bit of a free-thinker, and spoke contemptuously in his ordinary conversation of that class of agencies.

Having treated himself to a long last stare at these mysterious fabrics, Peter prepared to pursue his homeward way; having crossed the bridge and passed the mill, he arrived at the corner of the main-street of the little town, and casting a careless look up the Dublin road, his eye was arrested by a most unexpected spectacle.

This was no other than a column of foot-soldiers, marching with perfect regularity towards the village, and headed by an officer on horseback. They were at the far side of the turnpike, which was closed; but much to his perplexity he perceived that they marched on through it without appearing to sustain the least check from that barrier.

On they came at a slow march; and what was most singular in the matter was, that they were drawing several cannons along with them; some held ropes, others spoked the wheels, and others again marched in front of the guns and behind them, with muskets shouldered, giving a stately character of parade and regularity to this, as it seemed to Peter, most unmilitary procedure.

It was owing either to some temporary defect in Peter's vision, or to some illusion attendant upon mist and moonlight, or perhaps to some other cause, that the whole procession had a certain waving and vapoury character which perplexed and tasked his eyes not a little. It was like the pictured pageant of a phantasmagoria reflected upon smoke. It was as if every breath disturbed it; sometimes it was blurred, sometimes obliterated; now here, now there. Sometimes, while the upper part was quite distinct, the legs of the column would nearly fade away or vanish outright, and then again they would come out into clear relief, marching on with measured tread, while the cocked hats and shoulders grew, as it were, transparent, and all but disappeared.

Notwithstanding these strange optical fluctuations however, the column continued steadily to advance. Peter crossed the street from the corner near the old bridge, running on tip-toe, and with his body stooped to avoid observation, and took up a position upon the raised footpath in the shadow of the houses, where, as the soldiers kept the middle of the road, he calculated that he might, himself undetected, see them distinctly enough as they passed.

'What the div—, what on airth,' he muttered, checking the irreligious ejaculation with which he was about to start, for certain queer misgivings were hovering about his heart, notwithstanding the factitious courage of the whiskey bottle. 'What on airth is the manin' of all this? Is it the French that's landed at last to give us a hand and help us in airnest to this blessed repale? If it is not them, I simply ask who the div—, I mane who on airth are they, for such sogers as them I never seen before in my born days?'

By this time the foremost of them were quite near, and truth to say they were the queerest soldiers he had ever seen in the course of his life. They wore long gaiters and leather breeches, three-cornered hats, bound with silver lace, long blue coats, with scarlet facings and linings, which latter were shewn by a fastening which held together the two opposite corners of the skirt behind; and in front the breasts were in like manner connected at a single point, where and below which they sloped back, disclosing a long-flapped waistcoat of snowy whiteness; they had very large, long cross-belts, and wore enormous pouches of white leather hung extraordinarily low, and on each of which a little silver star was glittering. But what struck him as most grotesque and outlandish in their costume was their extraordinary display of shirt-frill in front, and of ruffle about their wrists, and the strange manner in which their hair was frizzled out and powdered under their hats, and clubbed up into great rolls behind. But one of the party was mounted. He rode a tall white horse, with high action and arching neck; he had a snow-white feather in his three-cornered hat, and his coat was shimmering all over with a profusion of silver lace. From these circumstances Peter concluded that he must be the commander of the detachment, and examined him as he passed attentively. He was a slight, tall man, whose legs did not half fill his leather breeches, and he appeared to be at the wrong side of sixty. He had a shrunken, weather-beaten, mulberry-coloured face, carried a large black patch over one eye, and turned neither to the right nor to the left, but rode on at the head of his men, with a grim, military inflexibility.

The countenances of these soldiers, officers as well as men, seemed all full of trouble, and, so to speak, scared and wild. He watched in vain for a single contented or comely face. They had, one and all, a melancholy and hang-dog look; and as they passed by, Peter fancied that the air grew cold and thrilling.

He had seated himself upon a stone bench, from which, staring with all his might, he gazed upon the grotesque and noiseless procession as it filed by him. Noiseless it was; he could neither hear the jingle of accoutrements, the tread of feet, nor the rumble of the wheels; and when the old colonel turned his horse a little, and made as though he were giving the word of command, and a trumpeter, with a swollen blue nose and white feather fringe round his hat, who was walking beside him, turned about and put his bugle to his lips, still Peter heard nothing, although it was plain the sound had reached the soldiers, for they instantly changed their front to three abreast.

'Botheration!' muttered Peter, 'is it deaf I'm growing?'

But that could not be, for he heard the sighing of the breeze and the rush of the neighbouring Liffey plain enough.

'Well,' said he, in the same cautious key, 'by the piper, this bangs Banagher fairly! It's either the Frinch army that's in it, come to take the town iv Chapelizod by surprise, an' makin' no noise for feard iv wakenin' the inhabitants; or else it's—it's—what it's—somethin' else. But, tundher-an-ouns, what's gone wid Fitzpatrick's shop across the way?'

The brown, dingy stone building at the opposite side of the street looked newer and cleaner than he had been used to see it; the front door of it stood open, and a sentry, in the same grotesque uniform, with shouldered musket, was pacing noiselessly to and fro before it. At the angle of this building, in like manner, a wide gate (of which Peter had no recollection whatever) stood open, before which, also, a similar sentry was gliding, and into this gateway the whole column gradually passed, and Peter finally lost sight of it.

'I'm not asleep; I'm not dhramin',' said he, rubbing his eyes, and stamping slightly on the pavement, to assure himself that he was wide awake. 'It is a quare business, whatever it is; an' it's not alone that, but everything about the town looks strange to me. There's Tresham's house new painted, bedad, an' them flowers in the windies! An' Delany's house, too, that had not a whole pane of glass in it this morning, and scarce a slate on the roof of it! It is not possible it's what it's dhrunk I am. Sure there's the big tree, and not a leaf of it changed since I passed, and the stars overhead, all right. I don't think it is in my eyes it is.'

And so looking about him, and every moment finding or fancying new food for wonder, he walked along the pavement, intending, without further delay, to make his way home.

But his adventures for the night were not concluded. He had nearly reached the angle of the short lane that leads up to the church, when for the first time he perceived that an officer, in the uniform he had just seen, was walking before, only a few yards in advance of him.

The officer was walking along at an easy, swinging gait, and carried his sword under his arm, and was looking down on the pavement with an air of reverie.

In the very fact that he seemed unconscious of Peter's presence, and disposed to keep his reflections to himself, there was something reassuring. Besides, the reader must please to remember that our hero had a *quantum sufficit* of good punch before his adventure commenced, and was thus fortified against those qualms and terrors under which, in a more reasonable state of mind, he might not impossibly have sunk.

The idea of the French invasion revived in full power in Peter's fuddled imagination, as he pursued the nonchalant swagger of the officer.

'Be the powers iv Moll Kelly, I'll ax him what it is,' said Peter, with a sudden accession of rashness. 'He may tell me or not, as he plases, but he can't be offinded, anyhow.'

With this reflection having inspired himself, Peter cleared his voice and began—

'Captain!' said he, 'I ax your pardon, captain, an' maybe you'd be so condescindin' to my ignorance as to tell me, if it's plasin' to yer honour, whether your honour is not a Frinchman, if it's plasin' to you.'

This he asked, not thinking that, had it been as he suspected, not one word of his question in all probability would have been intelligible to the person he addressed. He was, however, understood, for the officer answered him in English, at the same time slackening his pace and moving a little to the side of the pathway, as if to invite his interrogator to take his place beside him.

'No; I am an Irishman,' he answered.

'I humbly thank your honour,' said Peter, drawing nearer —for the affability and the nativity of the officer encouraged him—'but maybe your honour is in the *sarvice* of the King of France?'

'I serve the same King as you do,' he answered, with a sorrowful significance which Peter did not comprehend at the time; and, interrogating in turn, he asked, 'But what calls you forth at this hour of the day?'

'The *day*, your honour!—the night, you mane.'

'It was always our way to turn night into day, and we keep to it still,' remarked the soldier. 'But, no matter, come up here to my house; I have a job for you, if you wish to earn some money easily. I live here.'

As he said this, he beckoned authoritatively to Peter, who followed almost mechanically at his heels, and they turned up a little lane near the old Roman Catholic chapel, at the end of which stood, in Peter's time, the ruins of a tall, stone-built house.

Like everything else in the town, it had suffered a metamorphosis. The stained and ragged walls were now erect, perfect, and covered with pebble-dash; window-panes glittered coldly in every window; the green hall-door had a bright brass knocker on it. Peter did not know whether to believe his previous or his present impressions; seeing is believing, and Peter could not dispute the reality of the scene. All the records of his memory seemed but the images of a tipsy dream. In a trance of astonishment and perplexity, therefore, he submitted himself to the chances of his adventure.

The door opened, the officer beckoned with a melancholy air of authority to Peter, and entered. Our hero followed him into a sort of hall, which was very dark, but he was guided by the steps of the soldier, and, in silence, they ascended the stairs. The moonlight, which shone in at the lobbies, showed an old, dark wainscoting, and a heavy, oak banister. They passed by closed doors at different landing-places, but all was dark and silent as, indeed, became that late hour of the night.

Now they ascended to the topmost floor. The captain paused for a minute at the nearest door, and, with a heavy groan, pushing it open, entered the room. Peter remained at the threshold. A slight female form in a sort of loose, white robe, and with a great deal of dark hair hanging loosely about her, was standing in the middle of the floor, with her back towards them.

The soldier stopped short before he reached her, and said, in a voice of great anguish, 'Still the same, sweet bird—sweet bird! still the same.' Whereupon, she turned suddenly, and threw her arms about the neck of the officer, with a gesture of fondness and despair, and her frame was agitated as if by a burst of sobs. He held her close to his breast in silence; and honest Peter felt a strange terror creep over him, as he witnessed these mysterious sorrows and endearments.

'Tonight, tonight—and then ten years more—ten long years—another ten years.'

The officer and the lady seemed to speak these words together; her voice mingled with his in a musical and fearful wail, like a distant summer wind, in the dead hour of night, wandering through ruins. Then he heard the officer say, alone, in a voice of anguish—

'Upon me be it all, for ever, sweet birdie, upon me.'

And again they seemed to mourn together in the same soft and desolate wail, like sounds of grief heard from a great distance.

Peter was thrilled with horror, but he was also under a strange fascination; and an intense and dreadful curiosity held him fast.

The moon was shining obliquely into the room, and through the window Peter saw the familiar slopes of the Park, sleeping mistily under its shimmer. He could also see the furniture of the room with tolerable distinctness—the old balloon-backed chairs, a four-post bed in a sort of recess, and a rack against the wall, from which hung some military clothes and accoutrements; and the sight of all these homely objects reassured him somewhat, and he could not help feeling unspeakably curious to see the face of the girl whose long hair was streaming over the officer's epaulet.

Peter, accordingly, coughed, at first slightly, and afterward more loudly, to recall her from her reverie of grief; and, apparently, he succeeded; for she turned round, as did her companion, and both, standing hand in hand, gazed upon him fixedly. He thought he had never seen such large, strange eyes in all his life; and their gaze seemed to chill the very air around him, and arrest the pulses of his heart. An eternity of misery and remorse was in the shadowy faces that looked upon him.

If Peter had taken less whisky by a single thimbleful, it is probable that he would have lost heart altogether before these figures, which seemed every moment to assume a more marked and fearful, though hardly definable, contrast to ordinary human shapes.

'What is it you want with me?' he stammered.

'To bring my lost treasure to the churchyard,' replied the lady, in a silvery voice of more than mortal desolation.

The word 'treasure' revived the resolution of Peter, although a cold sweat was covering him, and his hair was bristling with horror; he believed, however, that he was on the brink of fortune, if he could but command nerve to brave the interview to its close.

'And where,' he gasped, 'is it hid—where will I find it?'

They both pointed to the sill of the window, through which the moon was shining at the far end of the room, and the soldier said—

'Under that stone.'

Peter drew a long breath, and wiped the cold dew from his face, preparatory to passing to the window, where he expected to secure the reward of his protracted terrors. But looking steadfastly at the window, he saw the faint image of a new-born child sitting upon the sill in the moonlight, with its little arms stretched toward him, and a smile so heavenly as he never beheld before.

At sight of this, strange to say, his heart entirely failed him, he looked on the figures that stood near, and beheld them gazing on the infantine form with a smile so guilty and distorted, that he felt as if he were entering alive among the scenery of hell, and shuddering, he cried in an irrepressible agony of horror—

'I'll have nothing to say with you, and nothing to do with you; I don't know what yez are or what yez want iv me, but let me go this minute, every one of yez, in the name of God.'

With these words there came a strange rumbling and sighing about Peter's ears; he lost sight of everything, and felt that peculiar and not unpleasant sensation of falling softly, that sometimes supervenes in sleep, ending in a dull shock. After that he had neither dream nor consciousness till he wakened, chill and stiff, stretched between two piles of old rubbish, among the black and roofless walls of the ruined house.

We need hardly mention that the village had put on its wonted air of neglect and decay, or that Peter looked around him in vain for traces of those novelties which had so puzzled and distracted him upon the previous night.

'Ay, ay,' said his grandmother, removing her pipe, as he ended his description of the view from the bridge, 'sure enough I remember myself, when I was a slip of a girl, these little white cabins among the gardens by the river side. The artillery sogers that was married, or had not room in the barracks, used to be in them, but they're all gone long ago.'

'The Lord be merciful to us!' she resumed, when he had described the military procession, 'it's often I seen the regiment marchin' into the town, jist as you saw it last night, acushla. Oh, voch, but it makes my heart sore to think iv them days; they were pleasant times, sure enough; but is not it terrible, avick, to think its what it was the ghost of the rigiment you seen? The Lord betune us an' harm, for it was nothing else, as sure as I'm sittin' here.'

When he mentioned the peculiar physiognomy and figure of the old officer who rode at the head of the regiment—

'*That*,' said the old crone, dogmatically, 'was ould Colonel Grimshaw, the Lord presarve us! he's buried in the churchyard iv Chapelizod, and well I remember him, when I was a young thing, an' a cross ould floggin' fellow he was wid the men, an' a devil's boy among the girls—rest his soul!'

'Amen!' said Peter; 'it's often I read his tombstone myself; but he's a long time dead.'

'Sure, I tell you he died when I was no more nor a slip iv a girl—the Lord betune us and harm!'

'I'm afeard it is what I'm not long for this world myself, afther seeing such a sight as that,' said Peter, fearfully.

'Nonsinse, avourneen,' retorted his grandmother, indignantly, though she had herself misgivings on the subject; 'sure there was Phil Doolan, the ferryman, that seen black Ann Scanlan in his own boat, and what harm ever kem of it?'

Peter proceeded with his narrative, but when he came to the description of the house, in which his adventure had had so sinister a conclusion, the old woman was at fault.

'I know the house and the ould walls well, an' I can remember the time there was a roof on it, and the doors an' windows in it, but it had a bad name about being haunted, but by who, or for what, I forget intirely.'

'Did you ever hear was there goold or silver there?' he inquired.

'No, no, avick, don't be thinking about the likes; take a fool's advice, and never go next or near them ugly black walls again the longest day you have to live; an' I'd take my davy, it's what it's the same word the priest himself I'd be afther sayin' to you if you wor to ax his raverence consarnin' it, for it's plain to be seen it was nothing good you seen there, and there's neither luck nor grace about it.'

Peter's adventure made no little noise in the neighbourhood, as the reader may well suppose; and a few evenings after it, being on an errand to old Major Vandeleur, who lived in a snug old-fashioned house, close by the river, under a perfect bower of ancient trees, he was called on to relate the story in the parlour.

The Major was, as I have said, an old man; he was small, lean, and upright, with a mahogany complexion, and a wooden inflexibility of face; he was a man, besides, of few words, and if *he* was old, it follows plainly that his mother was older still. Nobody could guess or tell *how* old, but it was admitted that her own generation had long passed away, and that she had not a competitor left. She had French blood in her veins, and although she did not retain her charms quite so well as Ninon de l'Enclos, she was in full possession of all her mental activity, and talked quite enough for herself and the Major.

'So, Peter,' she said, 'you have seen the dear, old Royal Irish again in the streets of Chapelizod. Make him a tumbler of punch, Frank; and Peter, sit down, and while you take it let us have the story.'

Peter accordingly, seated near the door, with a tumbler of the nectarian stimulant steaming beside him, proceeded with marvellous courage, considering they had no light but the uncertain glare of the fire, to relate with minute particularity his awful adventure. The old lady listened at first with a smile of goodnatured incredulity; her cross-examination touching the drinking-bout at Palmerstown had been teazing, but as the narrative proceeded she became attentive, and at length absorbed, and once or twice she uttered ejaculations of pity or awe. When it was over, the old lady looked with a somewhat sad and stern abstraction on the table, patting her cat assiduously meanwhile, and then suddenly looking upon her son, the Major, she said—

'Frank, as sure as I live he has seen the wicked Captain Devereux.'

The Major uttered an inarticulate expression of wonder.

'The house was precisely that he has described. I have told you the story often, as I heard it from your dear grandmother, about the poor young lady he ruined, and the dread-

ful suspicion about the little baby. *She*, poor thing, died in that house heart-broken, and you know he was shot shortly after in a duel.'

This was the only light that Peter ever received respecting his adventure. It was supposed, however, that he still clung to the hope that treasure of some sort was hidden about the old house, for he was often seen lurking about its walls, and at last his fate overtook him, poor fellow, in the pursuit; for climbing near the summit one day, his holding gave way, and he fell upon the hard uneven ground, fracturing a leg and a rib, and after a short interval died, and he, like the other heroes, lies buried in the little churchyard of Chapelizod.

THE GHOSTS AND THE GAME OF FOOTBALL

Patrick Kennedy

There was once a poor widow woman's son that was going to look for service, and one winter's evening he came to a strong farmer's house, and this house was very near an old castle. 'God save all here,' says he, when he got inside the door. 'God save you kindly,' says the farmer. 'Come to the fire.' 'Could you give me a night's lodging?' says the boy. 'That we will, and welcome, if you will only sleep in a comfortable room in the old castle above there; and you must have a fire and candlelight, and whatever you like to drink; and if you're alive in the morning I'll give you ten guineas.' 'Sure I'll be 'live enough if you send no one to kill me.' 'I'll send no one to kill you, you may depend. The place is haunted ever since my father died, and three or four people that slept in the same room were found dead next morning. If you can banish the spirits I'll give you a good farm and my daughter, so that you like one another well enough to be married.' 'Never say't twice. I've a middling safe conscience, and don't fear any evil spirit that ever smelled of brimstone.'

Well and good, the boy got his supper, and then they went up with him to the old castle, and showed him into a large kitchen, with a roaring fire in the grate, and a table, with a bottle and glass, and tumbler on it, and the kettle ready on the hob. They bade him good night and God speed, and went off as if they didn't think their heels were half swift enough.

'Well,' says he to himself, 'if there's any danger, this

prayer-book will be usefuller than either the glass or tumbler.' So he kneeled down and read a good many prayers, and then sat by the fire, and waited to see what would happen. In about a quarter of an hour, he heard something bumping along the floor overhead till it came to a hole in the ceiling. There it stopped, and cried out, 'I'll fall, I'll fall.' 'Fall away,' says Jack, and down came a pair of legs on the kitchen floor. They walked to one end of the room, and there they stood, and Jack's hair had like to stand upright on his head along with them. Then another crackling and whacking came to the hole, and the same words passed between the thing above and Jack, and down came a man's body, and went and stood upon the legs. Then comes the head and shoulders, till the whole man, with buckles in his shoes and knee-breeches, and a big flapped waistcoat and a three-cocked hat, was standing in one corner of the room. Not to take up your time for nothing, two more men, more old-fashioned dressed than the first, were soon standing in two other corners. Jack was a little cowed at first; but found his courage growing stronger every moment, and what would you have of it, the three old gentlemen began to kick a *puckeen* (football) as fast as they could, the man in the three-cocked hat playing again' the other two.

'Fair play is bonny play,' says Jack, as bold as he could; but the terror was on him, and the words came out as if he was frightened in his sleep; 'so I'll help *you*, sir.' Well and good, he joined the sport, and kicked away till his shirt was ringing wet, savin' your presence, and the ball flying from one end of the room to the other like thunder, and still not a word was exchanged. At last the day began to break, and poor Jack was dead beat, and he thought, by the way the three ghosts began to look at himself and themselves, that they wished him to speak.

So, says he, 'Gentlemen, as the sport is nearly over, and I done my best to please you, would you tell a body what is the reason of yous coming here night after night, and how could I give you rest, if it is rest you want?' 'Them is the wisest words,' says the ghost with the three-cocked hat, 'you ever said in your life. Some of those that came before you found courage enough to take a part in our game, but no one had *misnach* (energy) enough to speak to us. I am the father of the good man of the next house, that man in the left corner is *my* father, and the man on my right is my grandfather. From father to son we were too fond of money. We lent it at ten times the honest interest it was worth; we never paid a debt we could get over, and almost starved our tenants and labourers.

'Here,' says he, lugging a large drawer out of the wall; 'here is the gold and notes that we put together, and we were not honestly entitled to the one-half of it; and here,' says he, opening another drawer, 'are bills and memorandums that'll show who were wronged, and who are entitled to get a great deal paid back to them. Tell my son to saddle two of his best horses for himself and yourself, and keep riding day and night, till every man and woman we ever wronged be rightified. When that is done, come here again some night; and if you don't hear or see anything, we'll be at rest, and you may marry my grand-daughter as soon as you please.'

Just as he said these words, Jack could see the wall through his body, and when he winked to clear his sight, the kitchen was as empty as a noggin turned upside down. At the very moment the farmer and his daughter lifted the latch, and both fell on their knees when they saw Jack alive. He soon told them everything that happened, and for three days and nights did the farmer and himself ride about, till there wasn't a single wronged person left without being paid to the last farthing.

The next night Jack spent in the kitchen he fell asleep before he was after sitting a quarter of an hour at the fire, and in his sleep he thought he saw three white birds flying up to heaven from the steeple of the next church.

Jack got the daughter for his wife, and they lived comfortably in the old castle; and if ever he was tempted to hoard

up gold, or keep for a minute a guinea or a shilling from the man that earned it through the nose, he bethought him of the ghosts and the game of football.

HERTFORD O'DONNELL'S WARNING

Charlotte Riddell

Many a year, before chloroform was thought of, there lived in an old rambling house, in Gerrard Street, Soho, a clever Irishman called Hertford O'Donnell.

After Hertford O'Donnell he was entitled to write, MRCS for he had studied hard to gain this distinction, and the older surgeons at Guy's (his hospital) considered him one of the most rising operators of the day.

Having said chloroform was unknown at the time this story opens, it will strike my readers that, if Hertford O'Donnell were a rising and successful operator in those days, of necessity he combined within himself a larger number of striking qualities than are by any means necessary to form a successful operator in these.

There was more than mere hand skill, more than even thorough knowledge of his profession, then needful for the man, who, dealing with conscious subjects, essayed to rid them of some of the diseases to which flesh is heir. There was greater courage required in the manipulator or old than is altogether essential at present. Then, as now, a thorough mastery of his instruments, a steady hand, a keen eye, a quick dexterity were indispensable to a good operator; but, added to all these things, there formerly required a pulse which knew no quickening, a mental strength which never faltered, a ready power of adaptation in unexpected circumstances, fertility of resource in difficult cases, and a brave front under all emergencies.

If I refrain from adding that a hard as well as a courageous

36

heart was an important item in the programme, it is only out of deference to general opinion, which, amongst other strange delusions, clings to the belief that courage and hardness are antagonistic qualities.

Hertford O'Donnell, however, was hard as steel. He understood his work, and he did it thoroughly; but he cared no more for quivering nerves and shrinking muscles, for screams of agony, for faces white with pain, and teeth clenched in the extremity of anguish, than he did for the stony countenances of the dead, which so often in the dissecting room appalled younger and less experienced men.

He had no sentiment, and he had no sympathy. The human body was to him, merely an ingenious piece of mechanism, which it was at once a pleasure and a profit to understand. Precisely as Brunel loved the Thames Tunnel, or any other eingular engineering feat, so O'Donnell loved a patient on whom he had operated successfully, more especially if the ailment possessed by the patient were of a rare and difficult character.

And for this reason he was much liked by all who came under his hands, since patients are apt to mistake a surgeon's interest in their cases for interest in themselves; and it was gratifying to John Dicks, plasterer, and Timothy Regan, labourer, to be the happy possessors of remarkable diseases, which produced a cordial understanding between them and the handsome Irishman.

If he had been hard and cool at the moment of hacking them to pieces, that was all forgotten or remembered only as a virtue, when, after being discharged from hospital like soldiers who have served in a severe campaign, they met Mr O'Donnell in the street, and were accosted by that rising individual just as though he considered himself nobody.

He had a royal memory, this stranger in a strange land, both for faces and cases; and like the rest of his countrymen, he never felt it beneath his dignity to talk cordially to corduroy and fustian.

In London, as a Calgillan, he never held back his tongue from speaking a cheery or a kindly word. His manners were pliable enough, if his heart were not; and the porters, and the patients, and the nurses, and the students at Guy's were all pleased to see Hertford O'Donnell.

Rain, hail, sunshine, it was all the same; there was a life and a brightness about the man which communicated itself to those with whom he came in contact. Let the mud in the Borough be a foot deep or the London fog as thick as pea-soup, Mr O'Donnell never lost his temper, never muttered a surly reply to the gatekeeper's salutation, but spoke out blithely and cheerfully to his pupils and his patients, to the sick and to the well, to those below and to those above him.

And yet, spite of all these good qualities, spite of his handsome face, his fine figure, his easy address, and his unquestionable skill as an operator, the dons, who acknowledged his talent, shook their heads gravely when two or three of them in private and solemn conclave, talked confidentially of their younger brother.

If there were many things in his favour, there were more in his disfavour. He was Irish—not merely by the accident of birth, which might have been forgiven, since a man cannot be held accountable for such caprices of Nature, but by every other accident and design which is objectionable to the orthodox and respectable and representative English mind.

In speech, appearance, manner, taste, modes of expression, habits of life, Hertford O'Donnell was Irish. To the core of his heart he loved the island which he declared he never meant to re-visit; and amongst the English he moved to all intents and purposes a foreigner, who was resolved, so said the great prophets at Guy's, to rush to destruction as fast as he could, and let no man hinder him.

'He means to go the whole length of his tether,' observed one of the ancient wiseacres to another; which speech implied a conviction that Hertford O'Donnell having sold himself to the Evil One, had determined to dive the full length of his rope into wickedness before being pulled to that shore where even wickedness is negative—where there are no mad carouses, no wild, sinful excitements, nothing but impotent wailing and gnashing of teeth.

A reckless, graceless, clever, wicked devil—going to his natural home as fast as in London anyone possibly speed thither; this was the opinion his superiors, held of the man who lived all alone with a housekeeper and her husband (who acted as butler) in his big house near Soho.

Gerrard Street—made famous by De Quincey, was not then an utterly shady and forgotten locality; carriage-patients found their way to the rising young surgeon—some great personages thought it not beneath them to fee an individual whose consulting rooms were situated on what was even then considered the wrong side of Regent Street. He was making money, and he was spending it; he was over head and ears in debt—useless, vulgar debt—senselessly contracted, never bravely faced. He had lived at an awful pace ever since he came to London, a pace which only a man who hopes and expects to die young can ever travel.

Life was good, was it? Death, was he a child, or a woman, or a coward, to be afraid of that hereafter? God knew all about the trifle which had upset his coach, better than the dons at Guy's.

Hertford O'Donnell understood the world pretty thoroughly, and the ways thereof were to him as roads often traversed; therefore, when he said that at the Day of Judgment he felt certain he should come off as well as many of those who censured him, it may be assumed, that, although his views of post-mortem punishment were vague, unsatisfactory and infidel, still his information as to the peccadilloes of his neighbours was such as consoled himself.

And yet, living all alone in the old house near Soho Square, grave thoughts would intrude into the surgeon's mind—thoughts which were, so to say, italicised by peremptory letters, and still more peremptory visits from people who wanted money.

Although he had many acquaintances he had no single

friend, and accordingly these thoughts were received and brooded over in solitude—in those hours when, after returning from dinner, or supper, or congenial carouse, he sat in his dreary rooms, smoking his pipe and considering means and ways, chances and certainties.

In good truth he had started in London with some vague idea that as his life in it would not be of long continuance, the pace at which he elected to travel could be of little consequence; but the years since his first entry into the Metropolis were now piled one on the top of another, his youth was behind him, his chances of longevity, spite of the way he had striven to injure his constitution, quite as good as ever. He had come to that period in existence, to that narrow strip of tableland, whence the ascent of youth and the descent of age are equally discernible—when, simply because he has lived for so many years, it strikes a man as possible he may have to live for just as many more, with the ability for hard work gone, with the boom companions scattered, with the capacity for enjoying convivial meetings a mere memory, with small means perhaps, with no bright hopes, with the pomp and the circumstance and the fairy carriages, and the glamour which youth flings over earthly objects, faded away like the pageant of yesterday, while the dreary ceremony of living has to be gone through today and tomorrow and the morrow after, as though the gay cavalcade and the martial music, and the glittering helmets and the prancing steeds were still accompanying the wayfarer to his journey's end.

Ah! my friends, there comes a moment when we must all leave the coach, with its four bright bays, its pleasant outside freight, its cheery company, its guard who blows the horn so merrily through villages and along lonely country roads.

Long before we reach that final stage, where the black business claims us for its own special property, we have to bid goodbye to all easy, thoughtless journeying, and betake ourselves, with what zest we may, to traversing the common of reality. There is no royal road across it that ever I heard of. From the king on his throne to the labourer who vaguely

imagines what manner of being a king is, we have all to tramp across that desert at one period of our lives, at all events; and that period usually is when, as I have said, a man starts to find the hopes, and the strength, and the buoyancy of youth left behind, while years and years of life lie stretching out before him.

The coach he has travelled by drops him here. There is no appeal, there is no help; therefore, let him take off his hat and wish the new passengers good speed, without either envy or repining.

Behold, he has had his turn, and let whosoever will, mount on the box-seat of life again, and tip the coachman and handle the ribbons—he shall take that pleasant journey no more, no more for ever.

Even supposing a man's springtime to have been a cold and ungenial one, with bitter easterly winds and nipping frosts, biting the buds and retarding the blossoms, still it was spring for all that—spring with the young green leaves sprouting forth, with the flowers unfolding tenderly, with the songs of the birds and the rush of waters, with the summer before and the autumn afar off, and winter remote as death and eternity, but when once the trees have donned their summer foliage, when the pure white blossoms have disappeared, and the gorgeous red and orange and purple blaze of many-coloured flowers fills the gardens, then if there come a wet, dreary day, the idea of autumn and winter is not so difficult to realise. When once twelve o'clock is reached, the evening and night become facts, not possibilities; and it was of the afternoon, and the evening, and the night, Hertford O'Donnell sat thinking on the Christmas Eve, when I crave permission to introduce him to my readers.

A good-looking man ladies considered him. A tall, dark-complexioned, black-haired, straight-limbed, deeply divinely blue-eyed fellow, with a soft voice, with a pleasant brogue, who had ridden like a centaur over the loose stone walls in Connemara, who had danced all night at the Dublin balls, who had walked across the Bennebeola Mountains, gun in hand, day after day, without weariness, who had fished in every one of the hundred lakes you can behold from the top of that mountain near the Recess Hotel, who had led a mad, wild life in Trinity College, and a wilder, perhaps, while 'studying for a doctor'—as the Irish phrase goes—in Edinburgh, and who, after the death of his eldest brother left him free to return to Calgillan, and pursue the usual utterly useless, utterly purposeless, utterly pleasant life of an Irish gentleman possessed of health, birth, and expectations, suddenly kicked over the paternal traces, bade adieu to Calgillan Castle and the blandishments of a certain beautiful Miss Clifden, beloved of his mother, and laid out to be his wife, walked down the avenue without even so much company as a Gossoon to carry his carpet-bag, shook the dust from his feet at the lodge gates, and took his seat on the coach, never once looking back at Calgillan, where his favourite mare was standing in the stable, his greyhounds chasing one another round the home paddock, his gun at half-cock in his dressing-room and his fishing-tackle all in order and ready for use.

He had not kissed his mother, or asked for his father's blessing; he left Miss Clifden, arrayed in her brand-new riding-habit, without a word of affection or regret; he had spoken no syllable of farewell to any servant about the place; only when the old woman at the lodge bade him good morning and God-blessed his handsome face, he recommended her bitterly to look at it well for she would never see it more.

Twelve years and a half had passed since then, without either Miss Clifden or any other one of the Calgillan people having set eyes on Master Hertford's handsome face.

He had kept his vow to himself; he had not written home; he had not been indebted to mother or father for even a tenpenny-piece during the whole of that time; he had lived without friends; and he had lived without God—so far as God ever lets a man live without him.

One thing only he felt to be needful—money; money to

keep him when the evil days of sickness, or age, or loss of practice came upon him. Though a spendthrift, he was not a simpleton; around him he saw men, who, having started with fairer prospects than his own, were, nevertheless, reduced to indigence; and he knew that what had happened to others might happen to himself.

An unlucky cut, slipping on a piece of orange-peel in the street, the merest accident imaginable, is sufficient to change opulence to beggary in the life's programme of an individual, whose income depends on eye, on nerve, on hand; and, besides the consciousness of this fact, Hertford O'Donnell knew that beyond a certain point in his profession, progress was not easy.

It did not depend quite on the strength of his own bow and shield whether he counted his earnings by hundreds or thousands. Work may achieve competence; but mere work cannot, in a profession, at all events, compass fortune.

He looked around him, and he perceived that the majority of great men—great and wealthy—had been indebted for their elevation, more to the accident of birth, patronage, connection, or marriage, than to personal ability.

Personal ability, no doubt, they possessed; but then, little Jones, who lived in Frith Street, and who could barely keep himself and his wife and family, had ability, too, only he lacked the concomitants of success.

He wanted something or someone to puff him into notoriety—a brother at Court—a lord's leg to mend—a rich wife to give him prestige in Society; and in his absence of this something or someone, he had grown grey-haired and faint-hearted while labouring for a world which utterly despises its most obsequious servants.

'Clatter along the streets with a pair of fine horses, snub the middle classes, and drive over the commonalty—that is the way to compass wealth and popularity in England,' said Hertford O'Donnell, bitterly; and as the man desired wealth and popularity, he sat before his fire, with a foot on each hob, and a short pipe in his mouth, considering how he might best obtain the means to clatter along the streets in his carriage, and splash plebeians with mud from his wheels like the best.

In Dublin he could, by means of his name and connection, have done well; but then he was not in Dublin, neither did he want to be. The bitterest memories of his life were inseparable from the very name of the Green Island, and he had no desire to return to it.

Besides, in Dublin, heiresses are not quite so plentiful as in London; and an heiress, Hertford O'Donnell had decided, would do more for him than years of steady work.

A rich wife could clear him of debt, introduce him to fashionable practice, afford him that measure of social respectability which a medical bachelor invariably lacks, deliver him from the loneliness of Gerrard Street, and the domination of Mr and Mrs Coles.

To most men, deliberately bartering away their independence for money seems so prosaic a business that they strive to gloss it over even to themselves, and to assign every reason for their choice, save that which is really the influencing one.

Not so, however, with Hertford O'Donnell. He sat beside the fire scoffing over his proposed bargain—thinking of the lady's age, her money bags, her desirable house in town, her seat in the country, her snobbishness, her folly.

'It could be a fitting ending,' he sneered, 'and why I did not settle the matter tonight passes my comprehension. I am not a fool, to be frightened with old women's tales; and yet I must have turned white. I felt I did, and she asked me whether I were ill. And then to think of my being such an idiot as to ask her if she had heard anything like a cry, as though she would be likely to hear *that*, she with her poor parvenu blood, which I often imagine must have been mixed with some of her father's strong pickling vinegar. What a deuce could I have been dreaming about? I wonder what it really was.' And Hertford O'Donnell pushed his hair back off his forehead, and took another draught from the too familiar tumbler, which was placed conveniently on the chimney-piece.

'After expressly making up my mind to propose, too!' he mentally continued. 'Could it have been conscience—that myth, which somebody, who knew nothing about the matter, said, "Makes cowards of us all"? I don't believe in conscience; and even if there be such a thing capable of being developed by sentiment and cultivation, why should it trouble me? I have no intention of wronging Miss Janice Price Ingot, not the least. Honestly and fairly I shall marry her; honestly and fairly I shall act by her. An old wife is not exactly an ornamental article of furniture in a man's house; and I do not know that the fact of her being well gilded makes her look any handsomer. But she shall have no cause for complaint; and I will go and dine with her tomorrow, and settle the matter.'

Having arrived at which resolution, Mr O'Donnell arose, kicked down the fire—burning hollow—with the heel of his boot, knocked the ashes out of his pipe, emptied his tumbler, and bethought him it was time to go to bed. He was not in the habit of taking his rest so early as a quarter to twelve o'clock; but he felt unusually weary—tired mentally and bodily—and lonely beyond all power of expression.

'The fair Janet would be better than this,' he said, half aloud; and then, with a start and a shiver, and a blanched face, he turned sharply round, whilst a low, sobbing, wailing cry echoed mournfully through the room. No form of words could give an idea of the sound. The plaintiveness of the Æolian harp—that plaintiveness which so soon affects and lowers the highest spirits—would have seemed wildly gay in comparison with the sadness of the cry which seemed floating in the air. As the summer wind comes and goes amongst the trees, so that mournful wail came and went—came and went. It came in a rush of sound, like a gradual crescendo managed by a skilful musician, and died away in a lingering note, so gently that the listener could scarcely tell the exact moment when it faded into utter silence.

I say faded, for it disappeared as the coast line disappears in the twilight, and there was total stillness in the apartment.

Then, for the first time, Hertford O'Donnell looked at his dog, and beholding the creature crouched into a corner beside the fireplace, called upon him to come out.

His voice sounded strange even to himself, and apparently the dog thought so too, for he made no effort to obey the summons.

'Come here, sir,' his master repeated, and then the animal came crawling reluctantly forward with his hair on end, his eyes almost starting from his head, trembling violently, as the surgeon, who caressed him, felt.

'So you heard it, Brian?' he said to the dog. 'And so your ears are sharper than Miss Ingot's, old fellow. It's a mighty queer thing to think of, being favoured with a visit from a Banshee in Gerrard Street; and as the lady has travelled so far, I only wish I knew whether there is any sort of refreshment she would like to take after her long journey.'

He spoke loudly, and with a certain mocking defiance, seeming to think the phantom he addressed would reply; but when he stopped at the end of his sentence, no sound came through the stillness. There was a dead silence in the room —a silence broken only by the falling of cinders on the hearth and the breathing of his dog.

'If my visitor would tell me,' he proceeded, 'for whom this lamentation is being made, whether for myself, or for some member of my illustrious family, I should feel immensely obliged. It seems too much honour for a poor surgeon to have such attention paid him. Good Heavens! What is that?' he exclaimed, as a ring, loud and peremptory, woke all the echoes in the house, and brought his housekeeper, in a state of distressing dishabille, 'out of her warm bed', as she subsequently stated, to the head of the staircase.

Across the hall Hertford O'Donnell strode, relieved at the prospect of speaking to any living being. He took no precaution of putting up the chain, but flung the door wide. A dozen burglars would have proved welcome in comparison

with that ghostly intruder he had been interviewing; therefore, as has been said, he threw the door wide, admitting a
rush of wet, cold air, which made poor Mrs Coles' few
remaining teeth chatter in her head.

'Who is there? What do you want?' asked the surgeon,
seeing no person, and hearing no voice. 'Who is there? Why
the devil can't you speak?'

When even this polite exhortation failed to elicit an
answer, he passed out into the night and looked up the street
and down the street, to see nothing but the driving rain and
the blinking lights.

'If this goes on much longer I shall soon think I must be
either mad or drunk,' he muttered, as he re-entered the
house and locked and bolted the door once more.

'Lord's sake! What is the matter, sir?' asked Mrs Coles,
from the upper flight, careful only to reveal the borders of
her night-cap to Mr O'Donnell's admiring gaze. 'Is anybody
killed? Have you to go out, sir?'

'It was only a run-away ring,' he answered, trying to
reassure himself with an explanation he did not in his heart
believe.

'Run-away—I'd run away them!' murmured Mrs Coles,
as she retired to the conjugal couch, where Coles was, to
quote her own expression, 'snoring like a pig through it all'.

Almost immediately afterwards she heard her master
ascend the stairs and close his bedroom door.

'Madam will surely be too much of a gentlewoman to
intrude here,' thought the surgeon, scoffing even at his own
fears; but when he lay down he did not put out his light, and
made Brian leap up and crouch on the coverlet beside him.

The man was fairly frightened, and would have thought it
no discredit to his manhood to acknowledge as much. He
was not afraid of death, he was not afraid of trouble, he was
not afraid of danger; but he was afraid of the Banshee; and
as he lay with his hand on the dog's head, he recalled the
many stories he had been told concerning this family retainer
in the days of his youth.

He had not thought about her for years and years. Never before had he heard her voice himself. When his brother died she had not thought it necessary to travel up to Dublin and give him notice of the impending catastrophe. 'If she had, I would have gone down to Calgillan, and perhaps saved his life,' considered the surgeon. 'I wonder who this is for? If for me, that will settle my debts and my marriage. If I could be quite certain it was either of the old people, I would start tomorrow.'

Then vaguely his mind wandered on to think of every Banshee story he had ever heard in his life. About the beautiful lady with the wreath of flowers, who sat on the rocks below Red Castle, in the County Antrim, crying till one of the sons died for love of her; about the Round Chamber at Dunluce, which was swept clean by the Banshee every night; about the bed in a certain great house in Ireland, which was slept in constantly, although no human being ever passed in or out after dark; about that General Officer who, the night before Waterloo, said to a friend, 'I have heard the Banshee, and shall not come off the field alive tomorrow; break the news gently to poor Carry'; and who, nevertheless, coming safe off the field, had subsequently news about poor Carry broken tenderly and pitifully to him; about the lad, who, aloft in the rigging, hearing through the night a sobbing and wailing coming over the waters, went down to the captain and told him he was afraid they were somehow out of their reckoning, just in time to save the ship, which, when morning broke, they found but for his warning would have been on the rocks. It was blowing great guns, and the sea was all in a fret and turmoil, and they could sometimes see in the trough of the waves, as down a valley, the cruel black reefs they had escaped.

On deck the captain stood speaking to the boy who had saved them, and asking how he knew of their danger; and when the lad told him, the captain laughed, and said her ladyship had been outwitted that time.

But the boy answered, with a grave shake of his head,

that the warning was either for him or his, and that if he got safe to port there would be bad tidings waiting for him from home; whereupon the captain bade him go below, and get some brandy and lie down.

He got the brandy, and he lay down, but he never rose again; and when the storm abated—when a great calm succeeded to the previous tempest—there was a very solemn funeral at sea; and on their arrival at Liverpool the captain took a journey to Ireland to tell a widowed mother how her only son died, and to bear his few effects to the poor desolate soul.

And Hertford O'Donnell thought again about his own father riding full-chase across country, and hearing, as he galloped by a clump of plantation, something like a sobbing and wailing. The hounds were in full cry, but he still felt, as he afterwards expressed it, that there was something among those trees he could not pass; and so he jumped off his horse, and hung the reins over the branch of a Scotch fir, and beat the cover well, but not a thing could he find in it.

Then, for the first time in his life, Miles O'Donnell turned his horse's head *from* the hunt, and, within a mile of Calgillan, met a man running to tell him his brother's gun had burst, and injured him mortally.

And he remembered the story also, of how Mary O'Donnell, his great aunt, being married to a young Englishman, heard the Banshee as she sat one evening waiting for his return; and of how she, thinking the bridge by which he often came home unsafe for horse and man, went out in a great panic, to meet and entreat him to go round by the main road for her sake. Sir Edward was riding along in the moonlight, making straight for the bridge, when he beheld a figure dressed all in white crossing it. Then there was a crash, and the figure disappeared.

The lady was rescued and brought back to the hall; but next morning there were two dead bodies within its walls—those of Lady Eyreton and her still-born son.

Quicker than I write them, these memories chased one

another through Hertford O'Donnell's brain; and there was one more terrible memory than any, which would recur to him, concerning an Irish nobleman who, seated alone in his great town-house in London, heard the Banshee, and rushed out to get rid of the phantom, which wailed in his ear, nevertheless, as he strode down Piccadilly. And then the surgeon remembered how that nobleman went with a friend to the Opera, feeling sure that there no Banshee, unless she had a box, could find admittance, until suddenly he heard her singing up amongst the highest part of the scenery, with a terrible mournfulness, and a pathos which made the prima donna's tenderest notes seem harsh by comparison.

As he came out, some quarrel arose between him and a famous fire-eater, against whom he stumbled; and the result was that the next afternoon there was a new Lord, for he was killed in a duel with Captain Bravo.

Memories like these are not the most enlivening possible; they are apt to make a man fanciful, and nervous, and wakeful; but as time ran on, Hertford O'Donnell fell asleep, with his candle still burning, and Brian's cold nose pressed against his hand.

He dreamt of his mother's family—the Hertfords of Artingbury, Yorkshire, far-off relatives of Lord Hertford—so far off that even Mrs O'Donnell held no clue to the genealogical maze.

He thought he was at Artingbury, fishing; that it was a misty summer morning, and the fish rising beautifully. In his dreams he hooked one after another, and the boy who was with him threw them into the basket.

At last there was one more difficult to land than the others; and the boy, in his eagerness to watch the sport, drew nearer and nearer to the brink, while the fisher, intent on his prey, failed to notice his companion's danger.

Suddenly there was a cry, a splash, and the boy disappeared from sight.

Next instance he rose again, however, and then, for the first time, Hertford O'Donnell saw his face.

It was one he knew well.

In a moment he plunged into the water, and struck out for the lad. He had him by the hair, he was turning to bring him back to land, when the stream suddenly changed into a wide, wild, shoreless sea, where the billows were chasing one another with a mad demoniac mirth.

For a while O'Donnell kept the lad and himself afloat. They were swept under the waves, and came up again, only to see larger waves rushing towards them; but through all, the surgeon never loosened his hold, until a tremendous billow, engulfing them both, tore the boy from his grasp.

With the horror of his dream upon him he awoke, to hear a voice quite distinctly:

'Go to the hospital—go at once!'

The surgeon started up in bed, rubbing his eyes, and looked around. The candle was flickering faintly in its socket. Brian, with his ears pricked forward, had raised his head at his master's sudden movement.

Everything was quiet, but still those words were ringing in his ear:

'Go to the hospital—go at once!'

The tremendous peal of the bell over night, and this sentence, seemed to be simultaneous.

That he was wanted at Guy's—wanted imperatively—came to O'Donnell like an inspiration. Neither sense nor reason had anything to do with the conviction that roused him out of bed, and made him dress as speedily as possible, and grope his way down the staircase, Brian following.

He opened the front door, and passed out into the darkness. The rain was over, and the stars were shining as he pursued his way down Newport Market, and thence, winding in and out in a south-easterly direction, through Lincoln's Inn Fields and Old Square to Chancery Lane, whence he proceeded to St Paul's.

Along the deserted streets he resolutely continued his walk. He did not know what he was going to Guy's for. Some instinct was urging him on, and he neither strove to combat nor control it. Only once did the thought of turning back cross his mind, and that was the archway leading into Old Square. There he had paused for a moment, asking himself whether he were not gone stark, staring mad; but Guy's seemed preferable to the haunted house in Gerrard Street, and he walked resolutely on, determined to say, if any surprise were expressed at his appearance, that he had been sent for.

Sent for?—yea, truly; but by whom?

On through Cannon Street; on over London Bridge, where the lights flickered in the river, and the sullen splash of the water flowing beneath the arches, washing the stone piers, could be heard, now the human din was hushed and lulled to sleep. On, thinking of many things: of the days of his youth; of his dead brother; of his father's heavily-encumbered estate; of the fortune his mother had vowed she would leave to some charity rather than to him, if he refused to marry according to her choice; of his wild life in London; of the terrible cry he had heard over-night—that unearthly wail which he could not drive from his memory even when he entered Guy's, and confronted the porter, who said:

'You have been sent for, sir; did you meet the messenger?'

Like one in a dream, Hertford O'Donnell heard him; like one in a dream, also, he asked what was the matter.

'Bad accident, sir; fire; fell off a balcony—unsafe—old building. Mother and child—a son; child with compound fracture of thigh.'

This, the joint information of porter and house-surgeon, mingled together, and made a boom in Mr O'Donnell's ears like the sound of the sea breaking on a shingly shore.

Only one sentence he understood properly—'Immediate amputation necessary.' At this point he grew cool; he was the careful, cautious, successful surgeon, in a moment.

'The child you say?' he answered. 'Let me see him.'

The Guy's Hospital of today may be different to the Guy's Hertford O'Donnell knew so well. Railways have, I believe, swept away the old operating room; railways may have changed the position of the former accident ward, to reach which, in the days of which I am writing, the two surgeons had to pass a staircase leading to the upper stories.

On the lower step of this staircase, partially in shadow, Hertford O'Donnell beheld, as he came forward, an old woman seated.

An old woman with streaming grey hair, with attenuated arms, with head bowed forward, with scanty clothing, with bare feet; who never looked up at their approach, but sat unnoticing, shaking her head and wringing her hands in an extremity of despair.

'Who is that?' asked Mr O'Donnell, almost involuntarily.

'Who is what?' demanded his companion.

'That—that woman,' was the reply.

'What woman?'

'There—are you blind?—seated on the bottom step of the staircase. What is she doing?' persisted Mr O'Donnell.

'There is no woman near us,' his companion answered, looking at the rising surgeon very much as though he suspected him of seeing double.

'No woman!' scoffed Hertford. 'Do you expect me to disbelieve the evidence of my own eyes?' and he walked up to the figure, meaning to touch it.

But as he assayed to do so, the woman seemed to rise in the air and float away, with her arms stretched high up-over her head, uttering such a wail of pain, and agony, and distress, as caused the Irishman's blood to curdle.

'My God! Did you hear that?' he said to his companion.

'What?' was the reply.

Then, although he knew the sound had fallen on deaf ears, he answered:

'The wail of the Banshee! Some of my people are doomed!'

'I trust not,' answered the house-surgeon, who had an idea, nevertheless, that Hertford O'Donnell's Banshee lived in a whisky bottle, and would at some remote day make an end to the rising and clever operator.

With nerves utterly shaken, Mr O'Donnell walked forward to the accident ward. There with his face shaded from the light, lay his patient—a young boy, with a compound fracture of the thigh.

In that ward, in the face of actual danger or pain capable of relief the surgeon had never known faltering or fear; and now he carefully examined the injury, felt the pulse, inquired as to the treatment pursued, and ordered the sufferer to be carried to the operating room.

While he was looking out his instruments he heard the boy lying on the table murmur faintly:

'Tell her not to cry so—tell her not to cry.'

'What is he talking about?' Hertford O'Donnell inquired.

'The nurse says he has been speaking about some woman crying ever since he came in—his mother, most likely,' answered one of the attendants.

'He is delirious then?' observed the surgeon.

'No, sir,' pleaded the boy, excitedly, 'no; it is that woman —that woman with the grey hair. I saw her looking from the upper window before the balcony gave way. She has never left me since, and she won't be quiet, wringing her hands and crying.'

'Can you see her now?' Hertford O'Donnell inquired, stepping to the side of the table. 'Point out where she is.'

Then the lad stretched forth a feeble finger in the direction of the door, where clearly, as he had seen her seated on the stairs, the surgeon saw a woman standing—a woman with grey hair and scanty clothing, and upstretched arms and bare feet.

'A word with you, sir,' O'Donnell said to the house-surgeon, drawing him back from the table. 'I cannot perform this operation: send for some other person. I am ill; I am incapable.'

'But,' pleaded the other, 'there is no time to get anyone else. We sent for Mr West, before we troubled you, but he was out of town, and all the rest of the surgeons live so far away. Mortification may set in at any moment and—'.

'Do you think you require to teach me my business?' was the reply. 'I know the boy's life hangs on a thread, and that is the very reason I cannot operate. I am not fit for it. I tell you I have seen tonight that which unnerves me utterly. My hand is not steady. Send for someone else without delay. Say I am ill—dead!—what you please. Heavens! There she is again, right over the boy! Do you hear her?' and Hertford O'Donnell fell fainting on the floor.

How long he lay in that death-like swoon I cannot say; but when he returned to consciousness, the principal physician of Guy's was standing beside him in the cold grey light of the Christmas morning.

'The boy?' murmured O'Donnell, faintly.

'Now, my dear fellow, keep yourself quiet,' was the reply.

'The boy?' he repeated, irritably. 'Who operated?'

'No one,' Dr Lanson answered. 'It would have been useless cruelty. Mortification had set in and—'

Hertford O'Donnell turned his face to the wall, and his friend could not see it.

'Do not distress yourself,' went on the physician, kindly. 'Allington says he could not have survived the operation in any case. He was quite delirious from the first, raving about a woman with grey hair and—'

'I know,' Hertford O'Donnell interrupted; 'and the boy had a mother, they told me, or I dreamt it.'

'Yes, she was bruised and shaken, but not seriously injured.'

'Has she blue eyes and fair hair—fair hair all rippling and wavy? Is she white as a lily, with just a faint flush of colour in her cheek? Is she young and trusting and innocent? No; I am wandering. She must be nearly thirty now. Go, for God's sake, and tell me if you can find a woman you could imagine having once been as a girl such as I describe.'

'Irish?' asked the doctor; and O'Donnell made a gesture of assent.

'It is she then,' was the reply, 'a woman with the face of an angel.'

'A woman who should have been my wife,' the surgeon answered; 'whose child was my son.'

'Lord help you!' ejaculated the doctor. Then Hertford O'Donnell raised himself from the sofa where they had laid him, and told his companion the story of his life—how there had been bitter feud between his people and her people— how they were divided by old animosities and by difference of religion—how they had met by stealth, and exchanged rings and vows, all for naught—how his family had insulted hers, so that her father, wishful for her to marry a kinsman of his own, bore her off to a far-away land, and made her write him a letter of eternal farewell—how his own parents had kept all knowledge of the quarrel from him till she was utterly beyond his reach—how they had vowed to discard him unless he agreed to marry according to their wishes— how he left home, and came to London, and sought his fortune. All this Hertford O'Donnell repeated; and when he had finished, the bells were ringing for morning service— ringing loudly, ringing joyfully, 'Peace on earth, goodwill towards men'.

But there was little peace that morning for Hertford O'Donnell. He had to look on the face of his dead son, wherein he beheld, as though reflected, the face of the boy in his dream.

Afterwards, stealthily he followed his friend, and beheld, with her eyes closed, her cheeks pale and pinched, her hair thinner but still falling like a veil over her, the love of his youth, the only woman he had ever loved devotedly and unselfishly.

There is little space left here to tell of how the two met at last—of how the stone of the years seemed suddenly rolled away from the tomb of their past, and their youth arose and returned to them, even amid their tears.

She had been true to him, through persecution, through contumely, through kindness, which was more trying; through shame, and grief, and poverty, she had been loyal to the lover of her youth; and before the New Year dawned there came a letter from Calgillan, saying that the Banshee's wail had been heard there, and praying Hertford, if he were still alive, to let bygones be bygones, in consideration of the long years of estrangement—the anguish and remorse of his afflicted parents.

More than that. Hertford O'Donnell, if a reckless man, was honourable; and so, on the Christmas Day when he was to have proposed for Miss Ingot, he went to that lady, and told her how he had wooed and won, in the years of his youth, one who after many days was miraculously restored to him; and from the hour in which he took her into his confidence, he never thought her either vulgar or foolish, but rather he paid homage to the woman who, when she had heard the whole tale repeated, said, simply, 'Ask her to come to me till you can claim her—and God bless you both!'

HAND IN GLOVE

Elizabeth Bowen

Jasmine Lodge was favourably set on a residential, prettily-wooded hillside in the south of Ireland, overlooking a river and, still better, the roofs of a lively garrison town. Around 1904, which was the flowering period of the Miss Trevors, girls could not have had a more auspicious home—the neighbourhood spun merrily round the military. Ethel and Elsie, a spirited pair, garnered the full advantage—no ball, hop, picnic, lawn tennis, croquet or boating party was complete without them; in winter, though they could not afford to hunt, they trimly bicycled to all meets, and on frosty evenings, with their guitars, set off to *soirées*, snug inside their cab in their fur-tipped capes.

They possessed an aunt, a Mrs Varley de Grey, *née* Elysia Trevor, a formerly notable local belle, who, drawn back again in her widowhood to what had been the scene of her early triumphs, occupied a back bedroom in Jasmine Lodge. Mrs Varley de Grey had had no luck: her splashing match, in its time the talk of two kingdoms, had ended up in disaster—the well-born captain in a cavalry regiment having gone so far as to blow out his brains in India, leaving behind him nothing but her and debts. Mrs Varley de Grey had returned from India with nothing but seven large trunks crammed with recent finery; and she also had been impaired by shock. This had taken place while Ethel and Elsie, whose father had married late, were still unborn—so it was that, for as long as the girls recalled, their aunt had been the sole drawback to Jasmine Lodge. Their parents had orphaned them, somewhat thoughtlessly, by simultaneously dying of scarlet fever when Ethel was just out and Elsie soon to be—they were therefore left lacking a chaperone and, with their gift for putting everything to some use, propped the aunt up in order that she might play that role. Only when her peculiarities became too marked did they feel it necessary to withdraw her: by that time, however, all the surrounding ladies could be said to compete for the honour of taking into society the sought-after Miss Trevors. From then on, no more was seen or heard of Mrs Varley de Grey. ('Oh, just a trifle unwell, but nothing much!') She remained upstairs, at the back: when the girls were giving one of their little parties, or a couple of officers came to call, the key of her room would be turned in the outer lock.

The girls hung Chinese lanterns from the creepered veranda, and would sit lightly strumming on their guitars. Not less fascinating was their badinage, accompanied by a daring flash of the eyes. They were known as the clever Miss Trevors, not because of any taint of dogmatism or book-learning—no, when a gentleman cried, 'Those girls have brains!' he meant it wholly in admiration—but because of their accomplishments, ingenuity and agility. They took leading parts in theatricals, lent spirit to numbers of drawing-room games, were naughty mimics, and sang duets. Nor did their fingers lag behind their wits—they constructed lampshades, crêpe paper flowers and picturesque hats; and, above all, varied their dresses marvellously—no one could beat them for ideas, nipping, slashing or fitting. Once more allowing nothing to go to waste, they had remodelled the trousseau out of their aunt's trunks, causing sad old tulles and tarlatans, satins and *moiré* taffeta, to appear to have come from Paris only today. They re-stitched spangles, pressed ruffles crisp, and revived many a corsage of squashed silk roses. They went somewhat softly about that task, for the trunks were all stored in the attic immediately over the back room.

They wore their clothes well. 'A pin on either of those

two would look smart!' declared other girls. All that they were short of was evening gloves—they had two pairs each, which they had been compelled to buy. *What* could have become of Mrs Varley de Grey's presumably sumptuous numbers of this item, they were unable to fathom, and it was too bad. Had gloves been overlooked in her rush from India?—or, were they here, in that *one* trunk the Trevors could not get at? All other locks had yielded to pulls or pickings, or the sisters found keys to fit them, or they had used the tool-box; but this last stronghold defied them. In that sad little soiled silk sack, always on her person, Mrs Varley de Grey, they became convinced, hoarded the operative keys, along with some frippery rings and brooches— all true emeralds, pearls and diamonds having been long ago, as they knew, sold. Such contrariety on their aunt's part irked them—meanwhile, gaieties bore hard on their existing gloves. Last thing at nights when they came in, last thing in the evenings before they went out, they would manfully dab away at the fingertips. So, it must be admitted that a long whiff of benzine pursued them as they whirled round the ballroom floor.

They were tall and handsome—nothing so soft as pretty, but in those days it was a vocation to be a handsome girl; many of the best marriages had been made by such. They carried themselves imposingly, had good busts and shoulders, waists firm under the whalebone, and straight backs. Their features were striking, their colouring high; low on their foreheads bounced dark mops of curls. Ethel was, perhaps, the dominant one, but both girls were pronounced to be full of character.

Whom, and still more when, did they mean to marry? They had already seen regiments out and in; for quite a number of years, it began to seem, bets in the neighbourhood had been running high. Sympathetic spy-glasses were trained on the conspicuous gateway to Jasmine Lodge; each new cavalier was noted. The only trouble might be, their promoters claimed, that the clever Trevors were always so surrounded that they had not a moment in which to turn or choose. Or otherwise, could it possibly be that the admiration aroused by Ethel and Elsie, and their now institutional place in the local scene, scared out more tender feeling from the masculine breast? It came to be felt, and perhaps by the girls themselves, that, having lingered so long and so puzzlingly, it was up to them to bring off (like their aunt) a *coup*. Society around this garrison town had long plumed itself upon its romantic record; summer and winter, Cupid shot his darts. Lush scenery, the oblivion of all things else bred by the steamy climate, and perpetual gallivanting— all were conducive. Ethel's and Elsie's names, it could be presumed, were by now murmured wherever the Union Jack flew. Nevertheless, it was time they should decide.

Ethel's decision took place late one evening. She set her cap at the second son of an English marquess. Lord Fred had come on a visit, for the fishing, to a mansion some miles down the river from Jasmine Lodge. He first made his appearance, with the rest of the house party, at one of the more resplendent military balls, and was understood to be a man-about-town. The civilian glint of his pince-nez, at once serene and superb, instantaneously wrought, with his great name, on Ethel's heart. She beheld him, and the assembled audience, with approbation, looked on at the moment so big with fate. The truth, it appeared in a flash, was that Ethel, though so condescending with her charms, had not from the first been destined to love a soldier; and that here, after long attrition, her answer was. Lord Fred was, by all, at once signed over to her. For his part, he responded to her attentions quite gladly, though in a somewhat dazed way. If he did not so often dance with her— indeed, how could he, for she was much besought?—he could at least be perceived to gaze. At a swiftly organised river picnic, the next evening, he by consent fell to Ethel's lot—she had spent the foregoing morning snipping and tacking at a remaining muslin of Mrs Varley de Grey's, a very fresh forget-me-not-dotted pattern. The muslin did not survive the evening out, for when the moon should have risen, rain poured into the boats. Ethel's good-humoured drollery carried all before it, and Lord Fred wrapped his blazer around her form.

Next day, more rain; and all felt flat. At Jasmine Lodge, the expectant deck chairs had to be hurried in from the garden, and the small close rooms, with their greeneried windows and plentiful bric-à-brac, gave out a stuffy, resentful, indoor smell. The maid was out; Elsie was lying down with a migraine; so it devolved on Ethel to carry up Mrs Varley de Grey's tea—the invalid set very great store by tea, and her manifestations by door rattlings, sobs and mutters were apt to become disturbing if it did not appear. Ethel, with the not particularly dainty tray, accordingly entered the back room, this afternoon rendered dark by its outlook into a dripping uphill wood. The aunt, her visage draped in a cobweb shawl, was as usual sitting up in bed. '*Aha*,' she at once cried, screwing one eye up and glittering round at Ethel with the other, 'so what's all this in the wind today?'

Ethel, as she lodged the meal on the bed, shrugged her shoulders, saying: 'I'm in a hurry.'

'No doubt you are. The question is, will you get him?'

'Oh, drink your tea!' snapped Ethel, her colour rising.

The old wretch responded by popping a lump of sugar into her cheek, and sucking at it while she fixed her wink on her niece. She then observed: '*I* could tell you a thing or two!'

'We've had enough of *your* fabrications, Auntie!'

'Fabrications!' croaked Mrs Varley de Grey. 'And who's been the fabricator, I'd like to ask? Who's so nifty with the scissors and needle? Who's been going a-hunting in my clothes?'

'Oh, what a fib!' exclaimed Ethel, turning her eyes up. 'Those old musty miserable bundles of things of yours— would Elsie or I consider laying a finger on them?'

Mrs Varley de Grey replied, as she sometimes did, by heaving up and throwing the tray at Ethel. Nought, therefore, but cast-off kitchen china nowadays was ever exposed

to risk; and the young woman, not trying to gather the debris up, statuesquely, thoughtfully stood with her arms folded, watching tea steam rise from the carpet. Today, the effort required seemed to have been too much for Aunt Elysia, who collapsed on her pillows, faintly blue in the face. 'Rats in the attic,' she muttered. *'I've* heard them, rats in the attic! Now where's my tea?'

'You've had it,' said Ethel, turning to leave the room. However, she paused to study a photograph in a tarnished, elaborate silver frame. 'Really quite an Adonis, poor Uncle Harry.—From the first glance, you say, he never looked back?'

'My lovely tea,' said her aunt, beginning to sob.

As Ethel slowly put down the photograph, her eyes could be seen to calculate, her mouth hardened and a reflective cast came over her brow. Step by step, once more she approached the bed, and, as she did so, altered her tune. She suggested, in a beguiling tone: 'You said you could tell me a thing or two . . . ?'

Time went on; Lord Fred, though forever promising, still failed to come quite within Ethel's grasp. Ground gained one hour seemed to be lost the next—it seemed, for example, that things went better for Ethel in the afternoons, in the open air, than at the dressier evening functions. It was when she swept down on him in full plumage that Lord Fred seemed to contract. Could it be that he feared his passions? —she hardly thought so. Or, did her complexion not light up well? When there was a question of dancing, he came so late that her programme already was black with other names, whereupon he would heave a gallant sigh. When they did take the floor together, he held her so far at arm's length, and with his face turned so far away, that when she wished to address him she had to shout—she told herself this must be the London style, but it piqued her, naturally. Next morning, all would be as it was before, with nobody so completely assiduous as Lord Fred—but, through it all, he still never came to the point. And worse, the days of his visit were running out; he would soon be back in the heart of the London Season. 'Will you ever get him, Ethel, now, do you think?' Elsie asked, with trying solicitude, and no doubt the neighbourhood wondered also.

She conjured up all her fascinations. But was something further needed, to do the trick?

It was now that she began to frequent her aunt.

In that dank little back room looking into the hill, proud Ethel humbled herself, to prise out the secret. Sessions were close and long. Elsie, in mystification outside the door, heard the dotty voice of their relative rising, falling, with, now and then, bloodcurdling little knowing laughs. Mrs Varley de Grey was back in the golden days. Always, though, of a sudden it would break off, drop back into pleas, whimpers and jagged breathing. No doctor, though she constantly asked for one, had for years been allowed to visit Mrs Varley de Grey—the girls saw no reason for that expense, or for the interference which might follow. Aunt's affliction, they swore, was confined to the head; all she required was quiet, and that she got. Knowing, however, how gossip spreads, they would let no servant near her for more than a minute or two, and then with one of themselves on watch at the door. They had much to bear from the foetid state of her room.

'You don't think you'll kill her, Ethel?' the out-of-it Elsie asked. 'Forever sitting on top of her, as you now do. Can it be healthy, egging her on to talk? What's this attraction, all of a sudden?—whatever's this which has sprung up between you two? She and you are becoming quite hand-in-glove.'

Elsie merely remarked this, and soon forgot: she had her own fish to fry. It was Ethel who had cause to recall the words—for, the afternoon of the very day they were spoken, Aunt Elysia whizzed off on another track, screamed for what was impossible and, upon being thwarted, went into a seizure unknown before. The worst of it was, at the outset her mind cleared—she pushed her shawl back, reared up her unkempt grey head and looked at Ethel, unblinkingly studied Ethel, with a lucid accumulation of years of hate. 'You fool of a gawk,' she said, and with such contempt! 'Coming running to me to know how to trap a man. Could *you* learn, if it was from Venus herself? Wait till I show you beauty.—Bring down those trunks!'

'Oh, Auntie.'

'Bring them down, I say. I'm about to dress myself up.'

'Oh, but I cannot; they're heavy; I'm single-handed.'

'Heavy?—they came here heavy. But there've been rats in the attic.—*I* saw you, swishing downstairs in my *eau-de-nil*!'

'Oh, you dreamed that!'

'Through the crack of the door.—Let me up, then. Let us go where they are, and look—we shall soon see!' Aunt Elysia threw back the bedclothes and began to get up. 'Let's take a look,' she said, 'at the rats' work.' She set out to totter towards the door.

'Oh, but you're not fit!' Ethel protested.

'And when did a doctor say so?' There was a swaying: Ethel caught her in time and, not gently, lugged her back to the bed—and Ethel's mind the whole of this time was whirling, for tonight was the night upon which all hung. Lord Fred's last local appearance was to be, like his first, at a ball: tomorrow he left for London. So it must be tonight, at this ball, or never! How was it that Ethel felt so strangely, wildly confident of the outcome? It was time to begin on her coiffure, lay out her dress. Oh, tonight she would shine as never before! She flung back the bedclothes over the helpless form, heard a clock strike, and hastily turned to go.

'I will be quits with you,' said the voice behind her.

Ethel, in a kimono, hair half done, was in her own room, in front of the open glove drawer, when Elsie came in—home from a tennis party. Elsie acted oddly; she went at once to the drawer and buried her nose in it. 'Oh, my goodness,' she cried, 'it's all too true, and it's awful!'

'What is?' Ethel carelessly asked.

'Ethel dear, would you ever face it out if I were to tell you a certain rumour I heard today at the party as to Lord Fred?'

Ethel turned from her sister, took up the heated tongs and applied more crimps to her natural curliness. She said: 'Certainly; spit it out.'

'Since childhood, he's recoiled from the breath of benzine. He wilts away when it enters the very room!'

'Who says that's so?'

'He confided it to his hostess, who is now spitefully putting it around the country.'

Ethel bit her lip and put down the tongs, while Elsie sorrowfully concluded: 'And your gloves stink, Ethel, as I'm sure do mine.' Elsie then thought it wiser to slip away.

In a minute more, however, she was back, and this time with a still more peculiar air. She demanded: 'In what state did you leave Auntie? She was sounding so very quiet that I peeped in, and *I* don't care for the looks of her now at all!' Ethel swore, but consented to take a look. She stayed in there in the back room, with Elsie biting her thumb-nail outside the door, for what seemed an ominous length of time—when she did emerge, she looked greenish, but held her head high. The sisters' eyes met. Ethel said, stonily: 'Dozing.'

'You're certain she's *not* . . . ? She *couldn't* ever be—you know?'

'Dozing, I tell you,' Ethel stared Elsie out.

'If she *was* gone,' quavered the frailer sister, 'just think of it—why, we'd never get to the ball!—And a ball that everything hangs on,' she ended up, with a sacred but conspiratorial glance at Ethel.

'Reassure yourself. Didn't you hear me say?'

As she spoke Ethel, chiefly from habit, locked her late aunt's door on the outside. The act caused a sort of secret jingle to be heard from inside her fist, and Elsie asked: 'What's that you've got hold of, now?' 'Just a few little keys and trinkets she made me keep,' replied Ethel, disclosing

the small bag she had found where she'd looked for it, under the dead one's pillow. 'Scurry on now, Elsie, or you'll never be dressed. Care to make use of my tongs, while they're so splendidly hot?'

Alone at last, Ethel drew in a breath, and, with a gesture of resolution, retied her kimono sash tightly over her corset. She shook the key from the bag and regarded it, murmuring, 'Providential!', then gave a glance upward, towards where the attics were. The late spring sun had set, but an apricot afterglow, not unlike the light cast by a Chinese lantern, crept through the upper story of Jasmine Lodge. The cessation of all those rustlings, tappings, whimpers and moans from inside Mrs Varley de Grey's room had set up an unfamiliar, somewhat unnerving hush. Not till a whiff of singeing hair announced that Elsie was well employed did Ethel set out on the quest which held all her hopes. Success was imperative—she *must* have gloves. Gloves, gloves . . .

Soundlessly, she set foot on the attic stairs.

Under the skylight, she had to suppress a shriek, for a rat —yes, of all things!—leaped at her out of an empty hatbox; and the rodent gave her a wink before it darted away. Now Ethel and Elsie knew for a certain fact that there never *had* been rats in Jasmine Lodge. However, she continued to steel her nerves, and to push her way to the one inviolate trunk.

All Mrs Varley de Grey's other Indian luggage gaped and yawned at Ethel, void, showing its linings, on end or toppling, forming a barricade around the object of her search —she pushed, pitched and pulled, scowling as the dust flew into her hair. But the last trunk, when it came into view and reach, still had something select and bridal about it: on top, the initials E. V. de G. stared out, quite luminous in a frightening way—for indeed how dusky the attic was! Shadows not only multiplied in the corners but seemed to finger their way up the sloping roof. Silence pierced up through the floor from that room below—and, worst, Ethel had the sensation of being watched by that pair of fixed eyes she had not stayed to close. She glanced this way, that way, backward over her shoulder. But, Lord Fred was at stake!—she knelt down and got to work with the key.

This trunk had two neat brass locks, one left, one right, along the front of the lid. Ethel, after fumbling, opened the first—then, so great was her hurry to know what might be within that she could not wait but slipped her hand in under the lifted corner. She pulled out one pricelessly lacy top of what must be a bride-veil, and gave a quick laugh—must not this be an omen? She pulled again, but the stuff resisted, almost as though it were being grasped from inside the trunk —she let go, and either her eyes deceived her or the lace began to be drawn back slowly, in again, inch by inch. What was odder was, that the spotless finger-tip of a white kid glove appeared for a moment, as though exploring its way out, then withdrew.

Ethel's heart stood still—but she turned to the other lock. Was a giddy attack overcoming her?—for, as she gazed, the entire lid of the trunk seemed to bulge upward, heave and strain, so that the E. V. de G. upon it rippled.

Untouched by the key in her trembling hand, the second lock tore itself open.

She recoiled, while the lid slowly rose—of its own accord.

She should have fled. But oh, how she craved what lay there exposed!—layer upon layer, wrapped in transparent paper, of elbow-length, magnolia-pure white gloves, bedded on the inert folds of the veil. 'Lord Fred,' thought Ethel, 'now you're within my grasp!'

That was her last thought, nor was the grasp to be hers. Down on her knees again, breathless with lust and joy, Ethel flung herself forward on to that sea of kid, scrabbling and seizing. The glove she had seen before was now, however, readier for its purpose. At first it merely pounced after Ethel's fingers, as though making mock of their greedy course; but the hand within it was all the time filling out . . . With one snowy flash through the dusk, the glove clutched Ethel's front hair, tangled itself in her black curls and dragged her head down. She began to choke among the

sachets and tissue—then the glove let go, hurled her back, and made its leap at her throat.

It was a marvel that anything so dainty should be so strong. So great, so convulsive was the swell of the force that, during the strangling of Ethel, the seams of the glove split.

In any case, the glove would have been too small for her.

The shrieks of Elsie, upon the attic threshold, began only when all other sounds had died down . . . The ultimate spark of the once-famous cleverness of the Miss Trevors appeared in Elsie's extrication of herself from this awkward mess— for, who was to credit how Ethel came by her end? The sisters' reputation for warmth of heart was to stand the survivor in good stead—for, could those affections nursed in Jasmine Lodge, extending so freely even to the unwell aunt, have culminated in Elsie's setting on Ethel? No. In the end, the matter was hushed up—which is to say, is still talked about even now. Ethel Trevor and Mrs Varley de Grey were interred in the same grave, as everyone understood that they would have wished. What conversation took place under the earth, one does not know.

THE END OF THE RECORD

Sean O'Faolain

The news went around the poorhouse that there was a man with a recording van in the grounds. He was picking up old stories and songs.

'And they say that he would give you a five-shilling piece into your hand for two verses of an old song,' said Thomas Hunter, an old man from Coomacoppal, in West Kerry, forgetting that five-shilling pieces were no longer in fashion. 'Or for a story, if you have a good one.'

'What sort of stories would them be?' Michael Kivlehan asked skeptically. He was from the barony of Forth and Bargy, in County Wexford, and had been in the poorhouse for eleven years.

'Any story at all only it is to be an old story and a good story. A story about the fairies, or about ghosts, or about the way people lived long ago.'

'And what do he do with 'um when he have 'um?'

'Hasn't he a phonograph? And doesn't he give them out over the wireless? And doesn't everyone in Ireland be listening to them?'

'I wonder now,' said Michael Kivlehan, 'would he give me five shillings for the "Headless Horseman and the Coacha Bowr"?'

Thomas Hunter sighed.

'One time I had a grand story about Finn MacCool and the Scotch giant. But it is gone from me. And I'd be getting my fine five-shilling piece into my fist this minute if I could only announce it to him.'

THE END OF THE RECORD   71

The two old men sat on the sides of their beds and tried to remember stories. But it was other things they remembered and they forgot all about the man outside who had set them thinking of their childhood.

The doctor had taken the collector into the women's ward to meet Mary Creegan. She was sitting up in bed, alone in the long room; all the other women were out in the warm sun. As the two men walked up the bare floor the collector was trailing a long black cable from a microphone in his hand, and the doctor was telling him that she came from a place called Faill-a-ghleanna in West Cork.

'She should have lots of stories because her husband was famous for them. After he died she went a bit airy so they had to bring her to us. 'Twas a bit tough on her at first. Sixty years in the one cottage—and then to finish up here.' They stood beside her bed. 'I brought a visitor to see you, Mary,' he said in a loud voice.

She did not appear to see them. She was humming happily to herself. Her bony fingers were wound about an ancient rosary beads. Her white hair floated up above a face as tiny and as wrinkled as a forgotten crab apple. All her teeth were gone so that her face was as broad as it was long: it was as if the midwife had pressed the baby's chin and forehead between thumb and forefinger. The doctor gently laid his hand under the tiny chin and turned her face towards him. She smiled.

'Put down the kettle and wet the tay,' she ordered.

The doctor sat on the bed; so did the collector.

''Tis down, Mary, and two eggs in the pot. This poor man here is after coming a long way to talk to you. He's tired out.'

She turned and looked at the stranger. Encouraged by a brightening spark in the depths of her eyes he turned aside and murmured quietly into the microphone, 'Reggy? Recording ten seconds from . . . now.'

'It's a bad road,' she said. 'Ask Jamesy is he keeping that divil of a cow out of the cabbage.'

'She's all right,' the doctor cried into her ear. 'Jamesy is watching her. Be talking to us while we're waiting for the tay. You told me one time you saw a ghost. Is that true?'

She looked out of the window and her eyes opened and narrowed like a fish's gills as if they were sucking something in from the blue sky outside. The collector stealthily approached her chin with the microphone.

'Ghosts? Ayeh! Ha! My ould divil of a tailor is forever and always talkin' about 'um. But, sure, I wouldn't heed him. Bummin' and boashtin' he is from morning to night and never a needle to be shtuck in the shtuff. Where is he? Why don't you ask him to be talking to you about ghoshts?'

The doctor looked across the bed at the collector and raised his eyebrows.

'Maybe you don't believe in them yourself?' he mocked.

'I do *not* believe in 'um. But they're there. Didn't I hear tell of 'um from them that saw 'um? Aye, and often. And often! Aye'—still collecting her thoughts from the sky above the bakehouse chimney—'wasn't it that way the night Father Regan died? Huh! They called him Father Regan, but he was not a right priest. He was silenced for some wrong thing he did when he was a young priest, and they sent him to Faill-a-ghleanna to be doing penance for it. When his time came to die it was a bad, shtormy night. And when he sent for the parish priest to hear his confession the priest said he could not come. And that was a hard thing to do, for no man should refuse the dying. And they sent another messenger for the priest, and still the priest could not come. "Oh," said Father Regan, "I'm lost now." So they sent a third messenger. And for the third time the priest could not come. And on his way back wasn't the messenger shtopped on the road by a woman? It was Father Regan's own mother. "Go back," says she, "and if the candles by his bed light up," says she, "of their own accord," says she, "he is saved." And the messenger went back, and Father Regan gave wan look at him and he closed his eyes for the last time. With that all the people went on their knees. And they began to pray. If they did, there were three candles at the head of the dead priest. And didn't the one beside the window light up? And after a little while the candle beside the fire clevy lit up. And they went on praying. And the wind and the shtorm screaming about the house, and they watching the wick of the last candle. And, bit by bit, the way you'd blow up a fire with a bellows, didn't the candle over the priest's head light up until the whole room was like broad daylight.'

The old woman's voice suddenly became bright and hard.

'Isn't that tay ready a-yet? Domn and blosht it, ye'll have them eggs like bullets.' She looked alertly at the two men. 'Where am I? Where's Jamesy? What are ye doing to me?'

The doctor held her wrist. Her eyes faded. She sank back heavily.

'I thought,' she wailed, 'that it was how I saw a great brightness.'

The collector spoke one word into the microphone. The old woman had fainted. Overcome with regrets he began to apologise, but the doctor waved his hand at him.

'Excited. I'll send up the sister to give her an injection. Sometimes she loves to talk about old times. It does her good.'

They went out of the empty ward, the cable trailing softly. They passed the male ward. Michael Kivlehan and Thomas Hunter were sitting on their beds. As the doctor led the way downstairs, he said, 'When that generation goes it will be all over. Wait for me outside. There are a couple more. You might get bits and scraps from them.'

The engineer put his head out of the van and said, in the gloomy voice of all engineers, 'That might come through all right.'

When the doctor came out again they sat with a middle-aged man from Wicklow, named Fenelon. He had been on the roads until arthritis crippled him. When he counted the years he spoke in Urdu. He had scraps of the tinker's language which is called Shelta. He said:

'I often walked from Dublin to Puck, and that's a hundred

miles, without ever disturbing anything but a hare or a snipe. I'd make for Ross, and then cross to Callan, and by Slievenamon west to the Galtees.'

He did not see the microphone; he did not see his visitors; as the needle softly cut the disc he was seeing only the mountainy sheep that looked at him with slitted eyes, a thing as shaggy as themselves.

They moved on to an old woman who sang a love song for them in a cracked voice. She said she had learned it in Chicago. She gave them a poem of twelve verses about a voyage to the South Seas. They were finishing a disc with a very old man from Carlow when the sister came out and hastily beckoned to the doctor. As they folded up the cable he came back. He said, with a slow shake of the head:

'It's old Mary. I must leave ye. But ye have the best of them. The rest is only the shakings of the bag.'

When they had thanked him and were driving away, the collector said, eagerly:

'Pull up when we're out of the town. I want to play back those discs.'

They circled up and out of the town until its murmur was so faint that they could hear only the loudest cries of the playing children. There they played back the discs, and as they leaned towards the loud-speaker and the black record circled smoothly they could see, sideways through the window, the smoke of the hollow town. The last voice was Mary Cregan's.

'. . . and after a little while the candle beside the fire clevy lit up. And they went on praying. And the wind and the shtorm screaming about the house, and they watching the wick of the last candle. And, bit by bit, the way you'd blow up a fire with a bellows, didn't the candle over the priest's head light up until the whole room was like broad daylight . . . Isn't that tay ready a-yet? Domn and blosht it, ye'll have them eggs like bullets . . . Where am I? Where's Jamesy? What are ye doing to me? . . . I thought that it was how I saw a great brightness.'

The listeners relaxed. Then from the record came a low, lonely cry. It was the fluting of a bittern over moorland. It fluted sadly once again, farther away; and for a third time, almost too faint to be heard. Many times the two men played back those last few inches of disc. Every time they heard the bittern wailing over the mountains.

It was dusk. They laid the voices in a black box and drove away. Then they topped the hill, and the antennae of their headlamps began to probe the winding descent to the next valley.

2

HAUNTINGS

With a country as well populated with ghosts as Ireland, there are inevitably many different haunted localities. The range is enormous—from an ancient castle or a country mansion to a town house or a city flat—and there are even hauntings to be found on the remotest of the country's coastal islands. All these places, however, have a distinctive allure and atmosphere which over the years has provided inspiration for stories by some of the country's most versatile writers.

Bram Stoker (1847–1912) is best known for a single, classic horror novel, *Dracula*. His influence has been as great as that of Joseph Sheridan Le Fanu, for while Le Fanu may be regarded as the 'father' of the modern ghost story, all writers of vampire tales owe more than a nod of acknowledgement to Stoker's great story of the undead Count published almost a century ago, in 1897. Born in Clontarf, Dublin, Bram Stoker began his working life as a civil servant while nursing a passion for the theatre. He managed to secure for himself the part-time job of drama critic on the *Dublin Mail*, and a favourable review brought him to the attention of the great English actor-manager, Sir Henry Irving, who was touring the country. Offered the post of Irving's manager, Stoker enthusiastically accepted and for the next decade devoted himself to Sir Henry's career. In what little spare time he had, he also pursued his other interest, that of writing, and, apart from a couple of dozen short stories, composed several more horror novels—

including *The Jewel of Seven Stars* (1903), *The Lady of the Shroud* (1909) and *The Lair of the White Worm* (1911)— although none repeated the huge success of *Dracula*.

While it is true that Stoker was a great admirer of the works of several Irish supernatural writers, including Le Fanu, Patrick Kennedy and Gerald Griffin, unlike them he set very few of his stories in Ireland. One brilliant exception, however, is 'The Judge's House' which he contributed to the Christmas number of the English magazine *Holly Leaves*, published on 5 December, 1891. This story, of a young student who spends a night in a haunted town house and there encounters a vicious and dangerous spirit, may not have been ideal Christmas reading, but it is one of the most powerful and evocative short stories from Stoker's pen.

Appropriately a ghost story by Sir Henry Irving's manager is followed by a tale from one of Ireland's greatest twentieth-century theatrical figures, Michael MacLiammoir (1899–   ). Born in Cork, MacLiammoir has had a tremendous impact on the Irish theatrical scene, as an actor, scenic designer and dramatist. From 1928–1931 he was director of the Gaelic Theatre in Galway and later became a founder of the famous Dublin Gate Theatre. He was always interested in Irish legends and many of his plays, such as *Where Stars Walk* (1940), *Ill Met By Moonlight* (1946) and *Put Money in Thy Purse* (1952), are based on famous examples. His version of the love story of Midhir and Etain, in which the couple are reunited after death in the King's palace of Tara, was particularly notable for being transformed into a modern setting. He has also written a few short stories, of which 'The Servant', about a haunting in a Dublin flat, is as fine an example of a ghost story as one might hope to find.

L.A.G. Strong (1896–1958), the Anglo-Irish novelist and poet, was a great admirer of MacLiammoir and, like him, was interested in Irish legends and folkore. In his childhood many such tales had been told him by his mother who was a member of one of the oldest families in the country.

Indeed, his youth in Ireland had a strong influence on his verse—in such collections as *Dublin Days* (1921)—while his absorption with Irish supernatural tradition was revealed in novels like *Dewer Rides* (1929) and in several of the short stories collected in *Travellers* (1945) which won the James Tait Black Memorial Prize. He was also widely praised for his books about two famous Irishmen, John McCormack (1949), and James Joyce (1950). Strong was apparently inspired to write his story 'Let Me Go' in 1947, after one of his frequent return visits to Ireland. This tale of a bedraggled eighteenth-century ghost which haunts a decaying farmhouse is also in the very best tradition of Le Fanu.

A small town rectory provides the location for the strange and moving story 'Autumn Sunshine' by William Trevor (1928–   ). Born William Trevor Cox in County Cork, he grew up in a succession of little Irish towns as his father, who worked for the Bank of Ireland, was moved from one branch to another. The son remembers his father as a man who loved talking to people and telling stories, and after graduating from Trinity College, Dublin, he himself took to writing the novels and, particularly, short stories which have brought him international acclaim. His work has earned several major honours, including the Hawthornden Prize in 1964 and the Whitbread Literary Award in 1976, and he is a member of the Irish Academy of Letters and was made a CBE in Britain in 1977.

Because of his upbringing, William Trevor is to be found at his best when writing of small town life and people, invariably focusing on elements of disillusionment, the sordid and the depressing, with occasionally forays into the ghostly and the horrific. Indeed, he has written a number of supernatural stories—although not all set in Ireland—which have caused James F. Kilroy to describe him as 'a phlegmatic Poe', adding: 'To Trevor, horror is the dull, realistic stuff of everyday life.' A little of all these elements is to be found in 'Autumn Sunshine', written in 1981, a story whose unique handling of the supernatural endorses the claims of critics who have compared Trevor to that great English master of the ghost story, Charles Dickens.

The final story in this section, 'Aisling', is set about as far away from civilisation as it is possible to get: on the remote island of Inis Tuaisceart, where a youthful new priest discovers that he is sharing a primitive bothan (cabin) with another, very sinister, occupant. The author, Peter Tremayne, (Peter Berresford Ellis, 1943–   ) is one of the foremost modern Anglo-Irish supernatural fantasy writers, who has the distinction, alone among his contemporaries, of having had several of his short stories published in the leading Irish language literary journal, *Feasta*.

Tremayne, a contemporary of mine in London publishing thirty years ago, turned from journalism to writing literary and historical biographies, as well as fantasy stories based on Celtic myths and a continuing series of novels about Count Dracula (*Dracula Unborn*, 1977; *The Revenge of Dracula*, 1978; and so on). He believes that Bram Stoker's concepts have more to do with Irish folk legend and custom than with Transylvania. His passion for Celtic language and literature also inspired him to organise the first Celtic Book Fair in London which has subsequently became an annual event. 'Aisling' was published in an Irish language translation in *Feasta* in 1985 and is here making its first appearance in book form.

THE JUDGE'S HOUSE

Bram Stoker

When the time for his examination drew near Malcolm Malcolmson made up his mind to go somewhere to read by himself. He feared the attractions of the seaside, and also he feared completely rural isolation, for of old he knew its charms, and so he determined to find some unpretentious little town where there would be nothing to distract him. He refrained from asking suggestions from any of his friends, for he argued that each would recommend some place of which he had knowledge, and where he had already acquaintances. As Malcolmson wished to avoid friends he had no wish to encumber himself with the attention of friends' friends, and so he determined to look out for a place for himself. He packed a portmanteau with some clothes and all the books he required, and then took ticket for the first name on the local time-table which he did not know.

When at the end of three hours' journey he alighted at Benchurch, he felt satisfied that he had so far obliterated his tracks as to be sure of having a peaceful opportunity of pursuing his studies. He went straight to the one inn which the sleepy little place contained, and put up for the night. Benchurch was a market town, and once in three weeks was crowded to excess, but for the remainder of the twenty-one days it was as attractive as a desert. Malcolmson looked around the day after his arrival to try to find quarters more isolated than even so quiet an inn as 'The Good Traveller' afforded. There was only one place which took his fancy, and it certainly satisfied his wildest ideas regarding quiet; in fact, quiet was not the proper word to apply to it—desolation was the only term conveying any suitable idea of its isolation. It was an old rambling, heavy-built house of the Jacobean style, with heavy gables and windows, unusually small, and set higher than was customary in such houses, and was surrounded with a high brick wall massively built. Indeed, on examination, it looked more like a fortified house than an ordinary dwelling. But all these things pleased Malcolmson. 'Here,' he thought, 'is the very spot I have been looking for, and if I can only get opportunity of using it I shall be happy.' His joy was increased when he realised beyond doubt that it was not at present inhabited.

From the post-office he got the name of the agent, who was rarely surprised at the application to rent a part of the old house. Mr Carnford, the local lawyer and agent, was a genial old gentleman, and frankly confessed his delight at anyone being willing to live in the house.

'To tell you the truth,' said he, 'I should be only too happy, on behalf of the owners, to let anyone have the house rent free for a term of years if only to accustom the people here to see it inhabited. It has been so long empty that some kind of absurd prejudice has grown up about it, and this can be best put down by its occupation—if only,' he added with a sly glance at Malcolmson, 'by a scholar like yourself, who wants its quiet for a time.'

Malcolmson thought it needless to ask the agent about the 'absurd prejudice'; he knew he would get more information, if he should require it, on that subject from other quarters. He paid his three months' rent, got a receipt, and the name of an old woman who would probably undertake to 'do' for him, and came away with the keys in his pocket. He then went to the landlady of the inn, who was a cheerful and most kindly person, and asked her advice as to such stores and provisions as he would be likely to require. She threw up her hands in amazement when he told her where he was going to settle himself.

'Not in the Judge's House!' she said, and grew pale as she

spoke. He explained the locality of the house, saying that he did not know its name. When he had finished she answered:

'Aye, sure enough—sure enough the very place. It is the Judge's House sure enough.' He asked her to tell him about the place, why so called, and what there was against it. She told him that it was so called locally because it had been many years before—how long she could not say, as she was herself from another part of the country, but she thought it must have been a hundred years or more—the abode of a judge who was held in great terror on account of his harsh sentences and his hostility to prisoners at Assizes. As to what there was against the house itself she could not tell. She had often asked, but no one could inform her; but there was a general feeling that there was *something*, and for her own part she would not take all the money in Drinkwater's Bank and stay in the house an hour by herself. Then she apologised to Malcolmson for her disturbing talk.

'It is too bad of me, sir, and you—and a young gentleman, too—if you will pardon me saying it, going to live there all alone. If you were my boy—and you'll excuse me for saying it—you wouldn't sleep there a night, not if I had to go there myself and pull the big alarm bell that's on the roof!' The good creature was so manifestly in earnest, and was so kindly in her intentions, that Malcomson, although amused, was touched. He told her kindly how much he appreciated her interest in him, and added:

'But, my dear Mrs Witham, indeed you need not be concerned about me! A man who is reading for the Mathematical Tripos has too much to think of to be disturbed by any of these mysterious "somethings," and his work is of too exact and prosaic a kind to allow of his having any corner in his mind for mysteries of any kind. Harmonical Progression, Permutations and Combinations, and Elliptic Functions have sufficient mysteries for me!' Mrs Witham kindly undertook to see after his commissions, and he went himself to look for the old woman who had been recommended to him. When he returned to the Judge's House with her, after an interval of a couple of hours, he found Mrs Witham herself waiting with several men and boys carrying parcels, and an upholsterer's man with a bed in a cart, for she said, though tables and chairs might be all very well, a bed that hadn't been aired for mayhap fifty years was not proper for young bones to lie on. She was evidently curious to see the inside of the house; and though manifestly so afraid of the 'some-things' that at the slightest sound she clutched on to Malcom-son, whom she never left for a moment, went over the whole place.

After his examination of the house, Malcomson decided to take up his abode in the great dining-room, which was big enough to serve for all his requirements; and Mrs Witham, with the aid of the charwoman, Mrs Dempster, proceeded to arrange matters. When the hampers were brought in and unpacked, Malcomson saw that with much kind forethought she had sent from her own kitchen suf-ficient provisions to last for a few days. Before going she expressed all sorts of kind wishes; and at the door turned and said:

'And perhaps, sir, as the room is big and draughty it might be well to have one of those big screens put round your bed at night—though, truth to tell, I would die myself if I were to be so shut in with all kinds of—of "things," that put their heads round the sides, or over the top, and look on me!' The image which she had called up was too much for her nerves, and she fled incontinently.

Mrs Dempster sniffed in a superior manner as the landlady disappeared, and remarked that for her own part she wasn't afraid of all the bogies in the kingdom.

'I'll tell you what it is, sir,' she said; 'bogies is all kinds and sorts of things—except bogies! Rats and mice, and beetles; and creaky doors, and loose slates, and broken panes, and stiff drawer handles, that stay out when you pull them and then fall down in the middle of the night. Look at the wainscot of the room! It is old—hundreds of years old! Do you think there's no rats and beetles there! And do you imagine, sir, that you wont see none of them? Rats is bogies, I tell you, and bogies is rats; and don't you get to think anything else!'

'Mrs Dempster,' said Malcomson gravely, making her a polite bow, 'you know more than a Senior Wrangler! And let me say, that, as a mark of esteem for your indubitable soundness of head and heart, I shall, when I go, give you possession of this house, and let you stay here by yourself for the last two months of my tenancy, for four weeks will serve my purpose.'

'Thank you kindly, sir!' she answered, 'but I couldn't sleep away from home a night. I am in Greenhow's Charity, and if I slept a night away from my rooms I should lose all I have got to live on. The rules is very strict; and there's too many watching for a vacancy for me to run any risks in the matter. Only for that, sir, I'd gladly come here and attend on you altogether during your stay.'

'My good woman,' said Malcomson hastily, 'I have come here on purpose to obtain solitude; and believe me that I am grateful to the late Greenhow for having so organised his admirable charity—whatever it is—that I am perforce denied the opportunity of suffering from such a form of temptation! Saint Anthony himself could not be more rigid on the point!'

The old woman laughed harshly. 'Ah, you young gentlemen,' she said, 'you don't fear for naught; and belike you'll get all the solitude you want here.' She set to work with her cleaning; and by nightfall, when Malcomson returned from his walk—he always had one of his books to study as he walked—he found the room swept and tidied, a fire burning in the old hearth, the lamp lit, and the table spread for supper with Mrs Witham's excellent fare. 'This is comfort, indeed,' he said, as he rubbed his hands.

When he had finished his supper, and lifted the tray to the other end of the great oak dining-table, he got out his books again, put fresh wood on the fire, trimmed his lamp, and set himself down to a spell of real hard work. He went on without pause till about eleven o'clock, when he knocked off for a bit to fix his fire and lamp, and to make himself a cup of tea. He had always been a tea-drinker, and during his college life had sat late at work and had taken tea late. The rest was a great luxury to him, and he enjoyed it with a sense of delicious, voluptuous ease. The renewed fire leaped and sparkled, and threw quaint shadows through the great old room; and as he sipped his hot tea he revelled in the sense of isolation from his kind. Then it was that he began to notice for the first time what a noise the rats were making.

'Surely,' he thought, 'they cannot have been at it all the time I was reading. Had they been, I must have noticed it!' Presently, when the noise increased, he satisfied himself that it was really new. It was evident that at first the rats had been frightened at the presence of a stranger, and the light of fire and lamp; but that as the time went on they had grown bolder and were now disporting themselves as was their wont.

How busy they were! and hark to the strange noises! Up and down behind the old wainscot, over the ceiling and under the floor they raced, and gnawed, and scratched! Malcomson smiled to himself as he recalled to mind the saying of Mrs Dempster, 'Bogies is rats, and rats is bogies!' The tea began to have its effect of intellectual and nervous stimulus, he saw with joy another long spell of work to be done before the night was past, and in the sense of security which it gave him, he allowed himself the luxury of a good look round the room. He took his lamp in one hand, and went all around, wondering that so quaint and beautiful an old house had been so long neglected. The carving of the oak on the panels of the wainscot was fine, and on and round the doors and windows it was beautiful and of rare merit. There were some old pictures on the walls, but they were coated so thick with dust and dirt that he could not distinguish any detail of them, though he held his lamp as high as he could over his head. Here and there as he went round he saw some crack or hole blocked for a moment by the face of a rat with its bright eyes glittering in the light, but in an instant it was gone, and a squeak and a scamper followed. The thing that most struck him, however, was the rope of the great alarm bell on the roof, which hung down in a corner of the room on the right-hand side of the fireplace. He pulled up close to the hearth a great high-backed carved oak chair, and sat down to his last cup of tea. When this was done he made up the fire, and went back to his work, sitting at the corner of the table, having the fire to his left. For a little while the rats disturbed him somewhat with their perpetual scampering, but he got accustomed to the noise as one does to the ticking of a clock or to the roar of moving water; and he became so immersed in his work that everything in the world, except the problem which he was trying to solve, passed away from him.

He suddenly looked up, his problem was still unsolved, and there was in the air that sense of the hour before the dawn, which is so dread to doubtful life. The noise of the rats had ceased. Indeed it seemed to him that it must have ceased but lately and that it was the sudden cessation which had disturbed him. The fire had fallen low, but still it threw out a deep red glow. As he looked he started in spite of his *sang froid*.

There on the great high-backed carved oak chair by the right side of the fire-place sat an enormous rat, steadily glaring at him with baleful eyes. He made a motion to it as though to hunt it away, but it did not stir. Then he made the motion of throwing something. Still it did not stir, but showed its great white teeth angrily, and its cruel eyes shone in the lamplight with an added vindictiveness.

Malcomson felt amazed, and seizing the poker from the hearth ran at it to kill it. Before, however, he could strike it, the rat, with a squeak that sounded like the concentration of hate, jumped upon the floor, and, running up the rope of the alarm bell, disappeared in the darkness beyond the range of the green-shaded lamp. Instantly, strange to say, the noisy scampering of the rats in the wainscot began again.

By this time Malcomson's mind was quite off the problem; and as a shrill cock-crow outside told him of the approach of morning, he went to bed and to sleep.

He slept so sound that he was not even waked by Mrs Dempster coming in to make up his room. It was only when she had tidied up the place and got his breakfast ready and tapped on the screen which closed in his bed that he woke. He was a little tired still after his night's hard work, but a strong cup of tea soon freshened him up and, taking his book, he went out for his morning walk, bringing with him a few sandwiches lest he should not care to return till dinner time. He found a quiet walk between high elms some way outside the town, and here he spent the greater part of the day studying his Laplace. On his return he looked in to see Mrs Witham and to thank her for her kindness. When she saw him coming through the diamond-paned bay window of her sanctum she came out to meet him and asked him in. She looked at him searchingly and shook her head as she said:

'You must not overdo it, sir. You are paler this morning than you should be. Too late hours and too hard work on the brain isn't good for any man! But tell me, sir, how did you pass the night? Well, I hope? But, my heart! sir, I was glad when Mrs Dumpster told me this morning that you were all right and sleeping sound when she went in.'

'Oh, I was all right,' he answered smiling, 'the "some-things" didn't worry me, as yet. Only the rats; and they had a circus, I tell you, all over the place. There was one wicked looking old devil that sat up on my own chair by the fire, and wouldn't go till I took the poker to him, and then he ran up the rope of the alarm bell and got to somewhere up the wall or the ceiling—I couldn't see where, it was so dark.'

'Mercy on us,' said Mrs Witham, 'an old devil, and sitting on a chair by the fireside! Take care, sir! take care! There's many a true word spoken in jest.'

'How do you mean? 'Pon my word I don't understand.'

'An old devil! The old devil, perhaps. There! sir, you

needn't laugh,' for Malcomson had broken into a hearty peal. 'You young folks thinks it easy to laugh at things that makes older ones shudder. Never mind, sir! never mind! Please God, you'll laugh all the time. It's what I wish you myself!' and the good lady beamed all over in sympathy with his enjoyment, her fears gone for a moment.

'Oh, forgive me!' said Malcomson presently. 'Don't think me rude; but the idea was too much for me—that the old devil himself was on the chair last night!' And at the thought he laughed again. Then he went home to dinner.

This evening the scampering of the rats began earlier; indeed it had been going on before his arrival, and only ceased whilst his presence by its freshness disturbed them. After dinner he sat by the fire for a while and had a smoke; and then, having cleared his table, began to work as before. Tonight the rats disturbed him more than they had done on the previous night. How they scampered up and down and under and over! How they squeaked, and scratched, and gnawed! How they, getting bolder by degrees, came to the mouths of their holes and to the chinks and cracks and crannies in the wainscoting till their eyes shone like tiny lamps as the firelight rose and fell. But to him, now doubtless accustomed to them, their eyes were not wicked; only their playfulness touched him. Sometimes the boldest of them made sallies out on the floor or along the mouldings of the wainscot. Now and again as they disturbed him Malcomson made a sound to frighten them, smiting the table with his hand or giving a fierce 'Hsh, hsh,' so that they fled straightway to their holes.

And so the early part of the night wore on; and despite the noise Malcomson got more and more immersed in his work.

All at once he stopped, as on the previous night, being overcome by a sudden sense of silence. There was not the faintest sound of gnaw, or scratch, or squeak. The silence was as of the grave. He remembered the odd occurrence of the previous night, and instinctively he looked at the chair standing close by the fireside. And then a very odd sensation thrilled through him.

There, on the great old high-backed carved oak chair beside the fireplace sat the same enormous rat, steadily glaring at him with baleful eyes.

Instinctively he took the nearest thing to his hand, a book of logarithms, and flung it at it. The book was badly aimed and the rat did not stir, so again the poker performance of the previous night was repeated; and again the rat, being closely pursued, fled up the rope of the alarm bell. Strangely too, the departure of this rat was instantly followed by the renewal of the noise made by the general rat community. On this occasion, as on the previous one, Malcomson could not see at what part of the room the rat disappeared, for the green shade of his lamp left the upper part of the room in darkness, and the fire had burned low.

On looking at his watch he found it was close on midnight; and, not sorry for the *divertissement*, he made up his fire and made himself his nightly pot of tea. He had got through a good spell of work, and thought himself entitled to a cigarette; and so he sat on the great carved oak chair before the fire and enjoyed it. Whilst smoking he began to think that he would like to know where the rat disappeared to, for he had certain ideas for the morrow not entirely disconnected with a rat-trap. Accordingly he lit another lamp and placed it so that it would shine well into the right-hand corner of the wall by the fireplace. Then he got all the books he had with him, and placed them handy to throw at the vermin. Finally he lifted the rope of the alarm bell and placed the end of it on the table, fixing the extreme end under the lamp. As he handled it he could not help noticing how pliable it was, especially for so strong a rope, and one not in use. 'You could hang a man with it,' be thought to himself. When his preparations were made he looked around, and said complacently:

'There now, my friend, I think we shall learn something of you this time!' He began his work again, and though as before somewhat disturbed at first by the noise of the rats, soon lost himself in his propositions and problems.

Again he was called to his immediate surroundings suddenly. This time it might not have been the sudden silence only which took his attention; there was a slight movement of the rope, and the lamp moved. Without stirring, he looked to see if his pile of books was within range, and then cast his eye along the rope. As he looked he saw the great rat drop from the rope on the oak armchair and sit there glaring at him. He raised a book in his right hand, and taking careful aim, flung it at the rat. The latter, with a quick movement, sprang aside and dodged the missile. He then took another book, and a third, and flung them one after another at the rat, but each time unsuccessfully. At last, as he stood with a book poised in his hand to throw, the rat squeaked and seemed afraid. This made Malcomson more than ever eager to strike, and the book flew and struck the rat a resounding blow. It gave a terrified squeak, and turning on his pursuer a look of terrible malevolence, ran up the chair-back and made a great jump to the rope of the alarm bell and ran up it like lightning. The lamp rocked under the sudden strain, but it was a heavy one and did not topple over. Malcomson kept his eyes on the rat, and saw it by the light of the second lamp leap to a moulding of the wainscot and disappear through a hole in one of the great pictures which hung on the wall, obscured and invisible through its coating of dirt and dust.

'I shall look up my friend's habitation in the morning,' said the student, as he went over to collect his books. The third picture from the fireplace; I shall not forget.' He picked up the books one by one, commenting on them as he lifted them. '*Conic Sections* he does not mind, nor *Cycloidal Oscillations*, nor the *Principia*, nor *Quaternions*, nor *Thermodynamics*. Now for the book that fetched him!' Malcomson took it up and looked at it. As he did so he started, and a sudden pallor overspread his face. He looked round uneasily and shivered slightly, as he murmured to himself:

'The Bible my mother gave me! What an odd coincidence.'
He sat down to work again, and the rats in the wainscot
renewed their gambols. They did not disturb him, however;
somehow their presence gave him a sense of companionship.
But he could not attend to his work, and after striving to
master the subject on which he was engaged gave it up in
despair, and went to bed as the first streak of dawn stole in
through the eastern window.

He slept heavily but uneasily, and dreamed much; and
when Mrs Dempster woke him late in the morning he
seemed ill at ease, and for a few minutes did not seem to
realise exactly where he was. His first request rather surprised the servant.

'Mrs Dempster, when I am out today I wish you would get
the steps and dust or wash those pictures—specially that one
the third from the fireplace—I want to see what they are.'

Late in the afternoon Malcomson worked at his books in
the shaded walk, and the cheerfulness of the previous day
came back to him as the day wore on, and he found that
his reading was progressing well. He had worked out to a
satisfactory conclusion all the problems which had as yet
baffled him, and it was in a state of jubilation that he paid
a visit to Mrs Witham at 'The Good Traveller.' He found a
stranger in the cosy sitting-room with the landlady, who was
introduced to him as Dr Thornhill. She was not quite at
ease, and this, combined with the doctor's plunging at once
into a series of questions, made Malcomson come to the
conclusion that his presence was not an accident, so without
preliminary he said:

'Dr Thornhill, I shall with pleasure answer you any question you may choose to ask me if you will answer me one
question first.'

The doctor seemed surprised, but he smiled and answered
at once, 'Done! What is it?'

'Did Mrs Witham ask you to come here and see me and
advise me?'

Dr Thornhill for a moment was taken aback, and Mrs

Witham got fiery red and turned away; but the doctor was a frank and ready man, and he answered at once and openly:

'She did: but she didn't intend you to know it. I suppose it was my clumsy haste that made you suspect. She told me that she did not like the idea of your being in that house all by yourself, and that she thought you took too much strong tea. In fact, she wants me to advise you if possible to give up the tea and the very late hours. I was a keen student in my time, so I suppose I may take the liberty of a college man, and without offence, advise you not quite as a stranger.'

Malcomson with a bright smile held out his hand. 'Shake! as they say in America,' he said. 'I must thank you for your kindness and Mrs Witham too, and your kindness deserves a return on my part. I promise to take no more strong tea —no tea at all till you let me—and I shall go to bed tonight at one o'clock at latest. Will that do?'

'Capital,' said the doctor. 'Now tell us all that you noticed in the old house,' and so Malcomson then and there told in minute detail all that had happened in the last two nights. He was interrupted every now and then by some exclamation from Mrs Witham, till finally when he told of the episode of the Bible the landlady's pent-up emotions found vent in a shriek; and it was not till a stiff glass of brandy and water had been administered that she grew composed again. Dr Thornhill listened with a face of growing gravity, and when the narrative was complete and Mrs Witham had been restored he asked:

'The rat always went up the rope of the alarm bell?'

'Always.'

'I suppose you know,' said the Doctor after a pause, 'what the rope is?'

'No!'

'It is,' said the Doctor slowly, 'the very rope which the hangman used for all the victims of the Judge's judicial rancour!' Here he was interrupted by another scream from Mrs Witham, and steps had to be taken for her recovery. Malcomson having looked at his watch, and found that it was close to his dinner hour, had gone home before her complete recovery.

When Mrs Witham was herself again she almost assailed the Doctor with angry questions as to what he meant by putting such horrible ideas into the poor young man's mind. 'He has quite enough there already to upset him,' she added. Dr Thornhill replied.

'My dear madam, I had a distinct purpose in it! I wanted to draw his attention to the bell rope, and to fix it there. It may be that he is in a highly over-wrought state, and has been studying too much, although I am bound to say that he seems as sound and healthy a young man, mentally and bodily, as ever I saw—but then the rats—and that suggestion of the devil.' The doctor shook his head and went on. 'I would have offered to go and stay the first night with him but that I felt sure it would have been a cause of offence. He may get in the night some strange fright or hallucination; and if he does I want him to pull that rope. All alone as he is it will give us warning, and we may reach him in time to be of service. I shall be sitting up pretty late tonight and shall keep my ears open. Do not be alarmed if Benchurch gets a surprise before morning.'

'Oh, Doctor, what do you mean? What do you mean?'

'I mean this; that possibly—nay, more probably—we shall hear the great alarm bell from the Judge's House tonight,' and the Doctor made about as effective an exit as could be thought of.

When Malcomson arrived home he found that it was a little after his usual time, and Mrs Dempster had gone away —the rules of Greenhow's Charity were not to be neglected. He was glad to see that the place was bright and tidy with a cheerful fire and a well-trimmed lamp. The evening was colder than might have been expected in April, and a heavy wind was blowing with such rapidly-increasing strength that there was every promise of a storm during the night. For a few minutes after his entrance the noise of the rats ceased; but so soon as they became accustomed to his presence they began again. He was glad to hear them, for he felt once more the feeling of companionship in their noise, and his mind ran back to the strange fact that they only ceased to manifest themselves when that other—the great rat with the baleful eyes—came upon the scene. The reading-lamp only was lit and its green shade kept the ceiling and the upper part of the room in darkness, so that the cheerful light from the hearth spreading over the floor and shining on the white cloth laid over the end of the table was warm and cheery. Malcomson sat down to his dinner with a good appetite and a buoyant spirit. After his dinner and a cigarette he sat steadily down to work, determined not to let anything disturb him, for he remembered his promise to the doctor, and made up his mind to make the best of the time at his disposal.

For an hour or so he worked all right, and then his thoughts began to wander from his books. The actual circumstances around him, the calls on his physical attention, and his nervous susceptibility were not to be denied. By this time the wind had become a gale, and the gale a storm. The old house, solid though it was, seemed to shake to its foundations, and the storm roared and raged through its many chimneys and its queer old gables, producing strange, unearthly sounds in the empty rooms and corridors. Even the great alarm bell on the roof must have felt the force of the wind, for the rope rose and fell slightly, as though the bell were moved a little from time to time, and the limber rope fell on the oak floor with a hard and hollow sound.

As Malcomson listened to it he bethought himself of the doctor's words, 'It is the rope which the hangman used for the victims of the Judge's judicial rancour,' and he went over to the corner of the fireplace and took it in his hand to look at it. There seemed a sort of deadly interest in it, and as he stood there he lost himself for a moment in speculation as to who these victims were, and the grim wish of the Judge to have such a ghastly relic ever under his eyes. As he stood there the swaying of the bell on the roof still lifted the rope now and again; but presently there came a new sensation—

a sort of tremor in the rope, as though something was moving along it.

Looking up instinctively Malcomson saw the great rat coming slowly down towards him, glaring at him steadily. He dropped the rope and started back with a muttered curse, and the rat turning ran up the rope again and disappeared, and at the same instant Malcomson became conscious that the noise of the rats, which had ceased for a while, began again.

All this set him thinking, and it occurred to him that he had not investigated the lair of the rat or looked at the pictures, as he had intended. He lit the other lamp without the shade, and, holding it up, went and stood opposite the third picture from the fireplace on the right-hand side where he had seen the rat disappear on the previous night.

At the first glance he started back so suddenly that he almost dropped the lamp, and a deadly pallor overspread his face. His knees shook, and heavy drops of sweat came on his forehead, and he trembled like an aspen. But he was young and plucky, and pulled himself together, and after the pause of a few seconds stepped forward again, raised the lamp, and examined the picture which had been dusted and washed, and now stood out clearly

It was of a judge dressed in his robes of scarlet and ermine. His face was strong and merciless, evil, crafty, and vindictive, with a sensual mouth, hooked nose of ruddy colour, and shaped like the beak of a bird of prey. The rest of the face was of a cadaverous colour. The eyes were of peculiar brilliance and with a terribly malignant expression. As he looked at them, Malcomson grew cold, for he saw there the very counterpart of the eyes of the great rat. The lamp almost fell from his hand, he saw the rat with its baleful eyes peering out through the hole in the corner of the picture, and noted the sudden cessation of the noise of the other rats. However, he pulled himself together, and went on with his examination of the picture.

The Judge was seated in a great high-backed carved oak chair, on the right-hand side of a great stone fireplace where, in the corner, a rope hung down from the ceiling, its end lying coiled on the floor. With a feeling of something like horror, Malcomson recognised the scene of the room as it stood, and gazed around him in an awestruck manner as though he expected to find some strange presence behind him. Then he looked over to the corner of the fireplace— and with a loud cry he let the lamp fall from his hand.

There, in the judge's arm-chair, with the rope hanging behind, sat the rat with the Judge's baleful eyes, now intensified and with a fiendish leer. Save for the howling of the storm without there was silence.

The fallen lamp recalled Malcomson to himself. Fortunately it was of metal, and so the oil was not spilt. However, the practical need of attending to it settled at once his nervous apprehensions. When he had turned it out, he wiped his brow and thought for a moment.

'This will not do,' he said to himself. 'If I go on like this I shall become a crazy fool. This must stop! I promised the doctor I would not take tea. Faith, he was pretty right! My nerves must have been getting into a queer state. Funny I did not notice it. I never felt better in my life. However, it is all right now, and I shall not be such a fool again.'

Then he mixed himself a good stiff glass of brandy and water and resolutely sat down to his work.

It was nearly an hour when he looked up from his book, disturbed by the sudden stillness. Without, the wind howled and roared louder than ever, and the rain drove in sheets against the windows, beating like hail on the glass; but within there was no sound whatever save the echo of the wind as it roared in the great chimney, and now and then a hiss as a few raindrops found their way down the chimney in a lull of the storm. The fire had fallen low and had ceased to flame, though it threw out a red glow. Malcomson listened attentively, and presently heard a thin, squeaking noise, very faint. It came from the corner of the room where the rope hung down, and he thought it was the creaking of the rope on the floor as the swaying of the bell raised and lowered it.

Looking up, however, he saw in the dim light the great rat clinging to the rope and gnawing it. The rope was already nearly gnawed through—he could see the lighter colour where the strands were laid bare. As he looked the job was completed, and the severed end of the rope fell clattering on the oaken floor, whilst for an instant the great rat remained like a knob or tassel at the end of the rope, which now began to sway to and fro. Malcomson felt for a moment another pang of terror as he thought that now the possibility of calling the outer world to his assistance was cut off, but an intense anger took its place, and seizing the book he was reading he hurled it at the rat. The blow was well aimed, but before the missile could reach him the rat dropped off and struck the floor with a soft thud. Malcomson instantly rushed over towards him, but it darted away and disappeared in the darkness of the shadows of the room. Malcomson felt that his work was over for the night, and determined then and there to vary the monotony of the proceedings by a hunt for the rat, and took off the green shade of the lamp so as to insure a wider spreading light. As he did so the gloom of the upper part of the room was relieved, and in the new flood of light, great by comparison with the previous darkness, the pictures on the wall stood out boldly. From where he stood, Malcomson saw right opposite to him the third picture on the wall from the right of the fireplace. He rubbed his eyes in surprise, and then a great fear began to come upon him.

In the centre of the picture was a great irregular patch of brown canvas, as fresh as when it was stretched on the frame. The background was as before, with chair and chimney-corner and rope, but the figure of the Judge had disappeared.

Malcomson, almost in a chill of horror, turned slowly round, and then he began to shake and tremble like a man in a palsy. His strength seemed to have left him, and he was incapable of action or movement, hardly even of thought. He could only see and hear.

There, on the great high-backed carved oak chair sat the

judge in his robes of scarlet and ermine, with his baleful eyes glaring vindictively, and a smile of triumph on the resolute, cruel mouth, as he lifted with his hands a *black cap*. Malcomson felt as if the blood was running from his heart, as one does in moments of prolonged suspense. There was a singing in his ears. Without, he could hear the roar and howl of the tempest, and through it, swept on the storm, came the striking of midnight by the great chimes in the market place. He stood for a space of time that seemed to him endless still as a statue, and with wide-open, horror-struck eyes, breathless. As the clock struck, so the smile of triumph on the Judge's face intensified, and at the last stroke of midnight he placed the black cap on his head.

Slowly and deliberately the Judge rose from his chair and picked up the piece of the rope of the alarm bell which lay on the floor, drew it through his hands as if he enjoyed its touch, and then deliberately began to knot one end of it, fashioning it into a noose. This he tightened and tested with his foot, pulling hard at it till he was satisfied and then making a running noose of it, which he held in his hand. Then he began to move along the table on the opposite side to Malcomson keeping his eyes on him until he had passed him, when with a quick movement he stood in front of the door. Malcomson then began to feel that he was trapped, and tried to think of what he should do. There was some fascination in the Judge's eyes, which he never took off him, and he had, perforce, to look. He saw the Judge approach —still keeping between him and the door—and raise the noose and throw it towards him as if to entangle him. With a great effort he made a quick movement to one side, and saw the rope fall beside him, and heard it strike the oaken floor. Again the Judge raised the noose and tried to ensnare him, ever keeping his baleful eyes fixed on him, and each time by a mighty effort the student just managed to evade it. So this went on for many times, the Judge seeming never discouraged nor discomposed at failure, but playing as a cat does with a mouse. At last in despair, which had reached its climax, Malcomson cast a quick glance round him. The lamp seemed to have blazed up, and there was a fairly good light in the room. At the many rat-holes and in the chinks and crannies of the wainscot he saw the rats' eyes; and this aspect, that was purely physical, gave him a gleam of comfort. He looked around and saw that the rope of the great alarm bell was laden with rats. Every inch of it was covered with them, and more and more were pouring through the small circular hole in the ceiling whence it emerged, so that with their weight the bell was beginning to sway.

Hark! it had swayed till the clapper had touched the bell. The sound was but a tiny one, but the bell was only beginning to sway, and it would increase.

At the sound the Judge, who had been keeping his eyes fixed on Malcolmson, looked up, and a scowl of diabolical anger overspread his face. His eyes fairly glowed like hot coals, and he stamped his foot with a sound that seemed to make the house shake. A dreadful peal of thunder broke overhead as he raised the rope again, whilst the rats kept running up and down the rope as though working against time. This time, instead of throwing it, he drew close to his victim, and held open the noose as he approached. As he came closer there seemed something paralysing in his very presence, and Malcolmson stood rigid as a corpse. He felt the Judge's icy fingers touch his throat as he adjusted the rope. The noose tightened—tightened. Then the Judge, taking the rigid form of the student in his arms, carried him over and placed him standing in the oak chair, and stepping up beside him, put his hand up and caught the end of the swaying rope of the alarm bell. As he raised his hand the rats fled squeaking, and disappeared through the hole in the ceiling. Taking the end of the noose which was round Malcolmson's neck he tied it to the hanging-bell rope, and then descending pulled away the chair.

*   *   *

When the alarm bell of the Judge's House began to sound a crowd soon assembled. Lights and torches of various kinds appeared, and soon a silent crowd was hurrying to the spot. They knocked loudly at the door, but there was no reply. Then they burst in the door, and poured into the great dining-room, the doctor at the head.

There at the end of the rope of the great alarm bell hung the body of the student, and on the face of the Judge in the picture was a malignant smile.

THE SERVANT

Michael MacLiammoir

It was in London in the year 1916: a month or so before the Easter Rising. A very young boy, yet I was an experienced professional: I had been on the stage for nearly six years! And among my many grown-up friends—stage children are often more at home with adults than with each other—was an English actor I will call Kenneth Dane, though only the first name was his own.

A good actor, a French scholar, an ardent convert to the Catholic Church, an enthusiast about all things Irish, and a friend of Mabel Beardsley, the sister of the great artist. Altogether an interesting, companionable and charming man, who, although he was scarcely thirty, seemed to me almost middle-aged and an authority on all things under the sun.

On account, I suppose, of his Catholic faith, he was given a commission in an Irish Regiment of the British Army— we may as well call it the Munster Fusiliers—though he had never set a foot in Ireland in his life and on this chilly week-end of early spring in 1916 (he was in England for a few days' leave) he and I met at a week-end party in a lovely Georgian house on the river near Richmond.

The party was gay, noisy and sentimental with an atmosphere of 'let us be merry for tomorrow we die' after the manner of the times. Kenneth and I shared the bedroom lit by candles and lamps: electricity had not yet penetrated to the suburbs, and on the third night of our stay, as we were preparing for sleep, he said to me: 'Do you ever get premon-

itions? I do. I know, for example, that I'll never see you—
any of you—on this earth again, because I'm going to be
killed, you see. Oh, yes, I'm quite certain of it. In fact, I
could say "I know."'

My head at this period of my life was much more filled
with ghost stories than with sentiments of friendship and
my thoughts expressed themselves—as is the habit with my
thoughts—immediately. 'Promise me,' I said, 'that if you do
get killed you will come and tell me so.'

Suddenly he looked at me over the candlelight that separated our two beds. I was smoking my first cigarette and I
was immensely proud of it. He stubbed his out on an ashtray
'I'll come if God allows me—I'll come and tell you.'

I slept, youthful, heartless, and untroubled. When I
woke next morning the bed next to mine was empty: his
books, his clothes, his shaving things: all had been taken
away, there was a faint smell of brilliantine in the air,
that was all. And less than a week later, we received the
news! He had been killed three days after his return to
France.

Here I must repeat: I was youthful, heartless, and
untroubled. No ghost had come to me: no message from the
dead had arrived, no premonition had touched me, there
had been no sign. And, as the years went by, in spite of our
youthful vows of eternal friendship, I confess I forgot all
about him.

It was twenty years later—in 1936—that Hilton Edwards
and I, who some eight years previously had established the
Dublin Gate Theatre and done most of our early work, were
sharing a flat in a certain street that had a church like a
pepper-pot at the end of it. It was early Spring weather,
dark, gloomy, and ominous: we had engaged a new man-
servant, unknown to us but for his references from Trinity
College and an admission—or was it boast?—that he had
once served in the British Army. He was interviewed and I
felt he would be satisfactory.

'Don't knock on the door when you come up in the

morning at nine,' I told him: 'Just bring in the coffee, open the curtains, and that will wake me.'

'Yes, sir.'

Next morning, although after our heavy work in the theatre I sleep well as a rule, I awoke long before nine. I was vaguely disturbed: I wondered why, and finally concluded that it was because of the new man. Would he burn our trousers as he pressed them as his predecessor had done? Would he fill the bath to overflowing, make the coffee all wrong? Presently I heard him coming up the stairs, a church clock somewhere was striking the hour of nine, I remember thinking: 'He's punctual, anyway.'

The door opened softly and a British officer entered the room carrying a coffee tray.

I stared. The room was still dim with its drawn curtains and faint wintry light outside, but I could see him plainly. I thought: 'What is a British officer doing in Dublin in 1936?'

The man advanced into the room, and I saw that it was Kenneth Dane. In spite of the twenty years that had passed by since he died, there was no mistaking the spare figure: the light brown, smoothly-brushed hair: the lean, clean-shaven face. I almost shouted in my astonishment: 'Kenneth! Kenneth Dane!' And it was only then that I remembered his promise to me when I was a boy, and I said: 'You have come back to see me—after all!'

He nodded his head gravely: his lips, half smiling, moved as if in speech, but I heard no sound. He came close to the bed, set down the coffee tray on the table, and still with that old smile on his moving lips, still watching me intently, he turned and opened the curtains.

As the grey morning light streamed into the room, then that khaki-clad figure of the officer seemed to melt rapidly into that of a middle-aged, slightly stooping man: grey haired, and dressed in black trousers and a white linen coat. It was the new servant.

That was the only moment, I think, in which I felt any dismay. I gasped and almost wept, full of a strange, remote anguish: but, seeing the man staring at me in amazement, I made an effort, and muttered some foolish thing about a dream. But the servant's face was white.

'Excuse me, sir: but did you not call me Kenneth Dane, just now when I was coming in?'

'I did, yes . . . I'd been dreaming about a very old friend of mine . . .'

'Excuse me, sir: but it wouldn't be Captain Kenneth Dane, sir, would it?'

'Yes. He was an army man. Why do you ask?'

'It wouldn't be Captain Dane of the Munster Fusiliers, sir? Would it?'

'Yes, that was his Regiment. Why?'

'But I was his batman, sir. I was with him in France in 1916 when he got the bullet that killed him. Captain Dane, he died in my arms, sir.'

LET ME GO

L. A. G. Strong

'I never saw a ghost only the once,' said Mr Mangan, 'and then I not only saw him; I heard and smelt him. If he'd been a bit closer to me, I could have touched him.'

'Were you scared?' I asked.

'Divil the bit. He was so natural, I hardly realised he was a ghost, at first. And when I did, the poor fella looked so pitiful, he was so real in his speech and his squalor, so gentle and mild, sure no one could be afraid of him.'

Mr Mangan leaned forward and poked the fire till it blazed, and his enormous shadow leaped on the ceiling. The crockery on the dresser twinkled: an old lustre jug kept changing colour. Then he sat back, his rugged features impressive as a monolith in the firelight.

'It was in the county Tipperary, all of twenty-seven years ago. I have a queer clutch of cousins down there—if they're in it yet, indeed, for I never heard of them for years now, nor ever visited them saving that one time. I can't for the life of me remember what took me there, either, unless it was the races or a hurley match.

'They lived in a great barrack of a place, a kind of a country house come down to being a farm. The rooms were enormous. I was brought upstairs to put my bag in a bed-room big enough for a platoon. Ah, they were a strange lot, the oddest ever, for all they were my cousins. Three big black-bearded sons, all over six foot; a stout middle-aged sister with rosy cheeks, a thick waist, and the hint of a moustache, a meagre wistful old mother with an empty face and vague eyes, and, somewhere above stairs, an unseen father with asthma and an invincible objection to visitors. Maybe that was why none of them had married. They were well-to-do farming people, as far as I could see, but there was a depressed queerness about them that I couldn't fathom at all. Fine set-up, presentable, all but handsome, there they sat, the brothers and the sister, and not a word out of them. The house was dark and cold. It would have been deathly, even in August, only for a huge turf fire in an open stone fireplace, where you could have roasted an ox. Divil a sign of book or newspaper in the place, and, as dusk fell, the smallest lamp on earth, hanging from the rafters on a brass chain, and lighting dimly a wilderness of black hams, sides of bacon, and festooning onions.

'We ate in silence, only for the champing of jaws over the food. The table was long, and we sat so far away from one another that each was isolated. I essayed a remark or two, drew nothing but a grunt from one brother and a faded, absent smile from the mother, and shut up.

'When we'd done, the mother disappeared without a word, and the rest of us drew our chairs to the fire and sat in sombre silence. The turf sods smouldered away: now and then one would fall, sending up a shower of sparks and lighting the place far better than the little lamp, which only showed up the gloom.

'I'm an adaptable sort of lad, and was even more so then, so I sat with my thoughts and watched the fire. When one of the men spoke, it made me jump.

'"Where have you put our cousin to sleep, sister?"

'"Och," says she, "above in Grandfather's room."

'"Be dad," says black-beard number two, "it must be thirty year since any person slept there."

'"Never fear," says the sister, giving me a quite human smile. "There's a jar in the bed, and the clothes on it are hot out of the cupboard."

'I smiled and said something or other, but truth to tell I was relieved, for if there's one thing I've a dread of, it's a chill bed. There was another long silence, an hour maybe, and then the sister rose, lit an inch of candle in a heavy old brass candlestick, and gave me it, saying nothing at all.

'I took this candle, bade them all goodnight, getting a vague rumble by way of answer, and went up the wooden stair that led straight out of the room. At the bend I paused and looked down at them, the three black brothers and the old maid, musing there at the fire as if I had never existed.

'I had to go easy on the vast landing, for queer breezes sprang at me from nowhere, and made my candle gutter. At last I reached the room. The big four-poster bed stood in the middle, with the head facing the door. I felt in it. It was warm and welcoming. With the door shut behind me, my spirits rose. I'd be all right here, anyway, and tomorrow I could bid the house and its occupants goodbye and need never return.

'I got into bed, and put out the candle, with fresh pleasure, for it only emphasised the vast space of the room and the height of the ceiling. Now my world was small and warm and immediate. The moonlight that came in the windows fell on a high-backed chair and on the floor. They were tall, eighteenth century windows, two of them, uncurtained. The only curtains were a pair on either side of the bed, reaching perhaps half way along. I made to pull one back, but it was stiff; I thought of the possible shower of earwigs and such I might bring down, and let it be.

'For a time I couldn't sleep. My perplexity about the household had made my mind alert and clear. I tried various specifics, from reckoning sheep to trying to remember Scott's *Lady of the Lake*. Then I reconciled myself to being comfortable, and fell asleep, as so often happens when one has the sense so to relax oneself.

'I don't know what hour it was when I awoke, conscious that there was someone in the room: but the moonlight had walked away from the chair to another part of the floor, and a faint additional light came through the windows, as of approaching dawn. I noticed this, for I wasn't in the least bit scared. To this day, the divil nor a bench of bishops will ever persuade me but I was wide awake and with all my wits about me.

'I turned my head calmly to one side, and there was my visitor, close beside the bed. Did you ever see *She Stoops to Conquer?*'

'Many times.'

'You've saved me a deal of trouble, so: for there stood Tony Lumpkin, only a Tony in fear of the bailiffs, maybe, all his jauntiness and joking gone; aye, and most of his lout-ishness too, poor divil, for there he stood, downcast and miserable. His carroty hair was tied behind with a black bow, and his ruffles were dingy and stained with tobacco, or snuff, or port, or porter—maybe all four. He wore a shabby green velvet coat with breeches to match, and a yellow bro-cade sprigged waistcoat. He had grey worsted stockings on him, all in wrinkles, and black brogue shoes with gleaming paste buckles. He—'

'Wait a minute,' I exclaimed. 'On your own showing, the room was dark, but for a faint light from the windows and a patch of moonlight on the floor. How could you possibly see the detail of his clothes?'

Instead of exploding angrily as I expected, Mr Mangan gave me a candid smile.

'I can't tell you,' he confessed, 'except that I did see it. I have the feeling he sort of generated his own light, or else I was seeing him in another dimension, as it were. But, while at the same time I was perfectly well aware of the room about me, I did in fact see with what I can only call a kind of subdued clearness. I can't explain it.

'He had an anxious, monkey sort of a face, reddish and freckled, and a small forehead that suggested he wasn't over-burdened with brains. When he saw that I was looking at him, he gave me a poor propitiatory sort of a smile. His teeth were stained and irregular, and he could have done with a shave. I saw his hands then: they were coarse and the nails broken and dirty. He looked for all the world like a small broken fox-hunting squire.

'I was wondering what the divil to do, when suddenly he made a gawky bow and scraped his right foot on the floor.

' "Sarvint, sir. Sarvint," he said.

'The light seemed to get stronger: certainly I could see him more clearly. The metal buttons on his velvet coat shone in a dull sort of way, and he smelled strongly of bacon, turf, and stables. There he stood, pathetic, anxious, grinning at me.

'I cleared my throat. "I didn't hear you come in," I said. "Are you—are you staying here?"

' "Faith," said he, "I've stayed here this many's the year, and here I'll stay till I'm let depart. Yerrah," said he, "I'm a stranger to this place, for all I've been here so long. Thank God you spoke to me. Do ye know, you're the first man has addressed a civil word to me all the time since I came?"

' "Well," said I, raising myself on my elbow and smiling at him, "can I do anything for you at all?"

' "Indeed and you can, sir," said the small squire. "I hear tell that once a man's buried with the rites of the Church, he'll be let rest. Well, I amn't buried, sir, far from it, and my bag with a matter of a hundred and twenty-five guineas gone from me all these years. The way it is with me, sir, drifting around and looking on a million faces to find the one kind face, and me not knowing are they living persons or forlorn as I am, yerrah 'tis the hell of a life, sir, but you'll help me, sure I know you will. You're too fat and too kindly to be mean, and you're not afeard of me, and sure that's everything. It beats me," said he, fumbling apparently for his snuff box, "why folk do be in dread of a man in my state, for we couldn't hurt a flea, even if we wanted to."

' "Tell me," said I. "What happened to you?"

' "Aye, sir. What happened was this. It was towards the tail end of August, this very month and damme I believe this was the night, though I can't be sure, I'm a bit confused on me dates, so long after. I was sent to Dublin—"

'"Hold hard," I said. "What year was it? Do you remember that?"

'"Seventeen ninety-seven," says he. "There's no doubt of the year, anyway. I was sent into Dublin with a letter and a bag of one hundred and twenty-five guineas for a house in Thomas Street. Number eight. I was to deliver the bag and the letter there to a man who was to give me a receipt for them, and I was to come back without delay to Kilmallock. Them was my orders."

'"Who gave you the orders?"

'"Mr Ormonde. Ormonde of Kilmallock. I was employed there as a sort of a gentleman steward. I'd come down in the world, what with drinking and hunting and other things. Them was my orders. But, sir," his eyes opened wide at me, and his lower lip drooped, "divil a bit I ever set foot in Dublin. I was on a sorrel mare, with a pair of horse pistols—" he showed me with his hands, in pantomime that would have been comic if I hadn't been so sorry for the poor fella: I liked him well already—"a pair of horse pistols, a French cloak, and my glazed three-cornered hat without ere a cockade. It came on to blow and rain close by here, with thunder and lightning. The sorrel was nervous, and I was no better, so, seeing a light ahead, I came to this door below and knocked at it with the butt of my whip. A couple of hounds bayed their heads off in some distant part of the house, and presently the door was opened a few inches by a sulky-looking serving man with a lantern. I told him how it was with me, and begged shelter for the night for myself and the mare.

'"Without a word he came out on the steps and brought the mare away to the stables, at least I suppose he did. Then he came back and conducted me to the kitchen below. It was like a dining-room then. A mighty queer-lookin' fella was seated at the table, a tall man with a black beard on him, a rusty wig, and a dingy black dressing-gown. He was all sorts of a queer fella, for beards didn't be worn, only be philosophers and as—astrologers and mad lads o' that sort.

It gave me a turn, seeing him here, but he up polite enough and asked would I share his supper with him.

'"I was sharp set, so I agreed glad enough. The place looked poor, but the food was good and the wine better. It wasn't long before I was blathering, and the lad with the beard knew all about me. He was mighty friendly, I lost all dread of his beard, and after maybe the fifth bottle I was singing and soon fell under the table. I remember the serving man and another carrying me up to bed, from which I never woke, sir, not in the flesh that is, but as you see me now, and my guineas lost, and with them my soul, or near as no matter."

'And the tears began to come out of his comical puckered eyelids and to hang on the stubble on his chin.

'I was about to attempt some consoling remark, when there was a jag of bright blue lightning followed by a terrific crashing peal of thunder. Torrential rain dashed at the window, and roared like surf above the roof. I saw my poor friend the squire move slowly and sadly, as if his time was up and he not half done what he wanted to tell me: I watched him move towards the wall on my left, where I was staggered to see an old dark-coloured door I hadn't noticed in my inspection of the room. As I hope to be saved, my friend turned around to me, and he opening the door, and for the first time I took in his petty insignificant features. He was far shabbier and more soiled looking than I thought him to be at first. He smiled sadly at me, opened the door like any real man, and disappeared through it.

'I don't know how long I lay awake after that, and light slowly filling the room, but when it was broad day and maybe seven o'clock I turned and looked at the wall, and sorrow the sign of a door could I see in it or any of the walls. I got up and dressed and went down to the big kitchen. The three black-bearded brothers were at the table with their sister at the head, and the old mother at the bottom. All except herself were toying with their breakfast, a few pork chops with a wire basket of boiled eggs and a few gigantic home-made loaves in the middle of the table. I bade them good morning without breaking their grim taciturnity. After a while I took up my courage and, addressing the table in general, I told them of my strange visitor. This evoked no comment, and soon the three black brothers rose and went to their work in the fields. The sister went off to her dairy, leaving me with the old mother, who got her knitting and removed to a window seat.

'The thunder and rain had gone, and the sun shone brightly. Birds sang in the bushes, and I began to feel more like myself. I asked the old dame if I might smoke—she looked all of eighty in the morning light—and she nodded her white head. Emboldened, I drew my chair alongside, and asked her what she thought of my experience.

'She pushed her glasses up on her forehead, and laid down her knitting.

'"Och, there may be something in it. We were always a crossed family here and we haven't prospered as we might. My poor husband seemed under a cloud all his days, I never knew why. It might be the house, for I remember him telling me when we were married first that as a boy he heard his grandfather say there was murder done in this house."

'"When was it, ma'am?"

'"Ah, a long time ago. My husband knew nothing about it, only that someone was known to come here one summer night and never seen to go."

'"I wonder, ma'am," said I to her, "would your sons ever agree to go with me to my room and see is there ere a trace of that door? The Lord knows what may be under all those layers of paper."

'The old lady rather demurred to this, but my curiosity was up, and with a sort of obstinacy that surprised myself I put off leaving and stayed till the brothers came in for their mid-day dinner, when, to my surprise, the mother spoke up and put it to them. I got another surprise when one of the big brothers said, "Ah, what harm would it do anyway? God knows what may be in it, for we all know the sort of fortune we have had in this place."

'No sooner was the meal done, than we got a shovel and a couple of crowbars, and we four men went up to my bedroom. I pointed out the exact spot where the squireen had vanished. In a few minutes we had scaled off layers of wall paper, and there, sure enough, we had the bricked up doorway.

'The job had been solidly done, but it was the work of twenty minutes only for those great stalwart divils to break through. Soon there came a sort of a seeping gush of musty air, faint and frightening. I ran to open one of the two tall windows, but couldn't budge them. The brothers were digging on and taking no notice, so, feeling rather foolish, I slunk back to join them.

'Then one used his crowbar like a lever, and tumbled a heap of bricks away the far side of the hole, and we could clamber in. It was a sort of attic or lumber room, with a dull green piece of thick glass a foot square let into the roof for light. In the corner ahead was an old lidless, legless harpsichord with sagging wires. The rest of the furniture was a broken down chair, a bookcase with no books in it, and a bed. On the bed lay my friend of the night before. He was a mass of cobwebs. He had his green coat on, but ne'er a button—I suppose they had been cut off. His black brogues were on too, but they looked like bits of carved bog oak, and the paste buckles had ne'er a gleam to them. The grey worsted stockings had rotted, and the green velvet coat looked like moss covering the brown skeleton. At the base of the skull were a few traces still of the carroty hair.

'As we stood there in silence, tiny bits of cloth or fluff slowly disintegrated from the bed and softly drifted to the bare boards of the floor. There the squireen lay on his back, with his grisly arms outstretched.

'The brothers said never a word. No more did I. We left the room without ever a man looking back. I stayed maybe half an hour longer, and set out for home. I heard afterwards, in a round-about way, that the poor squire had been decently buried, and the family had taken a better and more prosperous turn.'

'Did you visit them again?'

'Never. I'm not a superstitious man, nor easily scared, but I had me enough of that house. Besides, my job was done. Do you know what gave me the worst turn of all?'

'No?'

'It wasn't the body. It wasn't even the faint smell in the room, like lilies. It was him saying to me that his host on that fatal evening, the lad he had supper with, was a tall lad with a black beard. That one thing gave me a chill that made it impossible for me to go near the place again. Odd, isn't it, the way things take a man?'

I agreed that it was odd.

'That's what I couldn't get out of my head,' Mr Mangan said. 'Many's the time I turned over the possibilities. Was the original black-bearded lad an ancestor, and so the curse fell on my cousins? Or did it fall on them because they chanced to have black beards too? And who put it on them? Not my poor friend, not the poor victim, I'm sure. Then who?'

'Was there a curse?' I suggested.

'Aye. Was there a curse—or were they blaming some ineptitude of their own on an outside thing?'

'You were there,' I said. 'How did the house strike you?'

Mr Mangan thought for a moment, then shivered.

'There was a curse,' he said. 'At least, there was something. I can feel, at this minute, the way it was going along that landing with my candle. And those big fellas, and the sister—all personable healthy human beings—ah yes. There was something, and I'm glad to think it's gone.'

AUTUMN SUNSHINE

William Trevor

The rectory was in County Wexford, eight miles from Enniscorthy. It was a handsome eighteenth-century house, with Virginia creeper covering three sides and a tangled garden full of buddleia and struggling japonica which had always been too much for its incumbents. It stood alone, seeming lonely even, approximately at the centre of the country parish it served. Its church—St Michael's Church of Ireland —was two miles away, in the village of Boharbawn.

For twenty-six years the Morans had lived there, not wishing to live anywhere else. Canon Moran had never been an ambitious man; his wife, Frances, had found contentment easy to attain in her lifetime. Their four girls had been born in the rectory, and had become a happy family there. They were grown up now, Frances's death was still recent: like the rectory itself, its remaining occupant was alone in the countryside. The death had occurred in the spring of the year, and the summer had somehow been bearable. The clergyman's eldest daughter had spent May and part of June at the rectory with her children. Another one had brought her family for most of August, and a third was to bring her newly married husband in the winter. At Christmas nearly all of them would gather at the rectory and some would come at Easter. But that September, as the days drew in, the season was melancholy.

Then, one Tuesday morning, Slattery brought a letter from Canon Moran's youngest daughter. There were two other letters as well, in unsealed buff envelopes which meant

118

that they were either bills or receipts. Frail and grey-haired in his elderliness, Canon Moran had been wondering if he should give the lawn in front of the house a last cut when he heard the approach of Slattery's van. The lawnmower was the kind that had to be pushed, and in the spring the job was always easier if the grass had been cropped close at the end of the previous summer.

'Isn't that a great bit of weather, Canon?' Slattery remarked, winding down the window of the van and passing out the three envelopes. 'We're set for a while, would you say?'

'I hope so, certainly.'

'Ah, we surely are, sir.'

The conversation continued for a few moments longer, as it did whenever Slattery came to the rectory. The postman was young and easy-going, not long the successor to old Mr O'Brien, who'd been making the round on a bicycle when the Morans first came to the rectory in 1952. Mr O'Brien used to talk about his garden; Slattery talked about fishing, and often brought a share of his catch to the rectory.

'It's a great time of year for it,' he said now, 'except for the darkness coming in.'

Canon Moran smiled and nodded; the van turned round on the gravel, dust rising behind it as it moved swiftly down the avenue to the road. Everyone said Slattery drove too fast.

He carried the letters to a wooden seat on the edge of the lawn he'd been wondering about cutting. Deirdre's hand-writing hadn't changed since she'd been a child; it was round and neat, not at all a reflection of the girl she was. The blue English stamp, the Queen in profile blotched a bit by the London postmark, wasn't on its side or half upside down, as you might possibly expect with Deirdre. Of all the Moran children, she'd grown up to be the only difficult one. She hadn't come to the funeral and hadn't written about her mother's death. She hadn't been to the rectory for three years.

'*I'm sorry,*' she wrote now. '*I couldn't stop crying actually. I've never known anyone as nice or as generous as she was. For ages I didn't even want to believe she was dead. I went on imagining her in the rectory and doing the flowers in church and shopping in Enniscorthy.*'

Deirdre was twenty-one now. He and Frances had hoped she'd go to Trinity and settle down, but although at school she'd seemed to be the cleverest of their children she'd had no desire to become a student. She'd taken the Rosslare boat to Fishguard one night, having said she was going to spend a week with her friend Maeve Coles in Cork. They hadn't known she'd gone to England until they received a picture postcard from London telling them not to worry, saying she'd found work in an egg-packing factory.

'*Well, I'm coming back for a little while now,*' she wrote, '*if you could put up with me and if you wouldn't find it too much. I'll cross over to Rosslare on the twenty-ninth, the morning crossing, and then I'll come on to Enniscorthy on the bus. I don't know what time it will be but there's a pub just by where the bus drops you so could we meet in the small bar there at six o'clock and then I won't have to lug my cases too far? I hope you won't mind going into such a place. If you can't make it, or don't want to see me, it's understandable, so if you don't turn up by half six I'll see if I can get a bus on up to Dublin. Only I need to get back to Ireland for a while.*'

It was, as he and Slattery had agreed, a lovely autumn. Gentle sunshine mellowed the old garden, casting an extra sheen of gold on leaves that were gold already. Roses that had been ebullient in June and July bloomed modestly now. Michaelmas daises were just beginning to bud. Already the crab-apples were falling, hydrangeas had a forgotten look. Canon Moran carried the letter from his daughter into the walled vegetable-garden and leaned against the side of the greenhouse, half sitting on a protruding ledge, reading the letter again. Panes of glass were broken in the greenhouse, white paint and putty needed to be renewed, but inside a vine still thrived, and was heavy now with black ripe fruit.

Later that morning he would pick some and drive into Enniscorthy, to sell the grapes to Mrs Roche in Slaney Street.

'*Love, Deirdre*: the letter was marvellous. Beyond the rectory the fields of wheat had been harvested, and the remaining stubble had the same tinge of gold in the autumn light; the beech-trees and the chestnuts were triumphantly magnificent. But decay and rotting were only weeks away, and the letter from Deirdre was full of life. '*Love, Deirdre*' were words more beautiful than all the season's glories. He prayed as he leaned against the sunny greenhouse, thanking God for this salvation.

*   *   *

For all the years of their marriage Frances had been a help. As a younger man, Canon Moran hadn't known quite what to do. He'd been at a loss among his parishioners, hesitating in the face of this weakness or that: the pregnancy of Alice Pratt in 1954, the argument about grazing rights between Mr Willoughby and Eugene Ryan in 1960, the theft of an altar cloth from St Michael's and reports that Mrs Tobin had been seen wearing it as a skirt. Alice Pratt had been going out with a Catholic boy, one of Father Hayes's flock, which made the matter more difficult than ever. Eugene Ryan was one of Father Hayes's also, and so was Mrs Tobin.

'Father Hayes and I had a chat,' Frances had said, and she'd had a chat as well with Alice Pratt's mother. A month later Alice Pratt married the Catholic boy, but to this day attended St Michael's every Sunday, the children going to Father Hayes. Mrs Tobin was given Hail Marys to say by the priest; Mr Willoughby agreed that his father had years ago granted Eugene Ryan the grazing rights. Everything, in these cases and in many others, had come out all right in the end: order emerged from the confusion that Canon Moran so disliked, and it was Frances who had always begun the process, though no one ever said in the rectory that she understood the mystery of people as well as he understood the teachings of the New Testament. She'd been a freckle-faced girl when he'd married her, pretty in her way. He was the one with the brains.

Frances had seen human frailty everywhere: it was weakness in people, she said, that made them what they were as much as strength did. And she herself had her own share of such frailty, falling short in all sorts of ways of the God's image her husband preached about. With the small amount of housekeeping money she could be allowed she was a spendthrift, and she said she was lazy. She loved clothes and often overreached herself on visits to Dublin; she sat in the sun while the rectory gathered dust and the garden became rank; it was only where people were concerned that she was practical. But for what she was her husband had loved her with unobtrusive passion for fifty years, appreciating her conversation and the help she'd given him because she could so easily sense the truth. When he'd found her dead in the garden one morning he'd felt he had lost some part of himself.

Though many months had passed since then, the trouble was that Frances hadn't yet become a ghost. Her being alive was still too recent, the shock of her death too raw. He couldn't distance himself; the past refused to be the past. Often he thought that her fingerprints were still in the rectory, and when he picked the grapes or cut the grass of the lawn it was impossible not to pause and remember other years. Autumn had been her favourite time.

*   *   *

'Of course I'd come,' he said. 'Of course, dear. Of course.'

'I haven't treated you very well.'

'It's over and done with, Deirdre.'

She smiled, and it was nice to see her smile again, although it was strange to be sitting in the back bar of a public house in Enniscorthy. He saw her looking at him, her eyes passing over his clerical collar and black clothes, and his thin quiet face. He could feel her thinking that he had aged, and putting it down to the death of the wife he'd been so fond of.

'I'm sorry I didn't write,' she said.

'You explained in your letter, Deirdre.'

'It was ages before I knew about it. That was an old address you wrote to.'

'I guessed.'

In turn he examined her. Years ago she'd had her long hair cut. It was short now, like a neat black cap on her head. And her face had lost its chubbiness; hollows where her cheeks had been made her eyes more dominant, pools of seaweed green. He remembered her child's stocky body, and the uneasy adolescence that had spoilt the family's serenity. Her voice had lost its Irish intonation.

'I'd have met you off the boat, you know.'

'I didn't want to bother you with that.'

'Oh, now, it isn't far, Deirdre.'

She drank Irish whiskey, and smoked a brand of cigarettes called Three Castles. He'd asked for a mineral himself, and the woman serving them had brought him a bottle of something that looked like water but which fizzed up when she'd poured it. A kind of lemonade he imagined it was, and didn't much care for it.

'I have grapes for Mrs Roche,' he said.

'Who's that?'

'She has a shop in Slaney Street. We always sold her the grapes. You remember?'

She didn't, and he reminded her of the vine in the greenhouse. A shop surely wouldn't be open at this hour of the evening, she said, forgetting that in a country town of course it would be. She asked if the cinema was still the same in Enniscorthy, a cement building halfway up a hill. She said she remembered bicycling home from it at night with her sisters, not being able to keep up with them. She asked after her sisters and he told her about the two marriages that had taken place since she'd left: she had in-laws she'd never met, and nephews and a niece.

They left the bar, and he drove his dusty black Vauxhall straight to the small shop he'd spoken of. She remained in the car while he carried into the shop two large chip-baskets full of grapes. Afterwards Mrs Roche came to the door with him.

'Well, is that Deirdre?' she said as Deirdre wound down the window of the car. 'I'd never know you, Deirdre.'

'She's come back for a little while,' Canon Moran explained, raising his voice a little because he was walking round the car to the driver's seat as he spoke.

'Well, isn't that grand?' said Mrs Roche.

Everyone in Enniscorthy knew Deirdre had just gone off, but it didn't matter now. Mrs Roche's husband, who was a red-cheeked man with a cap, much smaller than his wife, appeared beside her in the shop doorway. He inclined his head in greeting, and Deirdre smiled and waved at both of them. Canon Moran thought it was pleasant when she went on waving while he drove off.

In the rectory he lay wakeful that night, his mind excited by Deirdre's presence. He would have loved Frances to know, and guessed that she probably did. He fell asleep at half past two and dreamed that he and Frances were young again, that Deirdre was still a baby. The freckles on Frances's face were out in profusion, for they were sitting in the sunshine in the garden, tea things spread about them, the children playing some game among the shrubs. It was autumn then also, the last of the September heat. But because he was younger in his dream he didn't feel part of the season himself, or sense its melancholy.

*   *   *

A week went by. The time passed slowly because a lot was happening, or so it seemed. Deirdre insisted on cooking all the meals and on doing the shopping in Boharbawn's single shop or in Enniscorthy. She still smoked her endless cigarettes, but the peakiness there had been in her face when she'd first arrived wasn't quite so pronounced—or perhaps, he thought, he'd become used to it. She told him about the different jobs she'd had in London and the different places she'd lived in, because on the postcards she'd occasionally sent there hadn't been room to go into detail. In the rectory they had always hoped she'd managed to get a training of some sort, though guessing she hadn't. In fact, her jobs had been of the most rudimentary kind: as well as her spell in the egg-packing factory, there'd been a factory that made plastic earphones, a cleaning job in a hotel near Euston, and a year working for the Use-Us Office Cleansing Service. 'But you can't have liked any of that work, Deirdre?' he suggested, and she agreed she hadn't.

From the way she spoke he felt that that period of her life was over: adolescence was done with, she had steadied and taken stock. He didn't suggest to her that any of this might be so, not wishing to seem either too anxious or too pleased, but he felt she had returned to the rectory in a very different frame of mind from the one in which she'd left it. He imagined she would remain for quite a while, still taking stock, and in a sense occupying her mother's place. He thought he recognised in her a loneliness that matched his own, and he wondered if it was a feeling that their loneliness might be shared which had brought her back at this particular time. Sitting in the drawing-room while she cooked or washed up, or gathering grapes in the greenhouse while she did the shopping, he warmed delightedly to this theme. It seemed like an act of God that their circumstances should interlace this autumn. By Christmas she would know what she wanted to do with her life, and in the spring that followed she would perhaps be ready to set forth again. A year would have passed since the death of Frances.

'I have a friend,' Deirdre said when they were having a cup of coffee together in the middle of one morning. 'Someone who's been good to me.'

She had carried a tray to where he was composing next week's sermon, sitting on the wooden seat by the lawn at the front of the house. He laid aside his exercise book, and a pencil and a rubber. 'Who's that?' he inquired.

'Someone called Harold.'

He nodded, stirring sugar into his coffee.

'I want to tell you about Harold, Father. I want you to meet him.'

'Yes, of course.'

She lit a cigarette. She said, 'We have a lot in common. I mean, he's the only person . . .'

She faltered and then hesitated. She lifted her cigarette to her lips and drew on it.

He said, 'Are you fond of him, Deirdre?'

'Yes, I am.'

Another silence gathered. She smoked and drank her coffee. He added more sugar to his.

'Of course I'd like to meet him,' he said.

'Could he come to stay with us, Father? Would you mind? Would it be all right?'

'Of course I wouldn't mind. I'd be delighted.'

*　　*　　*

Harold was summoned, and arrived at Rosslare a few days later. In the meantime Deirdre had explained to her father that her friend was an electrician by trade and had let it fall that he was an intellectual kind of person. She borrowed the old Vauxhall and drove it to Rosslare to meet him, returning to the rectory in the early evening.

'How d'you do?' Canon Moran said, stretching out a hand in the direction of an excessively thin youth with a birthmark on his face. His dark hair was cut very short, cropped almost. He was wearing a black leather jacket.

'I'm fine,' Harold said.

'You've had a good journey?'

'Lousy, 'smatter of fact, Mr Moran.'

Harold's voice was strongly Cockney, and Canon Moran wondered if Deirdre had perhaps picked up some of her

English vowel sounds from it. But then he realised that most people in London would speak like that, as people did on the television and the wireless. It was just a little surprising that Harold and Deirdre should have so much in common, as they clearly had from the affectionate way they held one another's hand. None of the other Moran girls had gone in so much for holding hands in front of the family.

He was to sit in the drawing-room, they insisted, while they made supper in the kitchen, so he picked up the *Irish Times* and did as he was bidden. Half an hour later Harold appeared and said that the meal was ready: fried eggs and sausages and bacon, and some tinned beans. Canon Moran said grace.

Having stated that Co. Wexford looked great, Harold didn't say much else. He didn't smile much, either. His afflicted face bore an edgy look, as if he'd never become wholly reconciled to his birthmark. It was like a scarlet map on his left cheek, a shape that reminded Canon Moran of the toe of Italy. Poor fellow, he thought. And yet a birthmark was so much less to bear than other afflictions there could be.

'Harold's fascinated actually,' Deirdre said, 'by Ireland.'

Her friend didn't add anything to that remark for a moment, even though Canon Moran smiled and nodded interestedly. Eventually Harold said, 'The struggle of the Irish people.'

'I didn't know a thing about Irish history,' Deirdre said. 'I mean, not anything that made sense.'

The conversation lapsed at this point, leaving Canon Moran greatly puzzled. He began to say that Irish history had always been of considerable interest to him also, that it had a good story to it, its tragedy uncomplicated. But the other two didn't appear to understand what he was talking about and so he changed the subject. It was a particularly splendid autumn, he pointed out.

'Harold doesn't go in for anything like that,' Deirdre replied.

During the days that followed Harold began to talk more, surprising Canon Moran with almost everything he said. Deirdre had been right to say he was fascinated by Ireland, and it wasn't just a tourist's fascination. Harold had read widely: he spoke of ancient battles, and of the plantations of James I and Elizabeth, of Robert Emmet and the Mitchelstown martyrs, of Pearse and De Valera. 'The struggle of the Irish people' was the expression he most regularly employed. It seemed to Canon Moran that the relationship between Harold and Deirdre had a lot to do with Harold's fascination, as though his interest in Deirdre's native land had somehow caused him to become interested in Deirdre herself.

There was something else as well. Fascinated by Ireland, Harold hated his own country. A sneer whispered through his voice when he spoke of England: a degenerate place, he called it, destroyed by class-consciousness and the unjust distribution of wealth. He described in detail the city of Nottingham, to which he appeared to have a particular aversion. He spoke of unnecessary motorways and the stupidity of bureaucracy, the stifling presence of a Royal family. 'You could keep an Indian village,' he claimed, 'on what those corgis eat. You could house five hundred homeless in Buckingham Palace.' There was brainwashing by television and the newspaper barons. No ordinary person had a chance because pap was fed to the ordinary person, a deliberate policy going back into Victorian times when education and religion had been geared to the enslavement of minds. The English people had brought it on themselves, having lost their spunk, settling instead for consumer durables. 'What better can you expect,' Harold demanded, 'after the hypocrisy of that empire the bosses ran?'

Deirdre didn't appear to find anything specious in this line of talk, which surprised her father. 'Oh, I wonder about that,' he said himself from time to time, but he said it mildly, not wishing to cause an argument, and in any case his interjections were not acknowledged. Quite a few of the criticisms Harold levelled at his own country could be levelled at Ireland also and, Canon Moran guessed, at many countries throughout the world. It was strange that the two neighbouring islands had been so picked out, although once Germany was mentioned and the point made that developments beneath the surface there were a hopeful sign, that a big upset was on the way.

'We're taking a walk,' Harold said one afternoon. 'She's going to show me Kinsella's Barn.'

Canon Moran nodded, saying to himself that he disliked Harold. It was the first time he had admitted it, but the feeling was familiar. The less generous side of his nature had always emerged when his daughters brought to the rectory the men they'd become friendly with or even proposed to marry. Emma, the eldest girl, had brought several before settling in the end for Thomas. Linda had brought only John, already engaged to him. Una had married Carley not long after the death, and Carley had not yet visited the rectory: Canon Moran had met him in Dublin, where the wedding had taken place, for in the circumstances Una had not been married from home. Carley was an older man, an importer of tea and wine, stout and flushed, certainly not someone Canon Moran would have chosen for his second youngest daughter. But, then, he had thought the same about Emma's Thomas and about Linda's John.

Thomas was a farmer, sharing a sizeable acreage with his father in Co. Meath. He always brought to mind the sarcasm of an old schoolmaster who in Canon Moran's distant schooldays used to refer to a gang of boys at the back of the classroom as 'farmers' sons', meaning that not much could be expected of them. It was an inaccurate assumption but even now, whenever Canon Moran found himself in the company of Thomas, he couldn't help recalling it. Thomas was mostly silent, with a good-natured smile that came slowly and lingered too long. According to his father, and there was no reason to doubt the claim, he was a good judge of beef cattle.

Linda's John was the opposite. Wiry and suave, he was making his way in the Bank of Ireland, at present stationed in Waterford. He had a tiny orange-coloured moustache and was good at golf. Linda's ambition for him was that he should become the Bank of Ireland's manager in Limerick or Galway, where the insurances that went with the position were particularly lucrative. Unlike Thomas, John talked all the time, telling jokes and stories about the Bank of Ireland's customers.

'Nothing is perfect,' Frances used to say, chiding her husband for an uncharitableness he did his best to combat. He disliked being so particular about the men his daughters chose, and he was aware that other people saw them differently: Thomas would do anything for you, John was fun, the middle-aged Carley laid his success at Una's feet. But whoever the husbands of his daughters had been, Canon Moran knew he'd have felt the same. He was jealous of the husbands because ever since his daughters had been born he had loved them unstintingly. When he had prayed after Frances's death he'd felt jealous of God, who had taken her from him.

'There's nothing much to see,' he pointed out when Harold announced that Deirdre was going to show him Kinsella's Barn. 'Just the ruin of a wall is all that's left.'

'Harold's interested, Father.'

They set off on their walk, leaving the old clergyman ashamed that he could not like Harold more. It wasn't just his griminess: there was something sinister about Harold, something furtive about the way he looked at you, peering at you cruelly out of his afflicted face, not meeting your eye. Why was he so fascinated about a country that wasn't his own? Why did he refer so often to 'Ireland's struggle' as if that struggle particularly concerned him? He hated walking, he had said, yet he'd just set out to walk six miles through woods and fields to examine a ruined wall.

Canon Moran had wondered as suspiciously about Thomas and John and Carley, privately questioning every statement they made, finding hidden motives everywhere. He'd hated the thought of his daughters being embraced or even touched, and had forced himself not to think about that. He'd prayed, ashamed of himself then, too. 'It's just a frailty in you,' Frances had said, her favourite way of cutting things down to size.

He sat for a while in the afternoon sunshine, letting all of it hang in his mind. It would be nice if they quarrelled on their walk. It would be nice if they didn't speak when they returned, if Harold simply went away. But that wouldn't happen, because they had come to the rectory with a purpose. He didn't know why he thought that, but he knew it was true: they had come for a reason, something that was all tied up with Harold's fascination and with the kind of person Harold was, with his cold eyes and his afflicted face.

*   *   *

In March 1798 an incident had taken place in Kinsella's Barn, which at that time had just been a barn. Twelve men and women, accused of harbouring insurgents, had been tied together with ropes at the command of a Sergeant James. They had been led through the village of Boharbawn, the Sergeant's soldiers on horseback on either side of the procession, the Sergeant himself bringing up the rear. Designed as an act of education, an example to the inhabitants of Boharbawn and the country people around, the twelve had been herded into a barn owned by a farmer called Kinsella and there burned to death. Kinsella, who had played no part either in the harbouring of insurgents or in the execution of the twelve, was afterwards murdered by his own farm labourers.

'Sergeant James was a Nottingham man,' Harold said that evening at supper. 'A soldier of fortune who didn't care what he did. Did you know he acquired great wealth, Mr Moran?'

'No, I wasn't at all aware of that,' Canon Moran replied.

'Harold found out about him,' Deirdre said.

'He used to boast he was responsible for the death of a thousand Irish people. It was in Boharbawn he reached the thousand. They rewarded him well for that.'

'Not much is known about Sergeant James locally. Just the legend of Kinsella's Barn.'

'No way it's a legend.'

Deirdre nodded; Canon Moran did not say anything. They were eating cooked ham and salad. On the table there was a cake which Deirdre had bought in Murphy Flood's in Enniscorthy, and a pot of tea. There were several bunches of grapes from the greenhouse, and a plate of wafer biscuits. Harold was fond of salad cream, Canon Moran had noticed; he had a way of hitting the base of the jar with his hand, causing large dollops to spurt all over his ham. He didn't place his knife and fork together on the plate when he'd finished, but just left them anyhow. His fingernails were edged with black.

'You'd feel sick,' he was saying now, working the salad cream again. 'You'd stand there looking at that wall and you'd feel a revulsion in your stomach.'

'What I meant,' Canon Moran said, 'is that it has passed into local legend. No one doubts it took place; there's no question about that. But two centuries have almost passed.'

'And nothing has changed,' Harold interjected. 'The Irish people still share their bondage with the twelve in Kinsella's Barn.'

'Round here of course—'

'It's not round here that matters, Mr Moran. The struggle's world-wide; the sickness is everywhere actually.'

Again Deirdre nodded. She was like a zombie, her father thought. She was being used because she was an Irish girl; she was Harold's Irish connection, and in some almost frightening way she believed herself in love with him. Frances had once said they'd made a mistake with her. She had wondered if Deirdre had perhaps found all the love they'd offered her too much to bear. They were quite old when Deirdre was a child, the last expression of their own love. She was special because of that.

'At least Kinsella got his chips,' Harold pursued, his voice relentless. 'At least that's something.'

Canon Moran protested. The owner of the barn had been an innocent man, he pointed out. The barn had simply been a convenient one, large enough for the purpose, with heavy stones near it that could be piled up against the door before the conflagration. Kinsella, that day, had been miles away, ditching a field.

'It's too long ago to say where he was,' Harold retorted swiftly. 'And if he was keeping a low profile in a ditch it would have been by arrangement with the imperial forces.'

When Harold said that, there occurred in Canon Moran's mind a flash of what appeared to be the simple truth. Harold was an Englishman who had espoused a cause because it was one through which the status quo in his own country might be damaged. Similar such Englishmen, read about in newspapers, stirred in the clergyman's mind: men from Ealing and Liverpool and Wolverhampton who had changed their names to Irish names, who had even learned the Irish language, in order to ingratiate themselves with the new Irish revolutionaries. Such men dealt out death and chaos, announcing that their conscience insisted on it.

'Well, we'd better wash the dishes,' Deirdre said, and Harold rose obediently to help her.

*   *   *

The walk to Kinsella's Barn had taken place on a Saturday afternoon. The following morning Canon Moran conducted his services in St Michael's, addressing his small Protestant congregation, twelve at Holy Communion, eighteen at morning service. He had prepared a sermon about repentance, taking as his text St Luke, 15:32: '. . . *for this thy brother was dead, and is alive again; and was lost, and is found.*' But at the last moment he changed his mind and spoke instead of the incident in Kinsella's Barn nearly two centuries ago. He tried to make the point that one horror should not fuel another, that passing time contained its own forgiveness. Deirdre and Harold were naturally not in the church, but they'd been present at breakfast, Harold frying eggs on the kitchen stove, Deirdre pouring tea. He had looked at them and tried to think of them as two young people on holiday. He had tried to tell himself they'd come to the rectory for a rest and for his blessing, that he should be grateful instead of fanciful. It was for his blessing that Emma had brought Thomas to the rectory, that Linda had brought John. Una would bring Carley in November. 'Now, don't be silly,' Frances would have said.

'The man Kinsella was innocent of everything,' he heard his voice insisting in his church. 'He should never have been murdered also.'

Harold would have delighted in the vengeance exacted on an innocent man. Harold wanted to inflict pain, to cause suffering and destruction. The end justified the means for Harold, even if the end was an artificial one, a pettiness grandly dressed up. In his sermon Canon Moran spoke of such matters without mentioning Harold's name. He spoke of how evil drained people of their humour and compassion, how people pretended even to themselves. It was worse than Frances's death, he thought as his voice continued in the church: it was worse that Deirdre should be part of wickedness.

He could tell that his parishioners found his sermon odd, and he didn't blame them. He was confused, and naturally distressed. In the rectory Deirdre and Harold would be waiting for him. They would all sit down to Sunday lunch while plans for atrocities filled Harold's mind, while Deirdre loved him.

'Are you well again, Mrs Davis?' he inquired at the church door of a woman who suffered from asthma.

'Not too bad, Canon. Not too bad, thank you.'

He spoke to all the others, inquiring about health,

remarking on the beautiful autumn. They were farmers mostly and displayed a farmer's gratitude for the satisfactory season. He wondered suddenly who'd replace him among them when he retired or died. Father Hayes had had to give up a year ago. The young man, Father White, was always in a hurry.

'Goodbye so, Canon,' Mr Willoughby said, shaking hands as he always did, every Sunday. It was a long time since there'd been the trouble about Eugene Ryan's grazing rights; three years ago Mr Willoughby had been left a widower himself. 'You're managing all right, Canon?' he asked, as he also always did.

'Yes, I'm all right, thank you, Mr Willoughby.'

Someone else inquired if Deirdre was still at the rectory, and he said she was. Heads nodded, the unspoken thought being that that was nice for him, his youngest daughter at home again after all these years. There was forgiveness in several faces, forgiveness of Deirdre, who had been thoughtless to go off to an egg-packing factory. There was the feeling, also unexpressed, that the young were a bit like that.

'Goodbye,' he said in a general way. Car doors banged, engines started. In the vestry he removed his surplice and his cassock and hung them in a cupboard.

*   *   *

'We'll probably go tomorrow,' Deirdre said during lunch.

'Go?'

'We'll probably take the Dublin bus.'

'I'd like to see Dublin,' Harold said.

'And then you're returning to London?'

'We're easy about that,' Harold interjected before Deirdre could reply. 'I'm a tradesman, Mr Moran, an electrician.'

'I know you're an electrician, Harold.'

'What I mean is, I'm on my own; I'm not answerable to the bosses. There's always a bob or two waiting in London.'

For some reason Canon Moran felt that Harold was lying. There was a quickness about the way he'd said they were easy about their plans, and it didn't seem quite to make sense, the logic of not being answerable to bosses and a bob or two always waiting for him. Harold was being evasive about their movements, hiding the fact that they would probably remain in Dublin for longer than he implied, meeting other people like himself.

'It was good of you to have us,' Deirdre said that evening, all three of them sitting around the fire in the drawing-room because the evenings had just begun to get chilly. Harold was reading a book about Che Guevara and hadn't spoken for several hours. 'We've enjoyed it, Father.'

'It's been nice having you, Deirdre.'

'I'll write to you from London.'

It was safe to say that: he knew she wouldn't because she hadn't before, until she'd wanted something. She wouldn't write to thank him for the rectory's hospitality, and that would be quite in keeping. Harold was the same kind of man as Sergeant James had been: it didn't matter that they were on different sides. Sergeant James had maybe borne an affliction also, a humped back or a withered arm. He had ravaged a country that existed then for its spoils, and his most celebrated crime was neatly at hand so that another Englishman could make matters worse by attempting to make amends. In Harold's view the trouble had always been that these acts of war and murder died beneath the weight of print in history books, and were forgotten. But history could be rewritten, and for that Kinsella's Barn was an inspiration: Harold had journeyed to it as people make journeys to holy places.

'Yes?' Deirdre said, for while these reflections had passed through his mind he had spoken her name, wanting to ask her to tell him the truth about her friend.

He shook his head. 'I wish you could have seen your mother again,' he said instead. 'I wish she were here now.'

The faces of his three sons-in-law irrelevantly appeared in

his mind: Carley's flushed cheeks, Thomas's slow good-natured smile, John's little moustache. It astonished him that he'd ever felt suspicious of their natures, for they would never let his daughters down. But Deirdre had turned her back on the rectory, and what could be expected when she came back with a man? She had never been like Emma or Linda or Una, none of whom smoked Three Castles cigarettes and wore clothes that didn't seem quite clean. It was impossible to imagine any of them becoming involved with a revolutionary, a man who wanted to commit atrocities.

'He was just a farmer, you know,' he heard himself saying. 'Kinsella.'

Surprise showed in Deirdre's face. 'It was Mother we were talking about,' she reminded him, and he could see her trying to connect her mother with a farmer who had died two hundred years ago, and not being able to. Elderliness, he could see her thinking. 'Only time he wandered,' she would probably say to her friend.

'It was good of you to come, Deirdre.'

He looked at her, far into her eyes, admitting to himself that she had always been his favourite. When the other girls were busily growing up she had still wanted to sit on his knee. She'd had a way of interrupting him no matter what he was doing, arriving beside him with a book she wanted him to read to her.

'Goodbye, Father,' she said the next morning while they waited in Enniscorthy for the Dublin bus. 'Thank you for everything.'

'Yeah, thanks a ton, Mr Moran,' Harold said.

'Goodbye, Harold. Goodbye, my dear.'

He watched them finding their seats when the bus arrived and then he drove the old Vauxhall back to Boharbawn, meeting Slattery in his postman's van and returning his salute. There was shopping he should have done, meat and potatoes, and tins of things to keep him going. But his mind was full of Harold's afflicted face and his black-rimmed fingernails, and Deirdre's hand in his. And then flames burst from the straw that had been packed around living people in Kinsella's Barn. They burned through the wood of the barn itself, revealing the writhing bodies. On his horse the man called Sergeant James laughed.

Canon Moran drove the car into the rectory's ramshackle garage, and walked around the house to the wooden seat on the front lawn. Frances should come now with two cups of coffee, appearing at the front door with the tray and then crossing the gravel and the lawn. He saw her as she had been when first they came to the rectory, when only Emma had been born; but the grey-haired Frances was somehow there as well, shadowing her youth. 'Funny little Deirdre,' she said, placing the tray on the seat between them.

It seemed to him that everything that had just happened in the rectory had to do with Frances, with meeting her for the first time when she was eighteen, with loving her and marrying her. He knew it was a trick of the autumn sunshine that again she crossed the gravel and the lawn, no more than pretence that she handed him a cup and saucer. 'Harold's just a talker,' she said. 'Not at all like Sergeant James.'

He sat for a while longer on the wooden seat, clinging to these words, knowing they were true. Of course it was cowardice that ran through Harold, inspiring the whisper of his sneer when he spoke of the England he hated so. In the presence of a befuddled girl and an old Irish clergyman England was an easy target, and Ireland's troubles a kind of target also.

Frances laughed, and for the first time her death seemed far away, as her life did too. In the rectory the visitors had blurred her fingerprints to nothing, and had made of her a ghost that could come back. The sunshine warmed him as he sat there, the garden was less melancholy that it had been.

AISLING

Peter Tremayne

To my brother in Christ, Brother Antonio Urbino, **Ordinis Sancti Benedicti,** at the Pontifical Irish College, Rome; from his friend Father Máirtín Ó Meadhra, **Ordinis Praedicatorium,** priest at Inis Tuaisceart, in the county of Kerry, Ireland. September 11, 1852.

I have commenced writing this epistle to you today although I know not when I shall end it for the boats to this isolated, windswept rock of an island are so few and infrequent that it may be months before I can despatch it. I shall therefore content myself to begin my letter, to pick up my pen as and when I feel able, in order to tell you of the most extraordinary events that have occurred since I left the seminary at Rome and came hither as a priest to a handful of heathen.

I delight in writing to you in English, our common tongue, for I need practise in the language, there being no one in these parts who speaks or understands it in any degree. I find myself forgetting it from want of use which is troublesome for I have resolved, God willing, not to remain a rural priest all my life. English is a necessity if I am to move in the better parts of the country among the people of education and quality. For while our Irish tongue is spoken by many, it is now in a decline from which I doubt to see it recover. Two million of our population have been lost in recent years due to the most unprecedented famine; one million by death from starvation and attendant disease and

one million by migration to the Americas. Most of those
people were Irish-speaking and therefore their destruction
and going has dealt a blow to the language from which only
a miracle will allow recovery.

The cities of Ireland, in this particular, are English in
manner and speech and the remaining rural population will
eventually follow their example. Dublin, our chief city, is
representative, for only 3,426 souls are to be found there
who speak the tongue, of whom just 27 are in total ignorance
of English. Therefore, the only way to move in society is
through the English tongue. Yet in the remote area in which
I reside, ignorance is no handicap for here the old tongue is
strong and virile still.

But, my dear brother in Christ, I will come to particulars.

You will recall how we celebrated my ordination to the
Order of Preachers that last day which I spent in the Eternal
City? How I yearn for the hot Italian sunshine and the cool
white wine of the country. After I had bade farewell to you
and my tutors, I set out on the long journey to my native
land. It seems like a lifetime ago and yet it was only in the
Spring of this year. I reported myself to His Grace, the
Archbishop of Armagh, who is the apostelic delegate in this
country, for I had been given letters to bring him from Rome
among which was a warm letter of introduction and recommendation which the Father Prior of the Irish College
had written. I found His Grace most singularly occupied for
the Archbishop of Dublin had died but recently and His
Grace was to give up his See of Armagh for that of Dublin.
I had hoped, on the recommendation I brought with me,
that His Grace would take me to his new office and employ
me as some under-secretary in Dublin. God's will be done.

His Grace instructed me to repair to a tiny island off the
west coast of the county of Kerry to administer to the needs
of a small flock there. Having been born and raised in the
hills of Idagh, in the county of Kilkenny, I was informed
that my fluency in Irish was needed among a people who
spoke no other tongue. Being educated in the language, I

protested that the Irish of my native province of Leinster would differ to the dialect that was spoken in the western islands. The Archbishop rejected my protest and lectured me on the need to acquire the humility to accept God's purpose.

So it was that in the March of this year I came to this island.

If I had known then what I know now I would have prayed that a great wave had dashed the boat, which brought me, against the rocks and sent me to a watery death. God between me and all evil!

The island is called Inis Tuaisceart which means 'northerly island' for it is the most northerly island of a group called Na Blascaodaí, or, as some pronounce it in English, The Blaskets. They lay in a group off the coast of the Dingle Peninsula and are, indeed, the most westerly group of islands off the Irish coast. They are strange lumps of land, like the peaks of hills cut off from the mainland and surrounded by restless, brooding Atlantic waves. Islets surrounded by jagged granite rocks leaning seaward in a perpetual defence against the furious onslaught of the ocean.

Inis Tuaisceart, seen against the setting sun, is a curious serrated crag of an island, rising nearly six hundred feet above sea level at its highest point, shaped like the comb of a fighting cock.

It was late afternoon when I arrived, heralded by the haunted cry of the gulls and other soaring sea birds, curlews and plovers which flocked above the little craft which brought me from Dún Chaoin, a small village, isolated and lonely, yet the nearest point of civilization on the mainland. I had been three days at the village before a boat from the island had landed there. Six sun-bronzed and burly islandmen awaited me at the single quay of Dún Chaoin with their frail looking curragh or, as the natives call them, a *naomhóg,* which literally means a small boat. They are of light wooden lath framework, over which taut canvas is stretched and coated with tar. They are high bowed and ride lightly in the water so that they tend to skim the waves rather than slice through them.

'God and Mary to you Father,' cried one raw-boned man, greeting me in Irish. I replied courteously and asked if they had word of my coming and if they were waiting to take me to the island. A spokesman replied that they had not heard of me but nevertheless would transport me to the island if I so wished it. I confess, in spite of my disappointment at not getting a stipend in a more salubrious parish, I was eager to see what, after all, was to be my first living. So I placed my bags within the boat and climbed into the stern. The six short and almost bladeless oars caused a ripple in the water and the *naomhóg* worked its way out of the harbour, along the shoreline under the cliffs and then turned due west, running towards the dark silhouette of the island. It ran rapidly over the waves answering the faintest suggestion of a dipped oar. A tenor in the boat took up a lusty rowing chant and was answered by the other men in chorus, which seemed to lend an easy motion to their rowing.

''Tis a fair passage you are getting this day, Father,' confided the oarsman nearest to me. 'Sometimes the anger of the sea shuts off the island for weeks at a time.'

So we came pleasantly enough to Inis Tuaisceart, a brown jagged lump of rock which seemed so totally inhospitable that I was amazed to find that no less than forty souls resided there, trying to wrest their living from the dark waters which surrounded the island. Nestling among the grey granite boulders, which were strewn across the island, were several *clochán*. These, my brother, are stone built huts which are constructed without mortar and shaped like beehives. In these I found entire families resided. There were only a few better constructions among which was my church! Church! Forgive my bitterness for it was but a small oratory in which one man could scarcely stand. Yet it is consecrated for worship and dedicated to St Brendan whose reputation for voyaging in the west is legend.

I was later given to understand that few of my flock were native islanders. The inhabitants of these western islands usually dwell on An t-Oileán Mór, or the Great Island. It was during the recent famine years that many mainlanders came to the islands to escape the pestilence and hunger. Thus, where a few families dwelt, a whole village had sprung up. Such was the situation on Inis Tuaisceart.

The islanders gathered around me in curiosity as the boat came to shore. They were respectful and hands reached out to help me safely to dry land. Many a greeting was chorused and I replied in kind, finding that my dialect was readily understood by the majority. In spite of the courtesy with which I was received, I had the impression that the courtesy was for the cloth which I wore and behind that they watched me with veiled hostility and suspicion. There was respect but no welcome. As I moved among them I overheard one man say: 'By my baptism, isn't he but a slip of a child to be a priest?' And replied: 'Yerra, he has scarce learnt to shave and yet he will show us the way to salvation.' I stood hesitantly among them, my heart lacking resolution for the moment, wondering whether I should dare the Archbishop's fury and return to the mainland there and then. Some instinct made me brace my shoulders and ask if they knew where I was to stay.

Most of them turned away, muttering; suddenly finding important business to attend to about the island which necessitated them avoiding my company.

They all departed except for a young girl; she was no more than eighteen, I would say. Barefoot, as are most of the islanders, she was clad in a rag of a dress that had more holes in it than modesty would have allowed even in a city like Rome. Her figure would have rivalled the great marble statues of the masters in that city, so perfectly shaped was it. She was white skinned, her hair was flaming red, the setting sun kindling a furious fire in it as its bright rays slanted through the sky. Her eyes were reflective of the changing mood of the sea, seeming to change from quiet green to stormy grey with breath-taking ease. She carried herself proudly, her chin thrust forward.

'God and Mary to you, Father,' she said.

'God, Mary and Patrick to you, child,' I replied, my heart skipping a beat as I gazed at her untrammelled beauty. I may be a priest, my brother, but cannot a priest admire the beauty of God's creations?

'My name is Máire, Father,' she replied. 'I will show you to the priest's house.'

Before I had time to give her thanks, she had turned and strode away among the rocks towards the oratory, which lay just beyond the village. A short distance from the oratory was my house.

House! By my faith, Brother Antonio, if you could only see it to compare it with those dwellings we shared in Rome! Still, this 'house' was far better than the beehive huts of the natives. In fact, henceforth I shall call it by a more literal translation of the Irish word for it, which is *bothán* and is rendered as 'cabin.' It was a rectangular shell of roughly shaped stone, mortared with mud and washed with a yellow lime. The roof was thatched with rushes which rot easily in the heavy rains so that there is always a leak. Inside, the rafters are exposed. The interior walls are also lime washed and hung with a crucifix and a few religious paintings of cheap quality. There is just one room, the *seomra* as it is called. At one end is a bed, a chair or two, a cupboard and a washing basin. At the other end is a stone hearth, a great open chimney down which the light of day can be seen. Besides this stands an iron gallows-like construction with a swinging arm from which a cooking pot or kettle can be hung. This was my dwelling; I, who had slept in the marble chambers of the Vatican, hung with their silken drapes, ceilings painted by the great masters of the Renaissance. Yet God calls and we must obey His summons.

It was strange, I do not think I was imagining when I tell you that as I entered that house I felt a passing coldness. It made me shiver. There is a saying about such a feeling. They say that someone has walked on your grave. My mind was uneasy as I stood on that cold threshold. But the feeling swiftly passed and I dismissed its cause as the dampness and gloomy atmosphere of the cabin.

'I will light a fire for you, Father,' said the girl, Máire, as if she had read my thoughts.

'Is it long since there was a priest in this place, Máire?' I asked, watching her laying kindle in the hearth.

'Not since the start of the Great Hunger,' she replied. The natives here refer to the famine years by that title.

I frowned.

'Where do you go to mass or confession?'

Máire shrugged as she lit the fire.

'If the weather is fair we row to the mainland. But mostly the weather prevents us.'

I realised how badly these people stood in need of a priest. I thought of our mode of living in Rome; mass twice daily and two decades of the rosary on the toll of the Angelus bell three times a day. Yet these people go for months during the winter without the benefits of sacrament. I did learn afterwards that, because of their isolated station, the bishop had given dispensation to the people to make holy vows in matters of births, weddings and deaths until such occurrences could receive priestly blessing.

It took the girl some while before she was able to coax the kindle into flame and, when it was burning well, she laid the heavy sods of turf on it. Turf, or peat, is the substance which is burnt as fuel in these parts. It is slow burning and ideally suited for the stews and soups which are the people's main culinary art.

'There now, Father,' she said, standing up and dusting her rag of a dress, 'that should draw well but see to it that you feed it. Don't let it go out or you'll be feeling the cold. If you like, I'll come by each day and help you with the chores of the house until you are comfortably settled.'

I told her that this would suit me greatly.

I spent an uneasy night in that place. I told myself that it would take a few days to get used to the new situation, the curious smells, sounds and sights of this alien environment. I resigned myself to my restlessness and the discomforture of the damp and cold.

In the morning Máire returned with a basket of food.

'I have taken it upon myself to collect this from the islanders,' she said, setting it upon the table. 'There is a small packet of tea, some sugar, a few gulls' eggs and potatoes. Later today, the fishermen might return with a good catch in which case there will be fish to be had.'

Brother Antonio, this is the staple diet of these people. How they exist by it, I do not know, but fish and potatoes, now and again augmented by the eggs of sea birds, are their main nourishment. Tea is the beverage that everyone drinks and one must learn to take this with goat's milk, there being no cows on the island but just a few goats. For stronger liquor, an islander named Seán Rua, or Red John, distils a spirit from potatoes called *poitín*. Potatoes! Each dish of the day consists of potatoes and these are always boiled and eaten with a little salt from the sea dried in the sun. There is a song that the islanders sing whose words I shall transcribe for you:

> *Prátaí ar maidin*
> *Prátaí um nóin,*
> *'s dá n-éireochainn í*
> *Meadhon oídche*
> *Prátaí a gheobhainn!*

> Potatoes at morning,
> Potatoes at noon,
> and if I were to rise
> at midnight
> potatoes I'd get!

Now may you know the full extent of my comfortless existence on this island.

It would be tedious work to recount the personal details of the various islanders whom I gradually came to know in the course of my pastoral duties. Among them Seán Rua seemed their chief spokesman and leader. In the main they were courteous but it was clear that they regarded me as a stranger, an outsider in their society. My only friendly contact was with the girl Máire who helped me in adapting to the spartan community by relieving me of many burdensome domestic chores.

'Máire,' I said one day, 'I do not recall meeting your parents.'

'Nor will you,' she replied, 'for they are both dead.'

I made a sympathetic reply and asked who looked after her.

She laughed gaily.

'I look after myself.'

'But with whom do you live then?'

'With Diarmid Mac Maoláin.'

'And who is he?'

'A fisherman,' she replied, not understanding my question.

'I mean, what relation is he to you?'

'No relation,' she responded. 'He is just my man.'

'Ah, your husband? Are you married to him?'

She chuckled.

'Och, no, Father. I like him well enough but to marry you must be in love and I do not like him well enough to serve him all my days.'

I stared at her aghast.

'By my soul, child! You are living with Diarmid Mac Maoláin as his wife and are not married to him? I must resolve this right away. You and Diarmid must come to me this Saturday so that I may marry you.'

She sniffed coldly.

'Did I not say that I do not like him well enough to marry? I'm content until I can find a better man.'

My sensibilities were shocked.

'Holy Mary! You prefer to live with a man in carnal sin?
Child, do you know what you are saying?'

She pouted.

'By my baptism, child to you I am not! Why, you are
scarce a man yet.'

I coloured hotly. It is hard to be a priest and only twenty-
three summers to give weight to one's authority.

'I am your father in God,' I replied sternly.

'Priest you are ordained. It doesn't make you less of a
man or a boy for all that.'

She laughed at my mortified expression and stalked away.
That afternoon I sought out Diarmid Mac Maoláin.
Imagine my astonishment when I came across a man who
was elderly, with deep etched lines in his brown, weather
beaten face, his tousled hair bleached white by the sun. I
learnt that he was approaching sixty years in age but to my
eye he looked ancient for here, where man is in constant
battle with the inclement elements, nature prematurely ages
a man. For all his ancient look, Mac Maoláin was tall, mus-
cular and with narrow suspicious eyes. God's truth of it,
brother! How he had managed to persuade such a comely
young girl to share his bed, I cannot say. I will, however,
make this comment. Mac Maoláin was a native to the island
and owned his own *naomhóg,* cabin and nets. He was his
own master and wealthy by the meagre standards of the
island.

When I told him my business, he simply scowled.

'*Airiú,*' he replied, using the term which the islanders have
for 'indeed' or 'oh really?' '*Airiú,* Father. Marry Máire? It
will take more than the two of us combined to put a tether
on that one.'

'Explain yourself, man,' I demanded.

'Can you put a fence around the sea? Can you take the
sharp west wind or Spring and put it in a jar until summer?
Máire is a wild thing, a sprite, a free spirit. I am an old man,
Father. I merely thank God that she shares my house and,
thanks be, my bed when the mood is on her.'

I must have looked shocked.

'Do you not know how dire is the sin you commit?'

Mac Maoláin spat reflectively.

'I need no young boy to teach me the words of the Bible. I am a religious man but I am a man while you are a priest. I have a man's needs. I will accept this life which the girl offers and thanks be to God for it. Besides, I have said the words we were taught to say when no priest could reach the island because of the seas. Máire and I are vowed to each other in the eyes of the Blessed Virgin. We need no priest's blessing now.'

I had, as I have mentioned, learnt of this dispensation.

'And did Máire say the words, too?' I insisted.

I saw the answer in his shiftly glance.

'I said the words,' he muttered.

'Unless the words are freely said by both people then it is no vow before God.'

A red anger flushed his face. His blue eyes blazed suddenly as if in a battle fever. He took a step towards me, his great fisherman's hands clenching. I confess, I took an involuntary step backwards before his fury.

'Before God and man, Máire is mine! She is wife to me and no one will interfere in that. No one, be he bishop, cardinal or boy-priest!'

It took me a moment to recover my composure. Young though I am, I was still his pastor.

'Máire and you are living in sin,' I said evenly. 'I shall have no more to do with the pair of you until you make a full confession of your transgression before God and declare that you intend to marry according to the writ of Holy Mother Church.'

As I turned and walked away I heard his deep throated laughter.

'We lived well enough before you came. We can live well enough now . . . and after you have gone, we shall continue to live well enough.'

I strode back to my cabin and sat awhile in indignation,

meditating on the low standards of morality in the island. I do not recall how long I sat in front of the fire. I lost all track of the passing of time. I simply became aware that it was dark and that the fire was smouldering. There was a fierce coldness about the cabin and the quiet was so intense that it almost hurt my ears. I shivered and made to reach forward to stoke the fire but, as I did so, I caught sight of a shadow at the far end of the room.

The figure was plainly that of a man but that was as much as I could see in the gloom.

'Who are you?' I demanded.

There was no reply but, to my horror, the shadow raised an arm. I could see in the faint light from the glowing embers a silver flicker of light on an open razor held in the man's hand. Then there was a swift motion of the arm, a strangled cry, before the figure staggered forward and slumped down.

For a moment it was as if some force held me to my chair. I pushed myself suddenly forward, my face breaking into a cold sweat.

'In the name of God . . . !' I cried, hurrying forward to where I had seen the figure fall.

Oh, Brother Antonio, believe me, what horror froze my blood in my veins when I discovered there was no body on the floor. There was no one in the cabin except myself. I turned with a stifled exclamation of disbelief and searched for matches, lit my tiny lamp and stared incredulously. There was no doubt about it. I was alone in the cabin.

Was I asleep, do you say? Perhaps. As I thought about it, I tried to convince myself that I had been subject to some vile nightmare. Yet I recalled the scene vividly as if aware of all my senses. I pondered the vision a long time before falling into a troubled sleep.

Can you imagine my surprise, brother, when the next morning I was awakened from my slumber to find Máire boiling the kettle on the fire for my tea and preparing breakfast? I pushed myself up in my bed with a frown of displeasure.

'Máire!' I said sharply. 'Did I not make myself clear to you and Diarmid Mac Maoláin? I want to see you no more until you consent to marry in God's eyes.'

She looked at me as if I had made some amusing quip.

'*Amaidí chainte!*' she replied. My jaw dropped. I am not sure how I should render this into English but suffice to indicate that she told me I was speaking rubbish.

'You are not a grey haired old preacher so full of piety and age that you have forgotten how it is to feel young,' she went on. 'You are not that removed from this world that you do not feel the hot blood of youth coursing in your veins.'

In disgust, I clambered out of bed and, standing in my nightshirt, ordered her to leave my cabin. To my outraged horror, she came forward towards me with a mocking smile and pressed her young body against mine.

'Why, Father,' she sneered, 'I feel your body trembling. There is man enough left behind that priest's robe for you to appreciate my needs.'

God save me, brother, but she was the devil sent to tempt me. I closed my eyes and tried to shut my mind to the sensation of her soft warm body, from the smell of the wild summer fragrance in her soft hair.

'God help you, Máire!' I cried, suddenly finding the courage to push her roughly away.

She recovered her balance and stood in the middle of the cabin chuckling.

'God help you, Father,' she mimicked my tones. 'You were no more meant for the priesthood than I was meant to live my life on this God-forsaken island. Even if your mind does not accept the truth of what I say, your body admits it.'

I was stunned by her boldness.

'What wickedness is this?' I gasped.

'None that I know of. All I know is what I saw in your eyes when they met mine on the day you arrived from the mainland. I saw that your body and soul desired me, as I want you, even though your priest's mind seeks to reject me.'

I raised a hand to my brow in amazement. Was Christ tempted in this fashion, brother?

'Get out!' was all I could shout.

'How feebly your words are said, Father Máirtìn,' she whispered. 'Yes, I will leave. But I shall return, and shall keep returning until you admit what is truth and what is sham.'

I busied myself most of that day writing my first report on the parish to the bishop, determined to send it away to the mainland at the first opportunity. I tried to drive the image of that wilful girl from my mind. In the afternoon, I went to the oratory to baptise and bless five of the island's children born during the absence of a priest. That evening I went to visit Seán Rua in order to establish some confidence between the islanders and myself. After a glass or two of his *poitín*, Seán Rua unbent to confess that not only my age told against me but the fact that I was an *eachtrannach*, a stranger from another province, which made the islanders suspicious of me. Eventually, I returned to my cabin and prepared to retire.

At first I thought someone had opened the door, for the candle suddenly spluttered in my hand and the flames of the fire did a jig in the hearth. I felt a cold hand on my spine and shivered violently.

I turned towards the door fully expecting to see that it had blown open.

It was tight shut.

But there, there in the same gloomy corner, I could see the dark figure of a man, his back turned towards me. God look down on me! It was the same dream which I had before, yet I was not abed. How could this be dreaming? I was fully awake, a candle in my hand. Yet I was seeing this vision as clearly as I saw my own hearth and fire.

'Who are you?' I demanded. 'In the name of God, I tell you to speak!'

I raised my candle high and felt a curious constriction in my throat as I saw that the image was clad in the black robes of a priest.

Then the head turned slightly in my direction and in the flickering light I beheld its face. Jesus, Mary and Joseph, pray for me! Never have I beheld such a vision of suffering. From a bony skull, over which the skin was stretched like a taut parchment, two black eyes gazed forth like open windows into hell. And in those terrible tormented eyes there gleamed something else – a hopeless longing; a muted cry for help.

'Who are you?' I managed to blurt again.

Then, as on the previous occasion, I saw the arm raised, saw the flicker on the open blade of the razor, saw the blade descend to the man's throat with a strange jerking motion. There was a strangled gasp and the figure staggered forward a pace before collapsing.

Still, as I watched, my candle held high, the image disappeared.

I tried to raise my hand in genuflection and cry out the name of Our Saviour. What devil's vision was this? A priest committing suicide – the most unforgivable of all sins!

That night I spent in restless anxiety, aghast at what I had seen. I was up early and trying to kindle the fire to boil the kettle when the latch lifted and in came Máire. I was in a quandary of emotions. I know I should have thrown out that brazen vixen there and then but, after my nightmare, I was emotionally weakened and exhausted. The girl behaved as though nothing had happened between us on the previous day and I was content to let the situation remain so. It was selfish of me, but I needed someone to confide to, someone to whom I could recount that awesome nightmare. She alone of the islanders would make a sympathetic audience.

'That's a strange tale,' she conceded when I had done. 'But, surely, there's an easy understanding of it. You are a stranger here and unused to the island. Unfamiliarity creates strange dreams.'

'You mean that I was merely asleep and dreamt this spectre?' I asked her, almost hopefully. I found myself desiring the comfort in her voice. Oh, how weak this frail body of ours is; how weak its resolution.

She sat herself on my table and swung her long shapely legs, barely covered by her tattered dress.

'You say you saw the face of the image quite clearly? We usually put people we know into our dreams. Did you know the face?'

I shook my head thoughtfully, remembering that pleading, anguished countenance.

'It was no one that I recognised. No, of that I am sure. It was the face of a total stranger.'

Máire shrugged.

'There are three kinds of things that come to us when we are asleep; dreams that are only strange stories that pass through the mind in sleep; nightmares that are nothing but fears of the night; and then the *aisling* which is the vision of things that have been. Yours was only a nightmare.'

'How can I be sure?'

She smiled: 'And you a priest not to know?'

'What do you mean?'

'Here on the island there is a powerful charm against nightmares.'

'Charms!' I sneered in disgust.

'What are prayers but charms?' she countered.

'The *ortha an tromluí* is handed down from generation to generation as a protection. Churchmen have been saying it for centuries, my boy-priest.'

I glowered angrily at the girl.

'I will not have God taken into disrespect!' I thundered.

'I speak to the boy in the priest's coat, not to his God,' she retorted.

Anger moved me and I made to catch hold of her to throw her out. I caught her around the upper arms and she slid off the table towards me, her body so close up against mine that

I became aware of its soft contours. She was so close that her warm lips touched mine and – Angels preserve me! – I did not push her away until several long moments passed. Then I turned, my face hotly flushed, and rushed from the cabin.

What was it about this place, about these people, which was destroying my resolution in my vocation and the sacred vows that I had made to the Holy Mother Church? Was I but a weak man after all?

That evening, as I knelt in prayer, the ancient words of the *ortha an tromluí* came unbidden to my lips: 'Anne, the mother of Mary, and Mary, the mother of Jesus, and Elisabeth, the mother of John the Baptist. These three between me and the nightmare from tonight until a year from tonight and tonight itself. *In nomine Patris et Filli et Spiritus Sancti. Amen.*'

And in spite of this the vision came again.

I awoke in the night to find the room in darkness save for the spluttering from the dying fire. It was ice-cold again and so I climbed out of bed to stoke the fire. It was then that I turned and saw the dark figure dressed in the priest's robes; saw the gaunt, anguished face with those terrible pleading eyes turned in my direction. I could not mistake that mute cry for help from those hell-tormented eyes. Then I saw the upraised hand; saw the glint on the open razor. I tried to cry out, tried to stop the downward motion of the arm . . . then the vision vanished.

This was no nightmare, of that I was sure for here was I, standing in my nightshirt on the cold floor, fully awake and aware of my surroundings; aware of the cold; aware of the slow, ominous ticking of the clock on the shelf and the gentle roar of the sea outside.

When Máire came the next morning I found myself positively pleased to see her.

'It must be a dream,' she said dismissively. 'Didn't I tell you to say the *ortha an tromluí*?'

'God forgive me, I did say it,' I confessed.

She glanced at me, a fleeting smile faltering in the corner of her dimpled mouth.

'So?' She did not speak what was obviously in her mind. Instead she pursed her lips gravely and sighed. 'Then this is no nightmare. You must be seeing an *aisling*.'

I shivered and genuflected.

Brother Antonio, let me explain what this *aisling* is. It is the word we Irish have for a vision. Being an ancient Celtic people, we are much given to visions and vision-stories are a part of our old literature. Our beloved Saint Fursa, who founded monasteries in England before crossing to France where he died in the celebrated monastery he founded in Peronne in 649 *Anno Domini*, was the author of a great *aisling* tale, which is the first surviving such tale we have. Saints, scholars and poets have claimed to see an *aisling* and those who do are said to be the blessed of Christ.

As Máire was making the morning tea, I meditated on this.

If I was seeing an *aisling* of some past event, what did it portend? Had some poor priest taken his own life in the very cabin I now occupied? It was unthinkable that a priest could so neglect his vows as to commit such a mortal sin. Yet there it was. I had seen the vision and the vision was being shown me for a reason.

'Has anyone else seen such a vision on the island, Máire?' I asked, at length.

The girl shook her head vehemently.

'I would surely know if it were so.'

'You have never heard it spoken of that a priest took his own life here?'

She shook her head.

'Tell me, Máire, who knows the history of this island well? Who would know if there is a memory of some ancient deed the like of which I have been witnessing?'

'You must consult the *seanchaí*,' she said immediately. 'If there is but a vague recollection of such a deed, then he would know.'

I resolved to see the man at once.

Dael Mac an Bháird was the island's *seanchaí*, a sort of official storyteller who was the repository of all the history, genealogy, folklore and legend connected with the area. He was an old fellow who lived with his son in one of the *clochán*, spending his days in the tutoring of his son in the store of knowledge he held. The old man felt his time was approaching and oral traditions must be passed on. I went up to his *clochán* and found him seated outside, it being a fine day. He watched me come up the hillside to where he sat and greeted me courteously.

'Come safely, Father.'

'God bless all here,' I replied and took a seat on the sod beside him.

'I hear you are the man to recount the history of the island?' I made no preamble.

'I am the *seanchaí*,' he replied gravely. 'And so was my father and his father before that and all the sons of the poet before them.'

I must interject here, Brother Antonio, to tell you that the name Mac an Bháird means 'son of the poet' and hence his allusion to the fact.

'Do you know the history of the priests of this island?' I asked.

He paused and reflected.

'I do, by the faith.'

'Did ever a priest take his own life here?'

The old man raised his eyebrows in surprise.

'God stay us from evil! Where did you hear such a thing? For a priest to take his own life is a most grievous sin.'

'It is a terrible sin, yet did a priest ever do such a thing on this island?'

Mac an Bháird gazed long and thoughtfully at me and then heaved a deep sigh.

'There is such a tale, Father. I had it from my father and he from his and back many generations. Each *seanchaí* in turn has sworn never to tell anyone the tale other than the one who will fill his place.'

I made an impatient gesture.

'I must know the tale.'

The old man's eyes were troubled.

'I have sworn an oath only to tell the next *seanchaí* and no other.'

'I absolve you from that oath.'

He still hesitated and then I had a flash of inspiration.

'You may tell me in the nature of confession. By my soul, it shall go no further than the confessional.'

Mac an Bháird considered and looked relieved.

'It happened long ago when Cromwell was the scourge of our people. It happened when the Irish were being cleared from their lands, pushed westward across the River Shannon where they were ordered to reside on pain of death. Any Irish found east of the river was killed or shipped to the Barbados to be sold for labour. Priests were killed whenever the English encountered them and there was a five pound reward for the head of any priest. A few lucky ones were able to follow their flocks to be sold in the American colonies.'

I sighed impatiently. Who does not know that woeful history? The Irish folk memory of those savage days is as clear as ever it was.

'But what of this priest?' I pressed.

'He was a young priest; newly appointed to his flock. One night, so the tale goes, the English troopers rode down on his village, killing the old men and women and seizing the able-bodied and young children to take to the Barbados-bound ships. The young priest fled into the darkness. He did not stay with his people in this hour of peril. He deserted his flock and escaped alone to this island of Inis Tuaisceart where he thought no soldier would follow.

'*Airiú!* But his conscience followed him. He brooded on the desertion of his flock when they needed him. He pondered in his isolated melancholy until he could bear himself no longer. He was young. Perhaps that was his only sin.'

'Is that the tale?'

'That is all I know,' Mac an Bháird inclined his head.

I rose and gave a blessing on him and his house and departed.

When I returned to my cabin I found Diarmid Mac Maoláin waiting for me. He stood in front of the fire, his big hands clenching and unclenching in agitation. He would not gaze fully into my face but I could see jealous anger spread as a mask across his features. His face was flushed though anger were a small part of it for I smelt strong liquor on his breath.

'Do you think I am blind, Father?' were his first words, said without greeting or deference to my calling.

'I do not, Mac Maoláin,' I replied gravely. 'Why would you believe I do?'

Mac Maoláin made a gesture around the cabin.

'There is a woman's touch here and all the island knows it.'

'No harm in it,' I said defensively. 'Máire does her Christian duty in looking to the needs of her priest. 'Tis a pity that others of my parish are not so obliging as to help in the care of God's servants.'

Mac Maoláin stared at my bold front.

'So Máire is the model Christian now?' he sneered, after a hesitation. 'Was it not the other day that you wanted to see no more of her until she consented to be married? Now I find that she comes here every day . . .'

'That I might guide her to the truth of God,' I interrupted, the cold sweat breaking out on my face as I tried to still that small voice whispering in my ear: 'Thou shalt not bear false witness.' Oh Brother Antonio, I know above all people that false words are not only evil in themselves but they infect the soul with evil. To tell a falsehood is like the cut of a sabre for though the wound may heal, the scar of it will remain.

It was then that Mac Maoláin raised his eyes to mine. I

tried to meet his gaze boldly, eye to eye, soul to soul, but it was I who let my eyes drop before his.

'You are a young man, Father Máirtín,' he said softly now, his anger controlled. 'You are a priest but a young man nevertheless. And there is a handsomeness which shapes your features with an intelligent mind behind them. Who am I but a poor untutored fisherman? You are a stranger, a representative of a world that is strange but bewitching; a world which is alien but beguiling. Máire is like a summer's honey bee . . . she flits here and there among the flowers, attracted first by one and then by another; attracted to the beauty of one, then the colouring of another. I can see in her eyes what is in her heart.'

I tried to draw myself up and frown sternly.

'Man, are you forgetting that I am a priest? You are accusing me of a most dreadful sin or the contemplation of a dreadful sin. My marriage is with Holy Mother Church.'

Mac Maoláin stared at me for a long time before he finally spoke.

'*Airiú*, priests were not always celibate. Ask Dael Mac an Bháird the storyteller. I have heard that once even the Popes begat children. Because priests dress differently to other men and say words before an altar, it does not destroy their manhood.'

'I have heard enough, Mac Maoláin,' I said angrily. 'You cannot realise what you are saying nor what it is that you are accusing me of.'

Mac Maoláin leant suddenly forward and grasped my arm in a vice-like grip with an abruptness which caused my heart to pound.

'I know what is in Máire's mind. I know her soul. But I do not know what is in your soul, Father Máirtín. I have come here to say that a cloud of gloom spread over this island when you set foot here, it hovers over the island still. Go away! Go away, for you are not wanted here.'

I was livid with indignation.

'The cloud was here when I arrived on this bastion of

heathendom!' I snapped. 'The evil was here before my coming. Look into your own soul, Mac Maoláin. It is you who live in carnal sin, not I.'

He swore a terrible curse and turned towards the door.

The vision came at dusk this time.

Again I saw the shadowy figure, saw the black mantle of his calling, saw the pleading white tormented face turned towards me, saw the upraised hand, the gleaming razor.

It was only after the vision vanished that the thought occurred to me; this *aisling* was being shown to me and no one else on the island. Why? It was because I, too, was a priest and could bless this wraith with holy sacrament and absolve the sin. In giving the matter careful thought, I realised the truth of it. I was dealing with a troubled earth-bound spirit; an unquiet spirit seeking forgiveness for the desertion of his flock and that terrible act of self-destruction. Suddenly I became full of eagerness for the vision to re-appear so that I might perform this act of charity for a brother priest that his soul might finally rest in peace.

The following morning I arose early. I went down to the sea shore and started to walk along the sandy strand. I took with me my *Missal* to search its pages for an appropriate service of exorcism through which to absolve the earth-bound soul who haunted me. So engrossed was I in my meditative endeavours that I wandered quite a way from the village and did not stop on the strand until a clump of rocks barred my progress. I paused to consider whether I should climb around them or turn back to my cabin. Then I heard a cry of greeting which drove all other thoughts from my mind.

I turned my face seaward to see a white arm waving to me and I saw the red blaze of hair in the early morning light and knew it to be Máire.

I watched as she swum lazily towards the shore, her long white arms circling languorously in the blue waters.

'God save you,' she called as she came near the shore and

then, without shame, she rose from the frothy surf and came towards me, rose as naked as she had been on her birth.

God keep me from sin! I am a man! *I am a man!* My cheeks reddened yet I could not keep my eyes from drinking in the beauty of her body. I could see her examining me under lowered lashes and smiling demurely. I tried to clear my throat, tried to turn away from her, yet I could not. The sin of the flesh was beginning to make my body shake, my nerves tingle.

She stood there watching me as if aware of the tremendous struggle which coursed my body and soul. How well did she read my thoughts. She knew I would forsake all, send myself down into the bowels of hell, to touch her soft white body, to feel those warm red lips. She knew. Oh yes, she had always known.

'May I cover myself?' she asked coquettishly, nodding towards her tattered dress which lay discarded on some nearby rocks.

'No! Not yet!'

I could not believe that the voice which grunted from my throat was my own. I stood with the passion burning in my face.

She turned to me with a smile; a smile of triumph, took a step towards me and raised her arms as if in welcome. No word was spoken nor was any necessary. She had been right all along. I was a man!

Afterwards? The shame and horror of my deed drove me from her side without a word. With mortification heavy in my soul, I ran back to my cabin and threw myself on my knees, my arms held up in supplication for forgiveness. How I wished that I had never chanced along the sea shore; how I wished that I had never set foot on this island. But sin cannot be undone, only forgiven. Yet, Brother Antonio, how will I ever find the courage to confess this carnal sin? God knows and yet I find his terrible justice mild by comparison with the fears of my fellow brothers in Christ. How will they admonish me? You are my true friend, my brother in

Christ; tell me what I must do, Brother Antonio. How can I redeem myself?

It must have been about noon when I was torn from my feverish prayers of penance by the thundering of a fist on my cabin door. What new affliction was this? Was it Diarmid Mac Maoláin come seeking revenge? The thought of being revealed to the islanders made me hesitate before the door. Then the voice of Seán Rua sang out:

'God help us, Father! Are you in there?'

Trying to compose myself, I opened the door and stared at the circle of agitated faces which greeted me. There was Seán Rua, his face white, an expression of horror contorting his features.

'Come quickly, Father. Down to the strand.'

'What is it?' I demanded as he seized my arm and began to propel me forward.

'God have mercy on us, 'tis Máire. She is dead on the strand.'

I halted, rooted to the spot, my heart pumping wildly.

'I . . . I don't understand.'

'For the love you bear Christ, Father, come quickly now!' insisted Seán Rua. 'Hasn't Máire been killed by Diarmid Mac Maoláin?'

I was dragged forward like a man in a dream until we came to the spot near the rocks.

There lay Máire on the beach. She lay in that forlornly tattered dress of hers, as if sleeping on her side, one arm flung casually upwards, the other at her side. There was an ugly red welt across her skull. The instrument which made the wound was not hard to find for just beyond her lay a *sleaghán*. It is a special kind of spade with a wing at one side which the natives use for cutting the turf for their fires.

I knelt down beside her and felt for her pulse but it was obvious that she was gone from this world. God have mercy on her! I began to mutter the words of absolution.

When I had done, I stood up and looked round the gathered islanders.

'Where is Mac Maoláin?' I asked coldly. All feeling seemed to have departed. Perhaps it was the shock. I could not feel sorrow for poor Máire; I could not feel hate for Mac Maoláin nor could I feel guilt for myself. I was simply acting a part now. 'Is there proof that he did this thing?'

Seán Rua shuffled forward.

'I was yonder on the hill and saw the whole thing, Father. Máire was sitting on the rocks there and I saw Mac Maoláin come up to her. He was coming from the turf field yonder,' he jabbed a forefinger, 'and carried his *sleaghán* with him. I heard their voices raised in angry tones. God help me, but then I saw him raise his *sleaghán* and strike a cruel blow.'

He paused and there was a mumbling of amazement from those gathered.

'I cried out,' continued the man, 'and Mac Maoláin looked up and saw me. He dropped his *sleaghán* and ran along the strand towards the village.'

'That's the truth of it, surely,' intervened another man. 'He came hurrying along the strand and launched his *naomhóg*. Didn't I ask him where he was off to in such a bother and didn't he reply not a word?'

I bit my lip.

'So he is heading for the mainland?' I sighed, making a natural assumption.

'Not he,' responded the fisherman. 'I saw him heading for the back of the island.'

Seán Rua pointed to the greying skies against which black storm clouds were scurrying hither and thither.

"Tis a bad time to be in those waters, God save him. Maybe he means to give himself to God.'

'Give himself to God?' I asked bemused. 'What do you mean?'

It was the old *seanchaí*, Dael Mac an Bháird, who answered.

'In ancient times, Father, when a man had committed a terrible sin, it was the custom for him to row his *naomhóg* to the back of the island where the Atlantic seas crush against the granite cliffs, where the shore is inhospitable. There the man would wait for a coming storm. It was then up to God whether he drowned or survived. If he survived he was judged to have received God's forgiveness. It was the old justice.'

I cannot tell you, Brother Antonio, of the thousands of thoughts which coursed my mind. Had Mac Maoláin seen Máire and me together? Was it that which caused him such overpowering anger that he struck the life from the girl and now was as good as committing suicide himself? In my strange emotional numbness I made my way back to my cabin just as the storm broke over the island. God's will or not, I knew well what the fate of that man would be, alone in his canvas boat among the Atlantic swells. I knew also that I shared his sin; more than shared it. Máire's death, Mac Maoláin's death, were both my responsibility.

The skies continued to darken and only the occasional lightning bolt illuminated the interior of my cabin as I sat there before the hearth watching the fire that Máire had kindled flicker and die into embers and then the embers themselves fade into dead ashes.

Strangely, I felt akin to Mac Maoláin, felt his agony as he sat in his tossing *naomhóg*. I felt the salt seas hurling the little canvas craft hither and thither amidst the black frothing fury . . . hither and thither until—until it was rendered into pieces against the jagged granite cliffs; until it was sundered into a thousand pieces of matchwood; until the soul of Diarmid Mac Maoláin was sent abruptly into the next world.

I shivered involuntarily. There again came that feeling which I had felt so often now, the sudden coldness on my spine. Even as I prepared myself for what was to come, as I turned to stare into the gloom, a terrible cold dread seized me.

There stood the figure clad in the black robes of a priest. The flashing lightning at the window illuminated its pale, tormented, skull like features—the dark pleading eyes turned towards me.

I tried to push the thoughts of Máire and Mac Maoláin from my mind. I had to help this troubled soul, to give the young priest rest. He had deserted his flock and in his brooding misery had taken his life. Yet surely his sin only lay in his youth and inexperience?

'In the name of Christ and all His saints,' I cried, raising my crucifix to make the sign of the Blessed Cross. 'Peace be upon your soul! In Christ's Holy Name, forgiveness for your deed. Depart now in peace!'

The transformation was amazing. The skull-like face filled out and momentarily I saw the fresh-faced features of a handsome young man. The expression on that countenance was one of peace and exaltation. For a moment the young man's face gazed at me in wordless gratitude.

Then it was gone.

Oh my God! The face vanished but not the black robed shadow.

I stared in bewilderment.

A sudden searing flash of lightning across the island flickered on the upheld razor. I could see its wicked blade open, watch its swift downward stroke as impotently as I had watched it many times before.

Yet I had absolved the wretched spirit—had seen its departure with peace and joy!

There came another flash of lightning. I saw a new face staring back at me from the shadowy wraith. I could see the features as plainly as I saw the razor's descent, as plainly as I saw the vivid red welt across the throat just before the shadow fell and vanished from my sight.

I sprung backward screaming in terror, cold hands clutching at my palpitating heart.

We are all prisoners of consequences. Every deed must have a consequence to legitimise or cancel it and thus we must recompense the Creator for all our actions. I, who was not without grievous sin, did not have the power to absolve another without restitution.

The *aisling* was no longer a vision of the past. It was a

vision of the future. It is my atonement for my terrible sin and I pray God will forgive me.

When I stared at the face of the *aisling* it was as if I was staring into a mirror. The pleading white face was now my own!

Light a candle for the repose of my soul, my dear brother in Christ. Farewell.

3

FAERIE

The world of Faerie has a special place in Irish folklore: indeed traditions about the faerie folk—or *Daoine Sidh* as they are called in Gaelic, sometimes shortened to *Sidhe*— are to be found all over the country. These faeries, however, do not conform to the conventional picture fostered in countless storybooks, of miniature people. As W. B. Yeats wrote in his collection, *Irish Fairy and Folk Tales* (1893): 'Do not think the fairies are always little. Everything is capricious about them, even their size. They seem to take whatever size or shape pleases them. Their chief occupations are feasting, fighting and making love, and playing the most beautiful music. They have only one industrious person amongst them, the *lepra-caun*, the shoemaker.'

According to most folklore historians the faeries have been in existence since the days of antiquity and may possibly be the remnants of the early settlers of Ireland, the *Tuatha De Danān*. It has been pointed out that some of the most famous faeries in folklore have the same names as those of the old *Tuatha* heroes, and that the Faerie realm has its own hierarchy of kings, queens and chieftains, who gather in their special places, known as *raths*. Faeries are said to be friendly towards human beings if they are respected and not disturbed or attacked—although if they are angered they possess several weapons of retaliation including the power to bewitch or fire faerie darts which can paralyse men and animals. There is even a group of malignant faeries known as the *Lianhan Sidhe*.

Small wonder, then, that the *Sidhe* should have inspired a considerable number of excellent stories by Irish writers, among whom James Stephens (1882–1950) is particularly prominent. Stephens, who once claimed to have been born on the same day and at the same hour as his great friend, James Joyce, grew up in abject poverty and often dreamed of finding the fabled faerie gold. A small, perky little boy— remembered by his friends as looking rather like a leprechaun himself—he was raised in a Dublin orphanage after apparently being abandoned by his parents. He then worked briefly as a typist in a lawyer's office before discovering his talent for writing. In 1912 he published *The Crock of Gold*, an immediate best seller which reflected his fascination with the world of Faerie. In this and some of his later books he claimed (sincerely, but perhaps a little tongue-in-cheek) that he was setting out to create for Ireland 'a new mythology to take the place of the threadbare mythology of Greece and Rome'.

The culmination of James Stephens' research into the old epics and sagas of his native country was *Irish Fairy Tales*, which he published in 1920. In it he presented new narrative versions of the ancient stories, all told in his own, very distinctive style. Amongst these tales is 'The Carl of the Drab Coat' which at once transports the reader into a fantasy world—but a world which Stephens has made as accessible to us as our own.

Although the second story, 'The Curse of the Fires and of the Shadows' by W. B. Yeats (1865–1939), was actually written almost a quarter of a century before James Stephens' tale, it deals with a much later period, when the *Sidhe* had retreated to the periphery of human life and their intervention in mankind's affairs had become much more of a mystery. Like the story, its author is himself something of an enigma: for on the one hand we have William Butler Yeats, the Nobel prize-winning poet and generating force of Irish theatre, and on the other the self-styled mystic who believed implicitly in the supernatural and the occult. Yeats not only attempted to raise ghosts at séances, he also belonged to the Hermetic Order of the Golden Dawn, a secret society which practised alchemy and magic.

During his fifty-year quest for arcane knowledge, Yeats collected a wealth of folk tales from peasant sources, which he assembled in books such as *Irish Fairy and Folk Tales* and *The Celtic Twilight* (also published in 1893). In the latter, he suggested that while it was possible to doubt Hell and other Christian doctrines as 'inventions got up by the priests to keep people good', there was no doubting faeries and leprechauns 'for they stand to reason'. His unwavering defence of the supernatural has led many admirers of his poetry and plays to dismiss his other writings as nothing more than an aberration which he did not really expect to be taken seriously—a criticism that a reading of 'The Curse of the Fires and of the Shadows' will, I think, soon dispel. Important as Yeats undoubtedly is in the history of modern Irish poetry and drama, he also deserves credit—along with James Stephens—as a 'fabulist', the first of the Irish writers to popularise the old faerie stories in the form of modern fables.

Liam O'Flaherty (1897–1984) fought with the Republicans in the 1916 rising and had to flee the country to avoid arrest. It was while in exile in London that he began to write, in 1926 publishing his famous novel about the Irish insurrection, *The Informer*, which won the James Tait Black Memorial Prize and was later made into a classic Hollywood movie by John Ford. O'Flaherty's background, however, seemed to have destined him for a very different kind of life, for he was born on the Aran islands where he grew up speaking Gaelic and began training for the priesthood. Deciding he did not have a vocation for the Church, he served briefly in the British Army, being wounded in France, and after two years of travel around the world, returned to Dublin to join the Republicans.

As a writer O'Flaherty never forgot his origins or the folk tales that he had heard as a youngster on the Aran Islands, and his story 'The Fairy Goose' is clearly drawn from elements of Irish fable. It also offers a forceful comment on folk superstition and religious belief.

Frank O'Connor (1903–1966) has been called 'the Old Master of the Irish short story'. Like James Stephens he grew up in poverty, and it was W. B. Yeats who sensed his emerging talent and enrolled him into the work of the Abbey Theatre. Born Michael O'Donovan in Cork, the traumas of his childhood, followed by his experiences when he served in the Civil War and was captured, inspired his first excursions into fiction in which he revealed a deep insight into human loneliness as well as a feeling for the aspirations and weaknesses of men and women. The fame of his work later made him much in demand as a teacher in England and America, although his stories remained rooted in the people and places of Ireland. He was an intensely realistic writer, but well aware of the continuing influence of Irish folklore on the people, as his story 'The Old Faith' brilliantly shows.

Catherine Brophy (1941–   ) is the author of one of the most widely-praised Irish fantasy novels of recent years, *Dark Paradise*, which was published in 1991. Born in Dublin near Bray (the film studios there were once famous as the production centre for several of the most popular Hammer horror films), she was educated at University College and qualified as a teacher of deaf children. She has subsequently taught in a number of Irish schools and has also lectured on audiology. Her writing has embraced several genres, including historical fiction and SF, and since contributing to RTE's highly popular soap opera, 'Fair City' about life in Dublin, she has been appointed script editor of the series.

Her story 'The Science of Mirrors' is an ingenious tale which captures something of the faerie magic of old Ireland, through the experience of two girls who are as contemporary as any to be found in 'Fair City'.

THE CARL OF THE DRAB COAT

James Stephens

I

One day something happened to Fionn, the son of Uail; that is, he departed from the world of men, and was set wandering in great distress of mind through Faery. He had days and nights there and adventures there, and was able to bring back the memory of these.

That, by itself, is wonderful, for there are few people who remember that they have been to Faery or aught of all that happened to them in that state.

In truth we do not go to Faery, we become Faery, and in the beating of a pulse we may live for a year or a thousand years. But when we return the memory is quickly clouded, and we seem to have had a dream or seen a vision, although we have verily been in Faery.

It was wonderful, then, that Fionn should have remembered all that happened to him in that wide-spun moment, but in this tale there is yet more to marvel at; for not only did Fionn go to Faery, but the great army which he had marshalled to Ben Edair[1] were translated also, and neither he nor they were aware that they had departed from they had departed from the world until they came back to it.

Fourteen battles, seven of the reserve and seven of the regular Fianna, had been taken by the Chief on a great march and

1 The Hill of Howth.

175

manœuvre. When they reached Ben Edair it was decided to
pitch camp so that the troops might rest in view of the warlike
plan which Fionn had imagined for the morrow. The camp
was chosen, and each squadron and company of the host were
lodged into an appropriate place, so there was no over-
crowding and no halt or interruption of the march; for where
a company halted that was its place of rest, and in that place
it hindered no other company, and was at its own ease.

When this was accomplished the leaders of battalions
gathered on a level, grassy plateau overlooking the sea,
where a consultation began as to the next day's manœuvres,
and during this discussion they looked often on the wide
water that lay wrinkling and twinkling below them.

A roomy ship under great press of sail was bearing on Ben
Edair from the east.

Now and again, in a lull of the discussion, a champion
would look and remark on the hurrying vessel; and it may
have been during one of these moments that the adventure
happened to Fionn and the Fianna.

'I wonder where that ship comes from?' said Conán idly.
But no person could surmise anything about it beyond that
it was a vessel well equipped for war.

As the ship drew by the shore the watchers observed a tall
man swing from the side by means of his spear shafts, and
in a little while this gentleman was announced to Fionn, and
was brought into his presence.

A sturdy, bellicose, forthright personage he was indeed.
He was equipped in a wonderful solidity of armour, with a
hard, carven helmet on his head, a splendid red-bossed
shield swinging on his shoulder, a wide-grooved, straight
sword clashing along his thigh. On his shoulders under the
shield he carried a splendid scarlet mantle; over his breast
was a great brooch of burnt gold, and in his fist he gripped
a pair of thick-shafted, unburnished spears.

Fionn and the champions looked on this gentleman, and
they admired exceedingly his bearing and equipment.

'Of what blood are you, young gentleman?' Fionn

demanded, 'and from which of the four corners of the world do you come?'

'My name is Cael of the Iron,' the stranger answered, 'and I am son to the King of Thessaly.'

'What errand has brought you here?'

'I do not go on errands,' the man replied sternly, 'but on the affairs that please me.'

'Be it so. What is the pleasing affair which brings you to this land?'

'Since I left my own country I have not gone from a land or an island until it paid tribute to me and acknowledged my lordship.'

'And you have come to this realm—' cried Fionn, doubting his ears.

'For tribute and sovereignty,' growled that other, and he struck the haft of his spear violently on the ground.

'By my hand,' said Conán, 'we have never heard of a warrior, however great, but his peer was found in Ireland, and the funeral songs of all such have been chanted by the women of this land.'

'By my hand and word,' said the harsh stranger, 'your talk makes me think of a small boy or of an idiot.'

'Take heed, sir,' said Fionn, 'for the champions and great dragons of the Gael are standing by you, and around us there are fourteen battles of the Fianna of Ireland.'

'If all the Fianna who have died in the last seven years were added to all that are now here,' the stranger asserted, 'I would treat all of these and those grievously, and would curtail their limbs and their lives.'

'It is no small boast,' Conán murmured, staring at him.

'It is no boast at all,' said Cael, 'and, to show my quality and standing, I will propose a deed to you.'

'Give out your deed,' Fionn commanded.

'Thus,' said Cael with cold savagery. 'If you can find a man among your fourteen battalions who can outrun or outwrestle or outfight me, I will take myself off to my own country, and will trouble you no more.'

And so harshly did he speak, and with such a belligerent eye did he stare, that dismay began to seize on the champions, and even Fionn felt that his breath had halted.

'It is spoken like a hero,' he admitted after a moment, 'and if you cannot be matched on those terms it will not be from a dearth of applicants.'

'In running alone,' Fionn continued thoughtfully, 'we have a notable champion, Caelte mac Ronán.'

'This son of Ronán will not long be notable,' the stranger asserted.

'He can outstrip the red deer,' said Conán.

'He can outrun the wind,' cried Fionn.

'He will not be asked to outrun the red deer or the wind,' the stranger sneered. 'He will be asked to outrun me,' he thundered. 'Produce this runner, and we shall discover if he keeps as great heart in his feet as he has made you think.'

'He is not with us,' Conán lamented.

'These notable warriors are never with us when the call is made,' said the grim stranger.

'By my hand,' cried Fionn, 'he shall be here in no great time, for I will fetch him myself.'

'Be it so,' said Cael.

'And during my absence,' Fionn continued, 'I leave this as a compact, that you make friends with the Fianna here present, and that you observe all the conditions and ceremonies of friendship.'

Cael agreed to that.

'I will not hurt any of these people until you return,' he said.

Fionn then set out towards Tara of the Kings, for he thought Caelte mac Ronán would surely be there; 'and if he is not there,' said the champion to himself, 'then I shall find him at Cesh Corran of the Fianna.'

II

He had not gone a great distance from Ben Edair when he came to an intricate, gloomy wood, where the trees grew so thickly and the undergrowth was such a sprout and tangle that one could scarcely pass through it. He remembered that a path had once been hacked through the wood, and he sought for this. It was a deeply scooped, hollow way, and it ran or wriggled through the entire length of the wood.

Into this gloomy drain Fionn descended and made progress, but when he had penetrated deeply in the dank forest he heard a sound of thumping and squelching footsteps, and he saw coming towards him a horrible, evil-visaged being; a wild, monstrous, yellow-skinned, big-boned giant, dressed in nothing but an ill-made, mud-plastered, drab-coloured coat, which swaggled and clapped against the calves of his big bare legs. On his stamping feet there were great brogues of boots that were shaped like, but were bigger than, a boat, and each time he put a foot down it squashed and squirted a barrelful of mud from the sunk road.

Fionn had never seen the like of this vast person, and he stood gazing on him, lost in a stare of astonishment.

The great man saluted him.

'All alone, Fionn!' he cried. 'How does it happen that not one Fenian of the Fianna is at the side of his captain?'

At this inquiry Fionn got back his wits.

'That is too long a story and it is too intricate and pressing to be told, also I have no time to spare now.'

'Yet tell it now,' the monstrous man insisted.

Fionn, thus pressed, told of the coming of Cael of the Iron, of the challenge the latter had issued, and that he, Fionn, was off to Tara of the Kings to find Caelte mac Ronán.

'I know that foreigner well,' the big man commented.

'Is he the champion he makes himself out to be?' Fionn inquired.

'He can do twice as much as he said he would do,' the monster replied.

'He won't outrun Caelte mac Ronán,' Fionn asserted.

The big man jeered.

'Say that he won't outrun a hedgehog, dear heart. This Cael will end the course by the time your Caelte begins to think of starting.'

'Then,' said Fionn, 'I no longer know where to turn, or how to protect the honour of Ireland.'

'I know how to do these things,' the other man commented with a slow nod of the head.

'If you do,' Fionn pleaded, 'tell it to me upon your honour.'

'I will do that,' the man replied.

'Do not look any further for the rusty-kneed, slow-trotting son of Ronán,' he continued, 'but ask me to run your race, and, by this hand, I will be first at the post.'

At this the Chief began to laugh.

'My good friend, you have work enough to carry the two tons of mud that are plastered on each of your coat-tails, to say nothing of your weighty boots.'

'By my hand,' the man cried, 'there is no person in Ireland but myself can win that race. I claim a chance.'

Fionn agreed then.

'Be it so,' said he. 'And now, tell me your name?'

'I am known as the Carl of the Drab Coat.'

'All names are names,' Fionn responded, 'and that also is a name.'

They returned then to Ben Edair.

III

When they came among the host the men of Ireland gathered about the vast stranger; and there were some who hid their faces in their mantles so that they should not be seen to laugh, and there were some who rolled along the ground in merriment, and there were others who could only hold their mouths open and crook their knees and hang their arms and

stare dumbfoundedly upon the stranger, as though they were
utterly dazed.

Cael of the Iron came also on the scene, and he examined
the stranger with close and particular attention.

'What in the name of the devil is this thing?' he asked of
Fionn.

'Dear heart,' said Fionn, 'this is the champion I am putting
against you in the race.'

Cael of the Iron grew purple in the face, and he almost
swallowed his tongue through wrath.

'Until the end of eternity,' he roared, 'and until the very
last moment of doom I will not move one foot in a race
with this greasy, big-hoofed, ill-assembled resemblance of a
beggarman.'

But at this the Carl burst into a roar of laughter, so that
the eardrums of the warriors present almost burst inside of
their heads.

'Be reassured, my darling, I am no beggarman, and my
quality is not more gross than is the blood of the most delicate prince in this assembly. You will not evade your challenge in that way, my love, and you shall run with me or
you shall run to your ship with me behind you. What length
of course do you propose, dear heart?'

'I never run less than sixty miles,' Cael replied sullenly.

'It is a small run,' said the Carl, 'but it will do. From this
place to the Hill of the Rushes, Slieve Luachra of Munster,
is exactly sixty miles. Will that suit you?'

'I don't care how it is done,' Cael answered.

'Then,' said the Carl, 'we may go off to Slieve Luachra
now, and in the morning we can start our race there to
here.'

'Let it be done that way,' said Cael.

These two set out then for Munster, and as the sun was
setting they reached Slieve Luachra and prepared to spend
the night there.

IV

'Cael, my pulse,' said the Carl, 'We had better build a house or a hut to pass the night in.'

'I'll build nothing,' Cael replied, looking on the Carl with great disfavour.

'No!'

'I won't build house or hut for the sake of passing one night here, for I hope never to see this place again.'

'I'll build a house myself,' said the Carl, 'and the man who does not help in the building can stay outside of the house.'

The Carl stumped to a near-by wood, and he never rested until he had felled and tied together twenty-four couples of big timber. He thrust these under one arm and under the other he tucked a bundle of rushes for his bed, and with that one load he rushed up a house, well thatched and snug, and with the timber that remained over he made a bonfire on the floor of the house.

His companion sat at a distance regarding the work with rage and aversion.

'Now Cael, my darling,' said the Carl, 'if you are a man help me to look for something to eat, for there is game here.'

'Help yourself,' roared Cael, 'for all that I want is not to be near you.'

'The tooth that does not help gets no helping,' the other replied.

In a short time the Carl returned with a wild boar which he had run down. He cooked the beast over his bonfire and ate one half of it, leaving the other half for his breakfast. Then he lay down on the rushes, and in two turns he fell asleep.

But Cael lay out on the side of the hill, and if he went to sleep that night he slept fasting.

It was he, however, who awakened the Carl in the morning.

'Get up, beggarman, if you are going to run against me.'

The Carl rubbed his eyes.

'I never get up until I have had my fill of sleep, and there is another hour of it due to me. But if you are in a hurry, my delight, you can start running now with a blessing. I will trot on your track when I waken up.'

Cael began to race then, and he was glad of the start, for his antagonist made so little account of him that he did not know what to expect when the Carl would begin to run.

'Yet,' said Cael to himself, 'with an hour's start the beggarman will have to move his bones if he wants to catch on me,' and he settled down to a good, pelting race.

V

At the end of an hour the Carl awoke. He ate the second half of the boar, and he tied the unpicked bones in the tail of his coat. Then with a great rattling of the boar's bones he started.

It is hard to tell how he ran or at what speed he ran, but he went forward in great two-legged jumps, and at times he moved in immense one-legged, mud-spattering hops, and at times again, with wide-stretched, far-flung, terrible-tramping, space-destroying legs he ran.

He left the swallows behind as if they were asleep. He caught up on a red deer, jumped over it, and left it standing. The wind was always behind him, for he outran it every time; and he caught up in jumps and bounces on Cael of the Iron, although Cael was running well, with his fists up and his head back and his two legs flying in and out so vigorously that you could not see them because of that speedy movement.

Trotting by the side of Cael, the Carl thrust a hand into the tail of his coat and pulled out a fistful of red bones.

'Here, my heart, is a meaty bone,' said he, 'for you fasted all night, poor friend, and if you pick a bit off the bone your stomach will get a rest.'

'Keep your filth, beggarman,' the other replied, 'for I

would rather be hanged than gnaw on a bone that you have browsed.'

'Why don't you run, my pulse?' said the Carl earnestly; 'why don't you try to win the race?'

Cael then began to move his limbs as if they were the wings of a fly, or the fins of a little fish, or as if they were the six legs of a terrified spider.

'I am running,' he gasped.

'But try and run like this,' the Carl admonished, and he gave a wriggling bound and a sudden outstretching and scurrying of shanks, and he disappeared from Cael's sight in one wild spatter of big boots.

Despair fell on Cael of the Iron, but he had a great heart.

'I will run until I burst,' he shrieked, 'and when I burst, may I burst to a great distance, and may I trip that beggarman up with my burstings and make him break his leg.'

He settled then to a determined, savage, implacable trot.

He caught up on the Carl at last, for the latter had stopped to eat blackberries from the bushes on the road, and when he drew nigh, Cael began to jeer and sneer angrily at the Carl.

'Who lost the tails of his coat?' he roared.

'Don't ask riddles of a man that's eating blackberries,' the Carl rebuked him.

'The dog without a tail and the coat without a tail,' cried Cael.

'I give it up,' the Carl mumbled.

'It's yourself, beggarman,' jeered Cael.

'I am myself,' the Carl gurgled through a mouthful of black-berries, 'and as I am myself, how can it be myself? That is a silly riddle,' he burbled.

'Look at your coat, tub of grease!'

The Carl did so.

'My faith,' said he, 'where are the two tails of my coat?'

'I could smell one of them and it wrapped around a little

tree thirty miles back,' said Cael, 'and the other one was dishonouring a bush ten miles behind that.'

'It is bad luck to be separated from the tails of your own coat,' the Carl grumbled. 'I'll have to go back for them. Wait here, beloved, and eat blackberries until I come back, and we'll both start fair.'

'Not half a second will I wait,' Cael replied, and he began to run towards Ben Edair as a lover runs to his maiden or as a bee flies to his hive.

'I haven't had half my share of blackberries either,' the Carl lamented as he started to run backwards for his coat-tails.

He ran determinedly on that backward journey, and as the path he had travelled was beaten out as if it had been trampled by an hundred bulls yoked neck to neck, he was able to find the two bushes and the two coat-tails. He sewed them on his coat.

Then he sprang up, and he took to a fit and a vortex and an exasperation of running for which no description may be found. The thumping of his big boots grew as continuous as the pattering of hailstones on a roof, and the wind of his passage blew trees down. The beasts that were ranging beside his path dropped dead from concussion, and the steam that snored from his nose blew birds into bits and made great lumps of cloud fall out of the sky.

He again caught up on Cael, who was running with his head down and his toes up.

'If you won't try to run, my treasure,' said the Carl, 'you will never get your tribute.'

And with that he incensed and exploded himself into an eye-blinding, continuous, waggle and complexity of boots that left Cael behind him in a flash.

'I will run until I burst,' sobbed Cael, and he screwed agitation and despair into his legs until he hummed and buzzed like a blue-bottle on a window.

Five miles from Ben Edair the Carl stopped, for he had again come among blackberries.

He ate of these until he was no more than a sack of juice, and when he heard the humming and buzzing of Cael of the Iron he mourned and lamented that he could not wait to eat his fill. He took off his coat, stuffed it full of blackberries, swung it on his shoulders, and went bounding stoutly and nimbly for Ben Edair.

VI

It would be hard to tell of that was in Fionn's breast and in the hearts of the Fianna while they attended the conclusion of that race.

They discussed it unendingly, and at some moment of the day a man upbraided Fionn because he had not found Caelte the son of Ronán as had been agreed on.

'There is no one can run like Caelte,' one man averred.

'He covers the ground,' said another.

'He is light as a feather.'

'Swift as a stag.'

'Lunged like a bull.'

'Legged like a wolf.'

'He runs!'

These things were said to Fionn, and Fionn said these things to himself.

With every passing minute a drop of lead thumped down into every heart, and a pang of despair stabbed up to every brain.

'Go,' said Fionn to a hawk-eyed man, 'go to the top of this hill and watch for the coming of the racers.' And he sent lithe men with him so that they might run back in endless succession with the news.

The messengers began to run through his tent at minute intervals calling 'nothing,' 'nothing,' 'nothing,' as they paused and darted away.

And the words, 'nothing, nothing, nothing,' began to drowse into the brains of every person present.

'What can we hope from that Carl?' a champion demanded savagely.

'Nothing,' cried a messenger who stood and sped.

'A clump!' cried a champion.

'A hog!' said another.

'A flat-footed,'

'Little-winded,'

'Big-bellied,'

'Lazy-boned,'

'Pork!'

'Did you think, Fionn, that a whale could swim on land, or what did you imagine that lump could do?'

'Nothing,' cried a messenger, and was sped as he spoke.

Rage began to gnaw in Fionn's soul, and a red haze danced and flickered before his eyes. His hands began to twitch and a desire crept over him to seize on champions by the neck, and to shake and worry and rage among them like a wild dog raging among sheep.

He looked on one, and yet he seemed to look on all at once.

'Be silent,' he growled. 'Let each man be silent as a dead man.'

And he sat forward, seeing all, seeing none, with his mouth drooping open, and such a wildness and bristle lowering from that great glum brow that the champions shivered as though already in the chill of death, and were silent.

He rose and stalked to the tent-door.

'Where to, O Fionn?' said a champion humbly.

'To the hill-top,' said Fionn, and he stalked on.

They followed him, whispering among themselves, and keeping their eyes on the ground as they climbed.

VII

'What do you see?' Fionn demanded of the watcher.

'Nothing,' that man replied.

'Look again,' said Fionn.

The eagle-eyed man lifted a face, thin and sharp as though it had been carven on the wind, and he stared forward with an immobile intentness.

'What do you see?' said Fionn.

'Nothing,' the man replied.

'I will look myself,' said Fionn, and his great brow bent forward and gloomed afar.

The watcher stood beside, staring with his tense face and unwinking, lidless eye.

'What can you see, O Fionn?' said the watcher.

'I can see nothing,' said Fionn, and he projected again his grim, gaunt forehead. For it seemed as if the watcher stared with his whole face, aye, and with his hands; but Fionn brooded weightedly on distance with his puckered and crannied brow.

They looked again.

'What can you see?' said Fionn.

'I see nothing,' said the watcher.

'I do not know if I see or if I surmise, but something moves,' said Fionn. 'There is a trample,' he said.

The watcher became then an eye, a rigidity, an intense out-thrusting and ransacking of thin-spun distance. At last he spoke.

'There is a dust,' he said.

And at that the champions gazed also, straining hungrily afar, until their eyes became filled with a blue darkness and they could no longer see even the things that were close to them.

'I,' cried Conán triumphantly, 'I see a dust.'

'And I,' cried another.

'And I.'

'I see a man,' said the eagle-eyed watcher.

And again they stared, until their straining eyes grew dim with tears and winks, and they saw trees that stood up and sat down, and fields that wobbled and spin round and round in a giddy swirling world.

'There *is* a man,' Conán roared.

'A man there is,' cried another.

'And he is carrying a man on his back,' said the watcher. 'It is Cael of the Iron carrying the Carl on his back,' he groaned.

'The great pork!' a man gritted.

'The no-good!' sobbed another.

'The lean-hearted,'

'Thick-thighed,'

'Ramshackle,'

'Muddle-headed,'

'Hog!' screamed a champion.

And he beat his fists angrily against a tree.

But the eagle-eyed watcher watched until his eyes narrowed and became pin-points, and he ceased to be a man and became an optic.

'Wait,' he breathed, 'wait until I screw into one other inch of sight.'

And they waited, looking no longer on that scarcely perceptible speck in the distance, but straining upon the eye of the watcher as though they would penetrate it and look through it.

'It is the Carl,' he said, 'carrying something on his back, and behind him again there is a dust.'

'Are you sure?' said Fionn in a voice that rumbled and vibrated like thunder.

'It is the Carl,' said the watcher, 'and the dust behind him is Cael of the Iron trying to catch him up.'

Then the Fianna gave a roar of exultation, and each man seized his neighbour and kissed him on both cheeks; and they gripped hands about Fionn, and they danced round and round in a great circle, roaring with laughter and relief, in the ecstasy which only comes where grisly fear has been and whence that bony jowl has taken itself away.

VIII

The Carl of the Drab Coat came bumping and stumping and clumping into the camp, and was surrounded by a multitude that adored him and hailed him with tears.

'Meal!' he bawled, 'meal for the love of the stars!'

And he bawled, 'Meal, meal!' until he bawled everybody into silence.

Fionn addressed him.

'What for the meal, dear heart?'

'For the inside of my mouth,' said the Carl, 'for the recesses and crannies and deep-down profundities of my stomach. Meal, meal!' he lamented.

Meal was brought.

The Carl put his coat on the ground, opened it carefully and revealed a store of blackberries, squashed, crushed, mangled, democratic, ill-looking.

'The meal!' he groaned, 'the meal!'

It was given to him.

'What of the race, my pulse?' said Fionn.

'Wait, wait,' cried the Carl. 'I die, I die for meal and blackberries.'

Into the centre of the mess of blackberries he discharged a barrel of meal, and he mixed the two up and through, and round and down, until the pile of white-black, red-brown slibber-slobber reached up to his shoulders. Then he commenced to paw and impel and project and cram the mixture into his mouth, and between each mouthful he sighed a contented sigh, and during every mouthful he gurgled an oozy gurgle.

But while Fionn and the Fianna stared like lost minds upon the Carl, there came a sound of buzzing, as if a hornet or a queen of the wasps or a savage, steep-winged griffin was hovering about them, and looking away they saw Cael of the Iron charging on them with a monstrous extension and scurry of his legs. He had a sword in his hand, and there was nothing in his face but redness and ferocity.

Fear fell like night around the Fianna, and they stood with slack knees and hanging hands waiting for death. But the Carl lifted a pawful of his oozy slop and discharged this at Cael with such a smash that the man's head spun off his shoulders and hopped along the ground. The Carl then picked up the head and threw it at the body with such aim and force that the neck part of the head jammed into the neck part of the body and stuck there, as good a head as ever, you would have said, but that it had got twisted the wrong way round. The Carl then lashed his opponent hand and foot.

'Now, dear heart, do you still claim tribute and lordship of Ireland?' said he.

'Let me go home,' groaned Cael, 'I want to go home.'

'Swear by the sun and moon, if I let you go home, that you will send to Fionn, yearly and every year, the rent of the land of Thessaly.'

'I swear that,' said Cael, 'and I would swear anything to get home.'

The Carl lifted him then and put him sitting into his ship. Then he raised his big boot and gave the boat a kick that drove it seven leagues out into the sea, and that was how the adventure of Cael of the Iron finished.

'Who are you, sir?' said Fionn to the Carl.

But before answering the Carl's shape changed into one of splendour and delight.

'I am ruler of the Shí of Rath Cruachan,' he said.

Then Fionn mac Uail made a feast and a banquet for the jovial god, and with that the tale is ended of the King of Thessaly's son and the Carl of the Drab Coat.

THE CURSE OF THE FIRES AND OF THE SHADOWS

W. B. Yeats

One summer night, when there was peace, a score of Puritan troopers under the pious Sir Frederick Hamilton, broke through the door of the Abbey of the White Friars which stood over the Gara Lough at Sligo. As the door fell with a crash they saw a little knot of friars gathered about the altar, their white habits glimmering in the steady light of the holy candles. All the monks were kneeling except the abbot, who stood upon the altar steps with a great brazen crucifix in his hand. 'Shoot them!' cried Sir Frederick Hamilton, but none stirred, for all were new converts, and feared the crucifix and the holy candles. The white lights from the altar threw the shadows of the troopers up on to roof and wall. As the troopers moved about, the shadows began a fantastic dance among the corbels and the memorial tablets. For a little while all was silent, and then five troopers who were the body-guard of Sir Frederick Hamilton lifted their muskets, and shot down five of the friars. The noise and the smoke drove away the mystery of the pale altar lights, and the other troopers took courage and began to strike. In a moment the friars lay about the altar steps, their white habits stained with blood. 'Set fire to the house!' cried Sir Frederick Hamilton, and at his word one went out, and came in again carrying a heap of dry straw, and piled it against the western wall, and, having done this, fell back, for the fear of the crucifix and of the holy candles was still in his heart. Seeing this, the five troopers who were Sir Frederick Hamilton's body-guard darted forward, and taking each a holy candle set the straw in a blaze. The red tongues of fire rushed up and flickered from corbel to corbel and from tablet to tablet, and crept along the floor, setting in a blaze the seats and benches. The dance of the shadows passed away, and the dance of the fires began. The troopers fell back towards the door in the southern wall, and watched those yellow dancers springing hither and thither.

For a time the altar stood safe and apart in the midst of its white light; the eyes of the troopers turned upon it. The abbot whom they had thought dead had risen to his feet and now stood before it with the crucifix lifted in both hands high above his head. Suddenly he cried with a loud voice, 'Woe unto all who smite those who dwell within the Light of the Lord, for they shall wander among the ungovernable shadows, and follow the ungovernable fires!' And having so cried he fell on his face dead, and the brazen crucifix rolled down the steps of the altar. The smoke had now grown very thick, so that it drove the troopers out into the open air. Before them were burning houses. Behind them shone the painted windows of the Abbey filled with saints and martyrs, awakened, as from a sacred trance, into an angry and animated life. The eyes of the troopers were dazzled, and for a while could see nothing but the flaming faces of saints and martyrs. Presently, however, they saw a man covered with dust who came running towards them. 'Two messengers,' he cried, 'have been sent by the defeated Irish to raise against you the whole country about Manor Hamilton, and if you do not stop them you will be overpowered in the woods before you reach home again! They ride north-east between Ben Bulben and Cashel-na-Gael.'

Sir Frederick Hamilton called to him the five troopers who had first fired upon the monks and said, 'Mount quickly, and ride through the woods towards the mountain, and get before these men, and kill them.'

In a moment the troopers were gone, and before many moments they had splashed across the river at what is now called Buckley's Ford, and plunged into the woods. They followed a beaten track that wound along the northern bank of the river. The boughs of the birch and quicken trees mingled above, and hid the cloudy moonlight, leaving the pathway in almost complete darkness. They rode at a rapid trot, now chatting together, now watching some stray weasel or rabbit scuttling away in the darkness. Gradually, as the gloom and silence of the woods oppressed them, they drew closer together, and began to talk rapidly; they were old comrades and knew each other's lives. One was married, and told how glad his wife would be to see him return safe from this harebrained expedition against the White Friars, and to hear how fortune had made amends for rashness. The oldest of the five, whose wife was dead, spoke of a flagon of wine which awaited him upon an upper shelf; while a third, who was the youngest, had a sweetheart watching for his return, and he rode a little way before the others, not talking at all. Suddenly the young man stopped, and they saw that his horse was trembling. 'I saw something,' he said, 'and yet I do not know but it may have been one of the shadows. It looked like a great worm with a silver crown upon his head.' One of the five put his hand up to his forehead as if about to cross himself, but remembering that he had changed his religion he put it down, and said: 'I am certain it was but a shadow, for there are a great many about us, and of very strange kinds.' Then they rode on in silence. It had been raining in the earlier part of the day, and the drops fell from the branches, wetting their hair and their shoulders. In a little they began to talk again. They had been in many battles against many a rebel together, and now told each other over again the story of their wounds, and so awakened in their hearts the strongest of all fellowships, the fellowship of the sword, and half forgot the terrible solitude of the woods.

Suddenly the first two horses neighed, and then stood still, and would go no further. Before them was a glint of water, and they knew by the rushing sound that it was a river. They dismounted, and after much tugging and coaxing brought the horses to the river-side. In the midst of the water stood a tall old woman with grey hair flowing over a grey dress. She stood up to her knees in the water, and stooped from time to time as though washing. Presently they could see that she was washing something that half floated. The moon cast a flickering light upon it, and they saw that it was the dead body of a man, and, while they were looking at it, an eddy of the river turned the face towards them, and each of the five troopers recognised at the same moment his own face. While they stood dumb and motionless with horror, the woman began to speak, saying slowly and loudly: 'Did you see my son? He has a crown of silver on his head, and there are rubies in the crown.' Then the oldest of the troopers, he who had been most often wounded, drew his sword and cried: 'I have fought for the truth of my God, and need not fear the shadows of Satan,' and with that rushed into the water. In a moment he returned. The woman had vanished, and though he had thrust his sword into air and water he had found nothing.

The five troopers remounted, and set their horses at the ford, but all to no purpose. They tried again and again, and went plunging hither and thither, the horses foaming and rearing. 'Let us,' said the old trooper, 'ride back a little into the wood, and strike the river higher up.' They rode in under the boughs, the ground-ivy crackling under the hoofs, and the branches striking against their steel caps. After about twenty minutes' riding they came out again upon the river, and after another ten minutes found a place where it was possible to cross without sinking below the stirrups. The wood upon the other side was very thin, and broke the moonlight into long streams. The wind had arisen, and had begun to drive the clouds rapidly across the face of the moon, so that thin streams of light seemed to be dancing a grotesque dance among the scattered bushes and small fir-trees. The tops of the trees began also to moan, and the sound of it was like the voice of the dead in the wind; and the troopers remembered the belief that tells how the dead in purgatory are spitted upon the points of the trees and upon the points of the rocks. They turned a little to the south, in the hope that they might strike the beaten path again, but they could find no trace of it.

Meanwhile, the moaning grew louder and louder, and the dance of the white moon-fires more and more rapid. Gradually they began to be aware of a sound of distant music. It was the sound of a bagpipe, and they rode towards it with great joy. It came from the bottom of a deep, cup-like hollow. In the midst of the hollow was an old man with a red cap and withered face. He sat beside a fire of sticks, and had a burning torch thrust into the earth at his feet, and played an old bagpipe furiously. His red hair dripped over his face like the iron rust upon a rock. 'Did you see my wife?' he cried, looking up a moment; 'she was washing! she was washing!' 'I am afraid of him,' said the young trooper, 'I fear he is one of the Sidhe.' 'No,' said the old trooper, 'he is a man, for I can see the sun-freckles upon his face. We will compel him to be our guide;' and at that he drew his sword, and the others did the same. They stood in a ring round the piper, and pointed their swords at him, and the old trooper then told him that they must kill two rebels, who had taken the road between Ben Bulben and the great mountain spur that is called Cashel-na-Gael, and that he must get up before one of them and be their guide, for they had lost their way. The piper turned, and pointed to a neighbouring tree, and they saw an old white horse ready bitted, bridled, and saddled. He slung the pipe across his back, and, taking the torch in his hand, got upon the horse, and started off before them, as hard as he could go.

The wood grew thinner and thinner, and the ground began to slope up toward the mountain. The moon had already set, and the little white flames of the stars had come out everywhere. The ground sloped more and more until at last they rode far above the woods upon the wide top of the mountain. The woods lay spread out mile after mile below, and away to the south shot up the red glare of the burning town. But before and above them were the little white flames. The guide drew rein suddenly, and pointing upwards with the hand that did not hold the torch, shrieked out, 'Look; look at the holy candles!' and then plunged forward at a gallop. waving the torch hither and thither. 'Do you hear the hoofs of the messengers?' cried the guide. 'Quick, quick! or they will be gone out of your hands!' and he laughed as with delight of the chase. The troopers thought they could hear far off, and as if below them, rattle of hoofs; but now the ground began to slope more and more, and the speed grew more headlong moment by moment. They tried to pull up, but in vain, for the horses seemed to have gone mad. The guide had thrown the reins on to the neck of the old white horse, and was waving his arms and singing a wild Gaelic song. Suddenly they saw the thin gleam of a river, at an immense distance below, and knew that they were upon the brink of the abyss that is now called Lug-na-Gael, or in English the Stranger's Leap. The six horses sprang forward, and five screams went up into the air, a moment later five men and horses fell with a dull crash upon the green slopes at the foot of the rocks.

THE FAIRY GOOSE

Liam O'Flaherty

An old woman named Mary Wiggins got three goose eggs
from a neighbour in order to hatch a clutch of goslings. She
put an old clucking hen over the eggs in a wooden box with
a straw bed. The hen proved to be a bad sitter. She was
continually deserting the eggs, possibly because they were
too big. The old woman then kept her shut up in the box.
Either through weariness, want of air, or simply through
pure devilment, the hen died on the eggs, two days before
it was time for the shells to break.

The old woman shed tears of rage, both at the loss of her
hen, of which she was particularly fond, and through fear of
losing her goslings. She put the eggs near the fire in the
kitchen, wrapped up in straw and old clothes. Two days
afterwards, one of the eggs broke and a tiny gosling put out
its beak. The other two eggs proved not to be fertile. They
were thrown away.

The little gosling was a scraggy thing, so small and so
delicate that the old woman, out of pity for it, wanted to kill
it. But her husband said: 'Kill nothing that is born in your
house, woman alive. It's against the law of God.' 'It's a true
saying, my honest fellow,' said the old woman. 'What comes
into the world is sent by God. Praised be He.'

For a long time it seemed certain that the gosling was on
the point of death. It spent all the day on the hearth in the
kitchen nestling among the peat ashes, either sleeping or
making little tweaky noises. When it was offered food, it
stretched out its beak and pecked without rising off its

stomach. Gradually, however, it became hardier and went out of doors to sit in the sun, on a flat rock. When it was three months old it was still a yellowish colour with soft down, even though other goslings of that age in the village were already going to the pond with the flock and able to flap their wings and join in the cackle at evening time, when the setting sun was being saluted. The little gosling was not aware of the other geese, even though it saw them rise on windy days and fly with a great noise from their houses to the pond. It made no effort to become a goose, and at four months of age it still could not stand on one leg.

The old woman came to believe it was a fairy. The village women agreed with her after some dispute. It was decided to tie pink and red ribbons around the gosling's neck and to sprinkle holy water on its wing feathers.

That was done, and then the gosling became sacred in the village. No boy dare throw a stone at it, or pull a feather from its wing, as they were in the habit of doing with geese, in order to get masts for the pieces of cork they floated in the pond as ships. When it began to move about every house gave it dainty things. All the human beings in the village paid more respect to it than they did to one another. The little gosling had contracted a great affection for Mary Wiggins and followed her around everywhere, so that Mary Wiggins also came to have the reputation of being a woman of wisdom. Dreams were brought to her for unravelling. She was asked to set the spell of the Big Periwinkle and to tie the Knot of the Snakes on the sides of sick cows. And when children were ill, the gosling was brought secretly at night and led three times around the house on a thin halter of horse-hair.

When the gosling was a year old it had not yet become a goose. Its down was still slightly yellowish. It did not cackle, but made curious tweaky noises. Instead of stretching out its neck and hissing at strangers, after the manner of a proper goose, it put its head to one side and made funny noises like a duck. It meditated like a hen, was afraid of water and cleansed itself by rolling on the grass. It fed on bread, fish and potatoes. It drank milk and tea. It amused itself by collecting pieces of cloth, nails, small fish-bones and the limpet shells that are thrown in a heap beside dunghills. These pieces of refuse it placed in a pile to the left of Mary Wiggins' door. And when the pile was tall, it made a sort of nest in the middle of it and lay in the nest.

Old Mrs Wiggins had by now realised that the goose was worth money to her. So she became firmly convinced that the goose was gifted with supernatural powers. She accepted, in return for setting spells a yard of white frieze cloth for unravelling dreams, a pound of sugar for setting the spell of the Big Periwinkle and half a donkey's load of potatoes for tying the Knot of the Snakes on a sick cow's sides. Hitherto a kindly, humorous woman, she took to wearing her shawl in triangular fashion, with the tip of it reaching to her heels. She talked to herself or to her goose as she went along the road. She took long steps like a goose and rolled her eyes occasionally. When she cast a spell she went into an ecstasy during which she made inarticulate sounds, like: 'boum, roum, toum, kroum.'

Soon it became known all over the countryside that there was a woman of wisdom and a fairy goose in the village, and pilgrims came secretly from afar, at the dead of night, on the first night of the new moon, or when the spring tide had begun to wane.

The men soon began to raise their hats passing old Mary Wiggins' house, for it was understood, owing to the cure of Dara Foddy's cow, that the goose was indeed a good fairy and not a malicious one. Such was the excitement in the village and all over the countryside, that what was kept secret so long at last reached the ears of the parish priest.

The story was brought to him by an old woman from a neighbouring village to that in which the goose lived. Before the arrival of the goose, the other old woman had herself cast spells, not through her own merits but through those of

her dead mother, who had a long time ago been the woman
of wisdom in the district. The priest mounted his horse as
soon as he heard the news and galloped at a break-neck
speed towards Mary Wiggins' house, carrying his breviary
and his stole. When he arrived in the village, he dismounted
at a distance from the house, gave his horse to a boy and
put his stole around his neck.

A number of the villagers gathered and some tried to warn
Mary Wiggins by whistling at a distance, but conscious that
they had all taken part in something forbidden by the sacred
laws of orthodox religion they were afraid to run ahead of
the priest into the house. Mary Wiggins and her husband
were within, making little ropes of brown horse-hair, which
they sold as charms.

Outside the door, perched on her high nest, the little
goose was sitting. There were pink and red ribbons around
her neck and around her legs there were bands of black tape.
She was quite small, a little more than half the size of a
normal, healthy goose. But she had an elegant charm of
manner, an air of civilisation and a consciousness of great
dignity, which had grown out of the respect and love of the
villagers.

When she saw the priest approach she began to cackle
gently, making the tweaky noise that was peculiar to her.
She descended from her perch and waddled towards him,
expecting some dainty gift. For everybody who approached
her gave her a dainty gift. But instead of stretching out his
hand to offer her something and saying, 'Beadai, beadai,
come here,' as was customary, the priest halted and muttered something in a harsh, frightened voice. He became red
in the face and he took off his hat.

Then for the first time in her life, the little goose became
terrified. She opened her beak, spread her wings and lowered her head. She began to hiss violently. Turning around,
she waddled back to her nest, flapping her wings and raising
a loud cackle, just like a goose, although she had never been
heard to cackle loudly like a goose before. Clambering up

to her high nest, she lay there, quite flat, trembling violently.

The bird, never having known fear of human beings, never having been treated with discourtesy, was so violently moved by the extraordinary phenomenon of a man wearing black clothes, scowling at her and muttering, that her animal nature was roused and showed itself with disgusting violence.

The people, watching this scene, were astounded. Some took off their caps and crossed themselves. For some reason, it was made manifest to them that the goose was an evil spirit and not the good fairy which they had supposed her to be. Terrified of the priest's stole and breviary and of his scowling countenance, they were only too eager to attribute the goose's strange hissing and her still stranger cackle to supernatural forces of an evil nature. Some present even caught a faint rumble of thunder in the east and although it was not noticed at the time, an old woman later asserted that she heard a great cackle of strange geese afar off, raised in answer to the little fairy goose's cackle. 'It was,' said the old woman, 'certainly the whole army of devils offering her help to kill the holy priest.'

The priest turned to the people and cried, raising his right hand in a threatening manner.

'I wonder the ground doesn't open up and swallow you all. Idolators!'

'O father, blessed by the hand of God,' cried an old woman, the one who later asserted she had heard the devilish cackle afar off. She threw herself on her knees in the road. 'Spare us, father.'

Old Mrs Wiggins, having heard the strange noises, rushed out into the yard with her triangular shawl trailing and her black hair loose. She began to make vague, mystic movements with her hands, as had recently become a habit with her. Lost in some sort of ecstasy, she did not see the priest at first. She began to chant something.

'You hag,' cried the priest, rushing up the yard towards her, menacingly.

The old woman caught sight of him and screamed. But she faced him boldly.

'Come no farther!' she cried, still in an ecstasy, either affected, or the result of a firm belief in her own mystic powers.

Indeed it is difficult to believe that she was not in earnest, for she used to be a kind, gentle woman.

Her husband rushed out, crying aloud. Seeing the priest, he dropped a piece of rope he had in his hand and fled around the corner of the house.

'Leave my way, you hag!' cried the priest, raising his hand to strike her.

'Stand back!' she cried. 'Don't lay a hand on my goose.'

'Leave my way,' yelled the priest, 'or I'll curse you.'

'Curse, then,' cried the unfortunate woman, 'curse.'

Instead, the priest gave her a blow under the ear, which felled her smartly. Then he strode up to the goose's nest and seized the goose. The goose, paralysed with terror, was just able to open her beak and hiss at him. He stripped the ribbons off her neck and tore the tape off her feet. Then he threw her out of the nest. Seizing a spade that stood by the wall, he began to scatter the refuse of which the nest was composed.

The old woman, lying prostrate in the yard, raised her head and began to chant in the traditional fashion, used by women of wisdom.

'I'll call on the winds of the east and of the west, I'll raise the waves of the sea. The lightning will flash in the sky and there'll be great sounds of giants warring in the heavens. Blight will fall on the earth and calves with fishes' tails will be born of cows . . .'

The little goose, making tweaky noises, waddled over to the old woman and tried to hide herself under the long shawl. The people murmured at this, seeing in it fresh signs of devilry.

Then the priest threw down the spade and hauled the old woman to her feet, kicking aside the goose. The old woman, exhausted by her ecstasy and possibly seeking to gain popular support, either went into a faint or feigned one. Her hands and her feet hung limply. Again the people murmured. The priest, becoming embarrassed, put her sitting against the wall. Then he didn't know what to do, for his anger had exhausted his reason. He either became ashamed of having beaten an old woman, or he felt the situation was altogether ridiculous. So he raised his hand and addressed the people in a sorrowful voice.

'Let this be a warning,' he said sadly. 'This poor woman and . . . all of you, led astray by . . . foolish and . . . Avarice is at the back of this,' he cried suddenly in an angry voice, shaking his fist. 'This woman had been preying on your credulity, in order to extort money from you by her pretended sorcery. That's all it is. Money is at the back of it. But I give you warning. If I hear another word about this, I'll . . .'

He paused uncertainly, wondering what to threaten the poor people with. Then he added:

'I'll report it to the archbishop of the diocese.'

The people raised a loud murmur, asking forgiveness.

'Fear God,' he added finally, 'and love your neighbours.'

Then, throwing a stone angrily at the goose, he strode out of the yard and left the village.

It was then that the people began to curse violently and threaten to burn the old woman's house. The responsible people among them, however, chiefly those who had hitherto paid no respect to the superstition concerning the goose, restrained their violence. Finally, the people went home and Mary Wiggins' husband, who had been hiding in a barn, came and brought his wife indoors. The little goose, uttering cries of amazement, began to collect the rubbish once more, piling it in a heap in order to rebuild her nest.

That night, just after the moon had risen, a band of young men collected, approached Mary Wiggins' house and enticed the goose from her nest, by calling: 'Beadai, beadai, come here, come here.'

The little goose, delighted that people were again kind

and respectful to her, waddled down to the gate, making happy noises.

The youths stoned her to death.

And the little goose never uttered a sound, so terrified and amazed was she at this treatment from people who had formerly loved her and whom she had never injured.

Next morning, when Mary Wiggins discovered the dead carcase of the goose, she went into a fit, during which she cursed the village, the priest and all mankind.

And indeed it appeared that her blasphemous prayer took some effect at least. Although giants did not war in the heavens, and although cows did not give birth to fishes, it is certain that from that day the natives of that village are quarrelsome drunkards, who fear God but do not love one another. And the old woman is again collecting followers from among the wives of the drunkards. These women maintain that the only time in the history of their generation that there was peace and harmony in the village was during the time when the fairy goose was loved by the people.

THE OLD FAITH

Frank O'Connor

The Pattern at Kilmulpeter turned into a great day. Mass
was said in the ruins of the cathedral and the old bishop,
Dr Gallogly, preached. Father Devine, who was a bit of
an antiquarian, had looked up the details of St Mulpeter's
life for him. There were a lot of them, mostly contradic-
tory, and all very, very queer. It seemed that like most
of the saints of that remote period, St Mulpeter had put
to sea on a flagstone and floated ashore in Cornwall.
There, the seven harpers of the King had been put to death
through the curses of the Druids and the machinations of
the King's unfaithful wife. St Mulpeter miraculously
restored them to life, and through the great mercy of God,
they were permitted to sing a song about the Queen's
misbehaviour, which resulted in St Mulpeter turning her
into a pillar-stone and converting the King to the one true
faith.

The Bishop had been Professor of Dogmatic Theology in
the seminary; a job that had suited him excellently for he
was a man who dogmatised about everything. He was a tall,
powerfully built, handsome old man with a face that was
both broad and long, and high cheekbones that gave the
lower half of his face an air of unnatural immobility but drew
attention to the fine blue, anxious eyes. He had a quiet
manner and a low voice, but with a touch of the piledriver
about him.

For a dogmatic theologian he showed great restraint on
reading Devine's summary of the saint's life. He raised his

brows a few times, and then read it through again with an air of resignation.

'I suppose that's what you'd call allegorical, father,' he said anxiously.

'So long as you don't call it historical,' said Devine, who had a tongue he couldn't control.

The Bishop rarely showed signs of emotion, and he seemed quite unaffected by the scene in the ruined cathedral, though it impressed Devine—the crowds of country people kneeling in the wet grass among the tottering crosses and headstones, the wild countryside framed in the mullioned windows, and the big deeply-moulded clouds sailing overhead. The Bishop disposed neatly of St Mulpeter by saying that we couldn't all go to sea on flagstones, which required great faith in anyone who attempted it, but the family Rosary was just as good.

After Mass, Father Devine showed the Bishop and some of the other clergy round the ruins. Suddenly, a couple of men who had been hiding in the remains of a twelfth century chapel took to their heels. One of them stood on a low wall, looking down on the little group of clergymen with the expression of a terrified rabbit. The Bishop raised his umbrella and pointed it accusingly at him.

'Father Devine,' he said in a commanding tone, 'see what that fellow has.'

'I have nothing, Your Eminence,' wailed the man on the wall.

'You have a bottle behind your back,' said the Bishop sternly. 'What have you in that?'

'Nothing, Your Eminence, only a drop of water from the Holy Well.'

'Give it here to me till I see,' said the Bishop, and when Father Devine passed him the bottle he removed the cork and sniffed.

'I'd like to see the Holy Well that came out of,' he said ironically. 'Is it any use my preaching to ye about poteen?'

'Ah, 'tis a wild, windy quarter, Your Eminence,' said the man, beginning to scratch himself, 'and I have the rheumatics something terrible.'

'I'd sooner the rheumatics than the cirrhosis,' grunted the Bishop. 'Bring it with you, father,' he added to Devine, and strode on with his umbrella against his back.

The same night a few of them had dinner with him at the Palace—Father Whelan, an old parish priest, who was a cross between a saint and a half-wit; Father Fogarty, who was a bit of a firebrand, Devine and Canon Lanigan. The Bishop and the Canon never got on because the Canon's supporters were giving it out that the Bishop was doddering and needed a coadjutor. Besides, the Canon gave himself too many airs. He was tall and thin, with a long nose and a punchinello chin, and he let on to be an authority on Church history as well as on food and wine. That last item was enough to damn him in the Bishop's eyes, because he maintained almost *ex cathedra* that the best food and wine in the world were to be found on the restaurant car from Holyhead to Euston.

When Lanigan made a fool of himself by recommending Chateauneuf-du-Pape, the Bishop turned to Father Devine.

'Talking about drink, father,' he said with his anxious glare, 'what happened to the bottle of poteen you took off that fellow?'

'I suppose it's in the hall,' Father Devine said vaguely. 'I can assure you I wasn't indulging in it.'

'You could indulge in worse,' said the Bishop with a dirty look at the Canon. 'Many a good man was raised on it. Nellie,' he called, turning his head a few inches, 'bring in that bottle of poteen, if you can find it . . . You can have it in your tea,' he added to the Canon. 'Or is it coffee you want?'

'Oh, tea, tea,' sighed the Canon, offering it up. He knew only too well what the Bishop's coffee was like. According to the Bishop, it was the best bottled coffee in the world.

When the housekeeper brought in the poteen, the Bishop took out the cork and sniffed at the bottle again with an anxious air.

'I should have found out who made it,' he said. 'When they can't get the rye, they make it out of anything.'

'You seem to be quite an expert, my Lord,' said Devine with his waspish air.

'Why wouldn't I?' asked the Bishop. 'Didn't I make it myself? My poor father—God rest him!—had a still of his own. In milk he used to give it to me, for colds. Or like a liniment, rubbed on the chest. Not that I tasted it now in sixty, sixty-five years.'

He poured a stiff glass for each of them, and drank his own in a gulp without any change of expression. Then he looked anxiously at the others to see what they thought of it. Lanigan put on an air of consternation, but the Bishop knew that was only showing off. Father Fogarty drank it reverently, as though it were altar wine, but he was a nationalist and felt that anything that came from the people had to be treated accordingly. Father Devine disgraced himself; spluttered, choked, and then went petulantly off to the bathroom.

Meanwhile, the Bishop had decided that it was good poteen and treated them to another round, which they seemed to feel it might be disrespectful to refuse. Father Devine did refuse, and with a crucified air that the Bishop did not like at all. The Bishop, who knew everything and had one of the most venomously gossipy tongues in the diocese, was convinced that he was a model of Christian charity and had spoken seriously to Father Devine about his own sharpness.

'Was it on an island you made this stuff?' the Canon asked blandly.

'No,' replied the Bishop, who didn't know what irony was. 'A mountain.'

'A rather desolate one, I fancy,' Lanigan said dreamily.

'It had to be if you didn't want the police on top of you,'

said the Bishop. 'They'd have fifty men out at a time, scour-
ing the mountains.'

'And bagpipes!' said the Canon, bursting into an old
woman's cackle at the memory of the hilly road from Beaune
to Dijon with the vineyards at each side. 'It seems to go with
bagpipes.'

'There were no bagpipes,' the Bishop said shortly. 'As a
matter of fact,' he added nostalgically, 'it was very nice up
there on a summer's night. They'd hide the still in a hollow,
and then sit round and tell stories. Very queer stories, some
of them, like that Life of St Mulpeter Father Devine wrote
out for me.'

'Ah, the people were half-savage in those days,' the Canon
said.

'They were not,' the Bishop replied mildly, but from his
tone Father Devine knew he was very vexed. 'They were
more refined altogether.'

'Would you say so, my Lord?' asked Father Fogarty, who,
as a good nationalist was convinced the people were rushing
to perdition and that the only hope for them was to send
them all back to live in whitewashed cabins.

'Ah, a nicer class of people in every way,' Father Whelan
said mournfully. 'You wouldn't find the same nature at all
in them nowadays.'

'They had a lot of queer customs all the same, father,'
said the Bishop, who always spoke with peculiar affection
to Whelan. 'I remember they used to put the first mug of
poteen in hiding under a rock. Would that be something to
do with the fairies?' he asked Devine.

'Well, at any rate, you can't deny that the people today
are more enlightened,' the Canon said warmly.

'I deny it *in toto*,' retorted the Bishop. 'There's no comparison. The people were more intelligent altogether, better
balanced and better spoken. What would you say, Father
Whelan?'

'Oh, in every way, my Lord,' moaned Father Whelan,
taking out his pipe.

'And the superstitions, my Lord?' the Canon hissed superciliously. 'The ghosts and fairies and spells?'

'They might have good reason,' said the Bishop with a flash of his blue eyes.

'By God, you're right, my Lord,' said Fogarty, in a loud voice, and then, realising the attention he had attracted, he blushed and stopped short.

'"There are more things in heaven and earth, Horatio, than are dreamt of in our philosophy,"' added the Bishop complacently.

'Omar Khayyam,' whispered Father Whelan to Father Fogarty. 'He's a fellow you'd want to read. He said some very good things.'

'That's a useful quotation,' said the Canon, seeing he was getting the worst of it. 'I must remember that next time I'm preaching against fortune tellers.'

'I wouldn't bother,' the Bishop said curtly. 'There's no analogy. There was a parish priest in our place one time, a man called Muldoon. Father Whelan might remember him.'

'Con?' defined Father Whelan. 'I do, well. His nephew, Peter, was on the Chinese Mission.'

'A well-meaning man but a bit coarse, I thought,' said the Bishop.

'That was his mother's side of the family,' explained Whelan. 'His mother was one of the Clasheen Dempseys and they were always a rough lot.'

'Was she so?' the Bishop asked with a great air of enlightenment. 'I never knew that. It would explain a lot. He was always preaching against superstition, you might remember, and he had his knife in one poor old fellow up the Glen called Johnnie Ryan.'

'Johnnie the Fairies,' said Father Whelan. 'I knew him too.'

'I knew him well,' said the Bishop. 'A gentle poor man but a bit soft in the head. He was their Living Man.'

'Their what?' cried Father Devine in astonishment.

'Their Living Man,' said the Bishop.

'Whose Living Man?' asked Devine with a baffled air.

'The fairies',' explained the Bishop. 'They had to have a Living Man to go with them, or else they had no power. That was the way I heard it anyway. I remember him well playing the Fairy Music on his whistle. They taught it to him.'

'You wouldn't remember how it went?' Father Fogarty asked eagerly. Devine could see the scheme forming in his head, for the convent school orchestra to play it. He could even imagine it on the programme—'The Fairy Music, by kind permission of his Lordship the Bishop of Moyle.'

'I was never much good at remembering music,' said the Bishop. 'Anyway, I was only a child. Of course, there might be something in it. You'd often see queer lights on the mountain over our house. They said it was a fairy funeral. They had some story about a man from our place who interrupted a funeral like that one night. The fairies left down the coffin and ran away. The man opened the coffin and there was a girl inside. A fine-looking girl, too, I believe. When he breathed on her she woke up. They said she was from the Tuam direction—a changeling or something. I never checked the truth of it.'

'From Galway, I believe, my Lord,' Father Whelan said respectfully.

'Was it Galway?' asked the Bishop.

'I dare say with enough poteen in, a man could even believe that,' said the Canon indignantly.

'Still, Canon, strange things do happen,' said Father Fogarty.

'Why, then, indeed, they do,' agreed Father Whelan with a sigh.

'Was this something that happened to yourself, father?' the Bishop asked kindly, seeing the young man straining at the leash.

'It was, my Lord,' said Fogarty. ''Twas when I was a kid, going to school. I got fever very bad and the doctor gave me up. The mother—God rest her—was in a terrible state.

Then my aunt came to stay with us. She was a real old countrywoman. I remember them to this day arguing in the kitchen, about what they ought to do. "Don't be a fool, woman!" said my aunt. "You know there's ways."'

'Well, well, well,' Father Whelan said, shaking his head.

'Then my aunt came up with a scissors,' Father Fogarty continued excitedly. 'First, she cut off a bit of the end of my shirt, and then a bit of hair from behind my ear, and then a bit of fingernail, and she threw them in the fire. All the time she was muttering to herself like an old witch.'

'My! my! my!' exclaimed Father Whelan.

'And you got better?' said the Bishop with a quelling glance at the Canon.

'I got better, all right, but that wasn't the strangest part of it.' Fogarty leaned across the table, scowling, and dropped his eager, boyish voice to a whisper. 'Inside a year, her two sons, two of the finest young fellows you ever laid eyes on, died.' Then he sat back, took out a cigar and scowled again. 'Now, wasn't that extraordinary?' he asked. 'I say, wasn't it extraordinary?'

'Ah, whatever was waiting to get you,' Father Whelan said philosophically, emptying his pipe on to his plate. 'I suppose it had to get something. A similar thing happened an old aunt of my own. The cock used to sleep in the house, on a perch over the door—you know, the old-fashioned way. One night, the old woman had occasion, and when she went to the door, the cock crowed three times and dropped dead at her feet. Whatever was waiting for her, of course,' he added with a sigh. 'The cock gave them away, and they took their revenge on him.'

'Well! Well! Well!' the Canon exploded. 'I'm astonished at you, Father Whelan, absolutely astonished! How can you even repeat such old wives' tales?'

'I don't see what you have to be astonished about, Canon,' said the Bishop. 'It was no worse than what happened to Father Muldoon.'

'That was a bad business,' muttered Father Whelan, shaking his head.

'What happened to him?' asked Devine.

'I told you he was always denouncing old Johnnie,' said the Bishop. 'One day they had words and he struck the old man. It wasn't fair. The old man was too feeble. Within a month Muldoon got a breaking out on his knee.'

'Poor fellow, he lost the leg after,' Father Whelan said, stuffing his pipe again.

'I suppose next you'll say that was the fairies' revenge?' said the Canon, throwing discretion to the winds. It was too much for him, a man who knew Church history, had lived in France and was a connoisseur of wine.

'That was what Father Muldoon thought,' said the Bishop smugly.

'More fool he!' retorted the Canon.

'That's as may be, Canon,' said the Bishop. 'Anyway, the doctors couldn't do much for him. He went back up the Glen again to ask Johnnie's advice. "I had nothing to do with it, father," said Johnnie, "but you can tell the doctor from me that he might as well take the leg off you while he's at it." "Why so?" says Muldoon. "Because it was the Queen of the Fairies that fired the shot at you, father, and the Queen's wound never heals." No more it did,' added the Bishop. 'As you say, father, he ended his days on a peg leg.'

'He did, God rest him, he did,' muttered Father Whelan mournfully, and there was a long pause. It was clear that the Canon was routed, and soon after they all got up to go. Father Fogarty had left his car outside the Seminary, and the Bishop, in a benevolent mood, offered to guide them across the field by the footpath.

'No, I'll do that,' Devine said irritably. In his cranky way he was fond of the Bishop and he didn't want him perambulating through the fields at that hour.

'Ah, I need the little walk,' said the Bishop.

He, the Canon and Father Fogarty went first down the palace steps. Father Devine followed with Father Whelan, who went down sideways with the skirts of his coat held up.

'That was a very good drop of poteen,' the Bishop was saying. 'For some reason, bad poteen strikes at the extremities. I used to see the people at home, talking as clearly as yourself or myself, and then dropping off the chairs, paralysed. You'd have to take them home on a door. The head might be quite clear, but the legs would be like gateposts.'

'Father Devine,' Father Whelan whispered girlishly, stopping in his tracks.

'Yes, father, what is it?' Devine asked gently.

'What his Lordship said,' whispered Father Whelan guiltily. 'That's the way I feel. Like gateposts.'

And before the young priest could catch him, he put out one of the gateposts which failed to alight properly on its base: the other leaned slowly towards it, and he collapsed in an ungraceful parody of a ballet dancer's curtsey.

'Oh, my, my, my!' he exclaimed guiltily. Even in his liquor he was melancholy and gentle.

The other three turned round slowly, very slowly, to study him. To Devine they looked like sleep-walkers.

'Hah!' the Bishop said with quiet satisfaction. 'It wasn't as good as I thought. We'd want to mind ourselves.'

And off the three of them went, arm-in-arm, as though they recognised no responsibility to their fallen colleague. Paddy, the Bishop's 'boy', who had been anticipating trouble, immediately appeared, and he and Devine carried the old man back to the hallway. 'Father Whelan isn't feeling well,' he explained unnecessarily to the housekeeper. Then, the two of them took the hall bench and set out after the others. They were in time to see the collapse of the Canon, but in spite of it, the other two went on. Devine shouted a warning, but they ignored him. Father Fogarty had begun to chuckle hysterically. It occurred to Devine that he was already beginning to rehearse his story of 'the night I got drunk with the Bishop'.

Devine and Paddy left the Canon and pursued the other two. They had gone wildly astray, turning in a semi-circle round the field, till they were at the foot of the hill and before a high fence round the plantation. The Bishop never hesitated but began to climb the wall.

'I must be gone wrong, father,' he said anxiously. 'This never happened to me before. We'll go over the wall and up the wood.'

'I can't,' shouted Fogarty in a paroxysm of chuckles.

'Nonsense, father!' the Bishop said sternly, holding on to a bush and looking down at him from the top of the wall. 'Why can't you?'

'The fairies have me,' roared Fogarty.

'Pull yourself together, father,' the Bishop said sternly. 'You don't want to be making an exhibition of yourself.'

Next moment Fogarty was lying flat at the foot of the wall, laughing his head off. Devine shouted again to the Bishop, but the Bishop only turned his back contemptuously and slid down at the other side of the wall. They found him there under a tree in the starlight, quite powerless but full of wisdom, resignation and peace. When they lifted him on to the bench he reclined there, his hands crossed meekly on his breast, like an effigy on a tomb-chest.

'The most remarkable example of historical regression I've ever seen,' Devine told young Fogarty when he woke up later with a terrible head. 'I must write a paper on it for the Archaeological Society. I didn't mind your retreat into the Early Bronze Age so much, but I was afraid you'd forget yourselves and go neolithic on me all of a sudden.'

'Ah, how bad the neolithic fellows were!' groaned Fogarty. 'I'm damn full sure they never felt as bad as I do.'

'The neolithic fellows?' Devine said in mock surprise. 'And have the Bishop proposing to build Lanigan into the wall of the new cathedral? My dear fellow, believe me, you can take this historical regression business too far.'

THE SCIENCE OF MIRRORS

Catherine Brophy

Mullach pier stretches into the sea like an aged finger from a fist of rocky land. A cluster of lobster-pots, tied with blue and orange rope, were hunched against the pier wall. The unravelled ends streamed in the wind. A black tumulus climbed above brown mountains and spray. Down the boreen a turquoise van grunted and swayed. It drove to the end of the pier and stopped. The engine died and the chassis, home-painted and road-scarred, settled down on its axles.

Inside the van the passengers sat silent. They didn't need to speak. They were cautious and careful and happy to do their work unrecognised. After a time, each passed a palm over a worn black box with switches and dials and sat silent a while longer. Then they opened the doors.

Four lumpy, middle-aged women stepped out. They wore middle-aged clothes and carried worn-looking shopping-bags. The wind tossed them about making them clutch at their coats and tuck their hair into their scarves. Then, heads angled from the wind, they walked, in single file, back towards the land. They reached a dry-stone wall and sat behind it out of the wind. They sat with their legs straight out and the soles of their no-nonsense shoes to the sea. They took sandwiches from their bags and started to eat. They were the Mirror Women.

There are Mirror Women everywhere, but their presence is seldom suspected. They've been here since Maeve and Morrigan and have sisterhoods in every country in the world.

Though it's true their work is seldom needed in parts of Africa, the Amazon and certain isles and enclaves, generally they're kept busy. Their aim is enigmatic and their power works sideways, slyly, through a mirror.

The Mirror Women munched their sandwiches and washed them down with sweet hot tea from a flask. They tidied round them, threw crusts to the gulls and went to their bags. They took out their equipment, calibrated it and settled their focusers comfortably on their laps. They put on their glasses with the mirrors on the inside and made adjustments. Then they waited.

One of the nice things about their job was, that they could travel anywhere. They had scanned their circle from under may-bush hedgerows, from behind the stone pillars of gates, from picnic tables in main road lay-bys and down here by the sea. In fact there were certain technical advantages in having distance, limitations too, but then there's good and bad in everything. Their science was simple really, based on the principles of light refraction, particle physics and the strange, subversive properties of mirrors. And of women.

*   *   *

The Mirror Women had been watching them ever since the girls were fourteen, best friends and beautiful. At least Sarah and Mimi were beautiful, in very different ways. Sarah was auburn, with that thick, wavy, glowing hair that everyone wants to touch. And Mimi was dark. Not ordinary dark but black, blue-black, with tiny tendril curls around her face. Ger was not beautiful, in fact she was, well, plain is too strong a word, but she was ordinary, unformed and pasty. Sarah and Mimi were close as twins, as best-best friends, while Ger was next-best-friend to both. And the Mirror Women noted everything.

The three of them read magazines. No, devoured magazines. They spent whole afternoons, sometimes whole days, absorbed in *Cosmopolitan, IT, Nineteen, Marie Claire, Woman's Own* and *Vogue*, to mention just a few, searching, always searching for any clue that might inform how to be grown up. It was their favourite pastime. They grabbed excitedly at questionnaires, queried one another, ticked answers and totted scores to find out if they were good lovers, loyal friends, confident, party poopers, high fliers or jealous. They laughed, and argued over answers, joked about the results but inside, in her secret heart, each one was afraid she'd never match the ideal score.

They read each other's horoscopes aloud and hooted in derision when it said, 'beware a financial proposition from an acquaintance', but flushed with pleasure when it read, 'the 20th is excellent for romance' and 'the new moon on the 6th will bring a meeting with an interesting stranger.'

'"The first step to beauty is an honest assessment of your features."' Sarah read aloud from the 'Health and Beauty' page. '"Sit in front of a mirror in a good light and take a long hard look."'

The Mirror Women smiled and fine-tuned their focus.

The dressing table stool was wide enough for Sarah and Mimi to sit side by side, Ger stood behind them.

'"Be honest, for the only one you fool will be yourself."' read Sarah. She laid the magazine before them on the dressing table.

They examined the five 'before' faces alongside a feature called 'The Beautiful Illusion'. Then they turned the page to see the 'after' transformations. They put the magazine aside and looked, unsure and questioning, in the mirror.

The Mirror Women watched and waited.

'Come on Mimi, you go first,' said Sarah.

'No you.'

'No you, I asked first.'

Ger said nothing.

'All right, I'll go first,' said Sarah.

The girls stared at Sarah's reflection. The gold-glow, auburn hair framed milk-white skin so fine it showed the milk-blue veins. The lips, rose-pink, were pursed, the eyes grey-green with flecks of gold were searching deep inside themselves for signs. Beside her, Mimi's neat black eyebrows rucked in concentration, blue-black tendrils tumbled round her face, her iris-blue, blue eyes scanned Sarah's face for faults. Above them Ger's face floated, a pale and faintly freckled ghost.

'I'll start at the very top, with your hair. Will I?'

'All right.'

'Your hair's too coarse.' Mimi began.

'I know, it's impossible to manage.' Sarah laughed a little ruefully. 'Like a bewitched barleystack.'

The Mirror Women laughed ruefully as well.

'Your nose is hooked.'

Sarah raised a finger and flattened the tip of her nose.

'You're right,' she said, 'it is.'

'And your eyes, they're not green really, more like . . .' Mimi searched for a word that was accurate and not too damaging. '. . . like boiled gooseberries.'

'Boiled frogspawn,' Sarah said impatiently, 'with custard.'

There was silence for a moment.

'That's all,' said Mimi.

'Are you sure?'

'Sure.'

'You don't think my mouth's too wide?'

'No, your mouth's fine.'

'Sure?'

'Sure.'

Another silence.

'I think you're gorgeous-looking,' Ger mumbled, 'I wish I had your looks.'

Sarah shook off Ger's remark with a toss of her hair and examined the mirror accusingly.

'My hair is coarse,' she began.

'My nose is hooked.

'I've frogspawn eyes with custard . . . and,' she added hesitantly, 'I think I'm getting a double chin.'

'Let me see.' Mimi considered a moment. 'No, not yet,' she said. 'Though you might have a tendency.'

For a while Sarah sat slapping herself under the chin with the back of her hands like the women in the magazines advised.

The Mirror Women made adjustments, sighed and smiled a little sadly. Ger shifted impatiently, opened her mouth to speak . . .

'Come on, it's my turn now,' said Mimi, excited and scared to learn what she looked like. 'Promise to be honest, cross your heart and hope to die . . .'

Sarah licked her finger and crossed her forehead, lips and heart.

'Don't spare me anything,' begged Mimi, 'I'd prefer to know.'

'Cross my heart,' said Sarah.

The three young faces stared into the mirror again.

The Mirror Women sighed.

'You're hair's too curly and um . . . you're skin's a bit blotchy and, gosh, I've never noticed this before . . . your ears are pointy and stick out.'

'You're right,' said Mimi taking it as bravely as she could. She looked herself in her iris-blue, blue eyes.

'My hair's a frizz,' she said. 'My skin is blotched.'

'Oh you two make me sick,' said Ger grabbing her schoolbooks from the bed.

'My ears are pointy like a witch,' continued Mimi, 'and stick out far too far, also . . .' she leaned closer to the mirror, 'I think I'm getting frown lines on my forehead.'

The Mirror Women sighed, adjusted their lenses with the mirrors on the inside and made passes with their palms.

'I'm going home,' said Ger all tight and angry, and she left and slammed the door

Her friends didn't try to stop her, didn't even look round. They leaned forward, heads just touching, to examine their blemishes. Something in the mirror shimmered, a trick of light, a flaw perhaps, and the smooth young faces lost a little of their glow.

* * *

Ger came home, sighed and flopped grumpily into a chair, oppressed by her friend's beauty.

'It's not fair,' she complained.

'Sarah and Mimi?' her mother asked. 'Yes, they are beautiful, but you, you are a *joli laide.*'

Ger's mother had been an *au pair* in France once.

'That means plain.'

'No, it means you have a certain something that is beyond beauty, a style, a fascination, something that attracts both men and women, a . . .'

'*Je ne sais quoi*, I know, I know. It still means plain . . .'

'In France men appreciate all kinds of women . . .'

'Big deal. But we don't live in France.'

Yet up in her room she opened the wardrobe and gazed at herself in the long mirror.

The Mirror Women smiled and waited.

Her unformed face looked at her for a while then faded as she imagined Frenchmen, all black eyes, moustaches and aplomb, looking, looking. They would appreciate a *joli laide.* She twisted a wide, white scarf around her head and smiled back at the Frenchmen.

The Mirror Women laughed and made passes with their palms.

Some trick of light, some irregularity perhaps, cast a hint of ripple on the mirror. Ger's face gained a glow, looked somehow not so ordinary.

'The white scarf gives my features definition,' she told the mirror.

The Mirror Women smiled at one another.

'In fact I look quite interesting.'

Ger eyed the Frenchmen over one raised shoulder and

fluttered her fingers at the pavement-café women sipping Pernod.

*   *   *

How soon beauty fades, the headmaster thought as he saw Sarah and Mimi come out of the school door. They used to be delicious only a short time ago, delicious, creamy . . . he could hardly trust himself to think about it . . . delightful . . . but somehow they had coarsened. He was tired and near retirement and was the kind of man who remarked on hot high-summer days that the evenings were drawing in, who took solace in the dandruff on young men's collars, lines on women's necks. He watched the pupils climb on to the bus. So young, he thought, it's hard to believe that they could make their way in the world when they leave school in only six weeks' time. Well, he'd better get them organised.

He climbed aboard the bus and counted. Everyone was present. He took the driver's microphone and gave a speech about behaviour and being a credit to the school. The students cheered, and cat-called, this was their very last school trip. The three accompanying teachers smiled and hushed the noise, the driver revved his engine and the headmaster climbed down from the bus again.

A first-year came running to say that he was wanted on the phone. He returned to his office and sad-sweet thoughts of beauty fading.

*   *   *

When the school trip arrived at the Heritage Hostel the Warden allocated beds, boys on the ground floor, girls upstairs, eight bunk beds to a room. The Warden called Ger's name. She stepped forward bright-eyed and eager and rushed upstairs with her bags. Sarah and Mimi were left but they didn't mind. Ger was no longer their next-best friend

for friendships shift over four years and Ger spent more time
now at sports and debates and the kind of things that didn't
interest them.

'You two can have the small room on the left,' the Warden
said. 'Do you mind? You won't be with the others.'

They were glad for they preferred to be alone.

'Hey, we're in luck,' Mimi cried. 'This room has a mirror.'

It was screwed to the wall of an alcove and reached from
floor to ceiling.

The Mirror Women were ready, waiting.

'Full-length,' said Sarah, impressed with its size.

The Mirror Women smiled sadly.

Mimi locked the door. Then quickly, they stripped to their
underthings and stood side by side before the glass. Over
time it had become a ritual. First silence while they noted
all their faults and imperfections, all unsightly things, all
unacceptability. Then came the lamentations.

'My hair is coarse,' keened Sarah,
'My nose is hooked
I've frogspawn eyes in custard,
My breasts are flat
My stomach huge
I'm getting knock-knees too.'

'Too true, too true,' sang the Mirror Women and fingered
their focusers. 'Oh yes, too true.'

'My hair's a frizz,' wailed Mimi.

'My skin too blotched
My ears are pointy like a witch
And stick out far too far.
My forehead's lined
My waist's too thick
And I've got thunder thighs.'

'Sighs, sighs,' sang the Mirror Women. 'Sighs, sad
sighs.'

'Oh Mimi do you think I've developed a double chin?'
asked Sarah peering closer at herself.

'I'm afraid so,' Mimi answered.

The Mirror Women sighed one last sigh and made passes with their hands.

*   *   *

They had walked three winding miles when they came to the gate that might lead to the pre-Christian fort. Everyone stopped.

The teachers consulted maps and the Heritage Handbook. Some pupils stood waiting in groups, others wandered around.

'Keep together everybody, we don't want anyone lost,' a distracted teacher called.

Further on there was a turn left, down to the sea. Sarah looked at Mimi. Each knew the other's thought.

While pupils crowded round the gate and the teachers pointed up the hill, Mimi and Sarah ran away down the little sea-road stifling their laughter.

'I didn't want to see that old fort anyway,' said Mimi when they slowed down.

'I knew you didn't, I just knew! Neither did I.'

'Really?'

'Cross my heart, and then I got a sudden urge to see the sea,' said Sarah.

'I knew it, I knew it!' squealed Mimi, 'So did I.'

'Did you? Did you really?'

'Yes, cross my heart and hope to die.'

'We must be telepathic,' decided Sarah.

'I suppose it's 'cause we're best-best friends,' agreed Mimi.

The road petered into a rough boreen and they saw the pier. They saw the turquoise van resting on its axles, the streamered lobster pots, the big black cloud, the spray, the dry-stone wall. Behind the wall the Mirror Women, in their head scarves and their no-nonsense shoes, took off their glasses, put their focusers in their bags and got lumpily to their feet. They stood by the road waiting.

'Are you ready?' the Mirror Women asked when Mimi and Sarah drew level.

'We are,' the girls replied.

The Mirror Women led them to the van, climbed in and pushed up in their seats to make room.

'Come on,' they said.

The girls squeezed in beside the Mirror Women. Rain splattered on the rough fist of land with its gnarled finger stretched to the sea. The van doors clattered closed and they drove away.

4

LEPRECHAUNS

To many people outside Ireland, the leprechaun's name is probably as familiar as that of the banshee, although quite a few misconceptions exist about the precise nature of this little creature. Some sources use the word to describe all Irish faeries, but as W. B. Yeats explained, he is a quite individual member of that supernatural clan; other authorities have suggested that leprechauns are actually the last surviving members of the 'little people' who once occupied the British Isles, long before the arrival of the larger races from their scattered origins in Europe and Scandinavia. Writers supporting these theories have argued that on the one hand, the word 'leprechaun' is derived from *Luacharma 'n*, meaning pigmy, or, on the other, *Leith bhrogan*, the one-shoe maker.

Both sides, however, seem to agree that the leprechaun is a fairy shoemaker, about three feet high, dressed in red waistcoat and breeches, and wearing a cocked hat. His face is invariably wrinkled and tricky, for he is always looking to practise mischief on human beings and avoid capture at any cost, although he may reward any kindness which is shown towards him. As Yeats wrote in *The Celtic Twilight*: 'The leprechaun makes shoes continually and has grown very rich. Many treasure-crocks, buried in old war-time, has he now for his own.'

Such legends have made the leprechaun an obvious subject for supernatural tales, many of which were collected by Douglas Hyde (1862–1949), whose contributions in this field

—and in particular his volume *Beside the Fire: A Collection of Irish Gaelic Folk Stories* (1890)—have tended to be overshadowed by his greater fame as founder of the Gaelic League and first President of Ireland, from 1938 to 1945. Born in County Roscommon, he became fascinated by Irish language and lore as a young man and, after a classical education at Trinity College, Dublin, began to undertake the series of field trips which were to gather a rich trove of folk stories for use in his plays and books. His subsequent writings and lecture tours promoting Irish culture did much to foster interest in it in Ireland as well as America which he visited several times. Among Hyde's stories, the tale of 'Teig O 'Kane and the Corpse' is widely regarded as one of his best.

Thomas Crofton Croker (1798–1854) was also a great folklore collector who utilised the material from his field trips for short stories and books. Born in Cork, he published the first of his collections, *Fairy Legends and Traditions of the South of Ireland*, in 1825 and, according to James F. Kilroy, this 'helped to foster in Irish audiences a taste for fiction on native subjects'. The book is also said to have had an enduring effect on Sir Walter Scott and was later translated into German by the Brothers Grimm.

Croker's story 'The Haunted Cellar', taken from his book, introduces us to a particular kind of leprechaun, the Cluricaune, a mischievous and solitary little old man whose chief pleasure is getting drunk in wine cellars! Because of this habit, the Cluricaune is not the most welcome visitor in Irish houses, sometimes being referred to as 'that sottish elf' and occasionally as a *Naggeneen*, the Gaelic for a measure of drink and possibly the origin of the English word 'noggin'.

A quite different side of the leprechaun is featured in 'The Gollan' by the Anglo-Irish author A. E. Coppard (1873–1957). Coppard, who began his working life at the age of nine as a shop boy and then entered an ironworks, escaped from a life of drudgery when his first book, *Adam and Eve and Pinch Me*, written at home at night, became a best seller in 1921. Like so many others, Coppard had fallen under the spell of Irish legends and lore and was later to describe many of his short stories as 'modern folk tales'. Among those set in Ireland must be mentioned 'The Elixir of Youth' (1922), in which a faerie girl provides a man with the draught of eternal life and generates some very surprising results; 'Crotty Shinkwin' (1932), about two fishermen who discover a haunted island; and 'The Gollan', a story that Coppard wrote as a Christmas present for two Irish friends, Earl and Florence Fish. This tale of a foolish young man who earns a most unusual reward when he sets a leprechaun free is an outstanding example of Coppard's narrative skill.

Edward John Moreton Drax Plunkett, 18th Baron Dunsany (1878–1957), was, as his name might suggest, a larger-than-life character who combined the career of a soldier (he fought in both the Boer War and the First World War and was injured during the Easter Rising in 1916) with those of playwright for the Abbey Theatre, popular novelist and short story writer. He prided himself on his expertise as a big game hunter and chess player, and once claimed to be 'the worst dressed man in Ireland'. His stories of heroic fantasy, however, have caused him to be labelled 'one of Britain's most important fantasists' by critic Mike Ashley in his *Who's Who in Horror and Fantasy Fiction* (1977), and to be credited with 'fathering the invented fantasy world in short story form' through his collections *The Gods of Pegana* (1905), *Time and the Gods* (1906), *The Book of Wonder* (1912) and many more. The influence of these volumes can still be seen in much of the fantasy being written today, in both Britain and the United States.

Dunsany's inspiration for much of his work was clearly the Irish legends he had imbibed in the neighbourhood of his family home, a castle in County Meath. In later years, his reputation with the local people for eccentricity was increased when he cut a full-size cricket pitch in the castle grounds, so that he could organise matches with visiting friends from England. He was also a lover of tall stories, and in the character Jorkens created the archetypal line-shooter. Jorkens is a man who delights in spinning yarns that are told with sufficient verisimilitude to convince his friends in the Billiards Club that they *might* be true. In 'The Crock of Gold' (1948), taken from one of the five collections of Jorkens' adventures, the redoubtable narrator describes his experiences with a leprechaun. The story includes just the right mix of fantasy and fiction to show why the legend of this unique supernatural figure continues to exert such fascination.

TEIG O'KANE AND THE CORPSE

Douglas Hyde

There was once a grown-up lad in the County Leitrim, and he was strong and lively, and the son of a rich farmer. His father had plenty of money, and he did not spare it on the son. Accordingly, when the boy grew up he liked sport better than work, and, as his father had no other children, he loved this one so much that he allowed him to do in everything just as it pleased himself. He was very extravagant, and he used to scatter the gold money as another person would scatter the white. He was seldom to be found at home, but if there was a fair, or a race, or a gathering within ten miles of him, you were dead certain to find him there. And he seldom spent a night in his father's house, but he used to be always out rambling, and, like Shawn Bwee long ago, there was

'grádh gach cailin i mbrollach a léine,'

'the love of every girl in the breast of his shirt,' and it's many's the kiss he got and he gave, for he was very handsome, and there wasn't a girl in the country but would fall in love with him, only for him to fasten his two eyes on her, and it was for that someone made this *rann* on him—

'Look at the rogue, it's for kisses he's rambling,
　It isn't much wonder, for that was his way;
He's like an old hedgehog, at night he'll be scrambling
　From this place to that, but he'll sleep in the day.'

At last he became very wild and unruly. He wasn't to be seen day or night in his father's house, but always rambling or going on his *kailee* (night visit) from place to place and from house to house, so that the old people used to shake their heads and say to one another, 'It's easy seen what will happen to the land when the old man dies; his son will run through it in a year, and it won't stand him that long itself.'

He used to be always gambling and card-playing and drinking, but his father never minded his bad habits, and never punished him. But it happened one day that the old man was told that the son had ruined the character of a girl in the neighbourhood, and he was greatly angry, and he called the son to him, and said to him, quietly and sensibly —'Avic,' says he, 'you know I loved you greatly up to this, and I never stopped you from doing your choice thing whatever it was, and I kept plenty of money with you, and I always hoped to leave you the house and land, and all I had after myself would be gone; but I heard a story of you today that has disgusted me with you. I cannot tell you the grief that I felt when I heard such a thing of you, and I tell you now plainly that unless you marry that girl I'll leave house and land and everything to my brother's son. I never could leave it to anyone who would make so bad a use of it as you do yourself, deceiving women and coaxing girls. Settle with yourself now whether you'll marry that girl and get my land as a fortune with her, or refuse to marry her and give up all that was coming to you; and tell me in the morning which of the two things you have chosen.'

'Och! *Domnoo Sheery*! father, you wouldn't say that to me, and I such a good son as I am. Who told you I wouldn't marry the girl?' says he.

But his father was gone, and the lad knew well enough that he would keep his word too; and he was greatly troubled in his mind, for as quiet and as kind as the father was, he never went back on a word that he had once said, and there wasn't another man in the country who was harder to bend than he was.

The boy did not know rightly what to do. He was in love with the girl indeed, and he hoped to marry her sometime or other, but he would much sooner have remained another while as he was, and follow on at his old tricks—drinking, sporting, and playing cards; and, along with that, he was angry that his father should order him to marry, and should threaten him if he did not do it.

'Isn't my father a great fool,' says he to himself. 'I was ready enough, and only too anxious, to marry Mary; and now since he threatened me, faith I've a great mind to let it go another while.'

His mind was so much excited that he remained between two notions as to what he should do. He walked out into the night at last to cool his heated blood, and went on to the road. He lit a pipe, and as the night was fine he walked and walked on, until the quick pace made him begin to forget his trouble. The night was bright, and the moon half full. There was not a breath of wind blowing, and the air was calm and mild. He walked on for nearly three hours, when he suddenly remembered that it was late in the night, and time for him to turn. 'Musha! I think I forgot myself,' says he; 'it must be near twelve o'clock now.'

The word was hardly out of his mouth, when he heard the sound of many voices, and the trampling of feet on the road before him. 'I don't know who can be out so late at night as this, and on such a lonely road,' said he to himself.

He stood listening, and he heard the voices of many people talking through other, but he could not understand what they were saying. 'Oh, wirra!' says he, 'I'm afraid. It's not Irish or English they have; it can't be they're Frenchmen!' He went on a couple of yards further, and he saw well enough by the light of the moon a band of little people coming towards him, and they were carrying something big and heavy with them. 'Oh, murder!' says he to himself, 'sure it can't be that they're the good people that's in it!' Every *rib* of hair that was on his head stood up, and there fell a shaking on his bones, for he saw that they were coming to him fast.

He looked at them again, and perceived that there were about twenty little men in it, and there was not a man at all of them higher than about three feet or three feet and a half, and some of them were grey, and seemed very old. He looked again, but he could not make out what was the heavy thing they were carrying until they came up to him, and then they all stood round about him. They threw the heavy thing down on the road, and he saw on the spot that it was a dead body.

He became as cold as the Death, and there was not a drop of blood running in his veins when an old little grey *maneen* came up to him and said, 'Isn't it lucky we met you, Teig O'Kane?'

Poor Teig could not bring out a word at all, nor open his lips, if he were to get the world for it, and so he gave no answer.

'Teig O'Kane,' said the little grey man again, 'isn't it timely you met us?'

Teig could not answer him.

'Teig O'Kane,' says he, 'the third time, isn't it lucky and timely that we met you?'

But Teig remained silent, for he was afraid to return an answer, and his tongue was as if it was tied to the roof of his mouth.

The little grey man turned to his companions, and there was joy in his bright little eye. 'And now,' says he, 'Teig O'Kane hasn't a word, we can do with him what we please. Teig, Teig,' says he, 'you're living a bad life, and we can make a slave of you now, and you cannot withstand us, for there's no use in trying to go against us. Lift that corpse.'

Teig was so frightened that he was only able to utter the two words, 'I won't'; for as frightened as he was he was obstinate and stiff, the same as ever.

'Teig O'Kane won't lift the corpse,' said the little *maneen*, with a wicked little laugh, for all the world like the breaking of a *lock* of dry *kippeens*, and with a little harsh voice like the striking of a cracked bell. 'Teig O'Kane won't lift the corpse—make him lift it'; and before the word was out of his mouth they had all gathered round poor Teig, and they all talking and laughing through each other.

Teig tried to run from them, but they followed him, and a man of them stretched out his foot before him as he ran, so that Teig was thrown in a heap on the road. Then before he could rise up the fairies caught him, some by the hands and some by the feet, and they held him tight, in a way that he could not stir, with his face against the ground. Six or seven of them raised the body then, and pulled it over to him, and left it down on his back. The breast of the corpse was squeezed against Teig's back and shoulders, and the arms of the corpse were thrown around Teig's neck. Then they stood back from him a couple of yards, and let him get up. He rose, foaming at the mouth and cursing, and he shook himself, thinking to throw the corpse off his back. But his fear and his wonder were great when he found that the two arms had a tight hold round his own neck, and that the two legs were squeezing his hips firmly, and that, however strongly he tried, he could not throw it off, any more than a horse can throw off its saddle. He was terribly frightened then, and he thought he was lost. 'Ochone! for ever,' said he to himself, 'it's the bad life I'm leading that has given the good people this power over me. I promise to God and Mary, Peter and Paul, Patrick and Bridget, that I'll mend my ways for as long as I have to live, if I come clear out of this danger—and I'll marry the girl.'

The little grey man came up to him again, and said he to him, 'Now, Teig*een*,' says he, 'you didn't lift the body when I told you to lift it, and see how you were made to lift it; perhaps when I tell you to bury it, you won't bury it until you're made to bury it!'

'Anything at all that I can do for your honour,' said Teig, 'I'll do it,' for he was getting sense already, and if it had not been for the great fear that was on him, he never would have let that civil word slip out of his mouth.

The little man laughed a sort of laugh again. 'You're getting quiet now, Teig,' says he. 'I'll go bail but you'll be quiet enough before I'm done with you. Listen to me now, Teig O'Kane, and if you don't obey me in all I'm telling you to do, you'll repent it. You must carry with you this corpse that is on your back to Teampoll-Démus, and you must bring it into the church with you, and make a grave for it in the very middle of the church, and you must raise up the flags and put them down again the very same way, and you must carry the clay out of the church and leave the place as it was when you came, so that no one could know that there had been anything changed. But that's not all. Maybe that the body won't be allowed to be buried in that church; perhaps some other man has the bed, and, if so, it's likely he won't share it with this one. If you don't get leave to bury it in Teampoll-Démus, you must carry it to Carrick-fhad-vic-Orus, and bury it in the churchyard there; and if you don't get it into that place, take it with you to Teampoll-Ronan; and if that churchyard is closed on you, take it to Imlogue-Fada; and if you're not able to bury it there, you've no more to do than to take it to Kill-Breedya, and you can bury it there without hindrance. I cannot tell you what one of those churches is the one where you will have leave to bury that corpse under the clay, but I know that it will be allowed you to bury him at some church or other of them. If you do this work rightly, we will be thankful to you, and you will have no cause to grieve; but if you are slow or lazy, believe me we shall take satisfaction of you.'

When the grey little man had done speaking, his comrades laughed and clapped their hands together. 'Glic! Glic! Hwee! Hwee!' they all cried; 'go on, go on, you have eight hours before you till daybreak, and if you haven't this man buried before the sun rises, you're lost.' They struck a fist and a foot behind on him, and drove him on in the road. He was obliged to walk, and to walk fast, for they gave him no rest.

He thought himself that there was not a wet path, or a dirty *boreen*, or a crooked contrary road in the whole county, that he had not walked that night. The night was at times very dark, and whenever there would come a cloud across the moon he could see nothing, and then he used often to fall. Sometimes he was hurt, and sometimes he escaped, but he was obliged always to rise on the moment and to hurry on. Sometimes the moon would break out clearly, and then he would look behind him and see the little people following at his back. And he heard them speaking amongst themselves, talking and crying out, and screaming like a flock of sea-gulls; and if he was to save his soul he never understood as much as one word of what they were saying.

He did not know how far he had walked, when at last one of them cried out to him, 'Stop here!' He stood, and they all gathered round him.

'Do you see those withered trees over there?' says the old boy to him again. 'Teampoll-Démus is among those trees, and you must go in there by yourself, for we cannot follow you or go with you. We must remain here. Go on boldly.'

Teig looked from him, and he saw a high wall that was in places half broken down, and an old grey church on the inside of the wall, and about a dozen withered old trees scattered here and there round it. There was neither leaf nor twig on any of them, but their bare crooked branches were stretched out like the arms of an angry man when he threatens. He had no help for it, but was obliged to go forward. He was a couple of hundred yards from the church, but he walked on, and never looked behind him until he came to the gate of the churchyard. The old gate was thrown down, and he had no difficulty in entering. He turned then to see if any of the little people were following him, but there came a cloud over the moon, and the night became so dark that he could see nothing. He went into the churchyard, and he walked up the old grassy pathway leading to the church. When he reached the door, he found it locked. The door was large and strong, and he did not know what to do. At last he drew out his knife with difficulty, and stuck it in the wood to try if it were not rotten, but it was not.

'Now,' said he to himself, 'I have no more to do; the door is shut, and I can't open it.'

Before the words were rightly shaped in his own mind, a voice in his ear said to him, 'Search for the key on the top of the door, or on the wall.'

He started. 'Who is that speaking to me?' he cried, turning round; but he saw no one. The voice said in his ear again, 'Search for the key on the top of the door, or on the wall.'

'What's that?' said he, and the sweat running from his forehead; 'who spoke to me?'

'It's I, the corpse, that spoke to you!' said the voice.

'Can you talk?' said Teig.

'Now and again,' said the corpse.

Teig searched for the key, and he found it on the top of the wall. He was too much frightened to say any more, but he opened the door wide, and as quickly as he could, and he went in, with the corpse on his back. It was as dark as pitch inside, and poor Teig began to shake and tremble.

'Light the candle,' said the corpse.

Teig put his hand in his pocket, as well as he was able, and drew out a flint and steel. He struck a spark out of it, and lit a burnt rag he had in his pocket. He blew it until it made a flame, and he looked round him. The church was very ancient, and part of the wall was broken down. The windows were blown in or cracked, and the timber of the seats were rotten. There were six or seven old iron candlesticks left there still, and in one of these candlesticks Teig found the stump of an old candle, and he lit it. He was still looking round him on the strange and horrid place in which he found himself, when the cold corpse whispered in his ear, 'Bury me now, bury me now; there is a spade and turn the ground.' Teig looked from him, and he saw a spade lying beside the altar. He took it up, and he placed the blade under a flag that was in the middle of the aisle, and leaning all his weight on the handle of the spade, he raised it. When the first flag was raised it was not hard to raise the others near it, and he moved three or four of them out of their places. The clay that was under them was soft and easy to dig, but he had not thrown up more than three or four shovelfuls when he felt the iron touch something soft like flesh. He threw up three or four more shovelfuls from around it, and then he saw that it was another body that was buried in the same place.

'I am afraid I'll never be allowed to bury the two bodies in the same hole,' said Teig, in his own mind. 'You corpse, there on my back,' says he, 'will you be satisfied if I bury you down here?' But the corpse never answered him a word.

'That's a good sign,' said Teig to himself. 'Maybe he's getting quiet,' and he thrust the spade down in the earth again. Perhaps he hurt the flesh of the other body, for the dead man that was buried there stood up in the grave, and shouted an awful shout. 'Hoo! hoo!! hoo!!! Go! go!! go!!! or you're a dead, dead, dead man!' And then he fell back in the grave again. Teig said afterwards, that of all the wonderful things he saw that night, that was the most awful to him. His hair stood upright on his head like the bristles of a pig, the cold sweat ran off his face, and then came a tremour over all his bones, until he thought that he must fall.

But after a while he became bolder, when he saw that the second corpse remained lying quietly there, and he threw in the clay on it again, and he smoothed it overhead, and he laid down the flags carefully as they had been before. 'It can't be that he'll rise up any more,' said he.

He went down the aisle a little further, and drew near to the door, and began raising the flags again, looking for another bed for the corpse on his back. He took up three or four flags and put them aside, and then he dug the clay. He was not long digging until he laid bare an old woman without a thread upon her but her shirt. She was more lively than the first corpse, for he had scarcely taken any of the clay away from about her, when she sat up and began to cry,

'Ho, you *bodach* (clown)! Ha, you *bodach!* Where has he been that he got no bed?'

Poor Teig drew back, and when she found that she was getting no answer, she closed her eyes gently, lost her vigour, and fell back quietly and slowly under the clay. Teig did to her as he had done to the man—he threw the clay back on her, and left the flags down overhead.

He began digging again near the door, but before he had thrown up more than a couple of shovelfuls, he noticed a man's hand laid bare by the spade. 'By my soul, I'll go no further, then,' said he to himself; 'what use is it for me?' And he threw the clay in again on it, and settled the flags as they had been before.

He left the church then, and his heart was heavy enough, but he shut the door and locked it, and left the key where he found it. He sat down on a tombstone that was near the door, and began thinking. He was in great doubt what he should do. He laid his face between his two hands, and cried for grief and fatigue, since he was dead certain at this time that he never would come home alive. He made another attempt to loosen the hands of the corpse that were squeezed round his neck, but they were as tight as if they were clamped; and the more he tried to loosen them, the tighter they squeezed him. He was going to sit down once more, when the cold, horrid lips of the dead man said to him, 'Carrick-fhad-vic-Orus,' and he remembered the command of the good people to bring the corpse with him to that place if he should be unable to bury it where he had been.

He rose up, and looked about him. 'I don't know the way,' he said.

As soon as he had uttered the word, the corpse stretched out suddenly its left hand that had been tightened round his neck, and kept it pointing out, showing him the road he ought to follow. Teig went in the direction that the fingers were stretched, and passed out of the churchyard. He found himself on an old rutty, stony road, and he stood still again, not knowing where to turn. The corpse stretched out its bony hand a second time, and pointed out to him another road—not the road by which he had come when approaching the old church. Teig followed that road, and whenever he came to a path or road meeting it, the corpse always stretched out its hand and pointed with its fingers, showing him the way he was to take.

Many was the cross-road he turned down, and many was the crooked *boreen* he walked, until he saw from him an old burying-ground at last, beside the road, but there was neither church nor chapel nor any other building in it. The corpse squeezed him tightly, and he stood. 'Bury me, bury me in the burying-ground,' said the voice.

Teig drew over towards the old burying-place, and he was not more than about twenty yards from it, when, raising his eyes, he saw hundreds and hundreds of ghosts—men, women, and children—sitting on the top of the wall round about, or standing on the inside of it, or running backwards and forwards, and pointing at him, while he could see their mouths opening and shutting as if they were speaking, though he heard no word, nor any sound amongst them at all.

He was afraid to go forward, so he stood where he was, and the moment he stood, all the ghosts became quiet, and ceased moving. Then Teig understood that it was trying to keep him from going in, that they were. He walked a couple of yards forwards, and immediately the whole crowd rushed together towards the spot to which he was moving, and they stood so thickly together that it seemed to him that he never could break through them, even though he had a mind to try. But he had no mind to try it. He went back broken and dispirited, and when he had gone a couple of hundred yards from the burying-ground, he stood again, for he did not know what way he was to go. He heard the voice of the corpse in his ear, saying, 'Teampoll-Ronan,' and the skinny hand was stretched out again, pointing him out the road.

As tired as he was, he had to walk, and the road was neither short nor even. The night was darker than ever, and it was difficult to make his way. Many was the toss he got, and many a bruise they left on his body. At last he saw Teampoll-Ronan from him in the distance, standing in the middle of the burying-ground. He moved over towards it, and thought he was all right and safe, when he saw no ghosts nor anything else on the wall, and he thought he would never be hindered now from leaving his load off him at last. He moved over to the gate, but as he was passing in, he tripped on the threshold. Before he could recover himself, something that he could not see seized him by the neck, by the hands, and by the feet, and bruised him, and shook him, and choked him, until he was nearly dead; and at last he was lifted up, and carried more than a hundred yards from that place, and then thrown down in an old dyke, with the corpse still clinging to him.

He rose up, bruised and sore, but feared to go near the place again, for he had seen nothing the time he was thrown down and carried away.

'You corpse, up on my back?' said he, 'shall I go over again to the churchyard?'—but the corpse never answered him. 'That's a sign you don't wish me to try it again,' said Teig.

He was now in great doubt as to what he ought to do, when the corpse spoke in his ear, and said, 'Imlogue-Fada.'

'Oh, murder!' said Teig, 'must I bring you there? If you keep me long walking like this, I tell you I'll fall under you.'

He went on, however, in the direction the corpse pointed out to him. He could not have told, himself, how long he had been going, when the dead man behind suddenly squeezed him, and said, 'There!'

Teig looked from him, and he saw a little low wall, that was so broken down in places that it was no wall at all. It was in a great wide field, in from the road; and only for three or four great stones at the corners, that were more like rocks than stones, there was nothing to show that there was either graveyard or burying ground there.

'Is this Imlogue-Fada? Shall I bury you here?' said Teig. 'Yes,' said the voice.

'But I see no grave or gravestone, only this pile of stones,' said Teig.

The corpse did not answer, but stretched out its long fleshless hand to show Teig the direction in which he was to go. Teig went on accordingly, but he was greatly terrified, for he remembered what had happened to him at the last place. He went on, 'with his heart in his mouth,' as he said himself afterwards; but when he came to within fifteen or twenty yards of the little low square wall, there broke out a flash of lightning, bright yellow and red, with blue streaks in it, and went round about the wall in one course, and it swept by as fast as the swallow in the clouds, and the longer Teig remained looking at it the faster it went, till at last it became like a bright ring of flame round the old graveyard, which no one could pass without being burnt by it. Teig never saw, from the time he was born, and never saw afterwards, so wonderful or so splendid a sight as that was. Round went the flame, white and yellow and blue sparks leaping out from it as it went, and although at first it had been no more than a thin, narrow line, it increased slowly until it was at last a great broad band, and it was continually getting broader and higher, and throwing out more brilliant sparks, till there was never a colour on the ridge of the earth that was not to be seen in that fire; and lightning never shone and flame never flamed that was so shining and so bright as that.

Teig was amazed; he was half dead with fatigue, and he had no courage left to approach the wall. There fell a mist over his eyes, and there came a *soorawn* in his head, and he was obliged to sit down upon a great stone to recover himself. He could see nothing but the light, and he could hear nothing but the whirr of it as it shot round the paddock faster than a flash of lightning.

As he sat there on the stone, the voice whispered once more in his ear, 'Kill-Breedya'; and the dead man squeezed him so tightly that he cried out. He rose again, sick, tired, and trembling, and went forward as he was directed. The wind was cold, and the road was bad, and the load upon his back was heavy, and the night was dark, and he himself was nearly worn out, and if he had had very much farther to go he must have fallen dead under his burden.

At last the corpse stretched out its hand, and said to him, 'Bury me there.'

'This is the last burying-place,' said Teig in his own mind; 'and the little grey man said I'd be allowed to bury him in some of them, so it must be this; it can't be but they'll let him in here.'

The first faint streak of the *ring of day* was appearing in the east, and the clouds were beginning to catch fire, but it was darker than ever, for the moon was set, and there were no stars.

'Make haste, make haste!' said the corpse; and Teig hurried forward as well as he could to the graveyard, which was a little place on a bare hill, with only a few graves in it. He walked boldly in through the open gate, and nothing touched him, nor did he either hear or see anything. He came to the middle of the ground, and then stood up and looked round him for a spade or shovel to make a grave. As he was turning round and searching, he suddenly perceived what startled him greatly—a newly-dug grave right before him. He moved over to it, and looked down, and there at the bottom he saw a black coffin. He clambered down into the hole and lifted the lid, and found that (as he thought it would be) the coffin was empty. He had hardly mounted up out of the hole, and was standing on the brink, when the corpse, which had clung to him for more than eight hours, suddenly relaxed its hold of his neck, and loosened its shins from round his hips, and sank down with a *plop* into the open coffin.

Teig fell down on his two knees at the brink of the grave, and gave thanks to God. He made no delay then, but pressed down the coffin lid in its place, and threw in the clay over it with his two hands, and when the grave was filled up, he stamped and leaped on it with his feet, until it was firm and hard, and then he left the place.

The sun was fast rising as he finished his work, and the first thing he did was to return to the road, and look out for a house to rest himself in. He found an inn at last; and lay down upon a bed there, and slept till night. Then he rose up and ate a little, and fell asleep again till morning. When he awoke in the morning he hired a horse and rode home. He was more than twenty-six miles from home where he was, and he had come all that way with the dead body on his back in one night.

All the people at his own home thought that he must have left the country, and they rejoiced greatly when they saw him come back. Everyone began asking him where he had been, but he would not tell anyone except his father.

He was a changed man from that day. He never drank too much; he never lost his money over cards; and especially he would not take the world and be out late by himself of a dark night.

He was not a fortnight at home until he married Mary, the girl he had been in love with, and it's at their wedding the sport was, and it's he was the happy man from that day forward, and it's all I wish that we may be as happy as he was.

GLOSSARY—*Rann*, a stanza; *kailee* (*céilidhe*), a visit in the evening; *wirra* (*a mhuire*), 'Oh, Mary!' an exclamation like the French *dame*; *rib*, a single hair (in Irish, *ribe*); *a lock (glac)*, a bundle or wisp, or a little share of anything; *kippeen (cipín)*, a rod or twig; *boreen (bóithrín)*, a lane; *bodach*, a clown; *soorawn (suarán)*, vertigo. *Avic* (a Mhic) = my son, or rather, Oh, son. Mic is the vocative of Mac.

THE HAUNTED CELLAR

Thomas Crofton Croker

There are few people who have not heard of the Mac Carthies—one of the real old Irish families, with the true Milesian blood running in their veins as thick as buttermilk. Many were the clans of this family in the south; as the Mac Carthymore—and the Mac Carthy-reagh—and the Mac Carthy of Muskerry; and all of them were noted for their hospitality to strangers, gentle and simple.

But not one of that name, or of any other, exceeded Justin Mac Carthy, of Ballinacarthy, at putting plenty to eat and drink upon his table; and there was a right hearty welcome for every one who should share it with him. Many a wine-cellar would be ashamed of the name if that at Ballinacarthy was the proper pattern for one. Large as that cellar was, it was crowded with bins of wine, and long rows of pipes, and hogsheads, and casks, that it would take more time to count than any sober man could spare in such a place, with plenty to drink about him, and a hearty welcome to do so.

There are many, no doubt, who will think that the butler would have little to complain of in such a house; and the whole country round would have agreed with them, if a man could be found to remain as Mr Mac Carthy's butler for any length of time worth speaking of; yet not one who had been in his service gave him a bad word.

'We have no fault,' they would say, 'to find with the master, and if he could but get any one to fetch his wine from the cellar, we might every one of us have grown gray in the house and have lived quiet and contented enough in his service until the end of our days.'

''Tis a queer thing that, surely,' thought young Jack Leary, a lad who had been brought up from a mere child in the stables of Ballinacarthy to assist in taking care of the horses, and had occasionally lent a hand in the butler's pantry:—''Tis a mighty queer thing, surely, that one man after another cannot content himself with the best place in the house of a good master, but that every one of them must quit, all through the means, as they say, of the wine-cellar. If the master, long life to him! would but make me his butler, I warrant never the word more would be heard of grumbling at his bidding to go to the wine-cellar.'

Young Leary, accordingly watched for what he conceived to be a favourable opportunity of presenting himself to the notice of his master.

A few mornings after, Mr Mac Carthy went into his stable-yard rather earlier than usual, and called loudly for the groom to saddle his horse, as he intended going out with the hounds. But there was no groom to answer, and young Jack Leary led Rainbow out of the stable.

'Where is William?' inquired Mr Mac Carthy.

'Sir?' said Jack; and Mr Mac Carthy repeated the question.

'Is it William, please your honour?' returned Jack; 'why, then, to tell the truth, he had just *one* drop too much last night.'

'Where did he get it?' said Mr Mac Carthy; 'for since Thomas went away the key of the wine-cellar has been in my pocket, and I have been obliged to fetch what was drunk myself.'

'Sorrow a know I know,' said Leary, 'unless the cook might have give him the *least taste* in life of whiskey. But,' continued he, performing a low bow by seizing with his right hand a lock of hair, and pulling down his head by it, whilst his left leg, which had been put forward, was scraped back against the ground, 'may I make so bold as just to ask your honour one question?'

'Speak out, Jack,' said Mr Mac Carthy.

'Why, then, does your honour want a butler?'

'Can you recommend me one,' returned his master, with the smile of good-humour upon his countenance, 'and one who will not be afraid of going to my wine-cellar?'

'Is the wine-cellar all the matter?' said young Leary; 'devil a doubt I have of myself then for that.'

'So you mean to offer me your services in the capacity of butler?' said Mr Mac Carthy, with some surprise.

'Exactly so,' answered Leary, now for the first time looking up from the ground.

'Well, I believe you to be a good lad, and have no objection to give you a trial.'

'Long may your honour reign over us, and the Lord spare you to us!' ejaculated Leary, with another national bow, as his master rode off; and he continued for some time to gaze after him with a vacant stare, which slowly and gradually assumed a look of importance.

'Jack Leary,' said he, at length, 'Jack—is it Jack?' in a tone of wonder; 'faith, 'tis not Jack now, but Mr John, the butler;' and with an air of becoming consequence he strided out of the stable-yard towards the kitchen.

It is of little purport to my story, although it may afford an instructive lesson to the reader, to depict the sudden transition of nobody into somebody. Jack's former stable companion, a poor superannuated hound named Bran, who had been accustomed to receive many an affectionate pat on the head, was spurned from him with a kick and an 'Out of the way, sirrah.' Indeed, poor Jack's memory seemed sadly affected by this sudden change of situation. What established the point beyond all doubt was his almost forgetting the pretty face of Peggy, the kitchen wench, whose heart he had assailed but the preceding week by the offer of purchasing a gold ring for the fourth finger of her right hand, and a lusty imprint of good-will upon her lips.

When Mr Mac Carthy returned from hunting, he sent for Jack Leary—so he still continued to call his new butler. 'Jack,' said he, 'I believe you are a trustworthy lad, and here are the keys of my cellar. I have asked the gentlemen with whom I hunted today to dine with me, and I hope they may be satisfied at the way in which you will wait on them at table; but, above all, let there be no want of wine after dinner.'

Mr John having a tolerably quick eye for such things, and being naturally a handy lad, spread his cloth accordingly, laid his plates and knives and forks in the same manner he had seen his predecessors in office perform these mysteries, and really, for the first time, got through attendance on dinner very well.

It must not be forgotten, however, that it was at the house of an Irish country squire, who was entertaining a company of booted and spurred fox-hunters, not very particular about what are considered matters of infinite importance under other circumstances and in other societies.

For instance, few of Mr Mac Carthy's guests (though all excellent and worthy men in their way) cared much whether the punch produced after soup was made of Jamaica or Antigua rum; some even would not have been inclined to question the correctness of good old Irish whiskey; and, with the exception of their liberal host himself, every one in company preferred the port which Mr Mac Carthy put on his table to the less ardent flavour of claret—a choice rather at variance with modern sentiment.

It was waxing near midnight, when Mr Mac Carthy rung the bell three times. This was a signal for more wine; and Jack proceeded to the cellar to procure a fresh supply, but it must be confessed not without some little hesitation.

The luxury of ice was then unknown in the south of Ireland; but the superiority of cool wine had been acknowledged by all men of sound judgment and true taste.

The grandfather of Mr Mac Carthy, who had built the mansion of Ballinacarthy upon the site of an old castle which had belonged to his ancestors, was fully aware of this important fact; and in the construction of his magnificent wine-cellar had availed himself of a deep vault, excavated out of the solid rock in former times as a place of retreat and security. The descent to this vault was by a flight of steep stone stairs, and here and there in the wall were narrow passages —I ought rather to call them crevices; and also certain projections, which cast deep shadows, and looked very frightful when any one went down the cellar-stairs with a single light: indeed, two lights did not much improve the matter, for though the breadth of the shadows became less, the narrow crevices remained as dark and darker than ever.

Summoning up all his resolution, down went the new butler, bearing in his right hand a lantern and the key of the cellar, and in his left a basket, which he considered sufficiently capacious to contain an adequate stock for the remainder of the evening: he arrived at the door without any interruption whatever; but when he put the key, which was of an ancient and clumsy kind—for it was before the days of Bramah's patent—and turned it in the lock, he thought he heard a strange kind of laughing within the cellar, to which some empty bottles that stood upon the floor outside vibrated so violently that they struck against each other: in this he could not be mistaken, although he may have been deceived in the laugh, for the bottles were just at his feet, and he saw them in motion.

Leary paused for a moment, and looked about him with becoming caution. He then boldly seized the handle of the key, and turned it with all his strength in the lock, as if he doubted his own power of doing so; and the door flew open with a most tremendous crash, that if the house had not been built upon the solid rock would have shook it from the foundation.

To recount what the poor fellow saw would be impossible, for he seems not to have known very clearly himself: but what he told the cook next morning was, that he heard a roaring and bellowing like a mad bull, and that all the pipes

and hogsheads and casks in the cellar went rocking backwards and forwards with so much force that he thought every
one would have been staved in, and that he should have
been drowned or smothered in wine.

When Leary recovered, he made his way back as well as
he could to the dining-room, where he found his master and
the company very impatient for his return.

'What kept you?' said Mr Mac Carthy in an angry voice;
'and where is the wine? I rung for it half an hour since.'

'The wine is in the cellar, I hope, sir,' said Jack, trembling
violently; 'I hope 'tis not all lost.'

'What do you mean, fool?' exclaimed Mr Mac Carthy in
a still more angry tone: 'why did you not fetch some with
you?'

Jack looked wildly about him, and only uttered a deep
groan.

'Gentlemen,' said Mr Mac Carthy to his guests, 'this is too
much. When I next see you to dinner, I hope it will be in
another house, for it is impossible I can remain longer in
this, where a man has no command over his own wine-cellar,
and cannot get a butler to do his duty. I have long thought
of moving from Ballinacarthy; and I am now determined,
with the blessing of God, to leave it tomorrow. But wine
shall you have were I to go myself to the cellar for it.' So
saying, he rose from table, took the key and lantern from
his half-stupified servant, who regarded him with a look of
vacancy, and descended the narrow stairs, already
described, which led to his cellar.

When he arrived at the door, which he found open, he
thought he heard a noise, as if of rats or mice scrambling
over the casks, and on advancing perceived a little figure,
about six inches in height, seated astride upon the pipe of
the oldest port in the place, and bearing a spigot upon his
shoulder. Raising the lantern, Mr Mac Carthy contemplated
the little fellow with wonder: he wore a red night-cap on his
head; before him was a short leather apron, which now, from
his attitude, fell rather on one side; and he had stockings of

a light blue colour, so long as nearly to cover the entire of
his leg; with shoes, having huge silver buckles in them, and
with high heels (perhaps out of vanity to make him appear
taller). His face was like a withered winter apple; and his
nose, which was of a bright crimson colour, about the tip
wore a delicate purple bloom, like that of a plum; yet his
eyes twinkled

> 'like those mites
> Of candied dew in money nights—'

and his mouth twitched up at one side with an arch grin.

'Ha, scoundrel!' exclaimed Mr Mac Carthy, 'have I found
you at last? disturber of my cellar—what are you doing
there?'

'Sure, and master,' returned the little fellow, looking up
at him with one eye, and with the other throwing a sly glance
towards the spigot on his shoulder, 'a'n't we going to move
tomorrow? and sure you would not leave your own little
Cluricaune Naggeneen behind you?'

'Oh!' thought Mr Mac Carthy, 'if you are to follow me,
master Naggeneen, I don't see much use in quitting Ballinacarthy.' So filling with wine the basket which young Leary
in his fright had left behind him, and locking the cellar door,
he rejoined his guests.

For some years after Mr Mac Carthy had always to fetch
the wine for his table himself, as the little Cluricaune Naggeneen seemed to feel a personal respect towards him. Notwithstanding the labour of these journeys, the worthy lord
of Ballinacarthy lived in his paternal mansion to a good
round age, and was famous to the last for the excellence of
his wine, and the conviviality of his company; but at the time
of his death, that same conviviality had nearly emptied his
wine-cellar; and as it was never so well filled again, nor so
often visited, the revels of master Naggeneen became less
celebrated, and are now only spoken of amongst the legendary lore of the country. It is even said that the poor little

fellow took the declension of the cellar so to heart, that he became negligent and careless of himself, and that he has been sometimes seen going about with hardly a *skreed* to cover him.

THE GOLLAN

A. E. Coppard

There was once a peasant named Goose who had worked
his back crooked with never a Thank-ye from Providence or
Man, and he had a son, Gosling, whom the neighbours called
The Gollan for short. The Gollan was an obedient child and
strong, though not by nature very willing. He was so obedient that he would do without question whatever anybody
told him to do. One day he was bringing his mother three
eggs in a basket and he met a rude boy.

'Hoi,' called the rude boy, 'are those eggs the bouncing
eggs?'

'Are they?' enquired The Gollan.

'Try one and see,' the rude boy said.

The Gollan took one of the eggs from the basket and
dropped it to the ground, and it broke.

'Haw!' complained the rude one, 'you did not do it properly. How could an egg bounce if you dropped it so? You
must throw it hard and it will fly back into your hand like a
bird.'

So The Gollan took another and dashed it to the ground
and waited. But the egg only lay spilt at his feet.

'No, no, no! Stupid fellow!' the rude boy cried. 'Look.
Throw the other one up in the air as high as you can and all
three will bounce back into your basket.'

So The Gollan threw the last egg up on high, but it only
dropped beside the others and all lay in a slop of ruins.

'Oh dear! What will my mother say? Oh dear!' wept The
Gollan.

256

The rude boy merely put his thumb to his nose and ran off upon his proper business, laughing.

The Gollan grew up a great powerful fellow, and whatever anyone told him to do, it might be simple, it might be hard, he did it without repining, which shows that he had a kind heart anyway, though he had little enough inclination to work; indeed he had no wish to at all.

One day his father said to him: 'My son, you are full of strength and vigour, you are the prop of my old age and the apple of my two eyes. Take now these five and twenty pigs and go you to market and dispose of them. Beware of false dealing, and you may hear wonders.'

'What wonders should I hear?'

'Mum,' said his father, 'is the word. Say nothing and scare nobody.'

He gave him two noggins of ale and off went The Gollan. And it was a queer half and half day, however, but full of colour. There were poppies in the green corn, charlock in the swedes, and weak sunlight in the opaline sky. He tried to drive the pigs but they had their minds set upon some other matters and would not go where they should because of distractions and interruptions. There was the green corn, there were the swedes, and there were heifers in the lane, lambs afield, and hens in every hedge, so before he had gone a mile the pigs were all astray.

'I don't care where those pigs go,' then said The Gollan to himself. 'I don't trouble about those pigs as long as I have my strength and vigour.' So he lay down under a nut hazel-bush and was soon sleeping.

In the course of time—long or short makes no odds—he heard someone whistling shrilly, and waking up he looked about him to the right hand and to the left and soon saw a person caught hard and fast in a catchpole, a little plump man with a red beard and bright buckled shoes.

'Well met, friend!' the little man called out. 'Pray release me from this trap and I will make your fortune.'

So The Gollan went and put out all his strength and

vigour, with a heave and a hawk and a crash, until he had drawn the little plump man out of the trap and set him free.

'Thanks, friend,' said the leprechaun—for he was that and no less, not like any man you ever read about. 'You have done me a kind service. Ask any reward you will and I will give it.'

'Sir,' said the Gollan, 'there is no matter about that. I am the prop of my father's age and the apple of his two eyes. I have strength and vigour with which I work for what I need.'

'Unhappy is that man,' the leprechaun answered, 'who serves his need and not his choice. You have strength and vigour, but how do you use it?'

The Gollan drew himself up proudly: 'I can crack rocks and hew trees.'

'Well, then,' replied the other, 'crack on, and hew.'

'Alas,' The Gollan explained, 'I have four fingers and a thumb on one hand, four fingers and a thumb on the other, all of them able—but not one of them willing.' And he confided to the leprechaun that it was his doom and distress to be at the beck and call of everyone because of his strength and vigour, and he with no heart to refuse to do a deed required of him.

'That cannot be endured. I can easily remedy it,' said the leprechaun. 'I will make you invisible to mankind, except only when you are asleep. Nobody will be able to see you when you are awake and walking, therefore they will not be able to give you a task of any kind.'

So he made The Gollan invisible there and then, and no one saw The Gollan any more, save his parents when he was sleeping, and his life became a bed of roses and a bower of bliss. Where is The Gollan?—people would say. But though they knew he was thereabout they could not set eyes on him and they could not find him. If The Gollan were only with us—they would say—he would do this tiresome labour, he would do it well. But as he was no longer visible to them they could not catch him and they could not ask him. The Gollan would be about in the sunlight day after day doing

nothing at all, and got so blown up with pride that he
thought:

'I am invisible, no one can task me in my strength and
vigour. I am king of all the unseen world, and that is as good
as twenty of these other kings. I live as I choose, and I take
my need as I want it.'

But though it was all very grand to be invisible The Gollan
soon found out that there was small blessing on it. He could
be seen by none save when he slept, but the truth is neither
could *he* see anybody—man, woman, or child. No one could
hear *him*, but then he himself could hear no one—man,
woman, or child. It was the same way with smelling, touching and tasting. Animals and birds he could see, and he
could talk to them, but they were so hard of understanding
that he might as well have conversed with a monument or a
door. Sure, he had kept his wits but he had lost his five
senses, and that is cruel fortune.

After a while his heart grew weary for the sight of his
friends and the talk and sounds of people, he was tired of
seeing animals and birds only, so he went to a hawk he knew
that had the most piercing gaze, and said:

'Friend, lend me your two eyes for a while and I will pawn
you my own for their safe return.'

'Will I? Will I?' mused the hawk.

'You will!' The Gollan sternly said.

So they exchanged, but The Gollan was greatly deceived
by these hawk eyes. He went about wearing them far and
near, and he saw thousands of mice and birds and moles,
but those eyes never set their gaze on a single human creature, good, bad, or medium. What was worse, rascally
things, they never seemed to want to! The farther he wandered the more sure it became that those eyes were merely
looking out for moles and voles and such like. He saw nothing else except a jackass with fine upstanding ears straying
in a bethistled waste whom he accosted:

'Friend, lend me your two ears for a while. I will pawn
you my own for their safe return.'

'Will you? Won't you?' mused the ass.

'I will,' declared The Gollan, for he longed to hear human speech again, or a song to cheer him.

So they exchanged. But The Gollan was more deceived and bewildered than ever, for he never caught the sound of any pleasant human talk. What he heard was only an ass's bald portion, vile oaths, denunciations, and abuse. And although it all rushed into one ear and quickly fell out of the other it was not good hearing at all; it was not satisfactory. When he heard a pig grunting not far off he hastened to the pig, saying:

'Friend, lend me your nose. I will pawn you mine for its safe return.'

'Ask me no more,' said the pig, surveying him with a rueful smile as he suffered The Gollan to make the exchange.

But something kept The Gollan from smelling anything save what a pig may smell. Instead of flowers, the odour of fruit, or the cook's oven, the swinish nostrils delighted only in the vapours of swill and offal and ordure. Surely—thought The Gollan—it is better to be invisible and senseless than to live thus. So he tried no further, but gave back the eyes, the ears, and the nose and received his pledges again.

Now at that time the king of the land was much put about by the reason of a little pond that lay in front of his palace. It was a meagre patch of water and no ways good.

'If only this were a lake,' sighed the king, 'a great lake of blue water with neat waves and my ships upon it and my swans roving and my snipe calling and my fish going to and fro, my realm would be a great realm and the envy of the whole world.'

And one day, as he was wandering and wondering what he could do about this, he came upon The Gollan lying on a green bank drowsing and dreaming. Of course when the king set eyes on him he saw him and knew him.

'Hoi, Gollan!' the king roared at him. 'Stretch out that

water for me!' Just like that. The Gollan woke up and at once became invisible again, but he was so startled at being roared at that without thinking, just absent-mindedly, he stretched out the water of the king's pond and there and then it became a fine large lake with neat waves and ships and swans and such like, beautiful—though when he learned the right of it The Gollan was crabby and vexed, 'I am the king of the unseen world, and that's as good as any twenty of these other kings.' Still, he could not alter it back again. Whatever he did had to stay as it was once done: it could neither be changed nor improved.

However, by the reason of his fine new lake and ships the king's realm became the envy of all other nations, who began to strive after it and attack it. The king was not much of a one for martial dispositions and so the whole of his country was soon beleaguered and the people put to miserable extravagances.

Now although The Gollan could not directly see or hear anything of this, yet one way and another he came to know something of the misfortune, and then he was worn to a tatter with rage and fury by the reason he was such a great one for the patriotism. And he was powerless to help now his five senses were gone from him.

'O, what sort of a game is this,' he thought, 'now the world is in ruins and I have no more senses than a ghost or a stone! I had the heart of an ass when I took that red-haired villain out of his trap and had his reward. Reward! Take it back! Take it back, you palavering old crow of a catchpole! You have cramped me tight and hauled me to a grave. Take it back, you!'

'Well met, friend,' a voice replied, and there was the old leprechaun bowing before him. 'Your wish is granted.'

True it was. They were standing beside a field of corn ripe and ready, waving and sighing it was. The Gollan could hear once more, he could touch taste and smell again, and he could see his own royal king as clear as print on a page of history hurrying down the road towards them.

'What else can I do for you?' asked the little red-haired man.

'I fancy,' said The Gollan, jerking his thumb towards the king, 'he is running to ask me for a large great army.'

'You shall have that,' said the leprechaun, vanishing away at the king's approach.

'Gollan,' the king says, 'I want a large great army.'

'Yes, Sir,' says The Gollan. 'Will you have the grenadiers, the bombardiers, or men of the broad-sword?'

He said he would have the bombardiers.

Well, The Gollan made a pass of his hand over that field of corn, and the standing stalks at once began to whistle and sway sideways. Before you could blink a lash there they were, 50,000 men and noble men, all marking time, all dressed to glory with great helmets and eager for battle.

'Gollan,' says the king, 'will you undertake the command of this my noble army?'

'I will that, Sir.'

'Lead on, then,' says the king, 'and may the blood of calamity never splash upon one single rib of the whole lot of you.'

Which, it is good to say, it never did. The Gollan then marched them straightway to battle by the shore of the lake.

'Get ready now,' cried General Gollan, 'here comes the artill-airy with their big guns!'

The bombardiers began to prepare themselves and first gave a blast on their trumpets, but the enemy got ready sooner and fired off a blast on all their culverins, mortars, and whatnot. Ah, what a roar they let out of that huge and fatal cannonade! It would have frightened the trunk of a tree out of its own bark, and at the mere sound of it every man of General Gollan's army toppled to the earth like corn that is cut, never to rise again.

'What is it and all!' cried the distracted Gollan. 'Is this another joke of that palavering old crow of a catchpole? By the soul of my aunty!' he exclaimed, as he surveyed his exposed position amid all those fallen bombardiers, so neat, so gallant, so untimely dead, 'By the soul of my aunty I think I'd rather be invisible now!'

In a twink he *was* invisible once more, and his five senses gone again; but none of his friends ever had time to enquire what became of him because the conquering general painfully exterminated them all.

Unseen, unknown, the good Gollan lived on for many years in great privation, and when he at last came to die (though nobody knew even about that) he had grown mercifully wise and wrote his own epitaph—though nobody ever saw it:

To choose was my need, but need brooks no choosing.

THE CROCK OF GOLD

Lord Dunsany

I remember one day at the Billiards Club, when someone was mentioned who had been made an FRSW, and Jorkens was there. 'Oddly enough,' he said, 'I might once have been an FRSW myself, if I could have afforded it.'

'You don't become a Fellow of the Royal Society of Wise-acres for cash,' said one of us.

'I didn't say you did,' said Jorkens. 'But, if I could have afforded to have gone for it instead of going for cash, I should have had a pretty good chance of being elected. Why! A man was made a Fellow the other day, who had only discovered a new species of zebra. I had a much more curious specimen of zoology to tell them about, if I hadn't gone wandering after the cash instead. I had an opportunity for study that rarely occurs.'

'And why didn't you take it?' said Terbut.

'Because it was an opportunity,' said Jorkens. 'Does one ever take them?'

Somehow Terbut was not ready with any answer. So Jorkens continued awhile without more interruption. 'It was like this,' he said; 'in Ireland once; in Munster, near to a bog. I didn't think much of crocks of gold where rainbows end; but once when I saw one blazing upon the ground, turning the grass to an intenser green than anything you can imagine, and a hedge beyond it into purple and pink, and a leprechaun actually sitting in the middle of the patch where it touched the grass, then I could hardly doubt that there must be something in it, and that that was where he had buried his crock of gold.'

'A leprechaun,' exclaimed Terbut. 'What was it like?'

'That's what I should have studied more carefully,' said Jorkens. 'But I went instead for the crock of gold.'

'You did, did you?' said Terbut.

'I did,' said Jorkens. 'I said "Good morning" to the leprechaun. And he said "Good morning" rather sulkily. "I suppose you've buried your crock of gold there," I said.

'"It's no use denying it," said he. "But neither you nor anyone would ever find my crocks of gold if it wasn't for that damned rainbow that is always giving them away."

'"Well, I've found it," I said. "And, if the rainbow guided me here, it meant me to have it. And have it I will," I said.

'"You will not," said he.

'"I'm a bigger man than you," I said, "and finding's keeping where crocks of gold are concerned."

'For that is the custom of the country, and nobody calls it robbery to take his gold from a leprechaun. He counts no more than a political opponent. A leprechaun is mere game.

'"I'm off to get a spade," I said, "from the nearest cottage; and I'll mark the spot with something you can't pull up."

'For I'd stuck my stick in the ground and saw him eyeing it, and I took a bearing on a couple of trees with a compass I had on my watch-chain and jotted it down on paper.

'"You'll not pull up that," I said.

'But he knew nothing about compasses.

'And then he said, "And do you know what will happen if you dig up my crock of gold?"

'"I'll have some cash to spare," I said. "That's what will happen. And it hasn't happened for a very long time."

'"You will not," he said, "and I warn you. For if you start digging for that crock of gold, the crock and the rainbow and I, and the spade itself, will all turn into dreams."

'"Dreams be damned!" I said. "I'm going to get the crock."

'"It's only two foot down," said the leprechaun; "but it will be all a dream when you get it, crock and spade and rainbow and I myself."

'"Well," I said, "that's the kind of dream I like, and I'm going to get the spade."

'There was a little white-walled cottage beyond the rainbow, with an old brown thatch on it, nearly black in the hollows, except where a patch or two of pale-green oats were growing. And I went to the door and peered in over the upper half of it, which was open, and saw a man with a long thin beard, and asked him if he would be so good as to lend me a spade. Well, of course it was an odd request, and he looked a little doubtful, and I thought it was best to tell him the truth, for he would understand a thing like that. "There are rainbows about," I said, "and I'm going to dig for a crock of gold, and I'll give you one handful if you'll lend me the spade." Of course there was no danger of his going and getting the gold himself, because the end of the rainbow looked all different from where he was, and he hadn't seen the leprechaun. He was very obliging and lent me the spade, and thanked me for the offer of the handful. I might have got him to lend the spade for less, but I was in a hurry, for fear that the leprechaun should start to dig and try to remove his gold.

'"Many's the time," the old fellow said, "that I dug for them when I was young." And then he added kindly, "Maybe you'll find it." And away I went with the spade.

'The leprechaun was still there when I got back. He hadn't had time to dig up his gold and take it away, so he had not tried. "I warned you," he said. But I began to dig. I don't know if any of you have made money in shorter time, but I got down through two feet of that soft soil in little over five minutes. And there was the crock of gold, a pale-brown earthern crock with the top open, and the gold shining inside. Then for the first time I sat down to rest. Five minutes steady digging may not seem much, and isn't much to anyone that is accustomed to it. To anyone quite unaccustomed I've known it bring on lumbago that would drop a man in a heap. It didn't do that to me, but I was glad of a moment's rest; and so I sat down with my feet in the hole I had dug, one on each side of the neck of the crock of gold, and the rainbow glittering in my face. The little golden discs were shining between my feet, and I looked up at the leprechaun. "Well, there it is," I said. And all of a sudden I saw him beginning to fade. I couldn't believe it possible. I looked beyond him, and the rainbow was fading too! That startled me, and I looked hurriedly back at the crock. And that also was fading! Back I looked at the leprechaun, and he was nearly gone. "What did I tell you?" he cried out shrilly, and wholly disappeared. And then the crock went, and the rainbow, and the hole I had dug, and, even as he had said, the spade in my hand.

'All this while the echo of his last remark was floating over the fields, going down to the heather, and was taken up by a curlew that was flying over the bog. And the thought came to me, How on earth was I to explain to the man from whom I had borrowed the spade? Well, there was no sign left of crock, hole, rainbow or leprechaun, and so there was nothing to wait for, and I hurried back to the old white cottage to apologise and explain. And there was the man with the long, thin beard, indoors where I saw him last, and I leaned in through the door and began at once to apologise. "Ah, sure I never lent you a spade," he said, in those very words. I tried once more, but he still stuck to his point. And then I saw that the spade had gone with the crock so utterly into dreamland, that in this earth it had no existence, either at that time or ever. You see what I mean?'

At first it was not clear to me, or indeed to any of us. No one spoke, except to the waiter; and soon a scene unusual at the Billiards Club might have been observed, a group of members round Jorkens, each with a whiskey-and-soda, while Jorkens had none. With a moment or two for refreshment, and one or two for reflection, it soon became clear enough, and I think we saw what he meant.

5

DEVILRY

The Devil's role in Irish supernatural lore is as important as those of ghosts, faeries and leprechauns—although it is typical of the country and its people that he should be seen not entirely as a figure of evil and damnation. Writing in an excellent book, *Speak of the Devil* (1945), C. B. Boutell maintained, 'In the land of leprechauns and little people, the Devil easily passes as a logical and three-dimensional fellow and not in the least a figment of the imagination.' Another writer, the American folklorist Sterling North, wrote in the same book, 'St Patrick may have driven the snakes out of Ireland, but "The Old Serpent" in several of his Protean changes has been back for a nip of John Jameson on several occasions. In Ireland he speaks with a brogue as soft and easy as peat smoke on a misty morning, attends the Irish sweepstakes, and often confers with Oliver St John Gogarty.'

This section is a mixture of stories about devilry—one of them an excellent thriller, the remainder containing elements of the supernatural and even some macabre humour, but all illustrating the uniquely Irish approach to the figure of 'Old Nick'. It begins, appropriately, with a story featuring probably the oldest theme in this context: a pact between the Devil and a human being, with the man's soul as the price for great power and wealth. The story-teller is William Carleton (1794–1869) whose intimate knowledge of Irish peasant life—he was the youngest of 14 children of an impoverished County Tyrone farmer—has led John Wilson

Foster, in *Fictions of the Irish Literary Revival* (1987), to call him a 'natural, inventive and untutored genius' and the most significant figure in the nineteenth-century Irish folk-lore tradition. Carleton gleaned his knowledge of folklore from listening to the local story-tellers, and his ability to record their tales on paper came from rudimentary schooling at a couple of the 'hedge schools' which were then the only means of education available to the children of rural Ireland. As he was to say years later in his autobiography, 'My native place is a spot rife with old legends, tales, traditions, customs and superstitions, so that in my early youth they met me in every direction.'

After serving briefly as a member of a secret society, the Ribbonmen, fighting oppressive landlords, Carleton forsook his Catholic upbringing to become a Protestant and took up teaching in Dublin. He supplemented his meagre income by contributing sketches on rural life to the *Christian Examiner*, under his family name of Uilliam O Cearbhallain, and these were gathered together in 1830 to form the first volume of *Traits and Stories of the Irish Peasantry*. Further equally successful series followed, as well as novels like *The Evil Eye* (1850) and short stories which were all drawn from the supernatural lore he had gathered in Country Tyrone. 'The Three Wishes' perhaps most clearly demonstrates his talent, as well as presenting a classic story of the attempt by a plausible rogue to outwit the Devil.

Donn Byrne (1889–1928), the Irish-American author of 'Tale of the Piper', was a flamboyant character whose fiction expressed the wanderlust which had driven him round the world during his early life, through Europe, South America (where he was a cowhand) and America (where he worked as a garage hand in New York), before he began to pursue a literary career. Byrne, whose real name was Brian Oswald Donn-Byrne, grew up in Dublin and published his first stories in a number of the small magazines that flourished in the city around the turn of the century. He made his name with two novels, *Messer Marco Polo* (1921) and *Hangman's*

House (1926), which drew on his twin interests, travel and the supernatural, and these were followed by a number of outstanding short stories. 'Tale of the Piper', the story of a skilful, mysterious piper who comes to the village of Destiny but is quite unable to play any religious music when requested, was listed by the *Daily Express* in 1935 as 'one of the best thrillers of the century'.

Although John Millington Synge (1871–1909) has become widely associated with the Aran islands as a result of his great study of them, published in 1907, and several of his plays which were set there, he was in fact born near Dublin, and spent several years living in Paris before being encouraged by W. B. Yeats to visit the islands. There he settled amongst the people whose primitive ways and ancient traditions provided the material for the plays which made him famous: *In the Shadow of the Glen* (1903), *Riders to the Sea* (1904), *The Wells of the Saints* (1905) and the humorous masterpiece, *The Playboy of the Western World* (1907). The success of these plays at the Abbey Theatre—of which Synge was appointed a director in 1904—had a profound influence on the next generation of Irish playwrights.

Synge's enthusiasm for the supernatural can be traced back to his childhood, when he is said to have investigated a reputedly haunted redbrick Georgian house not far from his own home in the Rathmines district. It was his friendship with the mystic Yeats, however, and his time on the Aran islands, that really fired his interest, for as he wrote later, 'On these islands miracles enough happen every year to equip a divine emissary. Rye is turned into oats, storms are raised to keep evictors from the shore, cows that are isolated on lonely rocks bring forth calves, and other things of the same kind are common.' His story 'The Devil of a Rider' is not set on Aran, but its mixture of horse racing, gambling and not a little Irish superstition makes it linger in the mind long after it has been read.

Although it is now more than fifty years since James Joyce died, his fame is, if anything, greater than ever and his five major contributions to literature are all in print in many languages. Like Synge, Joyce (1882–1941) was born in the Rathmines district and knew all about its haunted house. There is also more than a hint in his novel *Ulysses* (1922) and in his collection of short stories, *Dubliners* (1914), of his interest in the supernatural.

In his writing Joyce, the man who once trained for a concert-platform career, used the techniques of musical composition to create a complex and individual form of fiction, but he was also a fine storyteller in the tradition of the Irish *seanchai* from whom he sprang. 'The Devil and the Cat' is just such a tale as one of these men might have told and, despite the fact that it is set in the Paris, where Joyce lived for much of his life, it is infused with Irish supernaturalism and ends by asking the question that must have crossed the minds of millions of Irish men and women over the years: Is the Devil an Irishman?

THE THREE WISHES

William Carleton

In ancient times there lived a man called Billy Dawson, and he was known to be a great rogue. They say he was descended from the family of the Dawsons, which was the reason, I suppose, of his carrying their name upon him.

Billy, in his youthful days, was the best hand at doing nothing in all Europe; devil a mortal could come next or near him at idleness; and, in consequence of his great practice that way, you may be sure that if any man could make a fortune by it he would have done it.

Billy was the only son of his father, barring two daughters, but they have nothing to do with the story I'm telling you. Indeed it was kind father and grandfather for Billy to be handy at the knavery as well as at the idleness, for it was well known that not one of their blood ever did an honest act, except with a roguish intention. In short, they were altogether a *dacent* connection and a credit to the name. As for Billy, all the villainy of the family, both plain and ornamental, came down to him by way of legacy, for it so happened that the father, in spite of all his cleverness, had nothing but his roguery to *lave* him.

Billy, to do him justice, improved the fortune he got. Every day advanced him farther into dishonesty and poverty, until, at the long run, he was acknowledged on all hands to be the completest swindler and the poorest vagabond in the whole parish.

Billy's father, in his young days, had often been forced to acknowledge the inconvenience of not having a trade, in consequence of some nice point in law, called the 'Vagrant Act,' that sometimes troubled him. On this account he made up his mind to give Bill an occupation, and he accordingly bound him to a blacksmith; but whether Bill was to *live* or *die* by *forgery* was a puzzle to his father—though the neighbors said that *both* was most likely. At all events, he was put apprentice to a smith for seven years, and a hard card his master had to play in managing him. He took the proper method, however, for Bill was so lazy and roguish that it would vex a saint to keep him in order.

'Bill,' says his master to him one day that he had been sunning himself about the ditches, instead of minding his business, 'Bill, my boy, I'm vexed to the heart to see you in such a bad state of health. You're very ill with that complaint called an *all-overness*; however,' says he, 'I think I can cure you. Nothing will bring you about but three or four sound doses every day of a medicine called "the oil o' the hazel." Take the first dose now,' says he, and he immediately banged him with a hazel cudgel until Bill's bones ached for a week afterward.

'If you were my son,' said his master, 'I tell you that, as long as I could get a piece of advice growing convenient in the hedges, I'd have you a different youth from what you are. If working was a sin, Bill, not an innocenter boy ever broke bread than you would be. Good people's scarce, you think; but however that may be, I throw it out as a hint, that you must take your medicine till you're cured, whenever you happen to get unwell in the same way.'

From this out he kept Bill's nose to the grinding stone, and whenever his complaint returned he never failed to give him a hearty dose for his improvement.

In the course of time, however, Bill was his own man and his own master, but it would puzzle a saint to know whether the master or the man was the more precious youth in the eyes of the world.

He immediately married a wife, and devil a doubt of it, but if *he* kept *her* in whisky and sugar, *she* kept *him* in hot water. Bill drank and she drank; Bill fought and she fought; Bill was idle and she was idle; Bill whacked her and she whacked Bill. If Bill gave her one black eye, she gave him another, *just to keep herself in countenance*. Never was there a blessed pair so well met, and a beautiful sight it was to see them both at breakfast time, blinking at each other across the potato basket, Bill with his right eye black, and she with her left.

In short, they were the talk of the whole town; and to see Bill of a morning staggering home drunk, his shirt sleeves rolled up on his smutted arms, his breast open, and an old tattered leather apron, with one corner tucked up under his belt, singing one minute and fighting with his wife the next —she, reeling beside him with a discolored eye, as aforesaid, a dirty ragged cap on one side of her head, a pair of Bill's old slippers on her feet, a squalling child on her arm—now cuffing and dragging Bill, and again kissing and hugging him! Yes, it was a pleasant picture to see this loving pair in such a state!

This might do for a while, but it could not last. They were idle, drunken, and ill conducted; and it was not to be supposed that they would get a farthing candle on their words. They were, of course, *dhruv* to great straits; and faith, they soon found that their fighting and drinking and idleness made them the laughing sport of the neighbors; but neither brought food to their *childhre*, put a coat upon their backs, nor satisfied their landlord when he came to look for his own. Still, the never a one of Bill but was a funny fellow with strangers, though, as we said, the greatest rogue unhanged.

One day he was standing against his own anvil, completely in a brown study—being brought to his wit's end how to make out a breakfast for the family. The wife was scolding and cursing in the house, and the naked creatures of children squalling about her knees for food. Bill was fairly at an amplush, and knew not where or how to turn himself, when a poor, withered old beggar came into the forge, tottering on his staff. A long white beard fell from his chin, and he looked as thin and hungry that you might blow him, one would think, over the house. Bill at this moment had been brought to his senses by distress, and his heart had a touch of pity toward the old man, for, on looking at him a second time, he clearly saw starvation and sorrow in his face.

'God save you, honest man!' said Bill.

The old man gave a sigh, and raising himself with great pain on his staff, he looked at Bill in a very beseeching way.

'Musha, God save you kindly!' says he. 'Maybe you could give a poor, hungry, helpless ould man a mouthful of something to ait? You see yourself I'm not able to work; if I was, I'd scorn to be beholding to anyone.'

'Faith, honest man,' said Bill, 'if you knew who you're speaking to, you'd as soon ask a monkey for a churnstaff as me for either mate or money. There's not a blackguard in the three kingdoms so fairly on the *shaughran* as I am for both the one and the other. The wife within is sending the curses thick and heavy on me, and the *childhre's* playing the cat's melody to keep her in comfort. Take my word for it, poor man, if I had either mate or money I'd help you, for I know particularly well what it is to want them at the present speaking; an empty sack won't stand, neighbor.'

So far Bill told him truth. The good thought was in his heart, because he found himself on a footing with the beggar; and nothing brings down pride, or softens the heart, like feeling what it is to want.

'Why, you are in a worse state than I am,' said the old man; 'you have a family to provide for, and I have only myself to support.'

'You may kiss the book on that, my old worthy,' replied Bill; 'but come, what I can do for you I will; plant yourself up here beside the fire, and I'll give it a blast or two of my bellows that will warm the old blood in your body. It's a cold, miserable, snowy day, and a good heat will be of service.'

'Thank you kindly,' said the old man; 'I *am* cold, and a

warming at your fire will do me good, sure enough. Oh, but it *is* a bitter, bitter day; God bless it!'

He then sat down, and Bill blew a rousing blast that soon made the stranger edge back from the heat. In a short time he felt quite comfortable, and when the numbness was taken out of his joints, he buttoned himself up and prepared to depart.

'Now,' says he to Bill, 'you hadn't the food to give me, but *what you could you did*. Ask any three wishes you choose, and be they what they may, take my word for it, they shall be granted.'

Now, the truth is, that Bill, though he believed himself a great man in point of 'cuteness, wanted, after all, a full quarter of being square, for there is always a great difference between a wise man and a knave. Bill was so much of a rogue that he could not, for the blood of him, ask an honest wish, but stood scratching his head in a puzzle.

'Three wishes!' said he. 'Why, let me see—did you say *three?*'

'Ay,' replied the stranger, 'three wishes—that was what I said.'

'Well,' said Bill, 'here goes—aha!—let me alone, my old worthy!—faith I'll overreach the parish, if what you say is true. I'll cheat them in dozens, rich and poor, old and young; let me alone, man—I have it here,' and he tapped his forehead with great glee. 'Faith, you're the sort to meet of a frosty morning, when a man wants his breakfast; and I'm sorry that I have neither money nor credit to get a bottle of whisky, that we might take our *morning* together.'

'Well, but let us hear the wishes,' said the old man; 'my time is short, and I cannot stay much longer.'

'Do you see this sledge hammer?' said Bill. 'I wish, in the first place, that whoever takes it up in their hands may never be able to lay it down till I give them lave; and that whoever begins to sledge with it may never stop sledging till it's my pleasure to release him.

'Secondly—I have an armchair, and I wish that whoever

sits down in it may never rise out of it till they have my consent.

'And, thirdly—that whatever money I put into my purse, nobody may have power to take it out of it but myself!'

'You Devil's rip!' says the old man in a passion, shaking his staff across Bill's nose. 'Why did you not ask something that would sarve you both here and hereafter? Sure it's as common as the market cross, that there's not a vagabone in His Majesty's dominions stands more in need of both.'

'Oh! By the elevens,' said Bill, 'I forgot that altogether! Maybe you'd be civil enough to let me change one of them? The sorra purtier wish ever was made than I'll make, if only you'll give me another chance at it.'

'Get out, you reprobate,' said the old fellow, still in a passion. 'Your day of grace is past. Little you knew who was speaking to you all this time. I'm St Moroky, you black-guard, and I gave you an opportunity of doing something for yourself and your family; but you neglected it, and now your fate is cast, you dirty, bog-trotting profligate. Sure, it's well known what you are! Aren't you a byword in every-body's mouth, you and your scold of a wife? By this and by that, if ever you happen to come across me again, I'll send you to where you won't freeze, you villain!'

He then gave Bill a rap of his cudgel over the head and laid him at his length beside the bellows, kicked a broken coal scuttle out of his way, and left the forge in a fury.

When Billy recovered himself from the effects of the blow and began to think on what had happened, he could have quartered himself with vexation for not asking great wealth as one of the wishes at least; but now the die was cast on him, and he could only make the most of the three he pitched upon.

He now bethought him how he might turn them to the best account, and here his cunning came to his aid. He began by sending for his wealthiest neighbors on pretence of busi-ness, and when he got them under his roof he offered them

the armchair to sit down in. He now had them safe, nor
could all the art of man relieve them except worthy Bill was
willing. Bill's plan was to make the best bargain he could
before he released his prisoners; and let him alone for knowing how to make their purses bleed. There wasn't a wealthy
man in the country he did not fleece. The parson of the
parish bled heavily; so did the lawyer; and a rich attorney,
who had retired from practice, swore that the Court of Chancery itself was paradise compared to Bill's chair.

This was all very good for a time. The fame of his chair,
however, soon spread; so did that of his sledge. In a short
time neither man, woman, nor child would darken his door;
all avoided him and his fixtures as they would a spring gun
or mantrap. Bill, so long as he fleeced his neighbors, never
wrought a hand's turn; so that when his money was out he
found himself as badly off as ever. In addition to all this, his
character was fifty times worse than before, for it was the
general belief that he had dealings with the old boy. Nothing
now could exceed his misery, distress, and ill temper. The
wife and he and their children all fought among one another.
Everybody hated them, cursed them, and avoided them.
The people thought they were acquainted with more than
Christian people ought to know. This, of course, came to
Bill's ears, and it vexed him very much.

One day he was walking about the fields, thinking of how
he could raise the wind once more; the day was dark, and
he found himself, before he stopped, in the bottom of a
lonely glen covered by great bushes that grew on each side.
'Well,' thought he, when every other means of raising money
failed him, 'it's reported that I'm in league with the old boy,
and as it's a folly to have the name of the connection without
the profit, I'm ready to make a bargain with him any day—
so,' said he, raising his voice, 'Nick, you sinner, if you be
convanient and willing, why stand out here; show your best
leg—here's your man.'

The words were hardly out of his mouth when a dark,
sober-looking old gentleman, not unlike a lawyer, walked

up to him. Bill looked at the foot and saw the hoof. 'Morrow, Nick,' says Bill.

'Morrow, Bill,' says Nick. 'Well, Bill, what's the news?'

'Devil a much myself hears of late,' says Bill; 'is there anything *fresh* below?'

'I can't exactly say, Bill; I spend little of my time down now; the Tories are in office, and my hands are consequently too full of business here to pay much attention to anything else.'

'A fine place this, sir,' says Bill, 'to take a constitutional walk in; when I want an appetite I often come this way myself—hem! *High* feeding is very bad without exercise.'

'High feeding! Come, come, Bill, you know you didn't taste a morsel these four-and-twenty hours.'

'You know that's a bounce, Nick. I eat a breakfast this morning that would put a stone of flesh on you, if you only smelt at it.'

'No matter; this is not to the purpose. What's that you were muttering to yourself a while ago? If you want to come to the brunt, here I'm for you.'

'Nick,' said Bill, 'you're complate; you want nothing barring a pair of Brian O'Lynn's breeches.'

Bill, in fact, was bent on making his companion open the bargain, because he had often heard that, in that case, with proper care on his own part, he might defeat him in the long run. The other, however, was his match.

'What was the nature of Brian's garment?' inquired Nick.

'Why, you know the song,' said Bill:

> '*Brian O'Lynn had no breeches to wear,*
> *So he got a sheep's skin for to make him a pair;*
> *With the fleshy side out and the woolly side in,*
> *"They'll be pleasant and cool," says Brian O'Lynn.*

'A *cool* pare would sarve you, Nick.'

'You're mighty waggish today, Misther Dawson.'

'And good right I have,' said Bill; 'I'm a man snug and

well to do in the world; have lots of money, plenty of good eating and drinking, and what more need a man wish for?'

'True,' said the other; 'in the meantime it's rather odd that so respectable a man should not have six inches of unbroken cloth in his apparel. You're as naked a tatter-demalion as I ever laid my eyes on; in full dress for a party of scarecrows, William?'

'That's my own fancy, Nick; I don't work at my trade like a gentleman. This is my forge dress, you know.'

'Well, but what did you summon me here for?' said the other; 'you may as well speak out, I tell you, for, my good friend, unless *you* do, *I* shan't. Smell that.'

'I smell more than that,' said Bill; 'and by the way, I'll thank you to give me the windy side of you—curse all sulphur, I say. There, that's what I call an improvement in my condition. But as you *are* so stiff,' says Bill, 'why, the short and long of it is—that—ahem—you see I'm—tut—sure you know I have a thriving trade of my own, and that if I like I needn't be at a loss; but in the meantime I'm rather in a kind of a so—so—don't you *take?*'

And Bill winked knowingly, hoping to trick him into the first proposal.

'You must speak aboveboard, my friend,' says the other. 'I'm a man of few words, blunt and honest. If you have anything to say, be plain. Don't think I can be losing my time with such a pitiful rascal as you are.'

'Well,' says Bill. 'I want money, then, and am ready to come into terms. What have you to say to that, Nick?'

'Let me see—let me look at you,' says his companion, turning him about. 'Now, Bill, in the first place, are you not as finished a scarecrow as ever stood upon two legs?'

'I play second fiddle to you there again,' says Bill.

'There you stand, with the blackguards' coat of arms quartered under your eye, and—'

'Don't make little of *black*guards,' said Bill, 'nor spake disparagingly of *your own* crest.'

'Why, what would you bring, you brazen rascal, if you were fairly put up at auction?'

'Faith, I'd bring more bidders than you would,' said Bill, 'if you were to go off at auction tomorrow. I tell you they should bid *downward* to come to your value, Nicholas. We have no coin *small* enough to purchase you.'

'Well, no matter,' said Nick. 'If you are willing to be mine at the expiration of seven years, I will give you more money than ever the rascally breed of you was worth.'

'Done!' said Bill. 'But no disparagement to my family, in the meantime; so down with the hard cash, and don't be a *neger*.'

The money was accordingly paid down; but as nobody was present, except the giver and receiver, the amount of what Bill got was never known.

'Won't you give me a luck penny?' said the old gentleman.

'Tut,' said Billy, 'so prosperous an old fellow as you cannot want it; however, bad luck to you, with all my heart! and it's rubbing grease to a fat pig to say so. Be off now, or I'll commit suicide on you. Your absence is a cordial to most people, you infernal old profligate. You have injured my morals even for the short time you have been with me, for I don't find myself so virtuous as I was.'

'Is that your gratitude, Billy?'

'Is it gratitude *you* speak of, man? I wonder you don't blush when you name it. However, when you come again, if you bring a third eye in your head you will see what I mane, Nicholas, ahagur.'

The old gentleman, as Bill spoke, hopped across the ditch on his way to *Downing* Street, where of late 'tis thought he possesses much influence.

Bill now began by degrees to show off, but still wrought a little at his trade to blindfold the neighbors. In a very short time, however, he became a great man. So long indeed as he was a *poor* rascal, no decent person would speak to him; even the proud servingmen at the 'Big House' would turn up their noses at him. And he well deserved to be made little of by others, because he was mean enough to make little of himself. But when it was seen and known that he had oceans of money, it was wonderful to think, although he was *now* a greater blackguard than ever, how those who despised him before began to come round him and court his company. Bill, however, had neither sense nor spirit to make those sunshiny friends know their distance; not he—instead of that he was proud to be seen in decent company, and so long as the money lasted, it was 'hail fellow well met' between himself and every fair-faced *spunger* who had a horse under him, a decent coat to his back, and a good appetite to eat his dinners. With riches and all, Bill was the same man still; but, somehow or other, there is a great difference between a rich profligate and a poor one, and Bill found it so to his cost in *both* cases.

Before half the seven years was passed, Bill had his carriage and his equipages; was hand and glove with my Lord This, and my Lord That; kept hounds and hunters; was the first sportsman at the Curragh; patronised every boxing ruffian he could pick up; and betted night and day on cards, dice, and horses. Bill, in short, *should* be a blood, and except he did all this, he could not presume to mingle with the fashionable bloods of his time.

It's an old proverb, however, that 'what is got over the Devil's back is sure to go off under it,' and in Bill's case this proved true. In short, the old boy himself could not supply him with money so fast as he made it fly; it was 'come easy, go easy,' with Bill, and so sign was on it, before he came within two years of his time he found his purse empty.

And now came the value of his summer friends to be known. When it was discovered that the cash was no longer flush with him—that stud, and carriage, and hounds were going to the hammer—whish! off they went, friends, relations, pot companions, dinner eaters, black-legs, and all, like a flock of crows that had smelt gunpowder. Down Bill soon went, week after week and day after day, until at last he was obliged to put on the leather apron and take to the hammer again; and not only that, for as no experience could make him wise, he once more began his taproom brawls, his quarrels with Judy, and took to his 'high feeding' at the dry potatoes and salt. Now, too, came the cutting tongues of all who knew him, like razors upon him. Those that he scorned because they were poor and himself rich now paid him back his own with interest; and those that he had measured himself with, because they were rich, and who only countenanced him in consequence of his wealth, gave him the hardest word in their cheeks. The Devil mend him! He deserved it all, and more if he had got it.

Bill, however, who was a hardened sinner, never fretted himself down an ounce of flesh by what was said to him or of him. Not he; he cursed, and fought, and swore, and schemed away as usual, taking in everyone he could; and surely none could match him at villainy of all sorts and sizes.

At last the seven years became expired, and Bill was one morning sitting in his forge, sober and hungry, the wife cursing him, and the children squalling as before; he was thinking how he might defraud some honest neighbour out of a breakfast to stop their mouths and his own, too, when who walks in to him but old Nick to demand his bargain.

'Morrow, Bill!' says he with a sneer.

'The Devil welcome you!' says Bill. 'But you have a fresh memory.'

'A bargain's a bargain between two *honest* men, any day,' says Satan; 'when I speak of *honest* men, I mean *yourself* and *me*, Bill'; and he put his tongue in his cheek to make game of the unfortunate rogue he had come for.

'Nick, my worthy fellow,' said Bill, 'have bowels; you wouldn't do a shabby thing; you wouldn't disgrace your own character by putting more weight upon a falling man. You know what it is to get a *comedown* yourself, my worthy; so just keep your toe in your pump, and walk off with yourself somewhere else. A *cool* walk will sarve you better than my company, Nicholas.'

'Bill, it's no use in shirking,' said his friend; 'your

swindling tricks may enable you to cheat others, but you won't cheat *me*, I guess. You want nothing to make you perfect in your way but to travel; and travel you shall under my guidance, Billy. No, no—I'm not to be swindled, my good fellow. I have rather a—a—better opinion of myself, Mr D., than to think that you could outwit one Nicholas Clutie, Esq.—ahem!'

'You may sneer, you sinner,' replied Bill, 'but I tell you that I have outwitted men who could buy and sell you to your face. Despair, you villain, when I tell you that *no attorney* could stand before me.'

Satan's countenance got blank when he heard this; he wriggled and fidgeted about and appeared to be not quite comfortable.

'In that case, then,' says he, 'the sooner I *deceive* you the better; so turn out for the *Low Countries*.'

'Is it come to that in earnest?' said Bill. 'And are you going to act the rascal at the long run?'

''Pon honor, Bill.'

'Have patience, then, you sinner, till I finish this horse-shoe—it's the last of a set I'm finishing for one of your friend the attorney's horses. And here, Nick, I hate idleness; you know it's the mother of mischief; take this sledge hammer and give a dozen strokes or so, till I get it out of hands, and then here's with you, since it must be so.'

He then gave the bellows a puff that blew half a peck of dust in Club-foot's face, whipped out the red-hot iron, and set Satan sledging away for bare life.

'Faith,' says Bill to him, when the shoe was finished, 'it's a thousand pities ever the sledge should be out of your hand; the great *Parra Gow* was a child to you at sledging, you're such an able tyke. Now just exercise yourself till I bid the wife and childhre good-by, and then I'm off.'

Out went Bill, of course, without the slightest notion of coming back; no more than Nick had that he could not give up the sledging, and indeed neither could he, but was forced to work away as if he was sledging for a wager. This was just what Bill wanted. He was now compelled to sledge on until it was Bill's pleasure to release him; and so we leave him very industriously employed, while we look after the worthy who outwitted him.

In the meantime Bill broke cover and took to the country at large; wrought a little journey work wherever he could get it, and in this way went from one place to another, till, in the course of a month, he walked back very coolly into his own forge to see how things went on in his absence. There he found Satan in a rage, the perspiration pouring from him in torrents, hammering with might and main upon the naked anvil. Bill calmly leaned back against the wall, placed his hat upon the side of his head, put his hands into his breeches pockets, and began to whistle *Shaun Gow's* hornpipe. At length he says, in a very quiet and good-humored way:

'Morrow, Nick!'

'Oh!' says Nick, still hammering away. 'Oh! you double-distilled villain (hech!), may the most refined, ornamental (hech!) collection of curses that ever was gathered (hech!) into a single nosegay of ill fortune (hech!) shine in the buttonhole of your conscience (hech!) while your name is Bill Dawson! I denounce you (hech!) as a doublemilled villain, a finished, hot-pressed knave (hech!), in comparison of whom all the other knaves I ever knew (hech!), attorneys included, are honest men. I brand you (hech!) as the pearl of cheats, a tiptop take-in (hech!). I denounce you, I say again, for the villainous treatment (hech!) I have received at your hands in this most untoward (hech!) and unfortunate transaction between us; for (hech!) unfortunate, in every sense, is he that has anything to do with (hech!) such a prime and finished impostor.'

'You're very warm, Nicky,' says Bill; 'what puts you into a passion, you old sinner? Sure if it's your own will and pleasure to take exercise at my anvil, *I'm* not to be abused for it. Upon my credit, Nicky, you ought to blush for using such blackguard language, so unbecoming your grave character. You cannot say that it was I set you a-hammering at the empty anvil, you profligate.

'However, as you are so very industrious, I simply say it would be a thousand pities to take you from it. Nick, I love industry in my heart, and I always encourage it, so work away; it's not often you spend your time so creditably. I'm afraid if you weren't at that you'd be worse employed.'

'Bill, have bowels,' said the operative; 'you wouldn't go to lay more weight on a falling man, you know; you wouldn't disgrace your character by such a piece of iniquity as keeping an inoffensive gentleman advanced in years, at such an unbecoming and rascally job as this. Generosity's your top virtue, Bill; not but that you have many other excellent ones, as well as that, among which, as you say yourself, I reckon industry; but still it is in generosity you *shine*. Come, Bill, honor bright, and release me.'

'Name the terms, you profligate.'

'You're above terms, William; a generous fellow like you never thinks of terms.'

'Good-by, old gentleman!' said Bill very coolly. 'I'll drop in to see you once a month.'

'No, no, Bill, you infern—a—a—. You excellent, worthy, delightful fellow, not so fast; not so fast. Come, name your terms, you sland—My dear Bill, name your terms.'

'Seven years more.'

'I agree; but—'

'And the same supply of cash as before, down on the nail here.'

'Very good; very good. You're rather simple, Bill; rather soft, I must confess. Well, no matter. I shall yet turn the tab —a—hem! You are an exceedingly simple fellow, Bill; still there will come a day, my *dear* Bill—there will come—'

'Do you grumble, you vagrant? Another word, and I double the terms.'

'Mum, William—mum; *tace* is Latin for a candle.'

'Seven years more of grace, and the same measure of the needful that I got before. Ay or no?'

'Of grace, Bill! Ay! Ay! Ay! There's the cash. I accept the terms. Oh, blood! The rascal—of grace! Bill!'

'Well, now drop the hammer and vanish,' says Billy; 'but what would you think to take this sledge, while you stay, and give me a—Eh! Why in such a hurry?' he added, seeing that Satan withdrew in double-quick time.

'Hello! Nicholas!' he shouted. 'Come back; you forgot something!' And when the old gentleman looked behind him, Billy shook the hammer at him, on which he vanished altogether.

Billy now got into his old courses; and what shows the kind of people the world is made of, he also took up with his old company. When they saw that he had the money once more and was sowing it about him in all directions, they immediately began to find excuses for his former extravagance.

'Say what you will,' said one, 'Bill Dawson's a spirited fellow that bleeds like a prince.'

'He's a hospitable man in his own house, or out of it, as ever lived,' said another.

'His only fault is,' observed a third, 'that he is, if anything, too generous and doesn't know the value of money; his fault's on the right side, however.'

'He has the spunk in him,' said a fourth; 'keeps a capital table, prime wines, and a standing welcome for his friends.'

'Why,' said a fifth, 'if he doesn't enjoy his money while he lives, he won't when he's dead; so more power to him, and a wider throat to his purse.'

Indeed, the very persons who were cramming themselves at his expense despised him at heart. They knew very well, however, how to take him on the weak side. Praise his generosity, and he would do anything; call him a man of spirit, and you might fleece him to his face. Sometimes he would toss a purse of guineas to this knave, another to that flatterer, a third to a bully, and a fourth to some broken-down rake—and all to convince them that *he* was a sterling friend —a man of mettle and liberality. But never was he known to help a virtuous and struggling family—to assist the widow or the fatherless, or to do any other act that was *truly* useful. It is to be supposed the reason of this was that as he spent it, as most of the world do, in the service of the Devil, by whose aid he got it, he was prevented from turning it to a good account. Between you and me, dear reader, there are more persons acting after Bill's fashion in the same world than you dream about.

When his money was out again, his friends played him the same rascally game once more. No sooner did his poverty become plain than the knaves began to be troubled with small fits of modesty, such as an unwillingness to come to his place when there was no longer anything to be got there. A kind of virgin bashfulness prevented them from speaking to him when they saw him getting out on the wrong side of his clothes. Many of them would turn away from him in the prettiest and most delicate manner when they thought he wanted to borrow money from them—all for fear of putting him to the blush for asking it. Others again, when they saw him coming toward their houses about dinner hour, would become so confused, from mere gratitude, as to think themselves in another place; and their servants, seized, as it were, with the same feeling, would tell Bill that their masters were 'not at home.'

At length, after traveling the same villainous round as before, Bill was compelled to betake himself, as the last remedy, to the forge; in other words, he found that there is, after all, nothing in this world that a man can rely on so firmly and surely as his own industry. Bill, however, wanted the organ of common sense, for his experience—and it was sharp enough to leave an impression—ran off him like water off a duck.

He took to his employment sorely against his grain, but he had now no choice. He must either work or starve, and starvation is like a great doctor—nobody tries it till every other remedy fails them. Bill had been twice rich; twice a gentleman among blackguards, but always a blackguard among gentlemen, for no wealth or acquaintance with decent society could rub the rust of his native vulgarity off him. He was now a common blinking sot in his forge; a drunken bully in the taproom, cursing and browbeating everyone as well as his wife; boasting of how much money he had spent in his day; swaggering about the high doings he carried on; telling stories about himself and Lord This at the Curragh; the dinners he gave—how much they cost him —and attempting to extort credit upon the strength of his former wealth. He was too ignorant, however, to know that he was publishing his own disgrace and that it was a mean-spirited thing to be proud of what ought to make him blush through a deal board nine inches thick.

He was one morning industriously engaged in a quarrel with his wife, who, with a three-legged stool in her hand, appeared to mistake his head for his own anvil; he, in the meantime, paid his addresses to her with his leather apron, when who steps in to jog his memory about the little agreement that was between them but old Nick. The wife, it seems, in spite of all her exertions to the contrary, was getting the worst of it; and Sir Nicholas, willing to appear a gentleman of great gallantry, thought he could not do less than take up the lady's quarrel, particularly as Bill had laid her in a sleeping posture. Now Satan thought this too bad, and as he felt himself under many obligations to the sex, he determined to defend one of them on the present occasion; so as Judy rose, he turned upon her husband and floored him by a clever facer.

'You unmanly villain,' said he, 'is this the way you treat your wife? 'Pon honor Bill, I'll chastise you on the spot. I could not stand by, a spectator of such ungentlemanly conduct, without giving you all claim to gallant—' Whack! The word was divided in his mouth by the blow of a churnstaff from Judy, who no sooner saw Bill struck than she nailed Satan, who 'fell' once more.

'What, you villain! That's for striking my husband like a murderer behind his back,' said Judy, and she suited the action to the word. 'That's for interfering between man and wife. Would you murder the poor man before my face, eh? If *he* bates me, you shabby dog you, who has a better right? I'm sure it's nothing out of your pocket. Must you have your finger in every pie?'

This was anything but *idle* talk, for at every word she gave him a remembrance, hot and heavy. Nicholas backed, danced, and hopped; she advanced, still drubbing him with great perseverance, till at length he fell into the redoubtable armchair, which stood exactly behind him. Bill, who had been putting in two blows for Judy's one, seeing that his enemy was safe, now got between the Devil and his wife, *a situation that few will be disposed to envy him.*

'Tenderness, Judy,' said the husband; 'I hate cruelty. Go put the tongs in the fire, and make them red-hot. Nicholas, you have a nose,' said he.

Satan began to rise but was rather surprised to find that he could not budge.

'Nicholas,' says Bill, 'how is your pulse? You don't look well; that is to say, you look worse than usual.'

The other attempted to rise but found it a mistake.

'I'll thank you to come along,' said Bill. 'I have a fancy to travel under your guidance, and we'll take the *Low Countries* in our way, won't we? Get to your legs, you sinner; you know a bargain's a bargain between two *honest* men, Nicholas, meaning *yourself* and *me*. Judy, are the tongs hot?'

Satan's face was worth looking at as he turned his eyes from the husband to the wife and then fastened them on the tongs, now nearly at a furnace heat in the fire, conscious at the same time that he could not move out of the chair.

'Billy,' said he, 'you won't forget that I rewarded you generously the last time I saw you, in the way of business.'

'Faith, Nicholas, it fails me to remember any generosity I ever showed you. Don't be womanish. I simply want to see what kind of stuff your nose is made of and whether it will stretch like a rogue's conscience. If it does we will flatter it up the *chimly* with red-hot tongs, and when this old hat is fixed on the top of it, let us alone for a weather-cock.'

'Have a *fellow feeling*, Mr Dawson; you know *we* ought not to dispute. Drop the matter, and I give you the next seven years.'

'We know all that,' says Billy, opening the red-hot tongs very coolly.

'Mr Dawson,' said Satan, 'if you cannot remember my friendship to yourself, don't forget how often I stood your father's friend, your grandfather's friend, and the friend of all your relations up to the tenth generation. I intended, also, to stand by your children after you, so long as the name of Dawson—and a respectable one it is—might last.'

'Don't be blushing, Nick,' says Bill; 'you are too modest; that was ever your failing; hould up your head, there's money bid for you. I'll give you such a nose, my good friend, that you will have to keep an outrider before you, to carry the end of it on his shoulder.'

'Mr Dawson, I pledge my honor to raise your children in the world as high as they can go, no matter whether they desire it or not.'

'That's very kind of you,' says the other, 'and I'll do as much for your nose.'

He gripped it as he spoke, and the old boy immediately sung out; Bill pulled, and the nose went with him like a piece of warm wax. He then transferred the tongs to Judy, got a ladder, resumed the tongs, ascended the chimney, and tugged stoutly at the nose until he got it five feet above the roof. He then fixed the hat upon the top of it and came down.

'There's a weathercock,' said Billy; 'I defy Ireland to show such a beauty. Faith, Nick, it would make the purtiest steeple for a church in all Europe, and the old hat fits it to a shaving.'

In this state, with his nose twisted up the chimney, Satan sat for some time, experiencing the novelty of what might be termed a peculiar sensation. At last the worthy husband and wife began to relent.

'I think,' said Bill, 'that we have made the most of the nose, as well as the joke; I believe, Judy, it's long enough.'

'What is?' says Judy.

'Why, the joke,' said the husband.

'Faith, and I think so is the nose,' said Judy.

'What do you say yourself, Satan?' said Bill.

'Nothing at all, William,' said the other; 'but that—ha! ha!—it's a good joke—an excellent joke, and a goodly nose, too, as it *stands*. You were always a gentlemanly man, Bill, and did things with a grace; still, if I might give an opinion on such a trifle—'

'It's no trifle at all,' says Bill, 'if you spake of the nose.'

'Very well, it is not,' says the other; 'still, I am decidedly of opinion that if you could shorten both the joke and the nose without further violence, you would lay me under very heavy obligations, which I shall be ready to acknowledge and *repay* as I ought.'

'Come,' said Bill, 'shell out once more, and be off for seven years. As much as you came down with the last time, and vanish.'

The words were scarcely spoken, when the money was at his feet and Satan invisible. Nothing could surpass the mirth of Bill and his wife at the result of this adventure. They laughed till they fell down on the floor.

It is useless to go over the same ground again. Bill was still incorrigible. The money went as the Devil's money always goes. Bill caroused and squandered but could never turn a penny of it to a good purpose. In this way year after year went, till the seventh was closed and Bill's hour come. He was now, and had been for some time past, as miserable a knave as ever. Not a shilling had he, nor a shilling's worth, with the exception of his forge, his cabin, and a few articles of crazy furniture. In this state he was standing in his forge as before, straining his ingenuity how to make out a breakfast, when Satan came to look after him. The old gentleman was sorely puzzled how to get at him. He kept skulking and sneaking about the forge for some time, till he saw that Bill hadn't a cross to bless himself with. He immediately changed himself into a guinea and lay in an open place where he knew Bill would see him. 'If,' said he, 'I once get into his possession, I can manage him.' The honest smith took the bait, for it was well gilded; he clutched the guinea, put it into his purse, and closed it up. 'Ho! Ho!' shouted the Devil out of the purse. 'You're caught, Bill; I've secured you at last, you knave you. Why don't you despair, you villain, when you think of what's before you?'

'Why, you unlucky ould dog,' said Bill, 'is it there you are? Will you always drive your head into every loophole that's set for you? Faith, Nick achora, I never had you bagged till now.'

Satan then began to tug and struggle with a view of getting out of the purse, but in vain.

'Mr Dawson,' said he, 'we understand each other. I'll give the seven years additional and the cash on the nail.'

'Be aisey, Nicholas. You know the weight of the hammer, that's enough. It's not a whipping with feathers you're going to get, anyhow. Just be aisey.'

'Mr Dawson, I grant I'm not your match. Release me, and I double the case. I was merely trying your temper when I took the shape of a guinea.'

'Faith and I'll try yours before I lave it, I've a notion.' He immediately commenced with the sledge, and Satan sang out with a considerable want of firmness. 'Am I heavy enough?' said Bill.

'Lighter, lighter, William, if you love me. I haven't been well latterly, Mr Dawson—I have been delicate—my health, in short, is in a very precarious state, Mr Dawson.'

'I can believe *that*,' said Bill, 'and it will be more so before I have done with you. Am I doing it right?'

'Bill,' said Nick, 'is this gentlemanly treatment in your own respectable shop? Do you think, if you dropped into my little place, that I'd act this rascally part toward you? Have you no compunction?'

'I know,' replied Bill, sledging away with vehemence, 'that

you're notorious for giving your friends a *warm* welcome.
Divil an ould youth more so; but you must be daling in bad
coin, must you? However, good or bad, you're in for a sweat
now, you sinner. Am I doin' it purty?'

'Lovely, William—but, if possible, a little more delicate.'

'Oh, how delicate you are! Maybe a cup o' tay would sarve
you, or a little small gruel to compose your stomach?'

'Mr Dawson,' said the gentleman in the purse, 'hold your
hand and let us understand one another. I have a proposal
to make.'

'Hear the sinner anyhow,' said the wife.

'Name your own sum,' said Satan, 'only set me free.'

'No, the sorra may take the toe you'll budge till you let
Bill off,' said the wife; 'hould him hard, Bill, barrin' he sets
you clear of your engagement.'

'There it is, my posy,' said Bill; 'that's the condition. If
you don't give *me* up, here's at you once more—and you
must double the cash you gave the last time, too. So, if
you're of that opinion, say *ay*—leave the cash and be off.'

The money appeared in a glittering heap before Bill, upon
which he exclaimed, 'The *ay* has it, you dog. Take to your
pumps now, and fair weather after you, you vagrant; but,
Nicholas—Nick—here, here—' The other looked back and
saw Bill, with a broad grin upon him, shaking the purse at
him. 'Nicholas, come back,' said he. 'I'm short a guinea.'
Nick shook his fist and disappeared.

It would be useless to stop now, merely to inform our
readers that Bill was beyond improvement. In short, he once
more took to his old habits and lived on exactly in the same
manner as before. He had two sons—one as great a blackguard as himself, and who was also named after him; the
other was a well-conducted, virtuous young man called
James, who left his father and, having relied upon his own
industry and honest perseverance in life, arrived afterward
to great wealth and built the town called Castle Dawson,
which is so called from its founder until this day.

Bill, at length, in spite of all his wealth, was obliged, as he himself said, 'to travel'—in other words, he fell asleep one day and forgot to awaken; or, in still plainer terms, he died.

Now, it is usual, when a man dies, to close the history of his life and adventures at once; but with our hero this cannot be the case. The moment Bill departed he very naturally bent his steps toward the residence of St Moroky, as being, in his opinion, likely to lead him toward the snuggest berth he could readily make out. On arriving, he gave a very humble kind of knock, and St Moroky appeared.

'God save your Reverence!' said Bill, very submissively.

'Be off; there's no admittance here for so poor a youth as you are,' said St Moroky.

He was now so cold and fatigued that he cared like where he went, provided only, as he said himself, 'he could rest his bones and get an air of the fire.' Accordingly, after arriving at a large black gate, he knocked, as before, and was told he would get *instant* admittance the moment he gave his name.

'Billy Dawson,' he replied.

'Off, instantly,' said the porter to his companions, 'and let His Majesty know that the rascal he dreads so much is here at the gate.'

Such a racket and tumult were never heard as the very mention of Billy Dawson created.

In the meantime, his old acquaintance came running toward the gate with such haste and consternation that his tail was several times nearly tripping up his heels.

'Don't admit that rascal,' he shouted; 'bar the gate—make every chain and lock and bolt fast—I won't be safe—and I won't stay here, nor none of us need stay here, if he gets in —my bones are sore yet after him. No, no—begone, you villain—you'll get no entrance here—I know you too well.'

Bill could not help giving a broad, malicious grin at Satan, and, putting his nose through the bars, he exclaimed, 'Ha! You ould dog, I have you afraid of me at last, have I?'

He had scarcely uttered the words, when his foe, who

stood inside, instantly tweaked him by the nose, and Bill felt as if he had been gripped by the same red-hot tongs with which he himself had formerly tweaked the nose of Nicholas.

Bill then departed but soon found that in consequence of the inflammable materials which strong drink had thrown into his nose, that organ immediately took fire, and, indeed, to tell the truth, kept burning night and day, winter and summer, without ever once going out from that hour to this.

Such was the sad fate of Billy Dawson, who has been walking without stop or stay, from place to place, ever since; and in consequence of the flame on his nose, and his beard being tangled like a wisp of hay, he has been christened by the country folk Will-O'-the-Wisp, while, as it were, to show the mischief of his disposition, the circulating knave, knowing that he must seek the coldest bogs and quagmires in order to cool his nose, seizes upon that opportunity of misleading the unthinking and tipsy night travelers from their way, just that he may have the satisfaction of still taking in as many as possible.

TALE OF THE PIPER

Donn Byrne

I first saw him as I rode from the Irish village into the gates of Destiny—a burly man with a moustache, a cheap suit of Glasgow reach-me-downs, a cap with a twisted brim, and the most evilly insolent eyes I have ever seen in a human face. At the sight of him Pelican, that wisest and steadiest of horses, reared; and I felt a savage gust of hatred rise in me.

'Now, who are you?' I asked; 'and what are you doing here?'

'The same question from me to you.' And his eyes were studiedly insulting.

An unaccountable rage made me tremble. I shook out the thong of the hunting-crop, and edged Pelican towards him.

'I am the Younger of Destiny,' I informed him; 'and when I pass, all folk in Destiny do me the honour of uncovering.'

He fumbled with his cap and took it off. His hair was shaggy and matted, like a wild man's.

'I am a piper your uncle, Sir Valentine Macfarlane, sent from the High Country of Scotland home here to await his coming.'

I said no more and rode in. My Aunt Jenepher told me of my Uncle Valentine's letter which Morag, her Islay maid, had read to her. My Uncle Valentine had met the man in an inn in Argyllshire, where he was stalking deer. 'None knows anything about him, and he is most reticent about himself; but I am persuaded he is the best piper in the world. Also, he may help revive the lost art of piping in Ireland.'

'Now, if he had only sent me a pair of Ayrshire plough-men,' I grumbled.

At dinner that night the man threw his reeds over his shoulder and played outside the dining-room window. He broke into the rollicking country air of the 'Palatine's Daughter.' I don't know what he did to it with the knowledge of his art, but out of that tune of frolicsome rural love-making he produced an atmosphere which made me uncomfortable, as though some cad were telling foul stories. He swung from that into 'Thorroo a Warralla,' the 'Funeral of the Barrel,' —a noted drinking song of how a barrel of porter went dry after a day's flax-pulling. But the picture evoked was not that of country men drinking healthily at a crossroads, but of a thieves' kitchen, where dreadful blowsy women, as of Hogarth, lay drunk with their rat-faced cut-purses . . .

'Stop that man, James Carabine,' said my Aunt Jenepher.

He played no more under our window, but in the Irish village the next day he piped 'The Desperate Battle,' that music that only a great piper can touch, and that night the only faction fight we had had in Destiny for forty years broke out and raged until the police from the neighbouring villages were rushed in. He played 'The Belles of Perth' to the men from the fields, and for days afterwards I saw maidservants and young girls in the farmhouses around with red eyelids. And a young under-gardener flung down his spade and said out of nothing, to nobody: 'I'm sick of the women in this untoward place.' And one morning I heard him play, 'Iss fada may an a walla shuh'—'I'm a long time in this one town'—and my own feet took an itch for the road.

I said to my Aunt Jenepher at luncheon, 'I was thinking now, with the winter coming, I'll give up hunting for this one season, and go and see Egypt maybe, or go as far as India. A young man ought to see the world a bit.'

'Shall we talk about it tonight, Kerry?' said my Aunt Jenepher.

She asked me to go with her into the garden after luncheon, and sent Carabine for the piper. He arrived with his instrument under his arm.

'You have never played for me yet, piper.'

'Your ladyship has never asked me.' There was a solid dignity about him.

'I suppose you have many tunes,' said my Aunt Jenepher.

'What I say now would be immodest in another man, but true in me: no piper has more tunes. I have the lost tunes of McCrimmon. I have tunes that were lost before McCrimmon's day—old, dark tunes. Also tunes of my own making.'

'Will you play me the tune of the fishermen, piper, as they raise the brown sails: "Christ, Who walked on the sea, guard us poor fisher folk"!'

'I am sorry, my lady, but I have not that tune.'

'Please play me Bruce's Hymn: "God of Battles"!'

'That also, my lady, is a tune I have not.'

'Then a merry song, piper, which you must know: "The Marriage Feast which took place in Cana"!'

He was stolid as a rock. 'I am afraid I have not that either.'

'One of your favourite tunes is: "I'm a long while in this one town"?'

He bowed with a nobleman's courtesy.

'It is a choice tune,' he said slowly, 'a darling tune.'

'Then play it, piper, then play it,' said my Aunt Jenepher. 'And as you are playing it'—she rose up suddenly from the seat and looked at him with her blind eyes—'in God's name, go!'

'I was to wait,' said the piper, 'until Sir Valentine returned.'

Both Carabine and I made a step towards him. My Aunt Jenepher must have felt us. 'Please, Kerry! Please, James Carabine!'

'Piper, my brother Valentine will not wish you to stay here an instant longer than I would have you stay, and I would not have you stay at all.'

'Then I had better go,' the piper said. And he swung his reeds to his shoulder; struck the piper's swagger.

'Do you need money for the road?' my Aunt Jenepher asked.

'I need nothing.'

'But you do, piper,' said my Aunt Jenepher softly. 'I shall pray for you tonight.'

He dropped the pipes from his shoulder and turned around. 'I thank your ladyship,' he said simply; 'but I fear it is late for that.'

'Nevertheless, I shall,' said my Aunt Jenepher.

He turned and went away from us down the garden path, and what became of him is not known. He did not play his pipes as he went, but held them crumpled under his arm, and his walk was more like the rapid amble of an animal than the step of a man. I was convinced that were I to look in the gravel I should find not a footprint of a man, but the slot of an animal. But I did not look. I was afraid.

THE DEVIL OF A RIDER

J. M Synge

There was a man of the name of Charley Lambert, and every horse he would ride in a race he would come in the first.

The people in the country were angry with him at last, and this law was made, that he should ride no more at races, and if he rode, any one who saw him would have the right to shoot him. After that there was a gentleman from that part of the country over in England, and he was talking one day with the people there, and he said that the horses of Ireland were the best horses. The English said it was the English horses were the best, and at last they said there should be a race, and the English horses would come over and race against the horses of Ireland, and the gentleman put all his money on that race.

Well, when he came back to Ireland he went to Charley Lambert, and asked him to ride on his horse. Charley said he would not ride, and told the gentleman the danger he'd be in. Then the gentleman told him the way he had put all his property on the horse, and at last Charley asked where the races were to be, and the hour and the day. The gentleman told him.

'Let you put a horse with a bridle and saddle on it every seven miles along the road from here to the racecourse on that day,' said Lambert, 'and I'll be in it.'

When the gentleman was gone, Charley stripped off his clothes and got into his bed. Then he sent for the doctor, and when he heard him coming he began throwing about his arms the way the doctor would think his pulse was up with the fever.

The doctor felt his pulse and told him to stay quiet till the next day, when he would see him again.

The next day it was the same thing, and so on till the day of the races. That morning Charley had his pulse beating so hard the doctor thought bad of him.

'I'm going to the races now, Charley,' said he, 'but I'll come in and see you again when I'll be coming back in the evening, and let you be very careful and quiet till you see me.'

As soon as he had gone Charley leapt up out of bed and got on his horse, and rode seven miles to where the first horse was waiting for him. Then he rode that horse seven miles, and another horse seven miles more, till he came to the racecourse.

He rode on the gentleman's horse and he won the race.

There were great crowds looking on, and when they saw him coming in they said it was Charley Lambert, or the devil was in it, for there was no one else could bring in a horse the way he did, for the leg was after being knocked off of the horse and he came in all the same.

When the race was over, he got up on the horse was waiting for him, and away with him for seven miles. Then he rode the other horse seven miles, and his own horse seven miles, and when he got home he threw off his clothes and lay down on his bed.

After a while the doctor came back and said it was a great race they were after having.

The next day the people were saying it was Charley Lambert was the man who rode the horse. An inquiry was held, and the doctor swore that Charley was ill in his bed, and he had seen him before the race and after it, so the gentleman saved his fortune.

THE DEVIL AND THE CAT

James Joyce

Beaugency is a tiny old town on a bank of the Loire, France's longest river. It is also a very wide river, for France, at least. At Beaugency it is so wide that if you wanted to cross it from one bank to the other you would have to take at least one thousand steps.

Long ago, the people of Beaugency, when they wanted to cross it, had to go in a boat for there was no bridge. And they could not make one for themselves or pay anyone else to make one. So what were they to do?

The devil, who is always reading the newspapers, heard about this sad state of theirs so he dressed himself and came to call on the lord mayor of Beaugency, who was named Monsieur Alfred Byrne. This lord mayor was very fond of dressing himself, too. He wore a scarlet robe and always had a great golden chain round his neck even when he was fast asleep in bed with his knees in his mouth.

The devil told the lord mayor what he had read in the newspaper and said he could make a bridge for the people of Beaugency so that they could cross the river as often as they wished. He said he could make as good a bridge as ever was made, and make it in one single night. The lord mayor asked him how much money he wanted for making such a bridge. No money at all, said the devil, all I ask is that the first person who crosses the bridge shall belong to me. Good, said the lord mayor.

The night came down, all the people in Beaugency went to bed and slept. The morning came. And when they put their heads out of their windows they cried: O Loire, what a fine bridge! For they saw a fine strong stone bridge thrown across the wide river.

All the people ran down to the head of the bridge and looked across it. There was the devil, standing at the other side of the bridge, waiting for the first person who should cross it. But nobody dared to cross it for fear of the devil.

Then there was a sound of bugles—that was a sign for the people to be silent—and the lord mayor M. Alfred Byrne appeared in his great scarlet robe and wearing his heavy golden chain round his neck. He had a bucket of water in one hand and under his arm—the other arm—he carried a cat.

The devil stopped dancing when he saw him from the other side of the bridge and put up his long spyglass.

All the people whispered to one another and the cat looked up at the lord mayor because in the town of Beaugency it was allowed that a cat should look at a lord mayor. When he was tired of looking at the lord mayor (because even a cat gets tired of looking at a lord mayor) he began to play with the lord mayor's heavy golden chain.

When the lord mayor came to the head of the bridge every man held his breath and every woman held her tongue.

The lord mayor put the cat down on the bridge and, quick as a thought, splash! he emptied the whole bucket of water over it.

The cat, who was now between the devil and the bucket of water, made up his mind quite as quickly and ran with his ears back across the bridge and into the devil's arms.

The devil was as angry as the devil himself.

Messieurs les Balgentiens, he shouted across the bridge, vous n'êtes pas de belles gens du tout! Vous n'êtes que des chats! And he said to the cat: Viens ici, mon petit chat! Tu as peur, mon petit chou-chat? Tu as froid, mon pau petit chou-chat? Viens ici, le diable t'emporte! On va se chauffer tous les deux.

And off he went with the cat.

And since that time the people of that town are called 'les chats de Beaugency'.

PS. The devil mostly speaks a language of his own called Bellsybabble which he makes up himself as he goes along, but when he is very angry he can speak quite bad French very well, though some who have heard him say that he has a strong Dublin accent.

6

REVENANTS

Most modern dictionaries define a revenant as 'one who returns after a long absence, especially from the dead', adding that nearly every civilisation, at some time in its history, has held beliefs that the dead come back in different visible or sensory forms. The revenant, it is said, can seem so like the living that the difference is only discernible with difficulty. In Irish supernatural lore the term embraces all manner of restless spirits—ghosts, demons, phantom animals and, most terrifying of all, the brotherhood of the undead, vampires. Funk and Wagnalls' authoritative *Dictionary of Folklore, Mythology and Legend* (1972) comments: 'Among Irish narrators, the story of the living corpse is commonplace—the corpse which for a brief period rises from its coffin to take part in the ceremony of the funeral. Spectral ghosts which appear as 'an apparition', 'a presence', 'a spook', 'a spectre' and 'a shrouded spirit' are all common, many of these being characterised by a wraithlike quality.'

In Irish lore it is believed that Revenants may be of either sex, of any age and from any social background. They return to complete unfinished business: to warn or inform, to revenge or protect, and in some instances even to re-enact their own deaths. Their capabilities are almost boundless and they have inspired a number of outstanding short stories.

'The Brown Man' by Gerald Griffin (1803–1840) is a tale of vampirism by one of the pioneer Irish folklore writers who may well have been an influence on Bram Stoker in the creation of his classic novel, *Dracula*. There is evidence among Stoker's papers, now held in America, that he had read the collection of stories in which it first appeared, *Holland-Tide; or Munster Popular Tales*, first published by Griffin in 1827; and there are similarities in the plot and characterisation which could easily have surfaced in Stoker's mind, consciously or unconsciously, as he was writing his tale of the vampire count.

Of the author himself, Griffin has been called 'one of Ireland's first Catholic writers in English', and he undoubtedly drew on his upbringing in a large Catholic farming family in Limerick for the stories collected in *Holland-Tide* which earned him sudden and considerable fame. The book was reviewed in England as enthusiastically as it had been in Ireland, one London reviewer declaring that it contained 'scenes which are hardly surpassed as to the truth and power by anything which has yet proceeded from the pen of Sir Walter Scott.' Other collections were to follow, but Griffin's career was tragically cut short in 1840 when he succumbed to an epidemic of typhus which swept through Cork where he was then living. His mark on the supernatural, however, and his influence on later writers of macabre fiction, had already been assured by tales such as 'The Brown Man'.

George Moore (1852–1933), the author of 'A Play-House in the Waste', differs from many of the other contributors to this volume in that he came from an upper-class South-West Irish background (his father was an MP and race horse owner). He was educated at a private Catholic boarding school in England and, after inheriting his father's estate, studied art for a time in Paris before becoming an agnostic and discovering his true metier as a writer in the realistic style of his hero, Emile Zola. The importance of Moore's decision to turn his back on painting may be judged by the fact that he is now regarded in literary circles as the founder of the modern Irish short story. Declaring to his publisher that 'the ordinary short story is about nothing', he proceeded to introduce the reading public to a wider and lower life than was found in the fashionable tales of the day. His fascination with the Irish way of life and its legendary tales never left him and found its way into collections such as *An Untilled Field* (1903) and *A Story-Teller's Holiday* (1918). The publication of *An Untilled Field* was a landmark in the history of the Irish short story and provided a model for much of the work of subsequent writers.

'A Play-House in the Waste', taken from the collection, also marks a significant step in the development of the ghost story, for in its account of a revenant—'a white thing gliding'—George Moore links the drama of the supernatural with an attack on the social conditions and poverty of rural Ireland. It deserves to be much better known and is certainly the equal of another story from the same book, 'Julia Cahill's Curse', which is frequently anthologised.

Daniel Corkery (1874–1964) is famous not only as a storyteller but also for his encouragement and literary influence on both Sean O'Faolain and Frank O'Connor. A promoter of Irish culture, he urged the two younger writers not to become provincial in their outlook and to do all they could in their work to promote their heritage. Despite this admonition, Corkery himself spent much of his life in the city of his birth, Cork; only his lameness, however, prevented him fighting in the Civil War and he worked enthusiastically for the Gaelic League and contributed plays to the Abbey Theatre.

Corkery wrote four volumes of short stories which draw on both the past and present to reveal the many facets of ordinary Irish life. In 'The Eyes of the Dead', which appeared in *The Stormy Hills* (1929), he focuses on a shipwreck victim who withdraws from active life only to find that there is no escape from the traumatic events of which he was the only survivor.

Benedict Kiely (1919–   ) was born in County Tyrone during the Civil War, and was introduced to the supernatural heritage of his native countryside through the folk tales of William Carleton who had lived in a neighbouring valley.

Indeed, his admiration for Carleton's ability as a story-teller shaped both his own writing and his interest in their common background. As a young man he trained for a time to be a priest, but forsook this calling for the study of history and literature at University College, Dublin, where his talent for writing was noticed and encouraged. His early work was mainly on political and literary themes, but he later branched out into novels, short stories and an acclaimed critical biography of his mentor, William Carleton.

Benedict Kiely's interest in ghostly dogs, a widespread phenomenon in Ireland, can be seen in several of his stories, including 'The Heroes in the Dark House', the tale of a folklore collector, Arthur Broderick, and the excellent 'Homes on the Mountain', in which he writes (in all probability referring to himself), 'In a spooky story I once read, the Black Hound of Kildare turned out to be the devil.' In 'The Dogs in the Great Glen' he takes the tradition further with his story of an American professor visiting Ireland to trace his grandfather and encountering a very strange pack of dogs. It is a story of mounting tension set amidst the rugged scenery and old superstitions for which Ireland is justifiably famous.

'The Green Grave and the Black Grave' by Mary Lavin (1912–   ) is, quite simply, one of the finest examples of Irish short story writing—a bringing together of all the elements initiated by the ancient *seanchai*, preserved by the collectors of folklore, and moulded and refined into an art form by the author's skill. Small wonder that she has been hailed by V. S. Pritchett as 'an artist with the power to present the surface of life rapidly, but as a covering for something else', while the novelist Joyce Carol Oates has no hesitation in calling her 'one of the finest short story writers'. Indeed, virtually her entire output has been short fiction.

An Irish-American, Mary grew up on an estate in County Meath, where a neighbour was the fantasy writer Lord Dunsany. He fostered her interest in the folklore of the country and encouraged her early stories, and it was he who read her first unpublished tales and discovered in them an 'astonishing insight reminiscent of the Russians' which made him suggest to her that she send some samples to the American magazine *Atlantic Monthly*. 'The Green Grave and the Black Grave' was the first of her stories to appear in this periodical (in its May 1940 issue) and the enthusiastic reception for her account of the reclaiming of the body of a drowned man from the sea by his wife's spirit inspired her to begin the career which has since proved so imaginative and productive. Lord Dunsany was also responsible for introducing her to the Irish literary circle, of which Sean O'Faolain and Frank O'Connor were members, and she was soon being ranked as one of their equals.

Since then, Mary Lavin has been heaped with honours by both Irish and American institutions, as well as becoming, in her turn, a major influence on the new generation of Irish short story writers. And with stories like 'The Green Grave and the Black Grave' she has also pointed out new directions in which the supernatural tale itself might go. There seems little doubt on the evidence available that the genre will continue to flourish and develop in Ireland in the years to come.

THE BROWN MAN

Gerald Griffin

The common Irish expression of 'the seven devils,' does not, it would appear, owe its origin to the supernatural influences ascribed to that numeral, from its frequent association with the greatest and most solemn occasions of theological history. If one were disposed to be fancifully metaphysical upon the subject, it might not be amiss to compare credulity to a sort of mental prism, by which the great volume of the light of speculative superstition is refracted in a manner precisely similar to that of the material, every day sun, the great refractor thus showing only *blue* devils to the dwellers in the good city of London, *orange* and *green* devils to the inhabitants of the sister (or rather step-daughter), island, and so forward until the seven component hues are made out, through the other nations of the earth. But what has this to do with the story? In order to answer that question, the story must be told.

In a lonely cabin, in a lonely glen, on the shores of a lonely lough, in one of the most lonesome districts of west Munster, lived a lone woman named Guare. She had a beautiful girl, a daughter named Nora. Their cabin was the only one within three miles round them every way. As to their mode of living, it was simple enough, for all they had was one little garden of white cabbage, and they had eaten that down to a few heads between them, a sorry prospect in a place where even a handful of *prishoc* weed was not to be had without sowing it.

It was a very fine morning in those parts, for it was only

snowing and hailing, when Nora and her mother were sitting at the door of their little cottage, and laying out plans for the next day's dinner. On a sudden, a strange horseman rode up to the door. He was strange in more ways than one. He was dressed in brown, his hair was brown, his eyes were brown, his boots were brown, he rode a brown horse, and he was followed by a brown dog.

'I'm come to marry you, Nora Guare,' said the Brown Man.

'Ax my mother fusht, if you plaise, sir,' said Nora, dropping him a curtsy.

'You'll not refuse, ma'am,' said the Brown Man to the old mother, 'I have money enough, and I'll make your daughter a lady, with servants at her call, and all manner of fine doings about her.' And so saying, he flung a purse of gold into the widow's lap.

'Why then the heavens speed you and her together, take her away with you, and make much of her,' said the old mother, quite bewildered with all the money.

'Agh, agh,' said the Brown Man, as he placed her on his horse behind him without more ado. 'Are you all ready now?'

'I am!' said the bride. The horse snorted, and the dog barked, and almost before the word was out of her mouth, they were all whisked away out of sight. After travelling a day and a night, faster than the wind itself, the Brown Man pulled up his horse in the middle of the Mangerton mountain, in one of the most lonesome places that eye ever looked on.

'Here is my estate,' said the Brown Man.

'A'then, is it this wild bog you call an estate?' said the bride.

'Come in, wife; this is my palace,' said the bridegroom.

'What! a clay-hovel, worse than my mother's!'

They dismounted, and the horse and the dog disappeared in an instant, with a horrible noise, which the girl did not know whether to call snorting, barking, or laughing.

'Are you hungry?' said the Brown Man. 'If so, there is your dinner.'

'A handful of raw white-eyes,[1] and a grain of salt!'

'And when you are sleepy, here is your bed,' he continued, pointing to a little straw in a corner, at sight of which Nora's limbs shivered and trembled again. It may be easily supposed that she did not make a very hearty dinner that evening, nor did her husband neither.

In the dead of the night, when the clock of Mucruss Abbey had just tolled one, a low neighing at the door, and a soft barking at the window were heard. Nora feigned sleep. The Brown Man passed his hand over her eyes and face. She snored. 'I'm coming,' said he, and he arose gently from her side. In half an hour after she felt him by her side again. He was cold as ice.

The next night the same summons came. The Brown Man rose. The wife feigned sleep. He returned, cold. The morning came.

The next night came. The bell tolled at Mucruss, and was heard across the lakes. The Brown Man rose again, and passed a light before the eyes of the feigning sleeper. None slumber so sound as they who *will* not wake. Her heart trembled, but her frame was quiet and firm. A voice at the door summoned the husband.

'You are very long coming. The earth is tossed up, and I am hungry. Hurry! Hurry! Hurry! if you would not lose all.'

'I'm coming!' said the Brown Man. Nora rose and followed instantly. She beheld him at a distance winding through a lane of frostnipt sallow trees. He often paused and looked back, and once or twice retraced his steps to within a few yards of the tree, behind which she had shrunk. The moon-light, cutting the shadow close and dark about her, afforded the best concealment. He again proceeded, and she followed. In a few minutes they reached the old Abbey of Mucruss. With a sickening heart she saw him enter the

1 A kind of potato

church-yard. The wind rushed through the huge yew-tree and startled her. She mustered courage enough, however, to reach the gate of the church-yard and look in. The Brown Man, the horse, and the dog, were there seated by an open grave, eating something; and glancing their brown, fiery eyes about in every direction. The moonlight shone full on them and her. Looking down towards her shadow on the earth, she started with horror to observe it move, although she was herself perfectly still. It waved its black arms, and motioned her back. What the feasters said, she understood not, but she seemed still fixed in the spot. She looked once more on her shadow; it raised one hand, and pointed the way to the lane; then slowly rising from the ground, and confronting her, it walked rapidly off in that direction. She followed as quickly as might be.

She was scarcely in her straw, when the door creaked behind, and her husband entered. He lay down by her side, and started.

'Uf! Uf!' said she, pretending to be just awakened, 'how cold you are, my love!'

'Cold, inagh? Indeed you're not very warm yourself, my dear, I'm thinking.'

'Little admiration I shouldn't be warm, and you laving me alone this way at night, till my blood is snow broth, no less.'

'Umph!' said the Brown Man, as he passed his arm round her waist. 'Ha! your heart is beating fast?'

'Little admiration it should. I am not well, indeed. Them pzaties and salt don't agree with me at all.'

'Umph!' said the Brown Man.

The next morning as they were sitting at the breakfast-table together, Nora plucked up a heart, and asked leave to go to see her mother. The Brown Man, who eat nothing, looked at her in a way that made her think he knew all. She felt her spirit die away within her.

'If you only want to see your mother,' said he, 'there is no occasion for your going home. I will bring her to you here. I didn't marry you to be keeping you gadding.'

The Brown Man then went out and whistled for his dog
and his horse. They both came; and in a very few minutes
they pulled up at the old widow's cabin-door.

The poor woman was very glad to see her son-in-law,
though she did not know what could bring him so soon.

'Your daughter sends her love to you, mother,' says the
Brown Man, the villain, 'and she'd be obliged to you for a
loand of a *shoot* of your best clothes, as she's going to give
a grand party, and the dress-maker has disappointed her.'

'To be sure and welcome,' said the mother; and making
up a bundle of clothes, she put them into his hands.

'Whogh! whogh!' said the horse as they drove off, 'that
was well done. Are we to have a mail of her?'

'Easy, ma-coppuleen, and you'll get your 'nough before
night,' said the Brown Man, 'and you likewise, my little
dog.'

'Boh!' cried the dog, 'I'm in no hurry—I hunted down a
doe this morning that was fed with milk from the horns of
the moon.'

Often in the course of that day did Nora Guare go to the
door, and cast her eye over the weary flat before it, to dis-
cern, if possible, the distant figures of her bridegroom and
mother. The dusk of the second evening found her alone in
the desolate cot. She listened to every sound. At length the
door opened, and an old woman, dressed in a new *jock*, and
leaning on a staff, entered the hut. 'O mother, are you
come?' said Nora, and was about to rush into her arms,
when the old woman stopped her.

'Whisht! whisht! my child!—I only stepped in before the
man to know how you like him? Speak softly, in dread he'd
hear you—he's turning the horse loose, in the swamp,
abroad, over.'

'O mother, mother! such a story!'

'Whisht! easy again—how does he use you?'

'Sarrow worse. That straw my bed, and them white-eyes
—and bad ones they are—all my diet. And 'tisn't that same,
only—'

'Whisht! easy, agin! He'll hear you, may be—Well?'

'I'd be easy enough only for his own doings. Listen, mother. The fusht night, I came about twelve o'clock—'

'Easy, speak easy, eroo!'

'He got up at the call of the horse and the dog, and staid out a good hour. He ate nothing next day. The second night, and the second day, it was the same story. The third—'

'Husht! husht! Well, the third night?'

'The third night I said I'd watch him. Mother, don't hold my hand so hard . . . He got up, and I got up after him . . . Oh, don't laugh, mother, for 'tis frightful . . . I followed him to Mucruss church-yard . . . Mother, mother, you hurt my hand . . . I looked in at the gate—there was great moonlight there, and I could see every thing as plain as day.'

'Well, darling—husht! softly! What did you see?'

'My husband by the grave, and the horse, . . . Turn your head aside, mother, for your breath is very hot . . . and the dog and they eating.—Ah, you are not my mother!' shrieked the miserable girl, as the Brown Man flung off his disguise, and stood before her, grinning worse than a blacksmith's face through a horse-collar. He just looked at her one moment, and then darted his long fingers into her bosom, from which the red blood spouted in so many streams. She was very soon out of all pain, and a merry supper the horse, the dog, and the Brown Man had that night, by all accounts.

A PLAY-HOUSE IN THE WASTE

George Moore

'It's a closed mouth that can hold a good story,' as the saying
goes, and very soon it got about that Father MacTurnan had
written to Rome saying he was willing to take a wife to his
bosom for patriotic reasons, if the Pope would relieve him
of his vow of celibacy. And many phrases and words from
his letter (translated by whom—by the Bishop or Father
Meehan? Nobody ever knew) were related over the Dublin
firesides, till at last out of the talk a tall gaunt man emerged,
in an old overcoat green from weather and wear, the tails
of it flapping as he rode his bicycle through the great
waste bog that lies between Belmullet and Crossmolina.
His name! We liked it. It appealed to our imagination.
MacTurnan! It conveyed something from afar like Hamlet
or Don Quixote. He seemed as near and as far from us
as they, till Pat Comer, one of the organisers of the IAOS,
came in and said, after listening to the talk that was going
round:

'Is it of the priest that rides in the great Mayo bog you are
speaking? If it is, you haven't got the story rightly.' As he
told us the story, so it is printed in this book. And we sat
wondering greatly, for we seemed to see a soul on its way
to heaven. But round a fire there is always one who cannot
get off the subject of women and blasphemy—a papist generally he is; and it was Quinn that evening who kept plaguing
us with jokes, whether it would be a fat girl or a thin that
the priest would choose if the Pope gave him leave to marry,
until at last, losing all patience with him, I bade him be silent,

322

and asked Pat Comer to tell us if the priest was meditating a new plan for Ireland's salvation.

'For a mind like his,' I said, 'would not stand still and problems such as ours waiting to be solved.'

'You're wrong there! He thinks no more of Ireland, and neither reads nor plans, but knits stockings ever since the wind took his play-house away.'

'Took his play-house away!' said several.

'And why would he be building a play-house,' somebody asked, 'and he living in a waste?'

'A queer idea, surely!' said another. 'A play-house in the waste!'

'Yes, a queer idea,' said Pat, 'but a true one all the same, for I have seen it with my own eyes—or the ruins of it, and not later back than three weeks ago, when I was staying with the priest himself. You know the road, all of you—how it straggles from Foxford through the bog alongside of bog-holes deep enough to drown one, and into which the jarvey and myself seemed in great likelihood of pitching, for the car went down into great ruts, and the horse was shying from one side of the road to the other, and at nothing so far as we could see.'

'There's nothing to be afeared of, yer honour; only once was he near leaving the road, the day before Christmas, and I driving the doctor. It was here he saw it—a white thing gliding, and the wheel of the car must have gone within an inch of the boghole.'

'And the doctor. Did he see it?' I said.

'He saw it too, and so scared was he that the hair rose up and went through his cap.'

'Did the jarvey laugh when he said that?' we asked Pat Comer; and Pat answered: 'Not he! Them fellows just speak as the words come to them without thinking. Let me get on with my story. We drove on for about a mile, and it was to stop him from clicking his tongue at the horse that I asked him if the bog was Father MacTurnan's parish.'

'Every mile of it, sir,' he said, 'every mile of it, and we

do be seeing him buttoned up in his old coat riding along the roads on his bicycle going to sick calls.'

'Do you often be coming this road?' says I.

'Not very often, sir. No one lives here except the poor people, and the priest and the doctor. Faith! there isn't a poorer parish in Ireland, and every one of them would have been dead long ago if it had not been for Father James.'

'And how does he help them?'

'Isn't he always writing letters to the Government asking for relief works? Do you see those bits of roads?'

'Where do those roads lead to?'

'Nowhere. Them roads stops in the middle of the bog when the money is out.'

'But,' I said, 'surely it would be better if the money were spent upon permanent improvements—on drainage, for instance.'

The jarvey didn't answer; he called to his horse, and not being able to stand the clicking of his tongue, I kept on about the drainage.

'There's no fall, sir.'

'And the bog is too big,' I added, in hope of encouraging conversation.

'Faith it is, sir.'

'But we aren't very far from the sea, are we?'

'About a couple of miles.'

'Well then,' I said, 'couldn't a harbour be made?'

'They were thinking about that, but there's no depth of water, and everyone's against emigration now.'

'Ah! the harbour would encourage emigration.'

'So it would, your honour.'

'But is there no talk about home industries, weaving, lace-making?'

'I won't say that.'

'But has it been tried?'

'The candle do be burning in the priest's window till one in the morning, and he sitting up thinking of plans to keep the people at home. Now, do ye see that house, sir, fornint

my whip at the top of the hill? Well, that's the play-house
he built.'

'A play-house?'

'Yes, yer honour. Father James hoped the people might
come from Dublin to see it, for no play like it had ever been
acted in Ireland before, sir!'

'And was the play performed?'

'No, yer honour. The priest had been learning them all
the summer, but the autumn was on them before they had
got it by rote, and a wind came and blew down one of the
walls.'

'And couldn't Father MacTurnan get the money to build
it up?'

'Sure, he might have got the money, but where'd be the
use when there was no luck in it?'

'And who were to act the play?'

'The girls and the boys in the parish, and the prettiest girl
in all the parish was to play Good Deeds.'

'So it was a miracle play,' I said.

'Do you see that man? It's the priest coming out of Tom
Burke's cabin, and I warrant he do be bringing him the
Sacrament, and he having the holy oils with him, for Tom
won't pass the day; we had the worst news of him last night.'

'And I can tell you,' said Pat Comer, dropping his story
for a moment and looking round the circle, 'it was a sad
story the jarvey told me. He told it well, for I can see the
one-roomed hovel full of peatsmoke, the black iron pot with
traces of the yellow stirabout in it on the hearth, and the
sick man on the pallet bed, and the priest by his side mumbling prayers together. Faith! these jarveys can tell a story
—none better.'

'As well as yourself, Pat,' one of us said. And Pat began
to tell of the miles of bog on either side of the straggling
road, of the hill-top to the left, with the play-house showing
against the dark and changing clouds; of a woman in a red
petticoat, a handkerchief tied round her head, who had flung
down her spade the moment she caught sight of the car, of

the man who appeared on the brow and blew a horn. 'For she mistook us for bailiffs,' said Pat, 'and two little sheep hardly bigger than geese were driven away.'

'A play-house in the waste for these people,' I was saying to myself all the time, till my meditations were interrupted by the jarvey telling that the rocky river we crossed was called the Greyhound—a not inappropriate name, for it ran swiftly . . . Away down the long road a white cottage appeared, and the jarvey said to me, 'That is the priest's house.' It stood on the hillside some little way from the road, and all the way to the door I wondered how his days passed in the great loneliness of the bog.

'His reverence isn't at home, yer honour—he's gone to attend a sick call.'

'Yes, I know—Tom Burke.'

'And is Tom better, Mike?'

'The devil a bether he'll be this side of Jordan,' the jarvey answered, and the housekeeper showed me into the priest's parlour. It was lined with books, and I looked forward to a pleasant chat when we had finished our business. At that time I was on a relief committee, and the people were starving in the poor parts of the country.

'I think he'll be back in about an hour's time, yer honour.' But the priest seemed to be detained longer than his house-keeper expected, and the moaning of the wind round the cottage reminded me of the small white thing the horse and the doctor had seen gliding along the road. 'The priest knows the story—he will tell me,' I said, and piled more turf on the fire—fine sods of hard black turf they were, and well do I remember seeing them melting away. But all of a sudden my eyes closed. I couldn't have been asleep more than a few minutes when it seemed to me a great crowd of men and women had gathered about the house, and a moment after the door was flung open, and a tall, gaunt man faced me.

'I've just come,' he said, 'from a deathbed, and they that have followed me aren't far from death if we don't succeed in getting help.'

I don't know how I can tell you of the crowd I saw round the house that day. We are accustomed to see poor people in towns cowering under arches, but it is more pitiful to see people starving in the fields on the mountain side. I don't know why it should be so, but it is. But I call to mind two men in ragged trousers and shirts as ragged, with brown beards on faces yellow with famine; and the words of one of them are not easily forgotten: 'The white sun of Heaven doesn't shine upon two poorer men than upon this man and myself.' I can tell you I didn't envy the priest his job, living all his life in the waste listening to tales of starvation, looking into famished faces. There were some women among them, kept back by the men, who wanted to get their word in first. They seemed to like to talk about their misery . . . and I said:

'They are tired of seeing each other. I am a spectacle, a show, an amusement for them. I don't know if you can catch my meaning?'

'I think I do,' Father James answered. And I asked him to come for a walk up the hill and show me the play-house.

Again he hesitated, and I said: 'You must come, Father MacTurnan, for a walk. You must forget the misfortunes of those people for a while.' He yielded, and we spoke of the excellence of the road under our feet, and he told me that when he conceived the idea of a play-house, he had already succeeded in persuading the inspector to agree that the road they were making should go to the top of the hill. 'The policy of the Government,' he said, 'from the first was that relief works should benefit nobody except the workers, and it is sometimes very difficult to think out a project for work that will be perfectly useless. Arches have been built on the top of hills, and roads that lead nowhere. A strange sight to the stranger a road must be that stops suddenly in the middle of a bog. One wonders at first how a Government could be so foolish, but when one thinks of it, it is easy to understand that the Government doesn't wish to spend money on works that will benefit a class. But the road that leads nowhere is difficult to make, even though starving men are employed upon it; for a man to work well there must be an end in view, and I can tell you it is difficult to bring even starving men to engage on a road that leads nowhere. If I'd told everything I am telling you to the inspector, he wouldn't have agreed to let the road run to the top of the hill; but I said to him: 'The road leads nowhere; as well let it end at the top of the hill as down in the valley.' So I got the money for my road and some money for my play-house, for of course the play-house was as useless as the road; a play-house in the waste can neither interest or benefit anybody! But there was an idea at the back of my mind all the time that when the road and the play-house were finished, I might be able to induce the Government to build a harbour.'

'But the harbour would be of use.'

'Of very little,' he answered. 'For the harbour to be of use a great deal of dredging would have to be done.'

'And the Government needn't undertake the dredging. How very ingenious! I suppose you often come here to read your breviary?'

'During the building of the play-house I often used to be up here, and during the rehearsals I was here every day.'

'If there was a rehearsal,' I said to myself, 'there must have been a play.' And I affected interest in the grey shallow sea and the erosion of the low-lying land—a salt marsh filled with pools.

'I thought once,' said the priest, 'that if the play were a great success, a line of flat-bottomed steamers might be built.'

'Sitting here in the quiet evenings,' I said to myself, 'reading his breviary, dreaming of a line of steamships crowded with visitors! He has been reading about the Oberammergau performances.' So that was his game—the road, the play-house, the harbour—and I agreed with him that no one would have dared to predict that visitors would have come from all sides of Europe to see a few peasants performing a miracle play in the Tyrol.

'Come,' I said, 'into the play-house and let me see how you built it.'

Half a wall and some of the roof had fallen, and the rubble had not been cleared away, and I said:

'It will cost many pounds to repair the damage, but having gone so far you should give the play a chance.'

'I don't think it would be advisable,' he muttered, half to himself, half to me.

As you may well imagine, I was anxious to hear if he had discovered any aptitude for acting among the girls and the boys who lived in the cabins.

'I think,' he answered me, 'that the play would have been fairly acted; I think that, with a little practice, we might have done as well as they did at Oberammergau.'

An odd man, more willing to discuss the play that he had chosen than the talents of those who were going to perform it, and he told me that it had been written in the fourteenth century in Latin, and that he had translated it into Irish.

I asked him if it would have been possible to organise an excursion from Dublin—'Oberammergau in the West.'

'I used to think so. But it is eight miles from Rathowen, and the road is a bad one, and when they got here there would be no place for them to stay; they would have to go all the way back again, and that would be sixteen miles.'

'Yet you did well, Father James, to build the play-house, for the people could work better while they thought they were accomplishing something. Let me start a subscription for you in Dublin.'

'I don't think that it would be possible—'

'Not for me to get fifty pounds?'

'You might get the money, but I don't think we could ever get a performance of the play.'

'And why not?' I said.

'You see, the wind came and blew down the wall. The people are very pious; I think they felt that the time they spent rehearsing might have been better spent. The play-house disturbed them in their ideas. They hear Mass on

Sundays, and there are the Sacraments, and they remember they have to die. It used to seem to me a very sad thing to see all the people going to America; the poor Celt disappearing in America, leaving his own country, leaving his language, and very often his religion.'

'And does it no longer seem to you sad that such a thing should happen?'

'No, not if it is the will of God. God has specially chosen the Irish race to convert the world. No race has provided so many missionaries, no race has preached the Gospel more frequently to the heathen; and once we realise that we have to die, and very soon, and that the Catholic Church is the only true Church, our ideas about race and nationality fade from us. *We* are here, not to make life successful and triumphant, but to gain heaven. That is the truth, and it is to the honour of the Irish people that they have been selected by God to preach the truth, even though they lose their nationality in preaching it. I do not expect you to accept these opinions. I know that you think very differently, but living here I have learned to acquiesce in the will of God.'

He stopped speaking suddenly, like one ashamed of having expressed himself too openly, and soon after we were met by a number of peasants, and the priest's attention was engaged; the inspector of the relief works had to speak to him; and I didn't see him again until dinner-time.

'You have given them hope,' he said.

This was gratifying to hear, and the priest sat listening while I told him of the looms already established in different parts of the country. We talked about half an hour, and then like one who suddenly remembers, the priest got up and fetched his knitting.

'Do you knit every evening?'

'I have got into the way of knitting lately—it passes the time.'

'But do you never read?' I asked, and my eyes went towards the bookshelves.

'I used to read a great deal. But there wasn't a woman in

the parish that could turn a heel properly, so I had to learn to knit.'

'Do you like knitting better than reading?' I asked, feeling ashamed of my curiosity.

'I have constantly to attend sick calls, and if one is absorbed in a book one doesn't like to put it aside.'

'I see you have two volumes of miracle plays!'

'Yes, and that's another danger: a book begets all kinds of ideas and notions into one's head. The idea of that play-house came out of those books.'

'But,' I said, 'you don't think that God sent the storm because He didn't wish a play to be performed?'

'One cannot judge God's designs. Whether God sent the storm or whether it was accident must remain a matter for conjecture; but it is not a matter of conjecture that one is doing certain good by devoting oneself to one's daily task, getting the Government to start new relief works, establishing schools for weaving. The people are entirely dependent upon me, and when I'm attending to their wants I know I'm doing right.'

The play-house interested me more than the priest's ideas of right and wrong, and I tried to get him back to it; but the subject seemed a painful one, and I said to myself: 'The jarvey will tell me all about it tomorrow. I can rely on him to find out the whole story from the housekeeper in the kitchen.' And sure enough, we hadn't got to the Greyhound River before he was leaning across the well of the car talking to me and asking if the priest was thinking of putting up the wall of the play-house.

'The wall of the play-house?' I said.

'Yes, yer honour. Didn't I see both of you going up the hill in the evening time?'

'I don't think we shall ever see a play in the play-house.'

'Why would we, since it was God that sent the wind that blew it down?'

'How do you know it was God that sent the wind? It might have been the devil himself, or somebody's curse.'

'Sure it is of Mrs Sheridan you do be thinking, yer honour, and of her daughter—she that was to be playing Good Deeds in the play, yer honour; and wasn't she wake coming home from the learning of the play? And when the signs of her wakeness began to show, the widow Sheridan took a halter off the cow and tied Margaret to the wall, and she was in the stable till the child was born. Then didn't her mother take a bit of string and tie it round the child's throat, and bury it near the play-house; and it was three nights after that the storm rose, and the child pulled the thatch out of the roof.'

'But did she murder the child?'

'Sorra wan of me knows. She sent for the priest when she was dying, and told him what she had done.'

'But the priest wouldn't tell what he heard in the confessional,' I said.

'Mrs Sheridan didn't die that night; not till the end of the week, and the neighbours heard her talking of the child she had buried, and then they all knew what the white thing was they had seen by the roadside. The night the priest left her he saw the white thing standing in front of him, and if he hadn't been a priest he'd have dropped down dead; so he took some water from the bog-hole and dashed it over it, saying, "I baptise thee in the name of the Father, and of the Son, and of the Holy Ghost!"'

The driver told his story like one saying his prayers, and he seemed to have forgotten that he had a listener.

'It must have been a great shock to the priest.'

'Faith it was, sir, to meet an unbaptised child on the roadside, and that child the only bastard that was ever born in the parish—so Tom Mulhare says, and he's the oldest man in the county.'

'It was altogether a very queer idea—this play-house.'

'It was indeed, sir, a quare idea, but you see he's a quare man. He has been always thinking of something to do good, and it is said that he thinks too much. Father James is a very quare man, your honour.'

THE EYES OF THE DEAD

Daniel Corkery

I

If he had not put it off for three years John Spillane's home-coming would have been that of a famous man. Bonfires would have been lighted on the hill-tops of Rossamara, and the ships passing by, twenty miles out, would have wondered what they meant.

Three years ago, the *Western Star*, an Atlantic liner, one night tore her iron plates to pieces against the cliff-like face of an iceberg, and in less than an hour sank in the waters. Of the 789 human souls aboard her one only had been saved, John Spillane, able seaman, of Rossamara in the county of Cork. The name of the little fishing village, his own name, his picture, were in all the papers of the world, it seemed, not only because he alone had escaped, but by reason of the manner of that escape. He had clung to a drift of wreckage, must have lost consciousness for more than a whole day, floated then about on the ocean for a second day, for a second night, and had arrived at the threshold of another dreadful night when he was rescued. A fog was coming down on the waters. It frightened him more than the darkness. He raised a shout. He kept on shouting. When safe in the arms of his rescuers his breathy, almost inaudible voice was still forcing out some cry which they interpreted as Help! Help!

That was what had struck the imagination of men—the half-insane figure sending his cry over the waste of waters, the fog thickening, and the night falling. Although the whole

333

world had read also of the groping rescue ship, of Spillane's bursts of hysterical laughter, of his inability to tell his story until he had slept eighteen hours on end, what remained in the memory was the lonely figure sending his cry over the sea.

And then, almost before his picture had disappeared from the papers, he had lost himself in the great cities of the States. To Rossamara no word had come from himself, nor for a long time from any acquaintance; but then, when about a year had gone by, his sister or mother as they went up the road to Mass of a Sunday might be stopped and informed in a whispering voice that John had been seen in Chicago, or, it might be, in New York, or Boston, or San Francisco, or indeed anywhere. And from the meagreness of the messages it was known, with only too much certainty, that he had not, in exchanging sea for land, bettered his lot. If once again his people had happened on such empty tidings of him, one knew it by their bowed and stilly attitude in the little church as the light whisper of the Mass rose and fell about them.

When three years had gone by he lifted the latch of his mother's house one October evening and stood awkwardly in the middle of the floor. It was nightfall and not a soul had seen him break down from the ridge and cross the roadway. He had come secretly from the ends of the earth.

And before he was an hour in their midst he rose up impatiently, timidly, and stole into his bed.

'I don't want any light,' he said, and as his mother left him there in the dark, she heard him yield his whole being to a sigh of thankfulness. Before that he had told them he felt tired, a natural thing, since he had tramped fifteen miles from the railway station in Skibbereen. But day followed day without his showing any desire to rise from the bedclothes and go abroad among the people. He had had enough of the sea, it seemed; enough too of the great cities of the States. He was a pity, the neighbours said; and the few of them who from time to time caught glimpses of him, reported him as not yet having lost the scared look that the ocean had left on him. His hair was grey or nearly grey, they said, and, swept back fiercely from his forehead, a fashion strange to the place, seemed to pull his eyes open, to keep them wide open, as he looked at you. His moustache also was grey, they said, and his cheeks were grey too, sunken and dark with shadows. Yet his mother and sister, the only others in the house, were glad to have him back with them; at any rate, they said, they knew where he was.

They found nothing wrong with him. Of speech neither he nor they ever had had the gift; and as day followed day, and week week, the same few phrases would carry them through the day and into the silence of night. In the beginning they had thought it natural to speak with him about the wreck; soon, however, they came to know that it was a subject for which he had no welcome. In the beginning also, they had thought to rouse him by bringing the neighbours to his bedside, but such visits instead of cheering him only left him sunken in silence, almost in despair. The priest came to see him once in a while, and advised the mother and sister, Mary her name was, to treat him as normally as they could, letting on that his useless presence was no affliction to them nor even a burden. In time John Spillane was accepted by all as one of those unseen ones, or seldom-seen ones, who are to be found in every village in the world— the bedridden, the struck-down, the aged—forgotten of all except the few faithful creatures who bring the cup to the bedside of a morning, and open the curtains to let in the sun.

II

In the nearest house, distant a quarter-mile from them, lived Tom Leane. In the old days before John Spillane went to sea, Tom had been his companion, and now of a night-time he would drop in if he had any story worth telling or if, on the day following, he chanced to be going back to Skibbereen, where he might buy the Spillanes such goods as they needed, or sell a pig for them, slipping it in among his own. He was a quiet creature, married, and struggling to bring up the little family that was thickening about him. In the Spillanes' he would, dragging at the pipe, sit on the settle, and quietly gossip with the old woman while Mary moved about on the flags putting the household gear tidy for the night. But all three of them, as they kept up the simple talk, were never unaware of the silent listener in the lower room. Of that room the door was kept open; but no lamp was lighted within it; no lamp indeed was needed, for a shaft of light from the kitchen struck into it showing one or two of the religious pictures on the wall and giving sufficient light to move about in. Sometimes the conversation would drift away from the neighbourly doings, for even to Rossamara tidings from the great world abroad would sometimes come; in the middle of such gossip, however, a sudden thought would strike Tom Leane, and, raising his voice, he would blurt out: 'But sure 'tis foolish for the like of me to be talking about these far-off places, and that man inside after travelling the world, over and thither.' The man inside, however, would give no sign whatever whether their gossip had been wise or foolish. They might hear the bed creak, as if he had turned with impatience at their mention of his very presence.

There had been a spell of stormy weather, it was now the middle of February, and for the last five days at twilight the gale seemed always to set in for a night of it. Although there was scarcely a house around that part of the south-west Irish coast that had not some one of its members, husband or brother or son, living on the sea, sailoring abroad or fishing the home waters or those of the Isle of Man—in no other house was the strain of a spell of disastrous weather so noticeable in the faces of its inmates. The old woman, withdrawn into herself, would handle her beads all day long, her voice every now and then raising itself, in forgetfulness, to a sort of moan not unlike the wind's, upon which the younger woman would chide her with a 'Sh! sh!' and bend vigorously upon her work to keep bitterness from her thoughts. At such a time she might enter her brother's room and find him raised on his elbow in the bed, listening to the howling winds, scared it seemed, his eyes fixed and wide open. He would drink the warm milk she had brought him, and hand the vessel back without a word. And in the selfsame attitude she would leave him.

The fifth night instead of growing in loudness and fierceness the wind died away somewhat. It became fitful, promising the end of the storm; and before long they could distinguish between the continuous groaning and pounding of the sea and the sudden shout the dying tempest would fling among the tree-tops and the rocks. They were thankful to note such signs of relief; the daughter became more active, and the mother put by her beads. In the midst of a sudden sally of the wind's the latch was raised, and Tom Leane gave them greeting. His face was rosy and glowing under his sou'wester; his eyes were sparkling from the sting of the salty gusts. To see him, so sane, so healthy, was to them like a blessing. 'How is it with ye?' he said, cheerily, closing the door to.

'Good, then, good, then,' they answered him, and the mother rose almost as if she would take him by the hand. The reply meant that nothing unforeseen had befallen them. He understood as much. He shook a silent head in the direction of the listener's room, a look of inquiry in his eyes, and this look Mary answered with a sort of hopeless upswing of her face. Things had not improved in the lower room.

The wind died away, more and more; and after some time streamed by with a shrill steady undersong; all through, however, the crashing of the sea on the jagged rocks beneath kept up an unceasing clamour. Tom had a whole budget of news for them. Finny's barn had been stripped of its roof; a window in the chapel had been blown in; and Largy's store of fodder had been shredded in the wind; it littered all the bushes to the east. There were rumours of a wreck somewhere; but it was too soon yet to know what damage the sea had done in its five days' madness. The news he had brought them did not matter; what mattered was his company, the knitting of their half-distraught household once again to humankind. Even when at last he stood up to go their spirits did not droop, so great had been the restoration.

'We're finished with it for a while anyhow,' Tom said, rising for home.

'We are, we are; and who knows, it mightn't be after doing all the damage we think.'

He shut the door behind him. The two women had turned towards the fire when they thought they again heard his voice outside. They wondered at the sound; they listened for his footsteps. Still staring at the closed door, once more they heard his voice. This time they were sure. The door reopened, and he backed in, as one does from an unexpected slap of rain in the face. The light struck outwards, and they saw a white face advancing. Some anxiety, some uncertainty, in Tom's attitude as he backed away from that advancing face, invaded them so that they too became afraid. They saw the stranger also hesitating, looking down his own limbs. His clothes were dripping; they were clung in about him. He was bare-headed. When he raised his face again, his look was full of apology. His features were large and flat, and grey as a stone. Every now and then a spasm went through them, and they wondered what it meant. His clab of a mouth hung open; his unshaven chin trembled. Tom spoke to him: 'You're better come in; but 'tis many another house would suit you better than this.'

They heard a husky, scarce-audible voice reply: 'A doghouse would do, or a stable.' Bravely enough he made an effort to smile.

'Oh, 'tisn't that at all. But come in, come in.' He stepped in slowly and heavily, again glancing down his limbs. The water running from his clothes spread in a black pool on the flags. The young woman began to touch him with her finger tips as with some instinctive sympathy, yet could not think, it seemed, what was best to be done. The mother, however, vigorously set the fire-wheel at work, and Tom built up the fire with bog-timber and turf. The stranger meanwhile stood as if half-dazed. At last, as Mary with a candle in her hand stood pulling out dry clothes from a press, he blurted out in the same husky voice, Welsh in accent:

'I think I'm the only one!'

They understood the significance of the words, but it seemed wrong to do so.

'What is it you're saying?' Mary said, but one would not have recognised the voice for hers, it was so toneless. He raised a heavy sailor's hand in an awkward taproom gesture: 'The others, they're gone, all of them.'

The spasm again crossed his homely features, and his hand fell. He bowed his head. A coldness went through them. They stared at him. He might have thought them inhuman. But Mary suddenly pulled herself together, leaping at him almost: 'Sh! Sh!' she said, 'speak low, speak low, low,' and as she spoke, all earnestness, she towed him first in the direction of the fire, and then away from it, haphazardly it seemed. She turned from him and whispered to Tom:

'Look, take him up into the loft, and he can change his clothes. Take these with you, and the candle, the candle.' And she reached him the candle eagerly. Tom led the stranger up the stairs, it was more like a ladder, and the two of them disappeared into the loft. The old woman whispered:

'What was it he said?'

''Tis how his ship is sunk.'

'Did he say he was the only one?'

'He said that.'

'Did himself hear him?' She nodded towards her son's room.

'No, didn't you see me pulling him away from it? But he'll hear him now. Isn't it a wonder Tom wouldn't walk easy on the boards!'

No answer from the old woman. She had deliberately

seated herself in her accustomed place at the fire, and now moaned out:

'Aren't we in a cruel way, not knowing how he'd take a thing!'

'Am I better tell him there's a poor seaman after coming in on us?'

'Do you hear them above! Do you hear them!'

In the loft the men's feet were loud on the boards. The voice they were half-expecting to hear they then heard break in on the clatter of the boots above:

'Mother! Mother!'

'Yes, child, yes.'

'Who's aloft? Who's going around like that, or is it dreaming I am?'

The sounds from above were certainly like what one hears in a ship. They thought of this, but they also felt something terrible in that voice they had been waiting for: they hardly knew it for the voice of the man they had been listening to for five months.

'Go in and tell him the truth,' the mother whispered. 'Who are we to know what's right to be done. Let God have the doing of it.' She threw her hands in the air.

Mary went in to her brother, and her limbs were weak and cold. The old woman remained seated at the fire, swung round from it, her eyes towards her son's room, fixed, as the head itself was fixed, in the tension of anxiety.

After a few minutes Mary emerged with a strange alertness upon her:

'He's rising! He's getting up! 'Tis his place, he says. He's quite good.' She meant he seemed bright and well. The mother said:

'We'll take no notice of him, only just as if he was always with us.'

'Yes.'

They were glad then to hear the two men in the loft groping for the stair head. The kettle began to splutter in the boil, and Mary busied herself with the table and tea cups.

III

The sailor came down, all smiles in his ill-fitting, haphazard clothes. He looked so overjoyed one might think he would presently burst into song.

'The fire is good,' he said. 'It puts life in one. And the dry clothes too. My word, I'm thankful to you, good people; I'm thankful to you.' He shook hands with them all effusively.

'Sit down now; drink up the tea.'

'I can't figure it out; less than two hours ago, out there . . .' As he spoke he raised his hand towards the little port-hole of a window, looking at them with his eyes staring. 'Don't be thinking of anything, but drink up the hot tea,' Mary said.

He nodded and set to eat with vigour. Yet suddenly he would stop, as if he were ashamed of it, turn half-round and look at them with beaming eyes, look from one to the other and back again; and they affably would nod back at him. 'Excuse me, people,' he would say, 'excuse me.' He had not the gift of speech, and his too-full heart could not declare itself. To make him feel at his ease, Tom Leane sat down away from him, and the women began to find something to do about the room. Then there were only little sounds in the room: the breaking of the eggs, the turning of the fire-wheel, the wind going by. The door of the lower room opened silently, so silently that none of them heard it, and before they were aware, the son of the house, with his clothes flung on loosely, was standing awkwardly in the middle of the floor, looking down on the back of the sailorman bent above the table. 'This is my son,' the mother thought of saying. 'He was after going to bed when you came in.'

The Welshman leaped to his feet, and impulsively, yet without many words, shook John Spillane by the hand, thanking him and all the household. As he seated himself again at the table John made his way silently towards the settle from which, across the room, he could see the sailor as he bent over his meal.

The stranger put the cup away from him, he could take no more; and Tom Leane and the womenfolk tried to keep him in talk, avoiding, as by some mutual understanding, the mention of what he had come through. The eyes of the son of the house were all the time fiercely buried in him. There came a moment's silence in the general chatter, a moment it seemed impossible to fill, and the sailorman swung his chair half-round from the table, a spoon held in his hand lightly: 'I can't figure it out. I can't nohow figure it out. Here I am, fed full like a prize beast; and warm—Oh, but I'm thankful—and all my mates,' with the spoon he was pointing towards the sea—'white, and cold like dead fish! I can't figure it out.'

To their astonishment a voice travelled across the room from the settle

'Is it how ye struck?'

'Struck! Three times we struck! We struck last night, about this time last night. And off we went in a puff! Fine, we said. We struck again. 'Twas just coming light. And off again. But when we struck the third time, 'twas like that!' He clapped his hands together; 'She went in matchwood! 'Twas dark. Why, it can't be two hours since!'

'She went to pieces?' the same voice questioned him.

'The *Nan Tidy* went to pieces, sir! No one knew what had happened or where he was. 'Twas too sudden. I found myself clung about a snag of rock. I hugged it. I hugged it.'

He stood up, hoisted as from within.

'Is it you that was on the look-out?'

'Me! We'd all been on the look-out for three days. My word, yes, three days. We were stupefied with it!'

They were looking at him as he spoke, and they saw the shiver again cross his features; the strength and warmth that the food and comfort had given him fell from him, and he became in an instant the half-drowned man who had stepped in to them that night with the clothes sagging about his limbs, ''Twas bad, clinging to that rock, with them all gone! 'Twas lonely! Do you know, I was so frightened I couldn't call out.'

John Spillane stood up, slowly, as if he too were being hoisted from within.

'Were they looking at you?'

'Who?'

'The rest of them. The eyes of them.'

'No,' the voice had dropped, 'no, I didn't think of that!' The two of them stared as if fascinated by each other.

'You didn't!' It seemed that John Spillane had lost the purpose of his questioning. His voice was thin and weak; but he was still staring with unmoving, puzzled eyes at the stranger's face. The abashed creature before him suddenly seemed to gain as much eagerness as he had lost: his words were hot with anxiety to express himself adequately:

'But now, isn't it curious, as I sat there, there at that table, I thought somehow they would walk in, that it would be right for them, somehow, to walk in, all of them!'

His words, his eager lowered voice, brought in the darkness outside, its vastness, its terror. They seemed in the midst of an unsubstantial world. They feared that the latch would lift, yet dared not glance at it, lest that should invite the lifting. But it was all one to the son of the house, he appeared to have gone away into some mood of his own; his eyes were glaring, not looking at anything or anyone close at hand. With an instinctive groping for comfort, they all, except him, began to stir, to find some little homely task to do: Mary handled the tea ware, and Tom his pipe, when a rumbling voice, very indistinct, stilled them all again. Words, phrases, began to reach them—that a man's eyes will close and he on the look-out, close in spite of himself, that it wasn't fair, it wasn't fair, it wasn't fair! And lost in his agony, he began to glide through them, explaining, excusing the terror that was in him: 'All round. Staring at me. Blaming me. A sea of them. Far, far! Without a word out of them, only their eyes in the darkness, pale like candles!'

Transfixed, they glared at him, at his roundshouldered

sailor's back disappearing again into his den of refuge. They could not hear his voice any more, they were afraid to follow him.

THE DOGS IN THE GREAT GLEN

Benedict Kiely

The professor had come over from America to search out his origins and I met him in Dublin on the way to Kerry where his grandfather had come from and where he had relations, including a grand-uncle, still living.

—But the trouble is, he said, that I've lost the address my mother gave me. She wrote to tell them I was coming to Europe. That's all they know. All I remember is a name out of my dead father's memories: the great Glen of Kanareen.

—You could write to your mother.

—That would take time. She'd be slow to answer. And I feel impelled right away to find the place my grandfather told my father about.

—You wouldn't understand, he said. Your origins are all around you.

—You can say that again, professor. My origins crop up like the bones of rock in thin sour soil. They come unwanted like the mushroom of Merulius Lacrimans on the walls of a decaying house.

—It's no laughing matter, he said.

—It isn't for me. This island's too small to afford a place in which to hide from one's origins. Or from anything else. During the war a young fellow in Dublin said to me: Mister, even if I ran away to sea I wouldn't get beyond the three-mile limit.

He said: But it's large enough to lose a valley in. I couldn't find the valley of Kanareen marked on any map or mentioned in any directory.

—I have a middling knowledge of the Kerry mountains, I said. I could join you in the search.

—It's not marked on the half-inch Ordnance Survey map.

—There are more things in Kerry than were ever dreamt of by the Ordnance Survey. The place could have another official name. At the back of my head I feel that once in the town of Kenmare in Kerry I heard a man mention the name of Kanareen.

We set off two days later in a battered, rattly Ford Prefect. Haste, he said, would be dangerous because Kanareen might not be there at all, but if we idled from place to place in the lackadaisical Irish summer we might, when the sentries were sleeping and the glen unguarded, slip secretly as thieves into the land whose legends were part of his rearing.

—Until I met you, the professor said, I was afraid the valley might have been a dream world my grandfather imagined to dull the edge of the first nights in a new land. I could see how he might have come to believe in it himself and told my father—and then, of course, my father told me.

One of his grandfather's relatives had been a Cistercian monk in Mount Melleray, and we went there hoping to see the evidence of a name in a book and to kneel, perhaps, under the high arched roof of the chapel close to where that monk had knelt. But, when we had traversed the corkscrew road over the purple Knockmealdowns and gone up to the mountain monastery through the forest the monks had made in the wilderness, it was late evening and the doors were closed. The birds sang vespers. The great silence affected us with something between awe and a painful, intolerable shyness. We hadn't the heart to ring a doorbell or to promise ourselves to return in the morning. Not speaking to each other we retreated, the rattle of the Ford Prefect as irreverent as dicing on the altar-steps. Half a mile down the road the mute, single-file procession of a group of women exercitants walking back to the female guest-house underlined the holy, unreal, unanswering stillness that had closed us out. It could easily have been that his grandfather never had a relative a monk in Mount Melleray.

A cousin of his mother's mother had, he had been told, been a cooper in Lady Gregory's Gort in the County Galway. But when we crossed the country westwards to Gort, it produced nothing except the information that apart from the big breweries, where they survived like birds or bison in a sanctuary, the coopers had gone, leaving behind them not a hoop or a stave. So we visited the woods of Coole, close to Gort, where Lady Gregory's house had once stood, and on the brimming lake-water among the stones, we saw by a happy poetic accident the number of swans the poet had seen.

Afterwards in Galway City there was, as there always is in Galway City, a night's hard drinking that was like a fit of jovial hysteria, and a giggling ninny of a woman in the bar who kept saying: You're the nicest American I ever met. You don't look like an American. You don't even carry a camera. You look like a Kerryman.

And in the end, we came to Kenmare in Kerry, and in another bar we met a talkative Kerryman who could tell us all about the prowess of the Kerry team, about the heroic feats of John Joe Sheehy or Paddy Bawn Brosnan. He knew so much, that man, yet he couldn't tell us where in the wilderness of mountains we might find the Glen of Kanareen. Nor could anybody else in the bar be of the least help to us, not even the postman who could only say that wherever it was, that is if it was at all, it wasn't in his district.

—It could of course, he said, be east over the mountain.

Murmuring sympathetically, the entire bar assented. The rest of the world was east over the mountain.

With the resigned air of men washing their hands of a helpless, hopeless case the postman and the football savant directed us to a roadside post-office twelve miles away where, in a high-hedged garden before an old grey-stone house with latticed windows and an incongruous, green, official post-office sign there was a child, quite naked, playing with a coloured, musical spinning-top as big as itself, and an old half-deaf man sunning himself and swaying in a rocking-chair, a straw hat tilted forwards to shade his eyes. Like Oisin remembering the Fenians, he told us he had known once of a young woman who married a man from a place called Kanareen, but there had been contention about the match and her people had kept up no correspondence with her. But the day she left home with her husband that was the way she went. He pointed. The way went inland and up and up. We followed it.

—That young woman could have been a relation of mine, the professor said.

On a rock-strewn slope, and silhouetted on a saw-toothed ridge where you'd think only a chamois could get by without broken legs, small black cows, accurate and active as goats, rasped good milk from the grass between the stones. His grandfather had told his father about those athletic, legendary cows and about the proverb that said: Kerry cows know Sunday. For in famine times, a century since, mountain people bled the cows once a week to mix the blood into yellow maize meal and provide a meat dish, a special Sunday dinner.

The road twisted on across moorland that on our left sloped dizzily to the sea, as if the solid ground might easily slip and slide into the depths. Mountain shadows melted like purple dust into a green bay. Across a ravine and quite alone on a long, slanting, brown knife blade of a mountain was a white house with a red door. The rattle of our pathetic little car affronted the vast stillness. We were free to moralise on the extent of all space in relation to the trivial area that limited our ordinary daily lives.

The two old druids of men resting from work on the leeward side of a turf-bank listened to our enquiry with the same attentive, half-conscious patience they gave to bird-cries or the sound of wind in the heather. Then they waved us ahead towards a narrow cleft in the distant wall of mountains as if they doubted the ability of ourselves and our conveyance to negotiate the gap and find the glen. They offered us strong tea and a drop out of a bottle. They watched us with kind irony as we drove away. Until the gap swallowed us and the hazardous, twisting track absorbed all our attention we could look back and still see them, motionless, waiting with indifference for the landslide that would end it all.

*   *   *

By a roadside pool where water-beetles lived their vicious secretive lives, we sat and rested, with the pass and the cliffs, overhung with heather, behind us and another ridge ahead. Brazenly the sheer rocks reflected the sun and semaphored at us. Below us, in the dry summer, the bed of a stream held only a trickle of water twisting painfully around piles of round black stones. Touch a beetle with a stalk of dry grass and the creature either dived like a shot or, angry at invasion, savagely grappled with the stalk.

—That silly woman in Galway, the professor said.

He dropped a stone into the pool and the beetles submerged to weather the storm.

—That day by the lake at Lady Gregory's Coole. The exact number of swans Yeats saw when the poem came to him. Upon the brimming water among the stones are nine and fifty swans. Since I don't carry a camera nobody will ever believe me. But you saw them. You counted them.

—Now that I am so far, he said, I'm half-afraid to finish the journey. What will they be like? What will they think of me? Will I go over that ridge there to find my grandfather's brother living in a cave?

Poking at and tormenting the beetles on the black mirror of the pool, I told him: Once I went from Dublin to near Shannon Pot, where the river rises, to help an American woman find the house where her dead woman friend had been reared. On her deathbed the friend had written it all out on a sheet of notepaper: Cross the river at Battle Bridge. Go straight through the village with the ruined castle on the right. Go on a mile to the crossroads and the labourer's cottage with the lovely snapdragons in the flower garden. Take the road to the right there, and then the second boreen on the left beyond the schoolhouse. Then stop at the third house on that boreen. You can see the river from the flag-stone at the door.

—Apart from the snapdragons it was exactly as she had written it down. The dead woman had walked that boreen as a barefooted schoolgirl. Not able to revisit it herself she entrusted the mission as her dying wish to her dearest friend. We found the house. Her people were long gone from it but the new tenants remembered them. They welcomed us with melodeon and fiddle and all the neighbours came in and collated the long memories of the townland. They feasted us with cold ham and chicken, porter and whisky, until I had cramps for a week.

—My only grip on identity, he said, is that a silly woman told me I looked like a Kerryman. My grandfather was a Kerryman. What do Kerrymen look like?

—Big, I said.

—And this is the heart of Kerry. And what my grand-father said about the black cows was true. With a camera I could have taken a picture of those climbing cows. And up that hill trail and over that ridge is Kanareen.

—We hope, I said.

*   *   *

The tired cooling engine coughed apologetically when we abandoned it and put city-shod feet to the last ascent.

—If that was the mountain my grandfather walked over in the naked dawn coming home from an all-night card-playing then, by God, he was a better man than me, said the pro-fessor.

He folded his arms and looked hard at the razor-cut edges of stone on the side of the mountain.

—Short of too much drink and the danger of mugging, he said, getting home at night in New York is a simpler operation than crawling over that hunk of miniature Mount Everest. Like walking up the side of a house.

He was as proud as Punch of the climbing prowess of his grandfather.

—My father told me, he said, that one night coming home from the card-playing my grandfather slipped down fifteen feet of rock and the only damage done was the ruin of one of two bottles of whisky he had in the tail-pockets of his greatcoat. The second bottle was unharmed.

The men who surfaced the track we were walking on had been catering for horses and narrow iron-hooped wheels. After five minutes of agonised slipping and sliding, wisdom came to us and we took to the cushioned grass and heather. As we ascended the professor told me what his grandfather had told his father about the market town he used to go to when he was a boy. It was a small town where even on market days the dogs would sit nowhere except exactly in the middle of the street. They were lazy town dogs, not active, loyal and intelligent like the dogs the grandfather had known in the great glen. The way the old man had described it, the town's five streets grasped the ground of Ireland as the hand of a strong swimmer might grasp a ledge of rock to hoist himself out of the water. On one side was the sea. On the other side a shoulder of mountain rose so steeply that the Gaelic name of it meant the gable of the house.

When the old man went as a boy to the town on a market day it was his custom to climb that mountain, up through furze and following goat tracks, leaving his shiny boots, that he only put on, anyway, when he entered the town, securely in hiding behind a furze bush. The way he remembered that mountain it would seem that twenty minutes active climbing brought him halfways to heaven. The little town was far

below him, and the bay and the islands. The unkempt coast-
line tumbled and sprawled to left and right, and westwards
the ocean went on for ever. The sounds of market day,
voices, carts, dogs barking, musicians on the streets, came
up to him as faint, silvery whispers. On the tip of one island
two tall aerials marked the place where, he was told, messages went down into the sea to travel all the way to America
by cable. That was a great marvel for a boy from the mountains to hear about: the ghostly shrill, undersea voices; the
words of people in every tongue of Europe far down among
the monstrous fish and shapeless sea-serpents that never saw
the light of the sun. He closed his eyes one day and it seemed
to him that the sounds of the little town were the voices of
Europe setting out on their submarine travels. That was the
time he knew that when he was old enough he would leave
the Glen of Kanareen and go with the voices westwards to
America.

—Or so he said. Or so he told my father, said the professor. Another fifty yards and we would be on top of the
ridge. We kept our eyes on the ground, fearful of the
moment of vision and, for good or ill, revelation. Beyond
the ridge there might be nothing but a void to prove that his
grandfather had been a dreamer or a liar. Rapidly, ner-
vously, he tried to talk down his fears.

—He would tell stories for ever, my father said, about
ghosts and the good people. There was one case of an old
woman whose people buried her—when she died, of course
—against her will, across the water, which meant on the far
side of the lake in the glen. Her dying wish was to be buried
in another graveyard, nearer home. And there she was, sitting in her own chair in the chimney corner, waiting for
them, when they came home from the funeral. To ease her
spirit they replanted her.

To ease the nervous moment I said: There was a polter-
geist once in a farmhouse in these mountains, and the police
decided to investigate the queer happenings, and didn't an
ass's collar come flying across the room to settle around the

sergeant's neck. Due to subsequent ridicule the poor man had to be transferred to Dublin.

Laughing, we looked at the brown infant runnel that went parallel to the path. It flowed with us: we were over the watershed. So we raised our heads slowly and saw the great Glen of Kanareen. It was what Cortez saw, and all the rest of it. It was a discovery. It was a new world. It gathered the sunshine into a gigantic coloured bowl. We accepted it detail by detail.

—It was there all the time, he said. It was no dream. It was no lie.

The first thing we realised was the lake. The runnel leaped down to join the lake, and we looked down on it through ash trees regularly spaced on a steep, smooth, green slope. Grasping from tree to tree you could descend to the pebbled, lapping edge of the water.

—That was the way, the professor said, the boys in his time climbed down to fish or swim. Black, bull-headed mountain trout. Cannibal trout. There was one place where they could dive off sheer rock into seventy feet of water. Rolling like a gentle sea: that was how he described it. They gathered kindling, too, on the slopes under the ash trees.

Then, after the lake, we realised the guardian mountain; not rigidly chiselled into ridges of rock like the mountain behind us but soft and gently curving, protective and, above all, noble, a monarch of mountains, an antlered stag holding a proud horned head up to the highest point of the blue sky. Green fields swathed its base. Sharp lines of stone walls, dividing wide areas of moorland sheep-grazing, marked man's grip for a thousand feet or so above sea-level then gave up the struggle and left the mountain alone and untainted. Halfways up one snow-white cloud rested as if it had hooked itself on a snagged rock and there it stayed, motionless, as step by step we went down into the glen. Below the cloud a long cataract made a thin, white, forked-lightning line, and, in the heart of the glen, the river that the cataract became, sprawled on a brown and green and golden patchwork bed.

—It must be some one of those houses, he said, pointing ahead and down to the white houses of Kanareen.

—Take a blind pick, I said. I see at least fifty.

They were scattered over the glen in five or six clusters.

—From what I heard it should be over in that direction, he said.

Small rich fields were ripe in the sun. This was a glen of plenty, a gold-field in the middle of a desert, a happy laughing mockery of the arid surrounding moors and mountains. Five hundred yards away a dozen people were working at the hay. They didn't look up or give any sign that they had seen two strangers cross the high threshold of their kingdom but, as we went down, stepping like grenadier guards, the black-and-white sheepdogs detached themselves from the haymaking and moved silently across to intercept our path. Five of them I counted. My step faltered.

—This could be it, I suggested with hollow joviality. I feel a little like an early Christian.

The professor said nothing. We went on down, deserting the comfort of the grass and heather at the side of the track. It seemed to me that our feet on the loose pebbles made a tearing, crackling, grinding noise that shook echoes even out of the imperturbable mountain. The white cloud had not moved. The haymakers had not honoured us with a glance.

—We could, I said, make ourselves known to them in a civil fashion. We could ask the way to your grand-uncle's house. We could have a formal introduction to those slinking beasts.

—No, let me, he said. Give me my head. Let me try to remember what I was told.

—The hearts of these highland people, I've heard, are made of pure gold, I said. But they're inclined to be the tiniest bit suspicious of town-dressed strangers. As sure as God made smells and shotguns they think we're inspectors from some government department: weeds, or warble-fly or horror of horrors, rates and taxes. With equanimity they'd see us eaten.

He laughed. His stride had a new elasticity in it. He was another man. The melancholy of the monastic summer dusk at Mount Melleray was gone. He was somebody else coming home. The white cloud had not moved. The silent dogs came closer. The unheeding people went on with their work.

—The office of rates collector is not sought after in these parts, I said. Shotguns are still used to settle vexed questions of land title. Only a general threat of excommunication can settle a major feud.

—This was the way he'd come home from the gambling cabin, the professor said, his pockets clinking with winnings. That night he fell he'd won the two bottles of whisky. He was only eighteen when he went away. But he was the tallest man in the glen. So he said. And lucky at cards.

The dogs were twenty yards away, silent, fanning out like soldiers cautiously circling a point of attack.

—He was an infant prodigy, I said. He was a peerless grand-father for a man to have. He also had one great advantage over us—he knew the names of these taciturn dogs and they knew his smell.

He took off his white hat and waved at the workers. One man at a haycock raised a pitchfork—in salute or in threat? Nobody else paid the least attention. The dogs were now at our heels, suiting their pace politely to ours. They didn't even sniff. They had impeccable manners.

—This sure is the right glen, he said. The old man was never done talking about the dogs. They were all black-and-white in his day, too.

He stopped to look at them. They stopped. They didn't look up at us. They didn't snarl. They had broad shaggy backs. Even for their breed they were big dogs. Their long tails were rigid. Fixing my eyes on the white cloud I walked on.

—Let's establish contact, I said, before we're casually eaten. All I ever heard about the dogs in these mountains is

that their family tree is as old as the Red Branch Knights.
That they're the best sheepdogs in Ireland and better than
anything in the Highlands of Scotland. They also savage you
first and bark afterwards.

Noses down, they padded along behind us. Their quiet
breath was hot on my calves. High up and far away the
nesting white cloud had the security of heaven.

—Only strangers who act suspiciously, the professor said.

—What else are we? I'd say we smell bad to them.

—Not me, he said. Not me. The old man told a story
about a stranger who came to Kanareen when most of the
people were away at the market. The house he came to visit
was empty except for two dogs. So he sat all day at the door
of the house and the dogs lay and watched him and said and
did nothing. Only once, he felt thirsty and went into the
kitchen of the house and lifted a bowl to go to the well for
water. Then there was a low duet of a snarl that froze his
blood. So he went thirsty and the dogs lay quiet.

—Hospitable people.

—The secret is touch nothing, lay no hand on property
and you're safe.

—So help me God, I said, I wouldn't deprive them of a
bone or a blade of grass.

Twice in my life I had been bitten by dogs. Once, walking
to school along a sidestreet on a sunny morning and simultaneously reading in *The Boy's Magazine* about a soccer
centre forward, the flower of the flock, called Fiery Cross
the Shooting Star—he was redheaded and his surname was
Cross—I had stepped on a sleeping Irish terrier. In retaliation, the startled brute had bitten me. Nor could I find it
in my heart to blame him, so that, in my subconscious, dogs
took on the awful heaven-appointed dignity of avenging
angels. The other time—and this was an even more dis-
quieting experience—a mongrel dog had come up softly
behind me while I was walking on the fairgreen in the town
I was reared in and bitten the calf of my leg so as to draw
spurts of blood. I kicked him but not resenting the kick, he

had walked away as if it was the most natural, legitimate thing in heaven and earth for a dog to bite me and be kicked in return. Third time, I thought, it will be rabies. So as we walked and the silent watchers of the valley padded at our heels, I enlivened the way with brave and trivial chatter. I recited my story of the four wild brothers of Adrigole.

—Once upon a time, I said, there lived four brothers in a rocky corner of Adrigole in West Cork, under the mountain called Hungry Hill. Daphne du Maurier wrote a book called after the mountain, but divil a word in it about the four brothers of Adrigole. They lived, I heard tell, according to instinct and never laced their boots and came out only once a year to visit the nearest town which was Castletownbere-haven on the side of Bantry Bay. They'd stand there, backs to the wall, smoking, saying nothing, contemplating the giddy market-day throng. One day they ran out of tobacco and went into the local branch of the Bank of Ireland to buy it and raised havoc because the teller refused to satisfy their needs. To pacify them the manager and the teller had to disgorge their own supplies. So they went back to Adrigole to live happily without lacing their boots, and ever after they thought that in towns and cities the bank was the place where you bought tobacco.

—That, said I with a hollow laugh, is my moral tale about the four brothers of Adrigole.

On a level with the stream that came from the lake and went down to join the valley's main river, we walked towards a group of four whitewashed, thatched farmhouses that were shining and scrupulously clean. The track looped to the left. Through a small triangular meadow a short-cut went straight towards the houses. In the heart of the meadow, by the side of the short-cut, there was a spring well of clear water, the stones that lined its sides and the roof cupped over it all white and cleansed with lime. He went down three stone steps and looked at the water. For good luck there was a tiny brown trout imprisoned in the well. He said quietly:

That was the way my grandfather described it. But it could hardly be the self-same fish.

He stooped to the clear water. He filled his cupped hands and drank. He stooped again, and again filled his cupped hands and slowly, carefully, not spilling a drop, came up the moist, cool steps. Then, with the air of a priest, scattering hyssop, he sprinkled the five dogs with the spring-water. They backed away from him, thoughtfully. They didn't snarl or show teeth. He had them puzzled. He laughed with warm good nature at their obvious perplexity. He was making his own of them. He licked his wet hands. Like good pupils attentively studying a teacher, the dogs watched him.

—Elixir, he said. He told my father that the sweetest drink he ever had was out of this well when he was on his way back from a drag hunt in the next glen. He was a great hunter.

—He was Nimrod, I said. He was everything. He was the universal Kerryman.

—No kidding, he said. Through a thorn hedge six feet thick and down a precipice and across a stream to make sure of a wounded bird. Or all night long waist deep in an icy swamp waiting for the wild geese. And the day of this drag hunt. What he most remembered about it was the way they sold the porter to the hunting crowd in the pub at the crossroads. To meet the huntsmen halfways they moved the bar out to the farmyard. With hounds and cows and geese and chickens it was like having a drink in Noah's Ark. The pint tumblers were set on doors lifted off their hinges and laid flat on hurdles. The beer was in wooden tubs and all the barmaids had to do was dip and there was the pint. They didn't bother to rinse the tumblers. He said it was the quickest-served and the flattest pint of porter he ever saw or tasted. Bitter and black as bog water. Completely devoid of the creamy clerical collar that should grace a good pint. On the way home he spent an hour here rinsing his mouth and the well-water tasted as sweet, he said, as silver.

The white cloud was gone from the mountain.

—Where did it go, I said. Where could it vanish to?
In all the wide sky there wasn't a speck of cloud. The mountain was changing colour, deepening to purple with the approaching evening.

*   *   *

He grasped me by the elbow, urging me forwards. He said: Step on it. We're almost home.

We crossed a crude wooden stile and followed the short-cut through a walled garden of bright-green heads of cabbage and black and red currant bushes. Startled, fruit-thieving birds rustled away from us and on a rowan tree a sated, impudent blackbird opened his throat and sang.

—Don't touch a currant, I said, or a head of cabbage. Don't ride your luck too hard.

He laughed like a boy half hysterical with happiness. He said: Luck. Me and these dogs, we know each other. We've been formally introduced.

—Glad to know you dogs, he said to them over his shoulder. They trotted behind us. We crossed a second stile and followed the short-cut through a haggard, and underfoot the ground was velvety with chipped straw. We opened a five-barred iron gate, and to me it seemed that the noise of its creaking hinges must be audible from end to end of the glen. While I paused to rebolt it he and the dogs had gone on, the dogs trotting in the lead. I ran after them. I was the stranger who had once been the guide. We passed three houses as if they didn't exist. They were empty. The people who lived in them were above at the hay. Towards the fourth thatched house of the group we walked along a green boreen, lined with hazels and an occasional mountain ash. The guardian mountain was by now so purple that the sky behind it seemed, by contrast, as silvery as the scales of a fish. From unknown lands behind the lines of hazels two more black-and-white dogs ran, barking with excitement, to join our escort. Where the hazels ended there was a house fronted by a low stone wall and a profusion of fuchsia. An old man sat on the wall and around him clustered the children of the four houses. He was a tall, broad-shouldered old man with copious white hair and dark side whiskers and a clear prominent profile. He was dressed in good grey with long, old-fashioned skirts to his coat—formally dressed as if for some formal event—and his wide-brimmed black hat rested on the wall beside him, and his joined hands rested on the curved handle of a strong ash plant. He stood up as we approached. The stick fell to the ground. He stepped over it and came towards us. He was as tall or, without the slight stoop of age, taller than the professor. He put out his two hands and rested them on the professor's shoulders. It wasn't an embrace. It was an appraisal, a salute, a sign of recognition.

He said: Kevin, well and truly we knew you'd come if you were in the neighbourhood at all. I watched you walking down. I knew you from the top of the glen. You have the same gait my brother had, the heavens be his bed. My brother that was your grandfather.

—They say a grandson often walks like the grandfather, said the professor.

His voice was shaken and there were tears on his face. So, a stranger in the place myself, I walked away a bit and looked back up at the glen. The sunlight was slanting now and shadows were lengthening on mountain slopes and across the small fields. From where I stood the lake was invisible, but the ashwood on the slope above it was dark as ink. Through sunlight and shadow the happy haymakers came running down towards us; and barking, playing, frisking over each other, the seven black-and-white dogs, messengers of good news, ran to meet them. The great glen, all happy echoes, was opening out and singing to welcome its true son.

Under the hazels, as I watched the running haymakers, the children came shyly around me to show me that I also was welcome. Beyond the high ridge, the hard mountain the card-players used to cross to the cabin of the gambling stood up gaunt and arrogant and leaned over towards us as if it were listening.

It was moonlight, I thought, not sunlight, over the great glen. From house to house, the dogs were barking, not baying the moon, but to welcome home the young men from the card-playing over the mountain. The edges of rock glistened like quartz. The tall young gambler came laughing down the glen, greatcoat swinging open, waving in his hand the one bottle of whisky that hadn't been broken when he tumbled down the spink. The ghosts of his own dogs laughed and leaped and frolicked at his heels.

THE GREEN GRAVE AND THE BLACK GRAVE

Mary Lavin

I

It was a body, all right. It was hard to see in the dark, and the scale-back sea was heaving up between them and the place where they saw the thing floating. But it was a body, all right.

'I knew it was a shout I heard,' said the taller of the two tall men in the black boat, that was out fishing for mackerel. He was Tadg Mor and he was the father of the less tall man, that was blacker in the hair than him and broader in the chest than him, but was called Tadg Beag because he was son to him. Mor means big and Beag means small, but Mor can be given to mean greater and Beag can be given to mean lesser than the greater.

'I knew it was a shout I heard,' said Tadg Mor.

'I knew it was a boat I saw and I dragging in the second net,' said Tadg Beag.

'I said the sound I heard was a kittwake, crying in the dark.'

'And I said the boat I saw was a black wave blown up on the wind.'

'It was a shout, all right.'

'It was a boat, all right.'

'It was a body, all right.'

'But where is the black boat?' said Tadg Beag.

'It must be that the black boat capsized,' said Tadg Mor, 'and went down into the green sea.'

'Whose boat was it, would you venture for to say?' said
Tadg Beag, pulling stroke for stroke at the sea.

'I'd venture for to say it was the boat of Eamon Og Murnan,' said Tadg Mor, pulling with his oar at the spittle-
painted sea.

The tall men rowed against the sharp up-pointing waves
of the scaly, scurvy sea. They rowed to the clumsy thing that
tossed on the tips of the deft green waves.

'Eamon Og Murnan,' said Tadg Mor, lifting clear his
silver-dripping oar.

'Eamon Og Murnan,' said Tadg Beag, lifting his clear,
dripping, silver oar.

It was a hard drag, dragging him over the arching sides of
the boat. His clothes logged him down to the water, and the
jutting waves jostled him back against the boat. His yellow
hair slipped from their fingers like floss, and the fibres of his
island-spun clothes broke free from their grip. But they got
him up over the edge of the boat, at the end of a black hour
that was only lit by the whiteness of the breaking wave. They
laid him down on the boards of the floor on their haul of
glittering mackerel and they spread the nets out over him.
But the scales of the fish glittered up through the net, and
so too the eyes of Eamon Og Murnan glittered up through
the nets. And the live glitter of those dead eyes put a strain
on Tadg Mor and he turned the body over on its face among
the fish, and when they had looked a time at the black corpse
with yellow hair set in the silver and opal casket of fishes,
they put the ends of the oars in the oarlocks and turned the
oar blades out again into the scurvy waves and turned their
boat back to the land.

'How did you know it was Eamon Og Murnan, and we
forty pointed waves away from him at the time of your nam-
ing his name?' said Tadg Beag to Tadg Mor.

'Whenever it is a thing that a man is pulled under by the
sea,' said Tadg Mor, 'think around in your mind until you
think out which man of all the men it might be that would
be the man most missed, and that man, that you think out

in your mind, will be the man that will be netted up on the shingle.'

'This is a man that will be missed mightily,' said Tadg Beag.

'He is a man that will be mightily bemoaned,' said Tadg Mor.

'He is a man that will never be replaced.'

'He is a man that will be prayed for bitterly and mightily.'

'And food will be set out for him every night in a bowl,' said Tadg Beag.

'The Brightest and the Bravest!' said Tadg Mor. 'Those are the words will be read over him—"The Brightest and the Bravest."'

The boat rose up on the points of the waves and clove down again between the points, and the oars of Tadg Mor and the oars of Tadg Beag split the points of many waves.

'How is it the green sea always greeds after the brightest and the bravest?' Tadg Beag asked Tadg Mor.

'And for the only sons?' asked Tadg Mor.

'And the men with one-year wives?'

'The one-year wife that's getting this corpse tonight,' said Tadg Mor, pointing down with his eyes, 'will have a black sorrow this night.'

'And every night after this night,' said Tadg Beag, because he was a young man and knew about such things.

'It's a great thing that he was not dragged down to the green grave, and that is a thing will lighten the nights of the one-year wife,' said Tadg Mor.

'It isn't many are saved out of the green grave,' said Tadg Beag.

'Kirnan Mor wasn't got,' said Tadg Mor.

'And Murnan Beag wasn't got.'

'Lorcan Mor wasn't got.'

'Tirnan Beag wasn't got.'

'It was three weeks and the best part of a night before the Frenchman with the leather coat was got, and five boats out looking for him.'

'It was seven weeks before Lorcan Mac Kinealy was got, and his eye sockets emptied by the gulls and the gannies.'

'And by the waves. The waves are great people to lick out your eyeballs!' said Tadg Mor.

'It was a good thing, this man to be got,' said Tadg Beag, 'and his eyes bright in his head.'

'Like he was looking up at the sky!'

'Like he was thinking to smile next thing he'd do.'

'He was a great man to smile, this man,' said Tadg Mor. 'He was ever and always smiling.'

'He was a great man to laugh, too,' said Tadg Beag. 'He was ever and always laughing.'

'Times he was laughing and times he was not laughing,' said Tadg Mor.

'Times all men stop from laughing,' said Tadg Beag.

'Times I saw this man and he not laughing. Times I saw him and he putting out in the black boat looking back at the inland woman where she'd be standing on the shore and her hair weaving the wind, and there wouldn't be any laugh on his face those times.'

'An island man should take an island wife,' said Tadg Beag.

'An inland woman should take an inland man.'

'The inland woman that took this man had a dreadful dread on her of the sea and the boats that put out in it.'

'I saw this woman from the inlands standing on the shore, times, from his putting out with the hard dry boat to his coming back with the shivering silver-belly boat.'

'He got it hard to go from her every night.'

'He got it harder than iron to go from her if there was a streak of storm gold in the sky at time of putting out.'

'An island man should not be held down to a woman from the silent inlands.'

'It was love talk and love looks that held down this man,' said Tadg Mor.

'The island women give love words and love looks too,' said Tadg Beag.

'But not the love words and the love looks of this woman,' said Tadg Mor.

'Times I saw her wetting her feet in the waves and wetting her fingers in the waves, and you'd see she was kind of lovering the waves so they'd bring him back to her.'

'Times he told me himself she had a dreadful dread of the green grave. "There dies as many men in the inlands as in the islands," I said. "Tell her that," I said. "I tell her that," said he. "'But they get the black-grave burial,' she says. 'They get the black-grave burial in clay that's blessed by two priests, and they get the speeding of the green sods thrown down by the kinsmen,' she says. "Tell her there's no worms in the green grave," I said to him. "I did," said he. "What did she say to that?" said I. "She said, 'The bone waits for the bone,'" said he. "What does she mean by that?" said I. "She gave another saying as her meaning to that saying," said he. "She said, 'There's no trouble in death when two go down together into the one black grave. Clay binds closer than love,' she said. 'But the green grave binds nothing,' she said. 'The green grave scatters,' she said. 'The green grave is for sons,' she said, 'and for brothers' she said, 'but the black grave is for lovers,' she said, 'and for husbands in the faithful clay under the jealous sods.'"

'She must be a great woman to make sayings,' said Tadg Beag.

'She made great sayings for that man every hour of the day, and she stitching the nets for him on the step while he'd be salting fish or blading oars.'

'She'll be glad us to have saved him from the salt green grave.'

'It's a great wonder but he was dragged down before he was got.'

'She is the kind of woman that always has great wonders happening round her,' said Tadg Mor. 'If she is a woman from the inlands itself, she has a great power in herself. She has a great power over the sea. Times and she on the cliff shore and her hair weaving the wind, like I told you, I'd

point my eyes through the wind across at where Eamon Og
would be in the waves back of me and there wouldn't be as
much as one white tongue of spite rising out of the waves
around his boat, and my black boat would be splattered over
every board of it with white sea spittle.'

'I heard tell of women like that. She took the fury out of
the sea and burnt it out to white salt in her own heart.'

II

The talk about the inland woman who fought the seas in her
heart was slow talk and heavy talk, and slow and heavy talk
was fit talk as the scurvy waves crawled over one another,
scale by scale, and brought the bitter boat back to the shore.

Sometimes a spiteful tongue of foam forked up in the dark
by the side of the boat and reached for the netted corpse on
the boards. When this happened Tadg Beag picked up the
loose end of the raggy net and lashed out with it at the sea.

'Get down, you scaly-belly serpent,' he said, 'and let the
corpse dry out in his dead-clothes.'

'Take heed to your words, Tadg Beag,' Tadg Mor would
say. 'We have the point to round yet. Take heed to your
words!'

'Here's a man took heed to his words and that didn't save
him,' said Tadg Beag. 'Here was a man was always singing
back song for song to the singing sea, and look at him now
lying there.'

They looked at him lying on his face under the brown web
of the nets in his casket of fish scales, silver and opal. And
as they looked another lick of the forked and venomous
tongue of the sea came up the side of the boat and strained
in towards the body. Tadg Beag beat at it with the raggy
net.

'Keep your strength for the loud knocking you'll have to
give on the wooden door,' said Tadg Mor. And Tadg Beag
understood that he was the one would walk up the shingle
and bring the death news to the one-year wife, who was

so strange among the island women with her hair weaving the wind at evening and her white feet wetted in the sea by day.

'Is it not a thing that she'll be, likely, out on the shore?' he said in a bright hope, pointing his eyes to where the white edge of the shore wash shone by its own light in the dark.

'Is there a storm tonight?' said Tadg Mor. 'Is there a high wind tonight? Is there a rain spate? Is there any sign of danger on the sea?'

'No,' said Tadg Beag, 'there are none of those things that you mention.'

'I will tell you the reason you ask that question,' said Tadg Mor. 'You ask that question because that question is the answer that you'd like to get.'

'It's a hard thing to bring news to a one-year wife, and she one that has a dreadful dread of the sea,' said Tadg Beag.

'It's good news you're bringing to the one-year wife when you bring news that her man is got safe to go down like any inlander into a black grave blessed and tramped down with the feet of his kinsmen on the sod.'

'It's a queer thing, him to be caught by the sea on a fine night with no wind blowing,' said Tadg Beag.

'On a fine night the women lie down to sleep, and if any woman has a power over the sea with her white feet in the water and her black hair on the wind and a bright fire in her heart, the sea can only wait until that woman's spirit is out of her body, likely back home in the inlands, and then the sea serpent gives a slow turn over on his scales, one that you wouldn't heed to, yourself, maybe and you standing up with no hold on the oars, and before there's time for more than the first shout out of you the boat is logging down to the depths of the water. And all the time the woman that would have saved you, with her willing and wishing for you, is in the deep bed of the dark sleep, having no knowledge of the thing that has happened until she hears the loud-handed knocking of the neighbour on the door outside.'

Tadg Beag knocked with his knuckles on the sideboards of the boat.

'Louder than that,' said Tadg Mor.

Tadg Beag knocked another louder knock on the boat sides.

'Have you no more knowledge than that of how to knock at a door in the fastness of the night, and the people inside the house buried in sleep and the corpse down on the shore getting covered with sand and the fish scales drying into him so tight that the fingernails of the washing women will be broken and split peeling them off him? Have you no more knowledge than that of how to knock with your knucklebones?'

Tadg Mor gave a loud knocking against the wet seat of the boat.

'That is the knock of a man that you might say knows how to knock at a door, daytime or night-time,' he said, and he knocked again.

And he knocked again, louder, if it could be that any knock he gave could be louder than the first knock. Tadg Beag listened and then he spoke, not looking at Tadg Mor, but looking at the oar he was rolling in the water.

'Two people knocking would make a loud knocking entirely, I would think,' he said.

'One has to stay with the dead,' said Tadg Mor.

Tadg Beag drew a long stroke on the oar and he drew a long breath out of his lungs and he took a long look at the nearing shore.

'What will I say,' he said, 'when she comes to my knocking?'

'When she comes to the knocking, step back a bit from the door, so's she'll see the wet shining on you, and so's she'll smell the salt water off you, and say in a loud voice that the sea is queer and rough this night.'

'She'll be down with her to the shore, if that's what I say, without waiting to hear more.'

'Say, then,' said Tadg Mor, pulling in the oar to slow the

boat a bit, 'say that there's news come in that a boat went down off beyond the point.'

'If I say that, she'll be down with her to the shore without waiting to hear more, and her hair flying and her white feet freezing on the shingle.'

'If that is so,' said Tadg Mor, 'then you'll have to stand back bold from the door and call out loudly in the night: "The Brightest and the Bravest!" '

'What will she say to that?'

'She'll say, "God bless them." '

'And what will I say to that?'

'You'll say, "God rest them." '

'And what will she say to that?'

'She'll say, "Is it in the black grave or the green grave?" '

'And what will I say to that?'

'You say, "God rest Eamon Og Murnan in the black grave in the holy ground, blessed by the priest and sodded by the people." '

'And what will she say to that?'

'She'll say, likely, "Bring him in to me, Tadg Beag!" '

'And what will I say to that?'

'Whatever you say after that, let it be loud and making echoes under the rafters, so she won't hear the sound of the corpse dragging up on the shingle, and when he's lifted up on to the scoured table, let whatever you say be loud then too, so's she won't be listening for the sound of the water drabbling down off his clothes on the floor!'

III

There was only the noise of the oars, then, till a shoaly sounding stole in between the oar strokes. It was the shoaly sounding of the irritable pebbles that were dragged back and forth on the shore by the tides.

They beached in a little while, and they stepped out among the sprawling waves and dragged the boat after them till it cleft its depth in the damp shingle.

'See that you give a loud knocking, Tadg Beag,' said Tadg Mor, and Tadg Beag set his head against the darkness and his feet were heard for a good time grinding down the shifting shingle as he made for the house of the one-year wife. The house was set in a sea field, and his feet did not sound down to the shore once he got to the dune grass of the sea field. But in another little while there was a loud sound of a fist knocking hard upon wood, stroke after stroke of a strong hand coming down on hard wood.

Tadg Mor, waiting with the body in the boat, recalled to himself all the times he went knocking on the island doors bringing news to the women of the death of their men, but island women were brought up in bitterness and they got life as well as death from the sea. They keened for their own, and it would be hard to know by their keening whether it was for their own men or the men of their neighbours they were keening. Island wives were the daughters of island widows. The sea gave food. The sea gave death. Life or death, it was all one thing in the end. The sea never lost its scabs. The sea was there before the coming of man. Island women knew that knowledge, but what knowledge had a woman from the inlands of the sea and its place in the world since the beginning of time? No knowledge. An inland woman had no knowledge to guide her when the loud knocking came on her door in the night.

Tadg Mor listened to the loud, hard knocking of his son Tadg Beag on the door of the one-year wife of Eamon Og Murnan that was lying in the silver casket of fishes on the floor of the boat, cleft fast in the shingle sand. The night was cold, the fish scales glittered even though it was dark. They glittered in the whiteness made by the breaking wave on the shore. The sound of the sea was sadder than the back of the head of the yellow-haired corpse, but still Tadg Mor was gladder to be down on the shore than up in the dune grass knocking at the one-night widow's door.

The knocking sound of Tadg Beag's knuckles on the wooden door was a human sound and it sounded good in

the ears of Tadg Mor for a time, but, like all sounds that
continue too long, it sounded soon to be as weird and
inhuman as the washing sound of the waves tiding in on the
shingle. Tadg Mor put up his rounded palms to his mouth
and shouted out to Tadg Beag to come back to the boat.
Tadg Beag came back running the shingle, and the air was
grained with sounds of sliding gravel.

'There's no one in the house where you were knocking,'
said Tadg Mor.

'I knocked louder on the door than you knocked on the
boat boards,' said Tadg Beag.

'I heard how you knocked,' said Tadg Mor; 'you knocked
well. But let you knock better when you go to the neighbour's house to find out where the one-night widow is from
her own home this night.'

'If I got no answer at one door, is it likely I'll get an answer
at another door?' said Tadg Beag. 'It was you yourself I
heard to say one time that the man that knows how a thing
is to be done is the man should do that thing when that thing
is to be done.'

'How is a man to get the knowledge of how to do a thing
if that man doesn't do that thing when that thing is to be
done?' said Tadg Mor.

Tadg Beag got into the boat again, and they sat there in
the dark. After four or maybe five waves had broken by
their side, Tadg Beag lifted the net and felt the clothes of
Eamon Og.

'The clothes is drying into him,' he said.

'If I was to go up with you to the house of Sean-bhean O
Suillebhein, who would there be to watch the dead?' said
Tadg Mor, and then Tadg Beag knew that Tadg Mor was
going with him and he had no need to put great heed on the
answer he gave to him.

'Let the sea watch him,' he said, putting a leg out over
the boat after the wave went back with its fistful of little
complaining pebbles.

'We must take him out of the boat first,' said Tadg Mor.

'Take hold of him there by the feet,' he said as he rolled back the net, putting it over the oar with each roll so it would not ravel and knot.

They lifted Eamon Og Murnan out of the boat, and the mackerel slipped about their feet into the place where he had left his shape. They dragged him up a boat length from the sprawling waves and they faced his feet to the shore, but when they saw that that left his head lower than his feet, because the shingle shelved greatly at that point, they faced him about again towards the scurvy waves that were clashing their sharp, pointy scales together and sending up spits of white spray in the air. The dead man glittered with the silver and verdigris scales of the mackerel that were clinging to his clothing over every part.

IV

Tadg Mor went up the sliding shingle in front of Tadg Beag, and Tadg Beag put his feet in the shelves that were made in the shingle by Tadg Mor, because the length of the step they took was the same length. The sea sounded in their ears as they went through the shingle, but by the time the first coarse dune grass scratched at their clothing the only sound that each could hear was the sound of the other's breathing.

The first cottage that rose out blacker than the night in their path was the cottage where Tadg Beag made the empty knocking. Tadg Mor stopped in front of the door as if he might be thinking of trying his hand at knocking, but he thought better of it and went on after Tadg Beag to the house that was next to that house, and that was the house of Sean-bhean O Suillebheain, one to know anything that eye or ear could know about those that lived within three right miles of her.

Tadg Mor hit the door of Sean-bhean O Suillebheain's house with a knock of his knuckles, and although it was a less loud knock than the echo of the knock that came down to the shore when Tadg Beag struck the first knock on the door of the wife of Eamon Og, there was a foot to the floor before he could raise his knuckle off the wood for another knock. A candle lit up and a shadow fell across the window-pane and a face came whitening at the door gap.

'You came to the wrong house this dark night,' said Sean-bhean O Suillebheain. 'The sea took all the men was ever in this house twelve years ago and two months and seventeen days.'

'It may be that we have no corpse for this house, but we came to the right house for all that,' said Tadg Mor. 'We came to this house for knowledge of the house across two sea fields from this house where we got no answer to our knocking with our knuckles,' said Tadg Mor.

'And I knocked with a stone up out of the ground, as well,' said Tadg Beag, coming closer.

The woman with the candle flame blowing drew back into the dark.

'Is it for the inland woman, the one-year's wife, you're bringing the corpse you have below in the boat this night?' she said.

'It is, God help us,' said Tadg Mor.

'It is, God help us,' said Tadg Beag.

'The Brightest and the Bravest,' said Tadg Mor.

'Is it a thing that you got no answer to your knocking?' said the old woman, bending out again with the blowing candle flame.

'No answer,' said Tadg Beag, 'and sturdy knocking.'

'Knocking to be heard above the sound of the sea,' said Tadg Mor.

'They sleep deep, the people from the inland?' said Tadg Beag, asking a question.

'The people of the inland sleep deep in the cottage in the middle of the field,' said Sean-bhean O Suillebheain, 'but when they're rooted up and set down by the sea their spirit never passes out of hearing of the step on the shingle. It's a queer thing entirely that you got no answer to your knocking.'

'We got no answer to our knocking,' said Tadg Mor and Tadg Beag, bringing their words together like two oars striking the one wave, one on this side of the boat and one on that.

'When the inland woman puts her face down on the feather pillow,' said Sean-bhean O Suillebheain, 'that pillow is but as the sea shells children put against their ears, that pillow has the sad crying voices of the sea.'

'Is it that you think she is from home this night?' said Tadg Mor.

'It must be a thing that she is,' said the old woman.

'Is it back to her people in the inlands she'll be gone?' said Tadg Beag, who had more than the curiosity of the night in him.

'Step into the kitchen,' said the old woman, 'while I ask Inghean Og if she saw Bean Eamuin Og go from her house this night.'

While she went into the room that was in from the kitchen, Tadg Beag put a foot inside the kitchen door, but Tadg Mor stayed looking down to the shore.

'If it is a thing the inland woman is from home entirely, where will we put Eamon Og, that we have below in the boat with his face and no sheet on it, and his eyes and no lids drawn down tight over them, and the fish scales sticking to him faster than they stuck to the mackerels when they swam beyond the nets, blue and silver and green?'

'Listen to Inghean Og,' said Tadg Beag, and he stepped a bit further into the kitchen of Sean-bhean O Suillebheain.

'Inghean Og,' came the voice of the old, old woman, 'is it a thing that the inland woman from two fields over went from her house this night?'

'It is a true thing that she went,' said Inghean Og, and Tadg Beag spoke to Tadg Mor and said, 'Inghean Og talks soft in the day, but she talks as soft as the sea in summer when she talks in the night in the dark.'

'Listen to what she says,' said Tadg Mor, coming in a step after Tadg Beag.

'Is it that she went to her people in the inlands?' said Sean-bhean O Suillebheain, who never left the island.

'The wife of Eamon Og never stirred a foot to her people in the inlands since the first day she came to the islands, in her blue dress with the beads,' said the voice of Inghean Og.

'Where did she go, then,' said the old woman, 'if it is a thing that she didn't go to her people in the inlands?'

'Where else but where she said she'd go?' said the voice of Inghean Og. 'Out in the boat with her one-year husband.'

There was sound of aged springs writhing in the room where Inghean Og slept, back behind the kitchen, and her voice was clearer and stronger, as if she were sitting up in the bed looking out at the black sea and the white points rising in it by the light of their own brightness.

'She said the sea would never drag Eamon Og down to the cold green grave and leave her to lie lonely in the black grave on the shore, in the black clay that held tight, under the weighty sods. She said a man and woman should lie in the one grave forever. She said a night never passed without her heart being burnt out to a cold white salt. She said that this night, and every night after, she'd go out with Eamon in the black boat over the scabby back of the sea. She said if ever he got the green grave, she'd get the green grave too, with her arms clinging to him closer than the weeds of the sea, binding them down together. She said that the island women never fought the sea. She said that the sea wanted taming and besting. She said the island women had no knowledge of love. She said there was a curse on the black clay for women that lay alone in it while their men floated in the caves of the sea. She said that the black clay was all right for inland women. She said that the black clay was all right for sisters and mothers. She said the black clay was all right for girls that died at seven years. But the green grave is the grave for wives, she said, and she went out in the black boat this night and she's going out every night after,' said Inghean Og.

'Tell her there will be no night after,' said Tadg Mor.

'Let her sleep till day,' said Tadg Beag. 'Time enough to tell her in the day,' and he strained his eyes behind the flutter-flame candle as the old woman came out from Inghean Og's room.

'You heard what she said,' said the old woman.

'It's a bad thing he was got,' said Tadg Beag.

'That's a thing was never said on this island before this night,' said Tadg Mor.

'There was a fire on every point of the cliff shore,' said the old woman, 'to light home the men who were dragging for Kirnan Mor.'

'And he never was got,' said Tadg Mor.

'There was a shroud spun for Tirnan Beag between the time of the putting out of the island boats to look for him and their coming back with the empty news in the green daylight,' said the old woman.

'Tirnan Beag was never got.'

'Kirnan Mor was never got.'

'Lorcan Mor was never got.'

'Murnan Beag was never got.'

'My four sons were never got,' said the old woman.

'The father of Inghean Og was never got,' said Tadg Beag, and he was looking at the shut door of the room where Inghean Og was lying in the dark; the candle shadows were running their hands over that door.

'The father of Inghean Og was never got,' said Tadg Beag again, forgetting what he was saying.

'Of all the men that had yellow coffins standing up on their ends by the gable, and all the men that had brown shrouds hanging up on the wall with the iron nail eating out its way through the yarn, it had to be the one man that should have never been got that was got,' said Tadg Beag, opening the top half of the door and letting in the deeper sound of the tide.

'That is the way,' said Tadg Mor.

'That is ever and always the way,' said the old woman.

'The sea is stronger than any man,' said Tadg Mor.

'The sea is stronger than any woman,' said Tadg Beag.

'The sea is stronger than women from the inland fields,' said Tadg Mor.

'The sea is stronger than *talk* of love,' said Tadg Beag, when he was out in the dark. It was too dark, after the candlelight, to see where the window was of Inghean Og's room, but he was looking where it might be while he buttoned over his jacket.

V

Tadg Mor and Tadg Beag went back to the shore over the sliding shingle, keeping their feet well on the shelving gravel, as they went towards the sprawling waves. The waves were up to the place where the sea-break was made that spring in the graywacke wall. The boat was floating free out of the cleft in the shingle.

The body of Eamon Og, that had glittered with fish scales of opal and silver and verdigris, was gone from the shore. They knew it was gone from the black land that was cut crisscross with grave cuts by the black spade and the shovel. They knew it was gone and would never be got.

'Kirnan Mor wasn't got.'

'Murnan Beag wasn't got.'

'Lorcan Mor wasn't got.'

'Tirnan Beag wasn't got.'

'The four sons of the Sean-bhean O Suillebheain were never got.'

'The father of Inghean Og wasn't got.'

The men of the island were caught down in the sea by the tight weeds of the sea. They were held in the tendrils of the sea anemone and the pricks of the sallow thorn, by the green sea grasses and the green sea reeds and the winding stems of the green sea daffodils. But Eamon Og Murnan would be held fast in the white sea arms of his one-year wife, who came from the inlands where women have no knowledge of the sea and have only a knowledge of love.

ACKNOWLEDGEMENTS

The editor and publishers are grateful to the following authors, publishers and agents for permission to reprint copyright stories: Random Century Publishers Ltd for 'Hand in Glove' by Elizabeth Bowen, 'Autumn Sunshine' by William Trevor, 'The Gollan' by A. E. Coppard, 'The Crock of Gold' by Lord Dunsany and 'The Eyes of the Dead' by Daniel Corkery; Peters, Fraser & Dunlop for 'Let Me Go' by L. A. G. Strong; *Dublin Evening Herald* for 'The Servant' by Michael MacLiammoir; A. M. Heath for 'Aisling' by Peter Tremayne; Macmillan & Co. Ltd for 'The Carl of the Drab Coat' by James Stephens, 'The Old Faith' by Frank O'Connor and 'The Green Grave and the Black Grave' by Mary Lavin; Victor Gollancz Ltd for 'The Fairy Goose' by Liam O'Flaherty and 'The Dogs in the Great Glen' by Benedict Kiely; A. P. Watt Ltd for 'The Science of Mirrors' by Catherine Brophy and 'The End of the Record' by Sean O'Faolain; *The Listener* for 'The Devil and the Cat' by James Joyce; and also New English Library for the use of the quotation from their edition of Funk and Wagnales' *Dictionary of Folklore, Mythology and Legend*.